D0363450

BAD MEMORY

BAD MEMORY

Duane Franklet

VICTOR GOLLANCZ
LONDON

First published in Great Britain 1997
by Victor Gollancz
An imprint of the Cassell Group
Wellington House, 125 Strand, London WC2R 0BB

A catalogue record for this book is
available from the British Library.

ISBN 0 575 06342 4

Typeset by Anneset, Weston-super-Mare, Somerset
Printed in Great Britain by
St Edmundsbury Press Ltd, Bury St Edmunds, Suffolk

97 98 99 5 4 3 2 1

Acknowledgments

For allowing me the time and space in which to write this book, I wish to thank my wife Barbara and my business partner David at Data Tracking Associates. Also the many good people at the University of Houston, my parents, sisters, and friends who have been supportive throughout.

Many thanks to my editor, Paul McCarthy, for all his skill and effort, and to my agent, Molly Friedrich, for giving the novel a chance. Special thanks to Sue Grafton, who saw the manuscript and was willing to help.

You have all lifted me up.

For my parents,
Beverly and Duane Sr.

1

Shawn Taylor steered his Honda Accord up the entrance ramp and knifed through three lanes of freeway traffic. Horns blew from all sides, but Shawn was listening to an R.E.M. tape. Loud.

A red pickup truck hung right off his back bumper, and Shawn tapped the brakes. *Bring it on,* he thought. *Asshole.* He waited until the truck backed off slightly, then he shifted into fifth and accelerated.

Traffic was still moving here, but he knew that up ahead he would almost certainly run into a packed mass of red tail-lights. It might not be L.A. or New York, but even in Oklahoma City you tried to get out of town as soon as the whistle sounded. Which made Shawn even angrier – he'd wasted precious minutes arguing, listening to his boss go on and on, clearly trying to cover his own ass; then he'd finally cleared off his desk and gotten the hell out.

That's what the boss had said, too. 'Don't worry, we'll pay you for the whole day. I want you to go ahead and leave now.' Which was a fine joke, waiting until three o'clock to come in and give him the ax.

As he came over the top of a small rise, there they all were, cars plugging the road far into the distance. He started down-shifting in a hurry, and as he came to a complete stop, he fought the temptation to wrench the steering wheel to the left and hop up on the shoulder, hit the gas again, and blow on past.

He wouldn't be making this trip again, anyway. His employer Garrett and Stevens had seen to that. They were freight handlers, with a thirty-person office in Oklahoma and smaller branches in Arkansas and Louisiana.

'Why don't you go on ahead and we'll pay you for the day?' Bastards. Like they were doing him a favor.

Not that he hadn't been warned. He'd known the stakes for three weeks after the office manager and the aging Garrett called him in for a meeting. It seemed they were unhappy with the progress he'd made installing their new network of PCs. Too many delays, they said. Missteps. They'd hired him because he was a mover, a problem solver. That's what he'd claimed in the interview, they said.

For God's sake, thought Shawn, wincing as he thought of it even now. It was as if they had a tape, rewound the thing, and kept playing it back. Giving him actual quotes from his interview. Finally, Garrett had declared, 'You better straighten up, young man. We hired a team player, not an ill-tempered maverick. We want this job done in three weeks, by Friday, July fourteenth,' and he shook a shriveled hand at Shawn with all the authority he could muster.

Shawn cursed, squeezing the wheel with his right hand. The old fucker didn't know a thing about computers. He'd never even used one. He had no idea what was involved, yet there he was giving out decrees.

The company was inefficient. Decrepit. How could Shawn Taylor help that? They made him put every damn purchase out for bid. Specs had to be drawn up, ads had to be placed. The process took weeks. Then he'd come under pressure from fellow employees, every one of whom seemed to have an uncle with some kind of hardware or software business who was trying to make a buck.

It wasn't even a large job. Thirty-two PCs and one, maybe two, network file servers. If they were willing to fight like dogs over this scrap, times had to be tough for the Oklahoma City computer integrators. But Shawn knew that much for a fact. He'd been out of work for seven months before finally landing this position, a job which, five years ago, he would never have considered.

He laid on the car horn for a good three seconds. Directly in front of him, some blue-haired lady had stalled her Datsun. A whole row of cars were inching by on the right and then jumping over in front of the stalled vehicle.

He could sense, more than hear, the Datsun's engine crank and stop. Crank and stop. 'Get that piece of shit off the road,' he shouted, but his words were drowned out in the wash of music coming from his own stereo.

Shawn slammed his hand down on the passenger seat. He was about to hit it again, when the Datsun shuddered and belched smoke. A small, acrid cloud drifted back and enveloped the Accord. Shawn tried not to inhale.

They advanced fifty feet and again came to a stop. It was not so much the losing of another job that got to him, but the prospect of looking for the next one. His latest search had required a rough seven months, scanning the want ads, spitting out résumés, doing his best at cold calls. And now that he'd been let go again, it was going to be even harder. He certainly didn't want anyone calling Garrett and Stevens for a reference.

Those were the cards he'd been dealt. Shitty cards. It seemed like, more and more in this country, that's what you got. You ordered a case of twenty-four Ethernet boards to put your machines on the network and three of them didn't work. You called in the cabling contractor to wire your jacks and fully a third of the network connections were inoperable until you got the contractor to send a crew out a second or third time. Everyone pointed to everyone else.

And then the fiasco that had sealed Shawn's fate. The machines themselves arrived and they had been completely misconfigured. The wrong software, the wrong memory, the wrong size hard drives – the whole order had been completely unusable. Shawn had thought he was going upscale by ordering from Simtec, which had a reputation for being the most reliable computer manufacturer in the world. The mistakes were totally inexplicable, and this after he'd already received the ultimatum. He tried to explain, but management had already made the decision.

Garrett had appeared solemnly in Shawn's office after lunch. 'You just don't seem to be able to get the job done,' Garrett told him, shaking his head. He fixed Shawn with his protruding eyes, then turned and walked out, leaving someone else to be the hatchet man.

Startled, Shawn glanced away from the backs of his hands.

He had been staring down toward the steering wheel, and the car had been physically jolted. He was dimly aware of horns blowing behind him, and he looked up and saw a long, open stretch of road in front of him. The red pickup was still in the rearview. That sonofabitch had bumped his car!

Shawn sped up and soon came to a halt again behind the Datsun. He reached over and flipped open his glove box. Ever since his father passed away and left him an assorted jackpot of firearms, Shawn had kept a small .38 inside.

'Fuck you,' he mouthed, and waved his middle finger in front of the mirror. Granny, he noticed, had again stalled out her car, and this made Shawn furious. This lady didn't even belong on the highway. Here she was holding him up, and then he gets bumped by some macho prick in a pickup truck.

He hit the steering wheel with both palms. He howled. Somebody had to get her off the road. He grabbed the .38 and kicked open his door.

'Get the fuck off the road!' he yelled, moving up alongside the Datsun. The woman had her window down, and she turned and gave him a surprised look. Her face was heavily wrinkled, and her lips seemed to snarl at him.

She said something he didn't hear, because the sound – the engines, horns, music, curses – had all become a steady, overpowering hum in his ear. He raised his arm and fired once, hitting the woman in the head, and the sound stopped.

Complete silence, except for one slow creak, which caused him to turn back. The driver of the pickup had started getting out. He had both feet on the ground. But now he looked as if he were shrinking back toward the interior of the vehicle.

Shawn took a step toward the pickup and fired twice. The first bullet hit the door, and the second knocked the driver back onto the concrete. The man got his hands up, pumping the air, as a dark stain spread down the front of his shirt.

Now it was absolutely quiet. There wasn't a single sound anywhere for Shawn to listen to. He liked that. He went over to the guardrail and sat down. He didn't hear the click of the hammer cocking back, and he thought triumphantly about never having to configure another computer as he lifted his hand and blew off the back of his own head.

2

The Simtec Corporation might call itself a campus, but it was really a small city. With twenty billion a year in revenues, the world's largest manufacturer of personal computers had been annexing property for ten years.

While not the mayor of this city, Barry Shepard was a respected alderman. As head of Simtec's TechDirect, and arguably the number three man in the company, Barry had been putting out fires ever since the new CEO had put a war council together and decided to pump up the mail order business. He'd been hired into marketing five years ago as an assistant director. After serving both there and in production, he'd been made a director. Barry was one of the few in upper management whom everyone seemed to get along with. He had a flexible style: at times he built a consensus; other times he simply made the tough choices. If anyone could make direct mail work, the CEO had told him, it was he.

Now this. Hundreds upon hundreds of their shipments had been either misconfigured or delivered to the wrong destination. The calls had begun to trickle in on Friday, but not in sufficient number to alert anyone to the magnitude of the problem. Monday had brought more calls and then, this morning, the dam had broken.

How could such a thing happen? You had a customer, a Mr. Sid Overstreet, who had just ordered a Star Pentium tower model with 16 megabytes of RAM and preloaded Windows, Excel, and WordPerfect. There it was right in his order, placed July 12 at 2:52 P.M. to JCJ, or June Jackson. What was then supposed to happen was, the order went to production, got pulled and configured, then came down the conveyor belt in a row of shipping cartons. Monitor, CPU, mouse, and manuals – three boxes with preprinted address labels already plastered on their sides.

This was one part of the operation that had worked flawlessly, only now when Mr. Overstreet in Prescott, Arizona, opened his box and pulled out his new computer, it wasn't a Pentium tower at all. Instead he'd gotten a desktop model, and the machine was preconfigured with Microsoft Word. The order wasn't even close, not even in the ballpark, and not only did this make Simtec look stupid, it made Mr. Overstreet *mad.*

It made Mr. Overstreet regret that he hadn't bought an AST, an IBM, or even a Macintosh. It made Mr. Overstreet wonder why he hadn't saved two hundred bucks and bought a Brand X out of the newspaper from a warehouse up the street. At least then he'd be able to charge out his front door and have someone to yell at. When Mr. Overstreet called Simtec's 1-800 Star Support number and wet his lips, mentally preparing himself to bitch somebody's brains out, all he got was a busy signal. So Mr. Overstreet got madder. He looked at the Simtec on his living-room floor and he wanted to kick it. He settled for tearing up the Styrofoam shipping blocks with his bare hands while Zeus, a two-year-old cocker spaniel, hid under the coffee table. Mr. Overstreet then tried the redial button on his phone for ten solid minutes, but he never got through, nor did he get through all morning. Four thousand other people just like him, all just as mad as he was, were trying to do the exact same thing.

Just before noon, a letter was dropped off at the front desk for Barry Shepard, TechDirect director. The letter made its way to his assistant, Gwen, who opened the letter, read a few lines, and caught her breath. She immediately stuffed it back in the envelope and placed it in a prominent place on his desk. She stuck a note on top that said, 'Hand-delivered downstairs.' The letter read like this:

Dear Mr. Shepard,

You may have been wondering about the recent mishap with your July 13 through 15 shipments. I am sure this has been a source of great concern, and I am glad to be able to offer some information as to the origins of your misfortune. Moreover, I am pleased to be able to provide you with a remedy that will protect you from ever having to experience this sort of embarrassment again.

As you are the party most directly affected, I thought it best to approach you directly. I am confident that you will be able to make a convincing argument to your superiors. I last counted 4,011 misshipments at $30 each, which makes a cash outlay of $120,330, but that minor inconvenience is the least of it. How can you estimate the lost goodwill that accompanies such a public display of ineptitude? I notice that 27 customers have canceled their orders altogether. I assure you that those 27 are only the beginning.

You might check the system for orders under your own name, by the way. The wife may be upset.

Enough. I am sure you are well aware, more so than even I, of the damage that has been wrought. Simtec will authorize a payment in the amount of one million dollars to alleviate your concerns regarding the recurrence of such an event. Have an affirmative answer by 5 P.M. tomorrow, Wednesday, July 19th, and we will proceed with payment. I will contact you at that time to discuss arrangements. Any indecisiveness on your part will be dealt with harshly. If called to conduct a second performance, I will escalate the price of my services fivefold. Splendid as it has been, let's have the show stop here.

It is not my desire to provoke a witch hunt. I am not one of your employees, I guarantee you, nor have I ever been. The game on this one revolved around your customer database residing on the computer you call Gandalf. We have come to know each other well. Sybase is a wonderful tool – I'd recommend it myself – but you've left so many holes it's frightening. At this point I'd expect you to lock Gandalf in a vault,

> but I have plenty of other convincing ways to earn my fee. As my father always warned, if you're going to fight with stones, you'd better carry a pocketful. A pocketful of stones I have, Mr. Shepard, some of them interesting and rarely found. Never found in one day, I might add.
>
> Shall we do business? I can hear the champagne popping in the halls of Michael Dell. I'll be in touch.

The letter was unsigned. Barry Shepard read it and sat back in his chair. Read it through again, a prickling sensation moving down his forearms. A group in TechDirect had been racing to debug these shipping errors since yesterday, but their efforts had been inconclusive.

He turned the paper over and examined it closely. Standard laser printer output – it could have come from the printer down the hall, or one halfway around the world. Gone were the days when you could match up a make and model of typewriter, narrow sales down to one geographic region, and finally discover the exact machine that had produced the letter due to some anomaly – the misshapen letter *p*.

He examined the envelope, finding that it, too, had been fed through a laser printer. The stamp, of a black woman apparently named Sarah Johnson, was uncanceled. Why the stamp? Had they originally intended to mail the letter? He turned the envelope and read the fine print along the edge of the stamp: Jazz Choreographer, 1931–1985. Barry was vaguely aware that perhaps he shouldn't be handling the letter so much, but at the same time, without making a conscious decision or choice, he knew that he was well clear of the realm of common forensics. Fingerprints and postmarks, crooked *p*'s, wiretaps, and phone traces. None of this was going to be of any help.

Barry stared a long moment at the picture of his wife, Claudia, sitting in a porch swing in their west Houston backyard. Then he dialed the extension for Jim Seidler, executive vice president of operations, and Karen Williams, chief counsel.

Less than one hour later, six people converged on the

boardroom in Simtec 3, the main administration building. Mike Spakovsky, the chief financial officer, had been called back from the airport just before boarding a plane for Singapore. President and CEO Diane Hughes, still in her first year at the helm, had been pulled out of a videotape session. Lastly, Chris Jacobs, director of security and internal affairs, sat at one end of the table casting furtive glances toward each new person who opened the door.

The room was opulent, built before the price wars had necessitated cuts in everything from staff RAM upgrades to the quality of the toilet paper used in the 113 company rest rooms. On one wall hung a large portrait of deceased Simtec founder John Sims.

The letter had been copied and distributed around the table, and Diane Hughes waited while everyone had a chance to finish reading. Spakovsky took the longest, but at last he looked up and said, 'Looks to me like the operations people screwed up.' A statement that made half the people in the room bristle.

'You voted against the server migration and you were against new cabling. Every time we want to spend any money or do anything with the infrastructure, you're the one crying like a baby. You want a return on investment, this is what you get.' Jim Seidler glared until Spakovsky looked away. Jim had been the man widely expected to become CEO before the surprise coup that had brought in Diane Hughes. He was still generally considered the one who ran the day-to-day operations of the company. Word on the street was that the Simtec board wanted marketing skills. They wanted a Lee Iacocca for the computer industry, and that had been the weakest part of Jim Seidler's résumé.

'This is something that could have been avoided,' Karen Williams said. 'Should have been avoided.'

Mike Spakovsky groaned, leaned forward and put his elbows on the table.

'I'd say that about sums it up,' Diane said. She'd seen enough and wanted to get them back on track. 'I want to frame this discussion by saying that we have two separate issues here. One, determining how this happened and ensuring that it never happens again, and two, determining our response and our immediate plan of action. I suggest that we not become involved in recriminations and finger-pointing. At this point, I don't have time to tolerate it. These are the cards we have been dealt. We have several decisions to make and we must make them right now.'

This was the style for which Diane Hughes had made herself loved and feared, both here at Simtec, and at Procter & Gamble before that. She was tough and analytical to a fault, known for squeezing an issue down to its essentials whether she understood it, or – as some asserted – even if not. As she spoke she made a series of rapid-fire notes on the legal pad in front of her.

'Barry, you began looking into this yesterday. Where do we stand?'

Barry shifted uneasily. *Should we have caught it sooner? Could more have been done?* 'We started receiving calls about mis-shipments yesterday morning. Not a huge number, but enough that I discussed the problem with both Diane and Jim. We isolated three areas of concern: the order-entry system used by the sales reps, the customer database itself, and the last link, the shipping queues in production. I immediately put three analysts to work. They made an on-line copy of the database and began hammering away at it. They worked well into last night without finding a definitive answer. A few programming glitches turned up, but nothing that would replicate the scrambled configurations.'

Chris Jacobs was a powerful man with a broad, heavy chest. His starched shirts were strained to accommodate him, such that he would sometimes appear physically uncomfortable, as he did now, leaning forward, frowning: 'What kind of glitches?'

'Small stuff. Irrelevant. I told them to keep looking, but this morning we've been swamped with damage control. Between eight A.M. and noon, we've had twelve hundred calls. That's where we now stand.'

'If this letter is accurate,' Diane said, 'you should expect several thousand more calls. Then we should see the call volume drop off. Keep us advised on how that goes.'

Barry nodded and said, 'The fact that we are all here right now indicates that we accept this letter as being genuine. We are dealing not only with someone who has cost us a good deal of money, but this person has been inside our system, our core operations, in ways we may not even know about ourselves. Moreover this person could be in a position to make matters worse.' He glanced around the table and saw reluctant agreement.

Diane's lips pinched together and she scribbled a note. 'Next,' she said. 'We must decide if this is to remain an internal matter. Should we approach any outside authority and, if so, which one? We must also assess if this person is capable of hitting us in some other way, as he claims. Can we be assured of our ability to keep him out?' Her quick grin looked like more of a grimace: 'By the way, I say *he* only as a matter of convention.

'I will be looking to you for arguments or rationale in favor and against. We will decide by consensus, or, if unable to reach agreement, I will decide. Karen, I'd like you to speak to the first matter. Do we keep this in-house or not?'

Karen Williams was a stern, attractive woman, who had once been queen of the Bluebonnet Bowl. Early in her career, this fact had caused many to underestimate her considerable talent in the courtroom. She said, 'If you're asking for a legal basis for the decision, we are not compelled to act one way or the other. But if you're asking for my personal opinion, I think that outside assistance could be extremely beneficial. We have neither the proper resources nor the experience to try and investigate this type of threat on our own.'

'What,' said Mike Spakovsky, 'and the cops will? Or the FBI?' Spakovsky was a sturdy, muscular man with a deep voice. He had a habit of never looking at you when he spoke, and that's what he did now, staring off into space as if it somehow gave his comments more weight. 'I have a hard time believing some law enforcement agency is going to come in here and have our whole system figured out in a matter of hours, or even days. The Houston police? Give me a break.'

'You're suggesting we handle it ourselves,' said Diane.

'I don't know about that. I'm saying to consider maybe we pay this guy and he goes away.'

'Hope he goes away.' Jim Seidler snorted.

'It could be a lot worse than a million dollars, Jim,' said Spakovsky.

'Yeah. The guy could come back next week asking for ten million. You cave in this easy, who's to say he won't?'

No one said anything.

Barry was glad Diane had kept a lid on the accusations. That wasn't what they needed right now. He looked down the table at the director of security. Chris Jacobs was high-strung and Barry had seen him pop off before, so he tried to keep his tone neutral. 'Chris, I'd like to hear your assessment of whether we can keep them out by tomorrow? Can we keep them out *today* for Christ's sake?'

'I wish I could tell you exactly how this is being done,' said Jacobs. He was shaking his head, and speaking with about half the volume of his usual, confident voice. 'You know, give me a few hours and a couple hundred lines of code and we'll be okay. I've got to be honest. It's hard to know where to start on this. It's clear they got into the Sybase server, which means they're on the token ring in Simtec ten. They could jump from there to any number of other places. Is it coming from inside the company? Are they off-site somewhere? What other things have been changed? They could be into payroll and accounting. They could be into R & D, production, they could be in the E-mail. So you go out and shut everything down, change every administrative and supervisory password in the company. Still, is there a program ticking out there, waiting to go off if we don't pay?'

The possibilities seemed to gradually sink in around the table.

Diane squirmed. 'We need a realistic damage report, damn it. Let's not go overthinking this. Surely you can eliminate some of those hypotheticals.'

Jacobs rubbed fiercely at the back of his strong neck. 'I can eliminate some of them faster than others,' he said at last.

Spakovsky stared at the wall and sighed. 'Can you imagine what would happen if springs and wires start poking out all over the place? What do you think the markets will make of that? I'll have analysts in here like a pack of wolves.'

'Surely this has happened to somebody else,' said Karen Williams. 'Surely we're not so . . . inept, for lack of a better word, that we're the easiest target in the *Fortune* 500.'

'Sure it has,' said Spakovsky. 'And they kept it quiet. Maybe they paid and got out from underneath. That's my point.'

Diane Hughes broke in, 'I think it's clear that Mike favors keeping this under wraps, from a publicity point of view. Another way of looking at it is this: If what we're concerned about is our responsibility to the shareholders, that obligation requires that we react in the most efficient manner possible, whatever that may be. Jim, you seem to think we can get a handle on this ourselves.'

'We can do what Chris suggested, have a mandatory change of password. We can monitor the networks for attempted log-ins twenty-four hours a day, if need be. We can run new cable, right down the hallways on a temporary basis if we have to. These things will do a lot of good, and there's more we can come up with. I suggest you put me, Barry, and Chris on a crisis management team. I'd rather spend a million dollars worth of overtime than pay this guy any money. So the stock moves two, five, ten points – I've seen it do that on a whim anyway. It'll bounce back.'

This statement made Spakovsky physically recoil from the table. The two men were so unlike one another – one a Harvard MBA and the other a University of Texas engineer – and they each brought such different perspectives to the table that they were rarely able to agree on anything.

Diane held up her clenched hands. 'That's one vote for paying and one against.' She raised an index finger on each hand. 'Karen?'

'You must realize this is not my area. I am not technically qualified to judge the measures Jim just mentioned. But, if there are immediate steps we can take to secure the system, and if they have a reasonable chance of being effective, I'd certainly go against paying, at this point.'

'Barry?'

'I don't want to pay. I'll tell you that right now. But we have to be absolutely clear on what's at stake. Did anyone see the story over the weekend about the systems manager who shot two people on a freeway in Oklahoma City? We had just sold that company thirty some-odd machines. They were one of the first bad shipments to go out. Thank God nobody tried to tie Simtec in as a possible cause of that mess.'

'The man was a mental case,' Spakovsky said. 'Don't be ridiculous.'

Barry clenched his back teeth together. He had the same hard feeling in his throat as when he'd first linked Simtec to the shootings. *Should he have caught it sooner? Could more have been done?* The article was small, and tucked away on page twenty-one, but it described the scenario leading up to the shooting. The man had been fired that same day. He was in charge of installing a computer system and, when Barry queried the database on the employer's name, Garrett and Stevens, his fears were confirmed.

'I woke up in the middle of the night thinking about that guy. If the machines had been right, would that still have happened? No one can say. All I know is that when someone orders equipment from us, I want the order to go out right. Every time.'

'I think that's something we all want,' Diane said. 'We're obviously dealing with an exceptional circumstance.'

'So? If it would bring those three people back, I'd pay the million dollars in a minute. You know that line in the letter, the one about check the system for your own orders? He'd bought fifty-three NoteStars with shipping destination to various addresses at Apple Computer in Cupertino. They were all due to be charged to my account and shipped, but we caught it right before they went out.'

'Great,' Jim Seidler said. 'A bastard with a sense of humor.'

'The point is, if they were able to do that kind of manipulation, there's absolutely no telling what else is in store. It makes me nervous just thinking about it. I'm against paying, but I also don't want to poke my finger in a hornet's nest. My approach would be to use the money as a way of stalling. Meanwhile we work like hell to figure out where they've been and what else they've done. If we did pay, I agree with Jim –

we'd have to be absolutely certain the one payoff would end it.'

'Barring any such assurance, what is your inclination?'

'Don't pay. We'll get through this. Chalk it up to a million-dollar wake-up call for antihack technology.'

'These people are no hacks,' said Chris Jacobs. 'I still have a hard time believing they don't have help on the inside.' He had been rereading the letter, and he pinched his lips together at the last sentence: 'Look at this line about Dell. You think they have a hand in this?'

'And broadcast it all over the place in a ransom letter? I doubt it,' said Diane. 'But as soon as resources permit, we will be investigating all avenues thoroughly. We'll look at the letter and how it got here. We'll tear apart the database. But those things will take time which right now we don't have. I count one for paying and two against. What's your opinion, Chris?'

Chris bit his lip. A breach like this fell squarely in his area of responsibility, and they had gone easy by not calling him out on the carpet. If there was any consolation, it was that he'd had little involvement with the TechDirect project. His people may have wired the offices, but they hadn't written the database. In that sense, there was a shared responsibility for this debacle. Still, he was probably the only one in the room, except for maybe Jim Seidler, who understood the scope of what they would have to do.

Frankly, he knew it couldn't be accomplished. Not only would they have to bring the company to a standstill, but it would wind up costing them much more than a million. As he ticked through the items in a lockdown scenario, a million was beginning to look cheap. Chris drew in a breath. 'Even if it backfires on us, I'd have to say we pay the money. Short of bringing the company to a halt, there's no way we can lock all the doors by tomorrow.'

'Damn right,' Spakovsky agreed. 'Now is not the time to go riding the range.'

Seidler pushed back his chair in disgust.

Diane Hughes was holding a slip of paper up in her right hand. 'I wrote this down before hearing Chris and Barry give their opinions. I wouldn't want anyone to think I was simply being argumentative.' She unfolded the paper and in big block letters everyone could read, Diane had printed DON'T PAY. 'I don't believe you let someone twist your arm, and I don't want to give out a red cent if we can possibly help it.'

Several around the table looked shocked.

'The vote is four to two. I would have liked more of a consensus. And Lord knows I hate to give anyone the chance to say, I told you so. Chris, Mike, I'm going to go against you on this. I need to go make phone calls and ensure that we have a fallback position, but for all practical purposes, we will proceed as if we're not paying. Jim, Chris, Barry, you should meet right now and discuss strategy. We need to work on the assumption that tomorrow evening we're going to be attacked.'

3

Barry Shepard lived on Houston's west side in a two-story brick house. Despite having former president George Bush move into the neighborhood three streets over, Barry liked to think of his dwelling and his personal tastes as modest. It was true that his street, Willow Creek Lane, was not ostentatious, but the security gates and guardhouse at the entrance still gave an air of privilege to the entire subdivision.

He pulled his white Grand Cherokee into the driveway at eleven o'clock and climbed wearily down from behind the wheel. His only child, seven-year-old Caroline, would be long asleep. He hadn't eaten since lunch, and his mouth watered at the heavy, spicy smell that hung in the air when he opened the back door to the kitchen. A note on the counter said: *Chicken tonight in oven.*

He got an empty plate, opened the oven door, and hauled out a baking dish slightly warm to the touch. Chicken in red sauce. He filled his plate and made a Scotch and water before going over to the kitchen table. What a day it had been. No one had clearly estimated the magnitude of the task that lay before them. Neither Karen Williams nor Mike Spakovsky had the technical background to be of any help. As Diane had directed, Barry, Jim, and Chris formulated the crisis plan.

The three had a brainstorming session that produced thirty-seven possible security measures. The list included surveillance sweep for bugs and phone taps, add packet signature to all network traffic, and concluded with: install tire shredders, which Chris Jacobs was keen on embedding in each of the parking lot exits. The three men assigned a weight to each item in terms of implementation speed, cost, and efficacy, and the weights combined to produce a ranked order and some semblance of a plan.

Point one on the plan thus became: passwords. Chris Jacobs drafted a memo requiring that everyone change all passwords by the end of the day. The memo referred to lax security and possible log-ins by unauthorized users, and they distributed copies of the memo to key personnel in all departments.

This set off a barrage of technical support phone calls as the request trickled down to end users. Some people had never changed their passwords and didn't know how to do it even if they wanted to. Barry's name was also at the top of the memo, and he soon began to get reports that dozens of employees could not be contacted. People were out of the office, in meetings, who knows where, which left no choice but to go in and change passwords administratively, effectively locking workers out of their own system until they were able to get in touch with a network administrator.

Changing passwords was routine maintenance. It was the kind of thing you could build right into the system. Everyone changes their passwords every three months. Mandatory behavior. But it was also the kind of maintenance that was easy to let slide. You didn't want to be inconvenient. You didn't want to be distrustful, or to make the system too unfriendly. Besides, people changed their passwords four times a year and they ended up having to write them down. Passwords ended up in files on hard drives, on scraps of paper in the tops of desk drawers. Barry had seen them scribbled on yellow stick-up notes dangling from the edges of monitors.

But being lax contributed to the disarray. They now appeared foolish and unprofessional, running around squawking at everyone to change their passwords this very minute. Barry sipped his drink and considered that you could walk into most companies in the United States and it would be the same way. Passwords wouldn't have changed in months, maybe not since the account was issued. They put up expensive glass-and-metal buildings and ringed them with security fences. They had checkpoints downstairs in the parking lots and sign-in desks in the lobby of each building. This was the pro forma way it had been done, while the real threat sneaked in over the phone lines, or came from a disgruntled employee who stayed late nights at the office.

Barry carved off a forkful of chicken. The whole house was quiet. Most of the floors were carpeted, and after only twelve years the foundation didn't yet make many of the settling noises that would come later. Nevertheless, Barry heard a faint noise on the stair and cocked his head. A shuffling sound in the corridor. He started to get up but then Claudia was in the doorway, looking at him sleepily.

'I heard the refrigerator,' she said, though she was normally a sound sleeper. 'What's up?'

Claudia was a litigator with Milford and Marks, one of the largest law firms in Houston. She listened to every word you said, and even though she hadn't pressed him on it at the time, Barry realized she must have guessed plenty when he called to say he'd be late.

'Trouble.'

She had medium-length brown hair that at the moment was very tousled, and she raised an eyebrow at this. 'Oh?'

'You know the shipments, the ones we've been sending all over hell and back, everywhere but the place they're supposed to go?'

'You mentioned it yesterday.'

'Well, it's a disaster. Someone broke into the system and sabotaged the whole program. We got a letter today asking for a million dollars or it'll happen again. We give an answer tomorrow.'

Claudia's eyes widened. She no longer looked sleepy.

'I should say, *I* got a letter, because the goddamned thing came addressed to me. None of this, by the way, leaves this kitchen.'

'Of course,' she said. 'Why would the letter come to you?'

'Because I was the one getting screwed, most likely.' He glanced up and noticed her worried expression. 'Look, I'm the one they chose to pick on for now. I have to believe that was just chance. They're not after me, personally. This is the company's hot potato. The letter came to me because I was supposed to take it to Diane, Jim – whoever they thought I'd take it to – and they expected me to be an advocate on behalf of payment.'

She considered that strategy for a moment. 'And were you? An advocate?'

Barry recalled the boardroom vote, only Chris and Mike in favor of payment. 'No, I wasn't. You can't buy your way out of everything.'

'How many machines are you talking about?'

'The letter says four thousand. So far, the letter speaks the truth.'

Claudia seemed to be making a calculation. Then she said, 'It could easily cost you more than a million anyway.'

Barry stabbed another piece of chicken and pushed his plate away. 'You sound exactly like Spakovsky. He wants to pay strictly because of economics, but I'm past that. I'd like to nail the bastard.'

'There's the whole theory of whether or not to pay ransom.'

'Exactly. Diane won't pay on principle. Seidler is just a hard-ass. That's two big votes right there. Karen Williams went along with us, too.'

'Miss I'm the Legal Franchise?' Claudia said distastefully. The two had met at various company functions and, contrary to what Barry had expected when he introduced them, they had not hit it off at all. This was unusual for his wife, who normally got along with everybody. Barry wondered if it wasn't some kind of professional jealousy – Karen in charge of a large legal division at a major corporation, and a beauty queen besides.

He said, 'I spoke to Karen after the meeting. She didn't have a legal problem with paying. It was much more of an ethical objection. I was really quite surprised.' He rose and carried his plate to the sink.

'How was the Y?' Barry meant their daughter Caroline's day at the YMCA day school. Toward the end of her first-grade school year, they had begun discovering that Caroline might have some kind of learning disability. The other kids were forging ahead in their handwriting and spelling exercises, while Caroline's pencil shook and sputtered like a wind-blown twig.

'Fine. She loves the swimming. She wants us to put in a pool.'

'She does, does she?' Barry said warily. He pictured only the vacuuming, measuring chlorine, and all the rest of it. 'I've been meaning to call and schedule a visit to the Stubblefields'. I found out more about his wife. She's a diagnostician at Hayes Middle School.'

Claudia looked away. The discovery had been hard on both of them. This was something that might go away as Caroline grew up. It might not. They were all going to have to work hard and be patient. 'Why don't we invite them over for dinner one weekend?' she said. 'We could be casual about it. She wouldn't even have to know she's being checked out.'

'That would be fine, but I can't do it until after we get past this crisis.' On the way into the hallway, he slipped an arm behind Claudia and pulled her in close for a kiss.

'I've still got to log on and check E-mail,' he said. 'I'll be up in a minute.'

'I'm going to wake up and do some work early,' she said, which for Claudia meant 5:00 A.M. 'You want me to reset the alarm?'

Barry shook his head. 'I'll get up with you. I'm looking at another hell day.' He pulled off his tie and flicked on the light in his downstairs study, where his computer and a wall full of software and manuals sat beside a set of French doors leading into the backyard.

He powered up the machine as an automatic light in the back corner by the garage flicked on. A cat moved along the fence and jumped out of sight. Probably to go sit on the hood of his car, he thought, as the Windows start-up screen pulled his attention back. As soon as it came up, he triggered a script that dialed into the office. The first thing Barry saw was not the usual Simtec log-on screen at all. Instead, he got a message that said:

> Attention: Only authorized Simtec employees are permitted to use this computer system. Anyone using this system consents to having all activities and keystrokes monitored by authorized security personnel.

> Any evidence of possible criminal activity may be provided to law enforcement officials and will be prosecuted to the fullest extent of the law.

Barry typed in his username and the cursor flickered after the password prompt, waiting. His hand started to move and then paused. He couldn't remember the password he'd assigned that very day. His mind was blank, so he tried the old standby BSimpson. Nothing. BARSHEP. Nope. ClElkins, which was short for Claudia Elkins, his wife's maiden name. No go, and the communications server logged him out. The *authorized security personnel* were going to have a field day.

Not only was this frustrating, he thought with some irony, it no doubt mirrored the experience of others all over the company. Barry sank back in his chair. Then he had another, less pleasant idea. Could it be possible? Could someone do this to them – actually change their usernames, scramble logins so that no one was capable of accessing the system at all?

He got up and walked to the kitchen to refill his drink, considering whether to call Greg Mitchell, one of the senior analysts for TechDirect, to see whether he was able to log in or not. The kitchen clock said 11:35. If they were locked out, he wanted to know now, so he picked up the kitchen phone and dialed. After two rings, the answering machine came on and Barry hung up. He stayed in the kitchen, leaning against the counter and sipping his drink.

BSimpson. He'd chosen Bart because he'd watched the show a few times and rather liked the little fellow. He could sympathize with Homer, too, trudging off to work every day for the tyrannical Mr. Burns at the nuclear plant. That's what Barry's job had been like before he'd left EDS in Dallas and moved to Houston.

EDS had been a twelve-year marathon. At first they were all-out, heady years, where he rose to senior analyst, project director, and finally settled in as manager of the southern region. Barry was good, and had been lucky enough to always find a boss who recognized that and moved him along. But as regional manager, the stagnation had set in. The heady years were gone and the bureaucracy pinched like a vise. Meanwhile

Simtec was down there taking risks and grabbing headlines in Houston. When a recruiter had called with a tempting offer, he'd closed his eyes and made the jump. How much and how fast things could change.

The nuclear plant! The password and the whole train of thought that had led up to it flashed back into memory. He'd been thinking about using the password HSimpson, but in a fit of paranoia, he had envisioned a hacker, sitting out there studying his other log-ins, trying Simpson characters, and easily breaking the new one. This had led to a series of rapid-fire connections. Mr. Burns at the nuclear plant. The doomed South Texas Nuclear Project down near Palacios. Leaks. And there it was, his new password: Pu239. He'd typed it in and promptly forgotten all about it.

Barry went back to the study and dialed in again. This time the password prompt appeared on screen and he typed the word, with deliberate keystrokes, pressing his lips together as he hit the return key. Go, he urged the machine. Let me in.

And it did. Hello, Barry Shepard, he was greeted. What's new?

Too much. If only this machine could know the trouble it had caused. He logged on to the mail server and found that he'd gotten seven messages since he'd last checked. Two were marked urgent.

The first was from Jim Seidler and it was straight to the point:

> Diane doesn't have a clue what we're in for. She comes from the land of dumb terminals. My building is in an uproar. Half the people had their passwords changed while they were off at lunch. A cabling crew managed to crash ADMIN1. Chaos. Let me know where you stand. – J.S.

It was true about Diane. She was familiar with a different kind of computing environment, where employees worked at what amounted to a monitor and keyboard, with nothing on the other end but a big mainframe. When they'd presented her with the crisis list, it was obvious she was lost.

The second note was from Spakovsky:

Barry. How are we ever going to keep this inside the company? Have you looked at the bulletin board? The messages are flying. This story gets out and we'll have press camped out on the front lawn. I can see the headlines – Simtec panics. Shuts out own employees. Give me a break, we're going to have to come up with something better than the memo that went around today. You shoot me an idea and I'll take it to Diane.

Barry skipped the other mail and responded to Jim:

Much the same for me. Will continue working it out tomorrow. Should I be recabling as well?

He read Spakovsky's note for the second time. Barry didn't like politics and he wondered how the hell he'd gotten caught in the middle of this. Didn't they have a public relations department for such things, with a staff of writers, strategists, and, if necessary, people trained in doublespeak?

He tapped out a brief reply:

If it's a big problem, I'd meet with media relations. How about going with the truth – we say someone hacked in here and messed up our shipping? We've taken immediate steps to eliminate recurrences. Just leave out the money part. I think the best bet is to go with as much of the truth as we can stand.

Barry hit send and leaned back while he scanned through the other messages. Item two on the crisis list was to tear apart the order-entry system. Barry had two notes from the team he'd put on this job. One was for his approval on Wednesday to requisition more equipment. They also wanted permission to contact the original lead programmer, who no longer worked at Simtec. The other three notes were from people who thought he might know their new passwords.

Good Lord, he thought. He couldn't even remember his own.

Wednesday morning arrived far too quickly. Barry had slept fitfully, at one point lying awake for an hour while he pictured a man somewhere – he imagined a youngish man, perhaps in his thirties – logged into the Simtec net, reading the day's memos, chuckling at the inept nature of their efforts, and downloading a fresh set of bugs and other destructive programs that would self-activate at a later date.

The problem with all this worrying was, you spent enough time thinking about this person and his capabilities began to seem superhuman. A company's information structure might be vulnerable, yes, but some things could not be done. You might be able to log on with a supervisory password and delete an entire network drive, with all its information, but you could not then leap from the wire itself and cross the room to delete the backup tapes that, at Simtec, were made on a nightly basis of all file servers and databases. Nor could you delete the hard drive on an individual computer, which, for better or worse, was where many people kept their important files anyway.

Or could you? The thought of this had left Barry wide-awake, staring up at the ceiling. He made a mental note to talk to Chris about how vulnerable the employees' local computers were from access over the network. Didn't they have antivirus programs that monitored for just this kind of activity? If not, they could go in one morning to a nightmare.

He showered and shaved mechanically. Flipping off the razor, he gave himself a once-over. Strong jawline. He could live with the grey that was spreading up the sides. The wrinkles were what bothered him, forming across his forehead like fault lines. Claudia said they were dignified, but damn, they looked worse on a morning like this. Ever since the orders had been misrouted he'd been getting five hours of sleep, and last night could have been no more than four. He shrugged into a shirt, grabbed a tie, and lumbered out to the kitchen. Claudia was just preparing to leave, shuffling some notes together that were spread out on the table.

'Good luck today,' she said.

'Somehow I think we got in this game too late for luck,' he said. He poured coffee. 'It's like this: Imagine walking into a courtroom, you've had a day to prepare, the opposition has had weeks, who knows, months.'

She looked at him quizzically. 'You've always got the

million-dollar out. If things are that bad, it's really not that much.'

Barry gave a tight-lipped grin 'Didn't I tell you that part? We don't pay today, it goes up to five.'

She came over and went up on tiptoes to give him a kiss. 'I think I'd better cancel dinner with the Williamses.'

He had forgotten all about it. The thought of getting badgered by Mr. Williams, then enduring endless golf stories as well as the occasional flirtation with Claudia, was more than he could stand. 'Oh God—' he said. 'Yes. Cancel. There's no way I can make it.'

'I'll tell them there's a little glitch in the software you've got to root out.'

'And that would be the truth.'

'Done. I'll get hold of Loretta and reschedule.' Claudia grabbed her briefcase and swung toward the back door. 'Caroline's supposed to be getting dressed. Make sure she remembers her swimsuit. And call me if it's going to be late, after midnight.'

Barry had twenty minutes to kill before depositing Caroline at the Thomases, four streets over. Claudia would manage evening pickup duties at the Y. He sipped coffee and tried to recall his middle-of-the-night inspirations, many of which he had thought were not so much paranoid as actual holes that needed looking into. He was about to pick up the phone and leave Chris Jacobs a voice mail when the back door opened again and Claudia said, 'Bee?'

This was what she had started calling him when they first met twelve years ago in Dallas, but the nickname had largely fallen into disuse. 'Bee? There's a box on the hood of your car. Did you leave it there?'

He returned the phone to its cradle and walked to a side window, where he could see the driveway. Sure enough, there was a shoebox-sized parcel on the middle of the Grand Cherokee's hood. 'Now what the hell is that?' he said and started for the back door. The parcel, standing there in the early-morning sunlight, carried a sense of foreboding, and Barry imagined, irrationally, that if the car hadn't been there, neither would the package. For the hundredth time, he wished he'd gotten rid of the old ski boat that sat like a useless fiberglass blimp, usurping half the garage.

He was almost to the car when Claudia came out saying, 'Barry, maybe you shouldn't touch it.'

He paused and let his hand drop. 'Why not?'

'There could be . . . I don't know, something bad in there. Something we don't want to open.'

'Like what, someone's foot in there? I don't think so. Maybe a tape with all the files off my hard drive, but not a foot.' He had another idea, but it didn't make any sense. 'Why would they do anything to me? I'm their messenger boy. Besides, they don't know yet whether we're paying or not.'

With a frustrated slap of the hand, he whacked the package off the hood and onto the ground on the other side of the car. Nothing happened. For a moment, he and Claudia were frozen, listening.

At last, she said, 'If you ask me, that was not smart. There could be anything in that box.'

'There could be Girl Scout cookies in that box. What am I supposed to do, call a cab and leave my car pinned here because I'm afraid to move a box?' He walked around the car and picked it up. It weighed very little, and through a crack in the top he could see green Styrofoam packing worms. He pulled the flaps open and shook the box slightly to one side. Some of the worms cascaded out onto the hood of the car. There was a piece of exposed gray plastic, which he reached in and took hold of with two fingers. Gently, the way he might have extracted a piece of crystal, he removed the object and held it up. A mobile phone, with a little card attached to its base that read: *Barry. We'll be in touch!*

Barry gripped the phone more firmly. 'A present,' he said. 'And guess who I'm going to get to talk to.'

The kitchen door opened and Caroline emerged behind them.

'I'm ready,' she called. 'But I can't find my shoes.'

'Just a minute. Daddy will help you find them,' Claudia said and then lowered her voice. 'They must have come between midnight and five A.M. I don't like that, the idea of someone coming up our driveway.'

Barry hit the power on button on the phone and dialed the number for the front gate. 'Hello? This is Barry Shepard. I was wondering if I could get a list of all the visitors who have come in since midnight last night.'

'They could have walked in,' said Claudia at his shoulder.

'No, no. Nothing's wrong. Just curious . . . I see. Yes, we did get the package. And what time was that? Four o'clock . . . I can understand why you didn't want to call. . . . No, forget the list. Did you happen to jot down the license plate, by chance? In case I want to call and speak to the driver? Yes, I understand . . . from now on, that'd be fine. Just as a precaution.'

He hit the off button. 'Courier service. The gate didn't want to call and wake us up.'

'A legit courier? Leave the package on the hood of the car?'

'I have no doubt if you pay an extra fifty bucks, you could get someone to climb up on the roof and drop it down the chimney. I'll call the courier, they're called Rabbit something-or-other, but I doubt our friends are stupid enough to pay by check.'

Claudia was shaking her head. 'I gotta go,' she said. 'You be careful. This is all getting way too involved.'

Barry noticed he had turned the phone off altogether and returned it to power on. He was going to have to keep the damn thing charged, he realized, and dug back in the box to find a charger and a cigarette lighter attachment.

He returned to the house long enough to get keys, a refill on coffee, and to help Caroline hunt down her Nike tennis shoes in the laundry room.

'What were they doing in there?' she asked, and Barry wondered, even though he willed himself not to have such thoughts, whether another child might have remembered where her Nikes were. Nonsense. Everybody lost track of things. They were kids.

Caroline planted a kiss on his cheek at the Thomases' doorstep, then he climbed back in the car and flipped on National Public Radio. They were doing a segment on baseball's three hot rookies. The only sport Barry really followed was basketball. What seemed like eons ago – he was now forty-six – he had attended the University of Virginia on a basketball scholarship. This was when six foot three was still a respectable height, and you could even hope to play forward without looking like a dwarf.

He listened to a few more minutes of baseball and flipped it off. How could they go in and register for a mobile phone? You had to fill out a questionnaire, show your driver's license, arrange for payment. He had two mobile phones, one for Claudia and another one for himself that he never used. He'd sworn off driving and talking ever since he had come within inches of plowing into a pickup truck stopped in the left lane on the freeway. At the last possible second he had swerved left up onto the shoulder, hurtled by the truck, glanced off the guardrail and then down onto the road again. If there hadn't been a shoulder, or if someone had been standing over there – he didn't even like to think about it.

He slowed and swung off the interstate onto the parkway that led to Simtec's corporate offices. He'd ask Gwen to track down Jay Starns, who, last he had heard, had left the company to go work for GTE Mobilnet.

The car clock read 6:32 when he pulled into the parking lot, and Barry was shocked at the number of cars. He'd expected his network administrators to be there already, but it appeared Chris Jacobs had mobilized half the company. He saw Diane's white BMW already in its slot, as well as Jim Seidler's Explorer with the mangled front fender. It had been six months since the accident, and Barry wondered why Jim hadn't had it fixed. The man had to be pulling down a base of three hundred thousand and change, but he drove around in what looked like a rattletrap. He'd also been going through a divorce, Barry remembered. Could be the car was the last thing on his mind.

Barry waved at the guard and was halfway past the counter when the man called out, 'Sorry, Mr. Shepard, I need to get you to sign in today. Mr. Jacobs insisted that every person, all the way up to the president, has to sign in and out. No visitors past the first floor.' The man looked sheepish.

'That's quite all right,' Barry said. 'Anyone tries to get by you without signing, you have my permission to shoot them.'

This had to be taken in jest, because the Simtec security guards didn't carry guns. 'You bet,' the man said. He looked up at Barry tentatively. 'Mr. Jacobs has us going back through every entry in our logs for the past two weeks. Something bad musta happened yesterday, huh?'

Barry started to say something, but then his mouth slid closed. 'We're looking into it,' he said finally. 'I don't want to start a bunch of hearsay. We've got some concerns and we'll have a much clearer picture soon. That's about all I can say.'

'I understand,' the man said, seeming to enjoy the intrigue. 'Good luck now, you hear?'

'I appreciate that.' Barry moved off down the hallway and took the stairs to the third floor. It was dark in his office, but he could see a light flashing on his phone. He flipped on the overheads, booted his computer, and tapped a key on the keyboard to start the E-mail package.

One message was marked urgent. Also a response from the message last night to Seidler. Barry punched up an official-looking memo from Chris Jacobs that Chris had taken the time to attach to his director of security letterhead. He had cc:ed all the vice presidents, Diane, and Jim.

> Please make sure that those responsible in your areas have performed the mandatory change of password for all user accounts. This includes all supervisory accounts, and you should caution your network administrators to check that no user has inadvertently been granted admin access.
>
> Any file server not on daily backup schedule should be backed up at the earliest possible time, even if it means slowing network traffic or temporarily bumping users off-line. A checklist for 214 known servers is attached. You will be relied upon to update the list and monitor compliance in your area.
>
> Senior analyst John Hardy is holding a meeting in P-110 at 10 A.M. to discuss database files and to establish a data integrity strategy. We will be targeting spare equipment to make certain mission-critical applications available on a hot-swap basis. An analyst or administrator in charge of each application should make plans to attend.

My staff is undertaking a complete review of all available dial-up lines, and we are temporarily canceling dial-in privileges, except on a special as-needed basis. Your understanding and cooperation are appreciated.

To this, Chris had appended a personal note:

Barry, we are going over all dial-in accounts. If they got in through a hole, we'll track them down. Your dial-in password is still active. Please change it if you haven't already. The only numbers available at this time will be 252-1011 to 1018. Request any additional access for your staff directly from me.

Barry ran his fingers up across his forehead, pressing in with the tips. He could already sense that tightening feeling in the middle of his chest, and for a moment he had the unmistakable thought that *they should have paid the money.* He rose from his chair to walk it off, went out to the kitchen facility in the outer hallway, and flipped on the coffeemaker. The cleaning cart was outside the door, and the countertops reeked of ammonia.

Even had they paid, he realized, they would have had to do this. They could no longer afford to be naive. He walked back to the office and looked at the response from Jim Seidler.

No, don't bother with recabling. I'm only doing it as a fail-safe to keep certain people on line. If the backbone needs to go down, I'm going to unhook and reroute them locally. Cheers.

Barry had to think that one through. If the backbone went down, meaning, most likely, that Chris Jacobs decided to shut down the fiber that connected all the buildings on the Simtec campus, what would that mean to him? Really, they'd be able to keep going pretty much autonomously. The customer service and the order databases were there on the same floor. As long as the hubs on his floor stayed operational, they'd be able to keep servicing customers and . . . his optimistic thoughts trailed off as he realized that the link to production would be severed. His orders were queued directly into production on an hourly basis. The whole sequence of shipments could be thrown off and, depending on how long the queues stayed down . . . you could have a shipping disruption that, coupled with what had already happened, could make them a laughingstock: TechDirect Can't Get It Right. And he remembered the letter: Champagne corks popping, all right, in the halls of Michael Dell.

Barry wondered again if maybe he hadn't been singled out. Much of Simtec's core business didn't compete with mail order. It was TechDirect that did. He scribbled a note on his desk: Line→Production. He was going to make sure that, if the connection went down, they would run a line out the window and down the sidewalk if they had to.

4

Barry was getting up to walk the floor when his phone rang and the LED display reported Diane Hughes.

'Good morning,' Barry said.

'Right. You got my message about the additional year on the service agreement?'

'Yes. I'm glad you and Jim approved it. The sales reps mention the upgrade and the customers think they're getting something for free.'

'They *are* getting something for free. Anything else? I'm about to meet with Jim.'

'I was given a cellular phone. It was dropped off at my house in the middle of the night, along with a note saying they would use it to get in touch.'

'Clever. I'll let Jim know. Any second thoughts about paying?'

'None that have stuck with me.'

'Good. My sense is that they fired their big guns first in an attempt to flush us out. We run at them waving cash in the air, do you really think that's going to end it? It won't. Let me tell you a story. I thought of this yesterday before we voted. A friend of mine was leaving the grocery store to go to her car. A man came up, pinned her against the door and she dropped her keys. The man had a knife and he ordered her to get inside the car. She flat out refused. In fact, she told him to go ahead and stab her. Do it right here in the parking lot, she told him. I'm not getting in that car. And you know what the man did? He ran off. She forced him to put up or shut up and, when it came down to it, he wasn't prepared to do it. Not in a public place.'

'That's one hell of a risk. Either way.'

'In my mind, by paying these people a million dollars, we're getting in that car. We're saying, "Drive me out to a field somewhere. Do whatever you want." Have you thought about what you're going to say when that phone rings?'

'Delay as long as I can. The decision is still being resolved. I can say we're trying to get in touch with one of our board members who can't be reached. They may not know this much about us, but Michael Gaines is in Greece right now.'

'That's a good idea,' she said. 'I have every confidence you'll handle it well. I need to run.' And she did, clicking off before he could answer.

Barry's assistant, Gwen, was a young black woman with a six-year-old phenomenon named Henry. He normally stayed with Gwen's mother, but one day Henry had come to the office and caused an uproar by beating the high score on the department's copy of Fury. Gwen, they learned, allowed Henry thirty minutes a day in front of the TV and unlimited time in front of their home computer. Someone had broadcast a message about Henry's score, and employees stopped in from all over the floor to watch him play.

Right now Gwen appeared in the doorway, watching Barry turn the cellular phone in his hands.

Without looking up, Barry said, 'Do you remember Jay Starns, who used to work for us as a junior programmer?'

'He left about a year and a half ago. I think to one of the cellular companies.' She seemed to draw the connection with the object in Barry's hands. 'Do you need another phone? I didn't think you were using it any more.'

'I'm rethinking that,' said Barry. He wondered how obvious the irony in his voice was. 'I recall him going to GTE. If you could, at some point this morning track down Jay's number. Someone ought to have it, personnel, or somebody in his old group. I'd like to give him a call.'

Gwen nodded.

'Also catch Greg Mitchell as soon as he comes in. In case I'm not available, tell him he's in charge of making sure everyone gets their passwords. He should sit at his desk all morning if he has to. Anyone calls about passwords, point them to Greg.'

She dawdled behind the doorway. 'New passwords,' she said. 'Mobile phones. I guess you can't really tell me what the fuss is all about?'

'The fuss is all about this: We think someone may have been hacking around in the network a few days ago. That's why the shipments were wrong. Maybe it was an accident, maybe it was on purpose, either way we've got to try and clamp down a little more than we have been.'

'Of course,' Gwen said gravely, though she looked pleased to have been let in on this information. She marched officiously back to her office.

Barry spent the next two hours going through all the servers and database engines that serviced TechDirect. He tabulated seventeen machines that he wanted to personally account for, checking that they had been backed up and stabilized. This entailed a string of E-mail, questions, assurances, and finally, slightly different contingency plans for each machine in the event they all went down anyway.

Seventeen servers. Seventeen little hearts that pumped the lifeblood of TechDirect. According to Chris Jacobs' memo, there must be close to two hundred servers in other areas. Barry had never realized there were so many.

He dispatched three employees to the 10:00 A.M. meeting called by Chris, and instructed them to carry off any spare equipment they could lay hands on. If they needed more, Barry would walk out to production with them and they'd take whatever they needed right off the line.

Thirty-two-year-old James Dupree parked his car in the shade of a massive live oak at Rice University. Dupree was lean, and he had a wide, boyish face that could easily have passed for that of a graduate student, or even an undergrad. The conservative gray suit, however, made him appear more along the lines of an up-and-coming young professor.

He walked through the campus, regarding the stately buildings with the same detached cynicism he reserved for all things academic. These people – from the youngest student to the most senior member of the faculty – knew nothing about what went on outside their august gated entrances.

They knew nothing about the heat of battle, Dupree thought, where he was perfecting his skills as a leader of men. A warrior.

He arrived punctually for his ten o'clock appointment, and predictably, the other party was late. Dupree punched quarters into a vending machine and ordered coffee, light and sugar. The tables in the building's small snack room were battered and stained, and he automatically chose one in the corner, with his back to the wall.

Simtec would be in the midst of chaos, and Dupree imagined this chaos with a mixture of amusement and resolution. It was good to sow disorder in the ranks of the opponent, but the only thing that counted, in the end, was the achievement of his objective. By whatever means necessary.

A middle-aged man in a rumpled shirt and tie appeared uncertainly in the doorway. He saw Dupree and shuffled over to the table.

'Some students caught me outside and started badgering me about their Friday project,' the man said, frowning. 'I hope I'm not late.'

'Not at all, Dr. Milstead. Please have a seat.'

The man seated himself and immediately began fidgeting. Dupree watched.

'I take it my last work was . . . satisfactory?' the man said.

'I wouldn't be here if it wasn't.'

Dupree relished this kind of power play. As a student in this professor's class, he would have received nothing but contempt, yet here he was with his thumb on the man's spine. Dupree had given no reason for this meeting. As the man who signed the checks, it was enough that he requested it.

With slow deliberation, as though he might change his mind at any moment, Dupree withdrew a diskette and a folded piece of paper from his pocket. The paper had a short descriptive paragraph of the programming work that Dupree desired, and the professor accepted it greedily.

Dupree sipped stale coffee, staring over the rim of the cardboard cup. However unwittingly they might have been conscripted, these were his troops. Right now they consisted of one twenty-six-year-old kid, uncommonly gifted in the arts of electronic manipulation; a loyal ex-con of questionable intelligence; and a rotating pool of three university Ph.D.'s whom, save for their ability to write computer code, Dupree considered utterly replaceable. Tucked away in their musty university cubbyholes, these men joyfully entered into temporary contracts doing under-the-table programming jobs for one Patrick Draper, of Data Security Incorporated. Draper's 800 number and false address in Mount Rose, Virginia, proved fertile soil. They did it for the money, the challenge, or out of misplaced patriotism. At least one professor had become convinced he was fighting the commies, the Libyans, or whatever devils his underworked imagination chose to conjure.

Dupree thought it nothing short of remarkable that he had forged these disparate ores into a weapon capable of success. He forked open his checkbook, pen poised to scribble a figure in the upper four digits.

The professor looked up and said, 'It's a modified SCSI driver. I can do this. I presume the driver's on this disk.'

'Correct. When it goes active, phase one will be of your own design. Phase two is to scramble the information on any attached hard drives.'

'The latter part is a snap.' The professor was on his own turf now, and he was emboldened. 'As long as they are SCSI drives, the driver handles communication to and from the drive. As indicated in the specifications, it can be triggered by date.'

A *snap*. Dupree almost smiled. He shaved several thousand from the price. 'And most network file servers would be using SCSI drives.'

'Certainly,' Milstead said. 'Though there are many different drivers—'

'I understand that. This is one specific implementation. What about the other requirements? The agency . . . excuse me,' Dupree waved a hand in the air, as though he might recall the words. 'The *application* calls for the maximum destructive capabilities.'

'You want to get to the workstations. This is more problematic, but of course it can be done.' Dr. Milstead stared intently at the instructions, mumbling his thoughts. 'You could wait until a workstation requests a file. An EXE file would perhaps be easiest. Then you patch into the header, if there's enough space, and send down the file. Yes, that might do it. It appears you wish to disable many network devices. Perhaps a large internetwork?' He looked up at Dupree, who simply raised an eyebrow.

'The machines will topple like dominoes,' Milstead continued. 'After a short time period, I'd expect any competent network staff to simply shut them all off. Disaster is clearly afoot. I'd advise that you wait no longer than ten minutes before entering phase two.'

Dupree's eyes narrowed into a look of shrewd appraisal, and the pen paused over the checkbook

Dr. Milstead leaned forward. A dry tongue darted out over his lips.

'Yes, indeed.' Dupree said, at last. 'Ten minutes it is. Something tells me you have a knack for this, Doctor.' The pen now continued, and the furrows in the professor's brow abated.

'We have something of a compressed time frame on this. The activation date is July twenty-fifth, but I need the file in thirty-six hours. Is that going to present any difficulty?'

The professor's eyes crackled with life. How much better this was than teaching the bubble-sort algorithm to two hundred freshmen in the intro class. How much more exciting than going over the Towers of Hanoi solution for the hundredth time. How much more profitable than teaching the same community college course from 6:00 to 8:00 P.M. on Tuesday and Thursday nights for the entire godforsaken semester.

'It will be done,' the professor said.

'You know the rules. There must be no discussion of this work with your colleagues. I can personally assure you, though, that your task is vital and does not go unnoticed.'

The professor nodded. He was accustomed to leisure and might ordinarily have stretched the project out for weeks. He might have to break this vow of secrecy and recruit his top graduate students to assist in pieces of the actual coding, but he could disguise the nature of the project. The time restraint was severe, and classes would be canceled. Advisory duties would be shifted to an underling. Extraordinary measures would have to be taken.

Dupree signed the check with the name Pat Draper and pushed it across the table. Half payment now, half upon completion. Dupree had a roomful of test equipment, and he intended to put the product through its paces.

The professor sat up straight in his chair, meaningfully folded and secreted away his payment.

'I will call in twenty-four hours to check on your progress,' Dupree said. He rose and extended his hand, then glanced at his watch and hurried out of the dingy snack room.

Instead of returning to his car, Dupree walked to the library and went directly to the computer science section on the second floor. This was often the cradle for his ideas. He would allow himself thirty minutes to browse, pulling books haphazardly from the shelves, waiting for serendipity to happen.

He had a Motorola flip-phone in his pocket, and he could direct his attack anytime, anywhere. In this particular battle, Dupree had more accurate intelligence than he had ever had before. He had been sought out and, for the first time, had a job handed to him on a silver platter. Nonetheless, he knew the Simtec Computer Corporation might well try a display of nerve.

James Dupree could feel the brush-off coming. All along, he had planned several moves ahead, and he would be ready.

At 10:45, Gwen buzzed with the information that Jay Starns did, in fact, work for GTE Mobilnet, and would Barry like for her to get Jay on the line?

'Sure,' said Barry, emerging from his thoughts about whether to start moving applications around between servers and, if so, could two servers handle the workload generated by even a fraction of the 560 people in his building?

She rang Jay and clicked off.

'Hello? Jay, I'm glad we were able to track you down.'

'You bet, Barry. What can I do for you?'

Barry had never known the man well. Jay had been doing a good job picking up the C programming language, and emptying his head of the useless notions they had taught him in school, but then the PC market had stumbled and Simtec started its layoffs. Jay had probably seen his number coming.

'Jay, the thing is, we've got a few phones here. Take this one, for example. It's a gray phone someone dropped off and now it's kicking around my office. Who knows if it's a Simtec phone, a personal phone, or who it's getting billed to. There must be some kind of way to track that sort of thing down.'

Jay laughed. 'You must be bored over there, Barry, to start worrying about things like that. Sure there's a way. Every phone has a serial number on it somewhere. On that one it's probably inside the battery compartment, and we can look it up from the number. It'll either be a GTE account or Houston Cellular. We have lost and stolen phones turn up all the time.'

Barry was cradling the receiver with his chin, pawing around on the mobile phone to get the plate off and see inside. Sure enough there were several different numbers in there. 'Okay,' he said. 'I've got it. There's a long number and a shorter one right under it.' He read out the nine-digit serial number. 'Are you able to look it up?'

'Hold on while I get to a terminal,' said Jay. He sounded amused. Ten seconds later he was back on. 'That comes up as one of yours. The account is only two weeks old.'

'The phone is registered to Simtec?'

'No,' said Jay. 'That's one of your personal phones. Barry Shepard on Willow Creek Lane, right? You say someone found it and dropped it off? You've only had it two weeks.'

'Hell, I don't know. I'm telling you, these phones are a mess over here. I ought to start putting labels on them. So this one is mine, you say, and it was added to my account two weeks ago?'

'That's right. You got any others you want to check?'

'I tell you what, Jay. Instead of wasting your time while I dig these all up, why don't I put together a list of all the numbers. Is there somebody in particular I should send it to?'

'Just fax it to my attention and I'll take care of it,' said Jay. 'No problem.'

'Thanks,' said Barry. 'You've been a big help.' He rang off and sat back in his chair. So, he was paying for his own phone.

How tidy. What he couldn't get over was that the bastards had it all planned out two weeks ago.

He was considering the implications when Gwen buzzed and one of Chris Jacobs' technical people came in with a gadget the size of a toaster under his arm.

'Looks like something I don't want to get,' Barry said.

'We cooked this up on short notice,' said the man, plopping the item down on Barry's desk as though he should be expecting it. 'It's primitive but will work well enough for what you want.'

Barry wondered if maybe he hadn't missed something somewhere. The guy was acting as if he'd ordered this thing, but he played along. 'Fine. Can you show me how it works?'

'Sure. Is this the phone?' The technician indicated the mobile phone sitting on Barry's desk.

'Yes.'

'Hmmm.' The man picked the phone up and struggled to get it fitted sideways in the box. He had apparently not expected the phone to be so large, because he had to undo some screws and adjust the width of the opening. When the phone slid comfortably in, he retightened the screws. 'Just answer the phone and set it in here like this, then press this button on the front to start the tape.'

So that's what this was about.

'It's just a modified speakerphone, with a little cassette recorder stuck in between. Here, let's try it out.' The man picked up the desk phone. 'What's the number?'

Barry shrugged and opened his hands. 'Beats me,' he said, thinking himself an idiot for not asking Jay Starns.

The technician frowned, the look on his face saying that he knew crap when he heard it. Here's a phone on the desk, they're going to record conversations on it, and Barry Shepard says he doesn't know the number. 'Whatever,' the man muttered, and turned to leave.

'What about those little suction cups?' Barry said. 'I think they sell them at Radio Shack. That would be a lot easier than this contraption.'

'Not on a mobile phone.' The technician's expression said, *You don't know much, big shot.*

'Can I take this thing with me?' said Barry. 'It'll work in the car, wherever?' He hadn't seen any cords.

'Four size D batteries. It doesn't turn on unless you hit the button. If I were you, I'd try it out first.' The man backed out of the doorway and disappeared.

So, thought Barry, they were trusting him to speak for the company, but they damn sure wanted to hear what he said. It put him in an awkward position, because the contraption on his desk made him realize he would rather they didn't hear his conversation. What if the conversation got ugly? What if he said the wrong thing? Christ, they'd probably sit in the boardroom and play it back, over and over again. You should have said this, Barry. What if you'd said that, Barry? You blew it, Barry.

Shit.

At noon, Barry thought getting up and moving around might do something for the knot in his stomach. He decided to walk the building and check on progress. The crisis team had done a good job conveying both what had to be done and that this was no ordinary fire drill. The air crackled with intensity. Ironically, the last time it had felt this way was the morning the company had come out with hundreds of pink slips. Greg Mitchell's desk was covered with scribbled notes, and Barry hated to think that this clutter was the repository for everyone's new passwords. But Greg affirmed that almost everyone had been able to resume working normally.

A cable crew was on the third floor, working on a rewiring scheme, and Barry paused to give them instructions about a backup line to the production center. Servers and databases were being backed up. Spare equipment was being configured. The knot in Barry's stomach began to dissipate. The only time he'd seen this much activity was when they'd set the whole thing up in the first place. Only this go-round it was even more vital that it be done now and done right.

At 12:20, there was an eruption in the phone bank. One of the telephone sales reps, April Rhodes, got the toughest call of her four-month Simtec career. She'd had people be short with her, pissed off that a network card wasn't in stock, or that the RAM upgrade was going to tack on another $149.

She'd had customers pissed off because they bought RAM as well as those who were pissed off because they hadn't. Why didn't you tell me? they said. I can't run shit with eight megabytes. Send me the goddamn RAM. I'm not going to be able to get my system up for a week.

That was about as bad as it got.

But this one said, 'You bitch. I've got to wait until you get this piece of crap back and then send me what I ordered?'

'We're sorry about that,' she said. 'We're all working overtime to make sure any problem is immediately rectified.'

'Well, April,' the man said. 'Then why don't you come over here and fuck me in the meantime?'

'Excuse me,' April said politely. 'I just need to verify the configuration and we can send it out. Possibly even today.'

'Possibly?' the man said. 'Do you have a brain? Did they pull a bunch of whores off the street to take orders?'

Her voice trembling, April said, 'You can give me your order now, or you can wait until somebody else gets around to calling you.'

'I'll give you my order. You can blow me. And the six other guys in my office, while we're waiting for your stupid ass to get this right.'

Which was about when April lost it. She started yelling into the phone. She yelled every obscenity she could think of. They came out of her mouth like fiery rockets and ricocheted off the walls. She tore off her two-hundred-dollar headset and strangled it. The entire phone room – thirty-five other TSRs and their customers – was shocked into absolute silence. April then leapt from her desk and ran out of the room crying.

No one knew what to do. After a minute, two of the others went out after her, finally locating April outside on the back steps of the building, still sobbing and cursing and balling her fists in the air. Somebody else went to find Barry Shepard, because, by God, he was paid six figures and this had to be one of the times he was supposed to earn it.

Barry asked them to bring April up to his office, which they did with much coaxing and arm-patting and handkerchiefs. Barry immediately assured her that no, she was not in trouble, and he spent the next fifteen minutes hearing everything the customer had told her, her responses, her restraint, and finally, how if she'd had the Lady Smith & Wesson she kept in the closet at home, she would have put a bullet in this man's head.

Barry looked up the man's address in the database. He reminded her the man was in Minneapolis, so forget about the bullet in the head. He declared they were not going to sell equipment to such a person, and this seemed to cheer April somewhat. Barry then dispatched an order for Federal Express to pick up the machine, he put a block on future orders from the man, and he gave April the rest of the day off.

Barry himself went and stood in front of the office refrigerator. Just as tension could flow from the top of a company downward, it could clearly move in the other direction as well. The anger and the stress started with the customers and boiled its way up into the front lines. The front lines heated up until the whole seething mass came straight in through your office doorway. Barry shook his head and got out a can of Coke. He leaned back and held the can against his forehead.

In the crawl space above the acoustical ceiling tiles, the air in Simtec 4 was eighty-four degrees and thick with dust. Ben Cooper pushed a flashlight along ahead of him, coming slowly down the metal service walkway on his hands and knees. There was supposed to be a light up there, but either the bulbs were gone or the circuit was out, so he'd play the flashlight up ahead for a few feet, checking for cobwebs, low girders, and other obstructions, and then he'd shuffle forward and repeat the process.

Ben was searching for several sets of unused computer wiring, a backup line supposedly stretching from one server room all the way to human resources. No one knew where these wires were or how to find them. Ben Cooper had been a Simtec employee since the beginning, just after he'd given up the two-weeks-on two-weeks-off routine of offshore oil drilling and taken the supply ship back into port for good. Ben Cooper said he remembered pulling that wiring in Simtec 4 with his own hands, and if Mr. Shepard said it had come to that, he'd go back up there and follow it inch by inch until he figured out where it all went.

It had come to that.

Unfortunately, Simtec 4 was one of the largest buildings on the campus, housing the TechDirect administration and analysts, the TSR facility, as well as the marketing department and a chunk of human resources. The three divisions were extremely interdependent electronically. Each shared common wiring, which had repeatedly been expanded over the company's initial years of spectacular growth. All three shared several application and file servers, and there were also a number of strictly local servers.

Two years ago, Barry had been put in charge of network operations for Simtec 4. Jim Seidler still officed there, but he didn't want the job, and the VP of marketing didn't grasp the issues involved.

Most of the time, the duty meant no more than attending monthly net-op meetings, helping to draft new policies and procedures and then disseminating the information. But Barry now had a formidable goal: to ensure that, should the network backbone that connected to all his disparate charges go down, he had at least one line to each group that could be counted on. If they had to, they could snap a cheap concentrator on the one good line and snake wiring across the floor to other priority machines in each office.

Ben heard a scuffling sound and he froze. Cobwebs and dirt and stale air he could take, but the one thing he didn't like the idea of was rats. And as he'd moved further and further away from the service door, never able to see more than about five feet ahead, he'd been wondering if there were any up there. He listened, his chest moving in and out while sweat ran down his neck, dripping off his nose onto the dusty ceiling tiles below the catwalk. The rustling sound continued, and it was vaguely comforting to hear it continue, unchanged now for the last minute. Far worse to have it stop, wondering where it was now, this very moment a damn furry thing right next to your hand or about to go up a pants leg.

He moved the flashlight around, tracing it over the conduit and ventilation shafts that ran the length of the building. The light paused when he saw a flicker of movement. Several fingers of heavy aluminum tape had blown loose on the ductwork, and the air was pushing them back and forth against one another. Looked like a job for the air-conditioning people, and Ben would try to remember to send them up. He moved ahead, adjusting his sweaty grip on the flashlight and occasionally mopping his forehead with a shirtsleeve.

What Ben could not see, and probably would never have seen even if the entire crawl space had been lit with a floodlight, was that three sections of the metal track ahead of his slow advance, someone had wedged a piece of cardboard in between the snaps that fastened the two sections together. It wasn't as if the section would fall. The twelve-inch walkway and the three-foot cable tray beside it were attached with metal rods to cement supports that anchored the fourth floor. Or even if it did fall, you might at worst land, *poof!* onto the ceiling tiles and come crashing through onto the top of somebody's desk. No, the cardboard was there for another reason.

The cardboard was there just in case somebody like Ben Cooper came snooping along, where Simtec employees usually had no reason to go. What Ben would also never see, and what investigators would later call an 'inadvertent electrical fault', was that an insulated wire had been sawed clear down to the bare copper, and that the copper was wedged into a groove in that section now isolated from the rest of the walkway. The unfortunate effect of which was to electrify the entire walkway from that point on with a power source connected back to a forty-amp breaker.

Ben Cooper inched ahead, separating out one set of gray wires on the cable tray beside him. He thought these were the ones he was looking for, because about every six feet another one of them went snaking off into the blackness where, he assumed, it went down the wall and out to a data jack in somebody's office. At the end of each wire you'd find anything and everything. A 286 with dual floppies. A host of middle-aged machines running Windows 3.x. Or the latest scorchers to enter the marketplace, complete with the latest Windows and all the most recent patches downloaded weekly from Microsoft OEM Direct. Given the sheer quantity and spectrum of equipment, most of the internal support technicians hadn't come up for air in years.

Ben decided he'd simply trace the wires to HR and see where they went. He bet he'd find several runs still sitting there coiled up in the ceiling.

He would not come near the wire, though, that ran off into a corner in a place where, if you made a precarious journey over a series of support girders, you might see the small dial-up box that would allow network access to anyone with a password that allowed them to get in. Even if he did see the box, Ben might have thought it a piece of Simtec's own equipment. He was not particularly computer literate, and it would have taken quite a leap to imagine a box that could sit there, right in his own building, and allow in more enemy than the Trojan horse.

The box was forty feet away, and the investigators, by the time they got that far, would be crouched over, the sweat pouring down their backs, the dirt accumulating in their nostrils. They would scan the immediate area and get the hell out.

Ben moved another twenty feet and paused. Sweat ran freely down his forearms now, and he rocked back onto his feet and squatted for a moment. He noticed a scrap of crumpled paper on the catwalk near his right foot and he picked it up. A green, one-day security pass. Ben envisioned a sloppy contractor throwing his pass down, and if he had only uncrumpled it and read the date, July 11, he might have paused for a moment and wondered who had been up here as recently as eight days before. No contractors should have been up in this ceiling for months. No one else went up in the ceiling unless they absolutely had to. Ben tucked the paper into his top pocket and rocked forward onto his hands and knees. Both hands came down on the other side of the break between sections twenty-three and twenty-four.

His hands clamped onto the grill with the flashlight pinned underneath his right thumb. The electricity came up both arms into his body and popped one shoulder out of its socket on the way through. It exited down through his right knee where it blew out his kneecap, shot down the rest of the walkway, and went to ground. There was a fraction of a second – Ben felt his forearms tighten, and thought *cramp* – when he knew he'd done it good this time. Too much work with the screwdriver and pliers, twisting and crimping and squeezing. Ben Cooper died in a flash of apprehension that this, at last, must be the dreaded carpal tunnel syndrome.

The breaker blew like it was supposed to, and Ben's body slumped forward onto the catwalk. Section number twenty-four was somewhat loose and it shifted slightly under the weight. A piece of folded-up cardboard fell from a crack and fluttered down onto the ceiling tiles below.

5

By four-thirty they were all in the Simtec 3 boardroom again: Chief Executive Officer Diane Hughes, Executive Vice President Jim Seidler, Vice President and Director of TechDirect Barry Shepard, Director of Security and Internal Affairs Chris Jacobs, Chief Financial Officer Mike Spakovsky, and Chief Counsel Karen Williams. Barry knew word of these meetings and who was in them got out and spread through the company by way of a very efficient grapevine. He wondered what others who were not invited to these meetings must be thinking, like the VP of marketing, the VP of worldwide sales, or the directors who presided over various smaller pieces of the company.

The vice president of marketing, an extremely serious, prune-faced man named Randall, had passed him in the hallway earlier with only the barest of nods. 'Barry,' he had muttered, and then walked on clutching a sheaf of papers and trying to move, Barry thought, as importantly as possible. Barry had been carrying his mobile phone and the taping device, which Randall eyed suspiciously but did not ask about.

The device now sat on the floor at Barry's feet and he prayed it didn't ring. The only thing worse than being taped would be to have the conversation right here in front of this entire crew.

Diane sat erect at the head of the table. Everything from her square-shouldered red jacket to her hair, close cropped on the sides, was precise and in place. 'As some or all of you are aware,' she started, 'we had a tragic mishap at approximately two-fifteen this afternoon. A workman named Ben Cooper was tracing some wiring. He somehow came into contact with live electricity and was killed, I am told, instantaneously.'

Barry was grateful she didn't say who requested that Ben perform the trace.

'No one is to blame here,' she said, echoing his own thoughts. 'But this does underscore the need for caution. These are urgent times, but did Mr. Cooper take a chance up there? Perhaps. Was he in too much of a hurry? We don't know.'

Oh, great, thought Barry. The implication here was that Ben might have been forced into carelessness. But the man was fully capable of handling the job. He knew what he was doing.

'Jim?'

Seidler looked haggard. His shirt collar and tie were askew, and he sat hunched over in his chair.

'They've already taken the body out,' he said. 'The area will be closed off until some investigators get in there and have a go at it. Barry, I'm sure they're going to want a statement as to what he was doing up there; then they can piece together what he did wrong. I'm told a loose wire came into contact with something he was standing on. It sounds like a freak accident to me. Totally unnecessary.'

Barry cleared his throat. 'After consulting with Karen, I've already given a brief account to the police for their report. Mr. Cooper was trying to find some unused wiring pairs that were apparently stretched to human resources at the time the building was originally cabled. We were in the process of creating a backup wiring plan that we could use in place of the backbone.'

Chris Jacobs had his shirtsleeves rolled up, exposing muscular forearms. He came forward onto his elbows, clearly agitated. 'We might want to talk about that later,' he said. 'There are times when that plan would be fine, but other times you wouldn't want to cut over, no matter what wiring you're on.'

Barry nodded, his fingers laced tightly together. He was well aware of the different scenarios.

'Hello?' said Spakovsky, across the table. 'I know it's tragic, and all that, and we should try and not have this happen again. But it has, and aren't there some other points to discuss? Like what is our liability on this?'

Diane glared. 'Mr. Cooper is married with two children. We will offer to honor his salary until age sixty, at which time the family would receive the usual retirement package. We will also offer a four-year college scholarship for each child to any Texas school of their choosing, providing they meet the admissions requirements.'

Numbers whirred in the CFO's head. Fifteen years at thirty-five thousand, retirement, eight years college – hell, they could go to SMU, which was probably twenty thousand a year – couldn't they make it any *state* school and put them in the good old University of Houston?

'Okay, that's about nine hundred thousand. Can we put some restrictions on which school they choose? Karen, do you think this will keep them from suing?'

Karen Williams said, 'My staff is preparing documents to support claims against the original contractor, the manufacturer of the wiring, and the structural components of the walkway and cabling system. We'll be ready.'

'One heck of a wiring fault, I'd say. But if the widow sues then she doesn't get the benefits, am I right?'

'Let's take that as it comes,' Diane said. She shot Spakovsky a stern glance.

'I'm sorry for the guy, all right? I didn't even know him, and I'm sorry about it. But we've got a company to run here. You think this won't play in the press? They love this stuff – the poor victimized family, left behind when Daddy got eaten by the corporate monster. It's all fine to have someone sit around and play the harp, but I'm going to have to go out and do damage control.'

'So this is what we've come to,' Barry said, addressing no one in particular. As usual, when he made a statement the others stopped bickering long enough to listen. 'We're arguing about how to avoid liability, how to pigeonhole an employee's children in the cheapest college possible. Some would argue that we have indeed become that corporate monster.'

No one filled the silence that followed. Spakovsky looked sullen. Karen Williams studied the wall.

In the back of his mind, Barry knew that Mike Spakovsky was, at times, correct. It had been this way from the moment he'd come aboard. The rest of them would range far afield, discussing some new project, or a new philosophy of doing business. Spakovsky always pulled them back, sometimes with annoying brusqueness, but he was anchored with a thick chain to corporate earnings, and the executive officers, in turn, were anchored to him.

That made the present discussion no more appetizing, and very ironic, considering Spakovsky's nine-hundred-thousand figure for the payoff to Cooper's family. Here they were, unwilling to pay out a million-dollar ransom, and it had already cost them close to that very same amount. When you added the overtime that had already been put in, the lost productivity from downed servers, and the password fiasco, they'd spent more than a million. The only good to come out of it was that they'd run a tougher and less vulnerable operation from this point on.

'Let's move on,' Diane said, finally. 'How's progress on the list?'

'We've had a mandatory change of password,' Chris Jacobs said. 'A great quantity of new equipment was distributed out to departmental teams this morning. They can use it for backup, testing, whatever they need. We're examining dial-up lines, visitor logs from all the security desks, and we've run reserve cabling on a limited basis.'

'Barry?'

'The group looking into order entry assures me that there is no software glitch, nothing built into the database that could scramble equipment configurations. It was either done manually or with an automated tool that was then erased. The latter is the most likely, as it would take a long time to key in changes to four thousand records.

'Almost certainly the person had access as a registered user, which means they had a password. Unfortunately, a lot of employees have authority to enter a configuration change. Customers call us all the time and tweak their orders. You know, "I was just over at my friend's house, and now I want a seventeen-inch monitor. I want more memory." Whatever. We get this all the time.'

'What about the change stamp?' Jim said, rubbing furiously at one watery eye.

More for Diane's benefit than anyone else in the room, Barry explained. 'He's talking about what happens when somebody enters a change. Their user ID is stamped into a change field along with the date and time. We're finding the altered records have been stamped with a variety of IDs. This means that, again, they either had multiple passwords and made each of the changes manually, or they had higher-level access and did it with a tool that utilized the other IDs.'

Diane was frowning.

'We've now restricted modification rights to one senior person per shift, and we've changed all existing passwords. I've got three TSRs assigned to do nothing but call and verify configurations. They choose customers at random and make phone contact prior to shipping. So far, no alterations have been found since Saturday.'

'He's now off in somebody else's sandbox,' Mike Spakovsky said gloomily.

No one took the bait.

It was at this moment that the cellular phone by Barry's right foot chirped violently. He'd never heard it ring before, and it took him completely by surprise. He looked around the room for a moment before he realized what it was, and that everyone was staring at him.

Barry hoisted the box up onto the table in front of him. The phone rang again insistently and Barry glared at it, feeling trapped. He pushed the answer button and slid the phone into the slot.

'Hello?' he said. 'This is Barry Shepard.'

'Barry,' came the voice through the speaker. 'This is *Hektor*. With a *k*, H-e-k-t-o-r. At least that's what we'll call me. As in, Hektor, scourge of the Akhaians.'

Damn! The tape wheels weren't turning. Barry hit the on switch.

'You probably don't get the reference.'

'No,' said Barry. 'I don't. You want to be called Hektor? All right. You're Hektor.'

'Like lambs to the slaughter,' came the voice of Hektor, with apparent satisfaction. Then, 'Hektor wants to know why he's being taped.'

Barry stared straight ahead, knowing he was going to have to ignore the others in the room and think on his feet. He made a split-second decision to go with the truth. This Hektor character might sound like a fool, he might try to project that image, but he was certainly not a fool at all.

'I'm going to tape the conversation whenever we talk,' said Barry. 'Our board insisted on it, if they're going to authorize that kind of payment. How do they know you're not some buddy of mine who's going to walk off with a pocketful of gold?'

Hektor seemed to think that was funny. He didn't seem half as nervous as Barry himself was.

'Is that what I'm going to do? Walk off with a pocketful of gold? I'd prefer a check, Barry. Can you keep the gold and write me a check?'

'It's up to the board,' said Barry. 'But we are unfortunately having a lot of trouble locating Michael Gaines, one of our board members. He's on vacation in Greece. That's the holdup, but we should have an answer soon.'

Hecktor was silent. Then he said, 'It's not up to the board. It's up to management. This is bad, Barry. I'm sorry about this.'

Barry's heart was pounding. Was the man bluffing? He seemed absolutely certain of what he was saying.

Less confidently, Barry said, 'I don't know what you're thinking. I can't just write a check for a million dollars. We've called Mykonos repeatedly to track down Gaines and get an answer.'

'Mykonos . . . hmm. What's the name of the place you're calling? I might want to call myself.'

'I don't know. I didn't take care of the details, but I can find out. Mr. Gaines will phone in the moment he is contacted.'

A long exhale.

'So be it,' said Hektor. 'I'll be in touch.'

The phone clicked off. Chris Jacobs and Karen Williams

erupted in spontaneous clapping. They seemed to think that Hektor had indicated acceptance of Barry's explanation, but then the others weighed in and they were not so sure. They spent the next ten minutes arguing over the meaning of the phrase *So be it.*

By 7:00 P.M., the network hadn't come crashing down. The phones were still ringing. New orders were coming in. Old orders were being verified. Everything would be okay. Barry stood and stretched his neck and shoulders, trying to placate the tension that had gathered in the middle of his upper back.

The phone rang in from an outside line and Barry's first fragile moment of optimism evaporated. He gave the telephone a baleful stare. On the third ring, he snatched up the receiver.

'Shepard.'

'Whoa,' Claudia's voice. 'Comfort call from the home front. We're making spaghetti and Caroline informs me that it will be ready precisely at eight o'clock.'

She waited, but when Barry didn't say anything she asked, 'How did it go today?'

'It went,' Barry said. 'The guy called right at five. He calls himself Hektor. *Hektor,* the asshole tells me, with a *k.* Scourge of somebody or other.'

'That would be the battle of Troy,' Claudia said. 'Hektor was a great warrior. Perhaps you're being attacked by a classicist.'

Barry knew she was trying to joke, but his lips only managed to pinch together in frustration.

'I take it you didn't pay the money.'

'Not yet. I tried to delay him but—' Barry considered for a moment if he should discuss this on the phone. He could, after all, be telling Hektor exactly what he wanted to know. 'We don't know if he was satisfied by the explanation. I was telling the truth. We've had trouble getting hold of the necessary board members.'

'I was watching the news here, Bee. I had the TV on, but I wasn't really paying attention. I heard something about a man being electrocuted out at Simtec today.'

'We had an accident. A worker was up in the ceiling following some wire and he must have gotten hold of the wrong thing.'

'That's awful,' she said, but she sounded relieved.

'What did they say on the news?'

'I was only half listening until I heard them mention Simtec. They said that a man was electrocuted and showed footage of paramedics out in the parking lot. It was pretty standard coverage. Why?'

'Just wanted to know how it appeared. Spakovsky pulled me aside and started jawing about how all this would look with the analysts. He likes to worry a lot, and when you spend too much time around him you start to worry yourself.'

'It sounds to me like you need to come home and have some spaghetti.'

'I'll be there as soon as I can,' he said. 'I need to finish typing up an accident report and I have a few things to check on.'

'We'll see you when you get here.'

He hung up the phone and swiveled back around to the typewriter. Not only the accident form, but the physical act of typing at a typewriter was a rarity. Most of Simtec's internal documents had been moved on-line. Personnel information, benefit and payroll arrangements, all could be accessed by a few mouse clicks. Barry was a self-taught typist, and he was so used to the flexibility of a word processor that his typed report was becoming a mess.

Under Accident Details, subheading Severity, he had first typed 'tragic' and then decided that was inappropriate. Many accidents were tragic. He used the correction ribbon to delete this word and type 'major'. He then realized that the correction only worked on the top copy and the subsequent copies now looked like gobbledygook. He x'ed out the whole thing, breathed out a long sigh, and wrote DECEASED in capital letters.

Section III said, Description of Job-related Duties During Which Accident Was Sustained. Barry typed, 'Tracing wire'. The form left a gap large enough for several sentences, so Barry added, 'Mr. Cooper had volunteered to trace several sets of unused wiring pairs to determine their presence and possible access points. As a maintenance worker, this function was well within the scope of Mr. Cooper's duties and capability.'

Barry read that back and wished he hadn't written 'volunteered to trace'. It made Cooper sound like a martyr. Also the last part was overly defensive. Barry weighed the prospects of another cross-out. *The hell with* it. He'd get Karen to sign off on the language before they made it official.

He was nearing the bottom of the form when he heard a knock at the door and Jim Seidler's voice said warmly, 'Barry. Imagine you still being here.'

'Yes,' Barry said. 'Imagine that.'

'I just wanted to stop by and have a chat. I think the phone call went well, by the way.'

'We'll know soon enough.'

'It was a good shot, anyway. And there may be nothing old Hektor can do about it. Hektor says, Pay me a million dollars. Wouldn't you have loved to answer, Barry says, Jump up my ass?'

Barry grinned at this. Jim Seidler could be all right, dead serious but able to joke sometimes, too, even when two steps from the precipice.

'I would have paid to see the look on his face.'

Jim had taken his tie off and had his collar unbuttoned. He handed Barry a printout and glanced about the office. 'We really need to get you a safe in here. I wanted to make sure you got a master list of the new administrative passwords. Add the TechDirect admins on there when you get a minute. There's the chance we'll have to go through this whole password exercise again.'

'I can certainly change passwords. My secondary account has supervisory access to all our servers, but Greg Mitchell's been handling most of that for me—'

Jim gave his head a quick, vigorous shake. 'No, I'd rather it be you. For the time being, we'd like to keep this within our own circle as much as possible.'

'Fine with me, but I won't be very efficient. The last time I did network admin was several years ago.'

'I'm just making sure we've got a handful of people we can go to and have the whole company covered. If it comes to that, you'd either delegate it out or have someone in here working at your elbow. I've got no problem with the way you're doing things. This is all a just-in-case scenario.'

Barry added a note, *Review Admin Procedures,* to the legal pad on his desk. He'd been adding and checking off items all day. 'No problem,' he said.

Jim seemed to relax and again adopt his social demeanor. 'You out of here soon?'

'Soon as I finish this report and check on my people.'

'Good,' Jim said. 'Get some sleep. Chris is going to have people here all night.'

6

Many Simtec users make the mistake of referring to Microsoft Windows as an operating system when, in reality, Windows is no more than a program, or a collection of programs, that provides a user interface that millions of people find convenient. The latest version of Windows was supposed to change all that and to make life easier in a variety of other ways, but many companies have been loath to make the switch.

The Simtec Corporation is no exception. Employees flocked to Windows in the late 1980s and now, whether the employee is using WordPerfect, Lotus 1-2-3, Word, Quark XPress or SPSS, chances are that employee is running it from a Windows environment.

For the younger personnel, so attached are they to their Windows that they hardly comprehend the presence of the true underlying operating system that, for fully half the employees at Simtec, is still good old DOS in one of its many incarnations. If these employees mistakenly exit out of Windows, they stare blankly at the screen which now holds a cursor, waiting patiently beside any one of a dozen drive letters: C, D, H, M, N, S. They do not have a clue what has happened or where to go from here, although the event swiftly and surely triggers a Pavlovian response. The employee catches his breath and types WIN, which more often than not is enough to bring him back to familiar territory and calm his beating heart.

The newest Windows had done little to change this situation. For the end user, the background processes that govern bootup, log-in scripts, and hardware configuration are still cloaked in a murky veil. One Simtec study estimated the cost of a wholesale Windows upgrade would cost the company as much as thirty million dollars, so this is to remain a slow metamorphosis.

Home computer users have always been astounded when they first examine Windows and attempt to sort through, and make sense of, the myriad files placed into what is usually the C:\windows directory. The user opens a file – it's a text file, so it should be something intelligible and relevant, right? – and the user might see something like:

> Wingtips=408080, C0C0C0, FFFFFF, 0, FFFFFF, 0, 808080, FFFFFF

Which is akin to opening the hood of your car and finding a small, glowing green ball instead of belts, hoses, spark plugs, and a radiator. Hoses can be replaced. Broken belts can be spotted. Wingtips=408080 is another matter entirely.

Inevitably, the user closes the hood to his or her computer, feeling somewhat chastened, and simply hopes the whole thing starts and runs the way it is supposed to. This happens every day, between thirty and forty million times, all across the United States of America.

In Simtec's accounting department, an area low on the priority list for hardware upgrades, John Hracek still sits down every day at an elderly 486 with Windows 3.11. The Windows application uses John's personal setup and gives him access to Excel, Mail, and a number of database entry and reporting tools. He finally got a tech to load Netscape six months earlier, but John found it slow, and he often worried about surfing the Net right into a big lagoon of trouble. People had been fired at Simtec for Internet abuse, and rumor had it that a crew in internal affairs logged and monitored the sites you visited.

Naomi, who sits near John in accounting, has the same exact setup except that, two years ago, she abandoned her mouse in favor of a big orange trackball. Naomi has been with Simtec for five years and she has approximately seventeen megabytes of data files stored on the server. In fact, in March she overran her original fifteen-megabyte limit and had to go to her network administrator to receive an additional authorization.

This basic scenario – an older or a newer machine, an older or a newer version of Microsoft Windows – repeated hundreds and hundreds of times across the company, is the way Simtec has worked, and until now, worked very well.

Just after midnight, a user began logging into one after another of the Simtec file servers. Four Simtec employees were watching twenty file servers at a time, waiting for the first sign of a failed log-in attempt or any indication that someone had tried to breach the system. Juggling their way through all the different possible targets, and trying to monitor the active user list to see what those people were up to, they completely failed to see the thirty-second strikes that were peppering the Simtec campus. Nothing appeared amiss, and no illegal log-in attempts were recorded, because the user had a valid administrative log-in and password stolen the day before when all the new passwords were created.

This user was dialing in from an apartment in southwest Houston, so the connection was somewhat slow. That didn't matter, though. All that was necessary was to make a simple change to a very simple file.

Every time John Hracek boots his machine in accounting a script is executed that sets up appropriate network drive mappings. It then copies a file into John's home directory on the file server. John doesn't know this. It really doesn't matter to John. The system works.

The young man who logged in at 12:18 A.M. to Simtec's server named PIGGY changed this command to copy an additional file into the user's home directory. John would also get a batch file that would run the next time he started Windows. The batch file would delete everything from that employee's home directory. It would then copy and launch a small executable file that scrambled the file and directory information on the employee's local hard drive, rendering everything there useless as well.

Certainly nothing kept this young man – logged on in the middle of the night with an administrator's password – from going in and deleting all the files in everyone's home directories himself. But his solution was elegant and much more satisfying. He changed one line and everything else took care of itself. The file even deleted itself from the home directory, leaving no immediate trace or explanation for what might have happened. The results were completely out of his hands.

The changes were made in fifteen minutes and the man disconnected. He popped the top on a bottle of beer, which was as close as he ever came to celebrating. He was enjoying himself and making good money. Far more than all his silly friends who had graduated and gone into entry-level data-processing positions, if they could find them. Others were bartending, going to grad school, living at home. As usual, he was the one who had come up a winner. If he did this for a while, with the knowledge he picked up he could probably walk into any company and name his price.

He opened the top desk drawer and took out a mobile phone. The phone was gray with a black leather sleeve, exactly the same model that had been given to Barry Shepard that morning.

'Mark here,' he said. No mistaking the enthusiasm in his voice. 'It's all done.'

'Were you thorough?' said a measured voice on the other end.

'No stone left unturned, no desktop untouched. Pure chaos in the morning. I'd love to be in there tomorrow to see what happens. Sometime we could contrive a way to get me on-site. It wouldn't be that hard.'

'Not a chance. It is out of the question. You will never be allowed to go into Simtec or any other company to sit around and gawk. What possible reason could there be for it?'

The young man became defensive. 'It would be useful. I could see certain things, like timing, the actual sequence of events. I could perfect some of my techniques.'

'We'll talk about that later. In the meantime, you need to have a backup plan and several new targets ready in case this is insufficient.'

'Don't worry about it. There's lots more I could do right now.'

'Then why didn't you do it?' The voice now aggravated. 'We're not trying to play cat and mouse.'

'You want to be convincing, right? And you want the money. You're not trying to destroy the company.'

'I couldn't care less about the company. The question is, Are we going to get paid on this? Now you're telling me that you held back. Maybe you didn't do enough.'

'That's not a question I can answer.'

'You be ready with a second plan, then.' The voice clicked off.

The young man slid the phone back into the desk. Bastards. They didn't understand that what he did was an *art*. He was not a simple technician. He was outsmarting the technicians.

He eyed a box UPS had delivered earlier with an evaluation copy of LAN Assist. Something new he would have to learn. The utility was popular, and he knew he would soon run into it. There were five inches of manuals, and he would be with them the rest of the night.

Barry Shepard couldn't sleep. He'd tossed and turned for an hour and finally decided to go downstairs for a glass of water.

Claudia was still awake. She had papers and notepads spread out all over the kitchen table. Barry had been so caught up in the events at Simtec that he had completely forgotten that she was going to trial this week.

'What's the case?' he asked, and plopped down into a chair beside her.

'Child custody. I hate family law, but they're parading me out there because I'm a female. We're representing the father, and they want the guy to look good.'

'Who's they?'

'Mainly the partner who's handling the case, but I'm sure several of them talk strategy.'

She had been passed over the year before to make partner, but they'd told her to stick it out for another year and she was a shoo-in. Hah. She knew this much: you were never a shoo-in, and with the current legal climate, many of the larger firms were holding back on new partners. They liked her courtroom skills, though, and they liked having a few women around for dirty work like this. They also liked her husband's position at one of Houston's favorite companies.

'You'd think the jurors would see right through it,' she went on. 'The wife gets a male to represent her in order to show she's not a castrating bitch, and the husband gets me. The kids, of course, get nobody.'

Barry glanced toward the darkened window leading out to the backyard. Over in the corner was an old tripod with a telescope mounted on top. The three of them had used it a week ago during a meteor shower. Barry started to consider – were he and Claudia ever to split – who would get custody of Caroline, but he quickly shook it off. The scenario was too hypothetical, too painful, to think about.

'You should have heard the other counsel,' she said. 'He had this big shtick he played during jury selection. He even managed to squeeze in that he was a Texas A & M alumnus, and that the woman he was defending went to Baylor. Anything to win sympathy votes.'

'You'd think that would work against him,' Barry said. 'What about all the people who didn't go to A & M?'

'It's BS is what it is. The subtext is, We're all Texans here. I'm a good ol' boy representing a good ol' girl.' She shook her head. 'It makes me sick. You want to tell him to just pick the jurors and shut up.'

'Do you think you'll win the case?' Barry asked.

'Probably. The husband has a lot of appeal, stable income, good testimonies from the neighbors. Plus there are eight men on the jury. On the other hand, it's hard to get the children away from the mother. You have to overcome a lot of prejudice. The funny thing is, neither one of them seem to be really bad people. Look at the parents a lot of kids get stuck with. They'd be lucky to have either one of these two. I guess that's the way it is.'

She looked sad, sitting there in the middle of the night trying to plan the destiny of somebody else's children. Barry came around behind her and started rubbing her neck. She closed her eyes and he could feel some of the tension ease out of her shoulders. Curiously, it also helped him relax to be reminded of that whole other world out there, where people came together and split apart and fought over children and houses and party boats and generally were much too concerned to worry about whether a computer got delivered across the country to some John Doe one day sooner or later.

He bent over and kissed his wife and she returned it – a good, long kiss, and letting him know it could go longer. Then he got a glass of water, went back up, and stretched out on the bed.

7

Thursday, July 20, the majority of Simtec employees arrived at the office early. The accounting department was no exception. With its refunds, credits, return authorizations, and thousands upon thousands of erroneous shipping and billing records, TechDirect had become an accounting nightmare. The harried workers talked amongst themselves: Surely heads would roll on this one.

If you weren't pulled into the TechDirect fiasco, you were roped into Mike Spakovsky's numbers machine. The fiscal quarter ended in eleven days and Mike demanded that figures, and accurate ones, be produced on time. Defining what *on time* meant depended on whom you were talking to.

Accounting might have liked a few weeks grace time after period end, but stock market analysts and industry watchdogs demanded numbers, at least preliminary numbers, long before the actual financials could even be tabulated. They wouldn't be happy no matter when they came out.

The chief financial officer had made a routine out of meeting with analysts and the press one week prior to the end of each fiscal quarter. He stressed at these meetings that the information was only a projection and that actual results could vary widely, but the watchdogs had come to sniff out the state of the company. Each quarterly meeting was expected to provide a window on the revenue and earnings totals to come.

In Simtec 7, where almost all company accounting took place, one entire floor was dedicated to handling purchases and requisitions. A dozen staffers were now involved with a last-minute summation of quarterly expenditures. Any requests received after 3:00 P.M. that day were to be put on hold for a week, effectively carrying them forward to the next quarterly statement.

Lights were flicking on in individual offices up and down the hallway. John Hracek, among several hundred others, made an early-morning trek between the nearest coffee machine and his desk. He removed his suit coat and hung it by the door, exchanging greetings with his co-workers. He knew that a stack of vouchers with lost or missing invoices awaited him at his desk, so he cut short the chitchat and returned to his chair.

He snapped on his 486 66 megahertz CPU and waited. Trial and error had taught John exactly the moment when he could begin typing his log-in sequence. His fingers flew over the keys and the Simtec menu system flashed briefly on the screen before John typed 3 for Windows and hit return.

Now this was interesting.

He got a message on screen telling him to wait, Windows had detected a slightly damaged file and would attempt to rebuild it. He heard the drive on his computer kick in, and John was impressed. Applications kept getting smarter and smarter. They diagnosed their own problems and damned if now they couldn't even fix themselves.

John might have asked himself, if he'd thought about it, why was his hard drive doing so much work when, in his case, he used Windows files that resided on a file server? But, then again, he might have imagined that the file needing repair was the Windows swap file, and a logical place for that to reside was, in fact, the local hard drive. John didn't know enough to think about why his drive was doing so much work, and he certainly couldn't have told you whether he was using a swap file, which he wasn't.

He stared at the screen, which said, *This may take a few minutes* . . . and he got up to go refill his coffee.

On his way back, he paused behind Naomi's desk and looked over her shoulder.

'My computer did the same thing,' he said.

'That's odd. I've never seen that before.'

John shrugged. 'It could be something to do with all the uproar yesterday. I know Trey was in here backing up the server in the middle of the day.'

'They do backups all the time,' Naomi said.

'Yeah, but normally the backups run unattended, in the middle of the night. During the day some of the files might have been in use. Maybe the backup corrupted one of the Windows files.'

She didn't say anything, but it did seem like a logical explanation.

'Anyway,' John said. 'It seems to be taking care of the problem itself.'

Naomi pursed her lips. 'They get us some new computers, we could run the new Windows and we wouldn't have problems like this.'

'You're an optimist,' John said. He didn't care what system they loaded, so long as it worked. He noticed that the message was gone from his screen, so he walked back over to his desk. Windows had not come up, but the H:\> prompt stood in the upper left corner of the screen.

H:, John knew, was his home directory on the network. This was where his user files resided, as well as any documents he cared to store on the network. He had once run speed comparisons to test whether he should store his files on the file server or his local hard drive. To his surprise, there had been no appreciable difference, but he ended up keeping most things on the local drive because that seemed more natural.

John typed WIN, thinking Windows had rectified its problems but had not launched itself.

Nothing happened.

Slightly annoyed, he typed DIR.

The cursor hesitated, then spat out No Files Found.

What was this? Somehow the whole machine had gotten screwed up. He had *lots* of files. He knew enough network terminology to be aware that the server did drive mappings, which was how he had a drive H: and Naomi and everyone else had a drive H:, but each of these H: drives was actually different and unique. That was the extent of John's network knowledge. Perhaps his drive H:, or the map to it, had been altered so that it now pointed off into space. How was he to get back to his original files?

Without saying anything, he walked over and stood behind

Naomi. He waited and, a minute later, her H:\> prompt appeared as well.

She immediately typed DIR.

No Files Found.

She glanced at him over her shoulder.

'Mine did the same thing,' he said.

'They've got the network completely fucked,' she said with her usual acid tongue. 'We might as well go get breakfast. We're not going to be able to do a damn thing.'

'I've got some paperwork I could take care of,' he said, half-heartedly eyeing a stack of bad vouchers.

'Where are you going to look them up? Come on, let's go downstairs. I'll buy you a donut.' She wiggled her fingers at him in the air.

This was the scenario in a number of offices all across the Simtec campus. Occasionally, an employee had left her computer on overnight. They had not even closed out of Windows. These were the lucky ones, but they also served to confirm to their co-workers that the applications were, in fact, operable. Hey, I'm up! You should be able to get in, too.

For a critical ten minutes, no one reported this strange behavior. The network gods were surely aware that there was a major SNAFU going on. They'd toggle a few switches, nudge a file or two – whatever it was they did – and everything would soon be back to normal. In twenty-three Simtec buildings, the ripples joined with the other ripples and became waves.

The waves crashed through entire offices, taking every scrap of data with them. Until one of the people watching an end-user boot up was Greg Mitchell, senior analyst for TechDirect. He read the corrupted file message on his screen and frowned. He noticed his hard drive come to life, and he thought that was doubly odd.

Greg picked up the phone and dialed technical services. The phone was busy, which meant someone was on-line and someone else was in the process of leaving a message in voice mail. Greg slapped his palm down on the desk. He dialed Chris Jacobs directly.

Chris was in the middle of a hunt through some old wiring

diagrams. He'd lost a segment of the wiring in Simtec 2, and he was about to send a crew over with a new network hub.

'Jacobs,' he said, sounding irritated.

'Chris, this is Greg Mitchell. How are you doing?'

'Okay, Greg. Lost a piece of the net in building 2. What's up?'

'Something I wanted to ask you about. I'm seeing an odd message from Windows. Right now, it's still on the screen. Something about a corrupted file, and Windows trying to rebuild it. The hard drive is active, and I find this a little odd.'

Chris leaned back in his chair. He preferred the time to thoroughly think through technical questions. It was his experience that easy answers often came back to haunt you. He considered the temp files that Windows made, as well as the swap file. He'd done a lot of experimenting with both, but that was some time ago. He didn't recall ever seeing a message like that.

'I don't know what to tell you, Greg. Let me get these guys headed over to 2. I'll send somebody over to check it out.'

'There it goes,' Greg said. 'I'm back to the H:\> prompt.'

They were silent except for Greg's tapping at the keyboard. He grunted, and then some more tapping.

'Chris?' he said finally. 'The home directory is gone. Wiped out. I went out to N: and backed down the complete path. I don't see a single file in there.'

Chris jolted up out of his chair.

'What do you mean, gone? How can it be gone?'

Greg didn't answer. He was clattering away on the keyboard, looking around to find the missing files. 'Uh oh,' Greg said. 'Oh, goddamnit!'

Chris's heart was racing. 'Greg? What's going on?'

'The hard drive . . . now it won't recognize the hard drive!'

Greg Mitchell knew these machines as well as anybody, and Chris believed him. His eyes were wild. *It was happening.* 'Don't let anyone else log in,' Chris said. 'I'll call you back.' He slammed the phone down.

A technician appeared in the doorway. 'We've got a problem, Mr. Jacobs. I've taken a zillion messages on voice mail.'

'Tell people not to get on the file servers,' Chris ordered.

'Put out a broadcast E-mail . . . shit! They won't be able to get it . . . go with voice mail. Broadcast an emergency voice message saying that no one should log in. Then start calling each office. No one logs in.' He sprinted up the hall to the support office, shouting out orders. Bring down the file servers, he barked. Get on a console and disable all log-ins.

He went over to a brand-new test machine and flipped it on. Chris waited, a tingling, prickly sensation forming at the base of his neck, until the machine began its network log-in. The message popped up that a file needed to be rebuilt and, after a few moments, the hard drive on the machine kicked in. Chris bent down and snapped the power off. This computer was brand new out of the box two days ago. Whatever was going on, it was capable of hitting everything they had.

His staff scrambled into action. They would have to examine each and every file server, and Chris clenched his fists. He knew they would never make it.

In Simtec 4, Barry was now standing behind Greg as he tried every way he could think of to get to the files on the hard drive. The files were simply no longer there.

'It's wiped out,' Greg confirmed under his breath.

Most of the other employees were milling about with confused looks on their faces. Across the room, Barry noticed somebody else had come in and turned on a machine. 'Don't log in!' he shouted. 'For Christ's sake, don't let anyone else log in!' He ran up the hallway to one of the data wiring closets and unlocked it with his master key.

It was another two minutes before he could trace down the lines to each file server and yank them out of their jacks. He had no way of knowing the extent of the damage. It would be hours before the scope of the assault became clear and before they would discover, with mind-numbing certainty, that either the files or the file information for 706 machines had been effectively erased.

John and Naomi had walked down to the first-floor snack bar for their donut. The snack bar was located in an open atrium, and they could hear the shouts up and down the hallways in Simtec 7.

Something major was going on. John kept frowning and glancing up toward the second floor. They better get back upstairs.

'Sounds like somebody won the lottery,' the cashier said.

Naomi handed over two dollars. 'Wouldn't that be nice? Hey, baby, I quit. I'll see you in the Bahamas.'

But it wasn't the lottery at all.

John and Naomi carried their donuts back toward their cubicles, and they were met in the doorway by Mary Allison. Mary had a balled-up handkerchief, and mascara was running in streaks down her face.

'It's all gone,' Mary said. 'All my work.'

'What do you mean it's all gone?' Naomi put a hand on Mary's arm.

'I got this message. The message said it was fixing something, but instead it deleted everything.' This statement brought a fresh supply of tears, and Mary hid behind the handkerchief.

They'd all gotten the exact same message, and John stepped to his machine and stabbed at the keyboard. Nothing. John Hracek took a seat on the desk behind him. The very first thing that came to his mind was the Norfolk Elementary School recipe book. It was a fund-raising project for his son's school, and he'd been putting the layout together on his lunch hour for the past month. He'd have to start over from scratch.

Then there were all the mail messages he'd saved from friends and colleagues. He still liked to go back and read the congratulatory notes he'd received after his promotion. He wanted those notes. Also the many letters he'd carefully composed to his mother. He wanted those, too. His contact manager – basically an electronic Rolodex – held over three thousand contacts. No. He simply couldn't afford to lose that.

John dropped his donut in the trash. The bite he'd taken felt like a small rock in his stomach. His mouth was dry. Parched.

Mary Allison was still blubbering away to his left, but John got up and wandered out of the office. He gazed blankly down the hallway. The place seemed unfamiliar. Where was the water fountain? He'd never needed water so badly in his entire life.

The next two hours at Simtec were pure pandemonium. Alternating reports came out of the security and technical office and filtered down through each of the divisional heads. At first, no one could use Windows. Next it appeared you could use Windows, if you were capable of doing so without logging in to the network. Perhaps it only affected certain versions of Windows, or only users in certain areas.

At that point employees were so worried, and so many of them had seen co-workers lose everything, that they didn't want to boot their machines no matter what they were told. Vice presidents wanted to be briefed on the problem, and they were miffed at having to appear out of the loop.

Meanwhile Chris Jacobs had a team working furiously to figure out what had gone wrong. They set up a half dozen different machines side by side, performing various functions on each: start Windows, log into a file server, log out, check mail, transfer files. In this way, they quickly narrowed to a trigger in the log-in sequence.

Of course, when asked to do so, Chris could not guarantee that this was the only threat. So, depending on the confidence and risk-taking tolerance of their respective division heads, some of the offices were told not to resume work at all, and others were told they could operate freely, so long as they stayed off the file servers.

At about this point in the melee, support specialist Kelly Ford was tracing the Windows start-up sequence used by the older machines, and she made a second Eureka! A line in a batch file executed by the main menu had also been changed. That change was then tracked down and examined, and a similar bug was rooted out. A malicious, deviously small bug that had nonetheless proven enormously potent.

Chris ordered his staff to search for similar traps in every script, batch file, and menu sequence used on any of the 214 Simtec file servers. He then went back to his office to call Diane Hughes and Jim Seidler. What had occurred was horrendous, and he dreaded the call he was about to make.

The upper executives all had phones that identified the caller on an LED panel, and Diane picked up for Chris Jacobs immediately.

'You must have some news for me,' she said in her characteristically direct manner.

'We've found how it happened. He made clever, very small changes to some files, but it was enough to do quite a job.'

'By what I'm hearing, yes, it was. Let's talk first about how this was done. You say he changed a file . . .'

'Changed log-in scripts, to be exact. Also, on some machines, a batch file involved in starting Windows. The file itself is not a Windows file. A batch file triggers other activities – copies files over the network, launches executable programs, that kind of thing. I've got my people examining all similar files for tampering. So far, it's not widespread.'

'That's what I would expect,' Diane said. 'Once you find the first one, the game is up. How was it done?'

'The person had to have administrative access to do this. You can't just log on as Jane Doe and make that kind of change.'

'And it was done since we changed passwords yesterday?'

Chris paused. His first impulse was to say yes, the man must have somehow gotten a high-level password, but that wasn't necessarily the case. A file could have been installed with a timer. On such and such date, it unfolds and swaps itself out. Unlikely, but it might be possible.

'I can't say. We know the file was changed last night. Whether it was physically done at that time, or whether it was simply triggered automatically I don't yet know.'

'So there's no need to change passwords again. It wouldn't do us any good anyway, I suppose. If he got hold of the last change, he, or they, could get this one, too.'

'That's a fair assumption. Other changes could be made by automatic trigger. The person could have inside help, or there's always the possibility the guy is a system engineer who knows more than any of us.'

'You're saying someone could be better than you and all your staff?'

'It's possible he could know a back way into a file server

that nobody on the outside would find in a million years. Anything's possible. Lots of companies build features into their products that are never meant to be released to the public. They get taken out during Beta testing, or they get left in. Almost every program on the shelf has undocumented features, but a trapdoor that could allow this to happen is a complete breach of confidence.'

'I see.' She seemed to be weighing her options. 'Let me ask you this, this person was in a position – no matter exactly how he did it – to delete entire file servers, right? Every application gone, am I correct?'

'I would have to believe so.'

'So . . . he chose not to.'

Diane didn't understand, thought Chris. Like many people, she focused on the applications, the big files.

'He had his reasons,' Chris said. 'By waiting until each machine came up, and appearing to have the servers behave normally, he was able to get to all the individual files on people's hard drives. Many users don't back up their own files. They know better, but they don't do it. No copy exists anywhere but on that person's hard drive. If he blanks a whole server, so what? We restore from tape and nobody loses anything.'

The distinction seemed to sink in, and in a bitter voice Diane said, 'How shrewd.'

Chris said nothing.

'That was my next topic, the extent of the damage. I understand people have lost important data files.'

'Some have. In the best case, they never booted up. In some cases, they hit the off switch in the middle of the process. The worst case is, they lost everything.'

'But there are recovery programs, right? I know it's a lot of work, but the files can be brought back.'

Chris measured his answer. It depended on how the destruction was carried out. Sure, you could recover a file that had been inadvertently deleted, but a scrambled drive? And expect it to come back exactly as it was before? He wasn't so sure.

'We're going to try our best,' Chris said.

'That's all I can ask,' Diane said. 'And Chris, just let me say this. I'm going to meet with Jim and discuss much of what you've told me and our ability to keep it from happening again. However it comes out, I want you to understand that I know you have done your absolute best at all times. And that you've been placed in extremely difficult circumstances.'

He didn't know how to answer. It sounded like a death sentence.

'Thank you,' he said finally.

'I'll be in touch,' she said.

At 1:00 P.M., Barry Shepard, Jim Seidler, Chris Jacobs, Mike Spakovsky, and Karen Williams, as well as the vice presidents who had not been included in the earlier talks, were all assembled in the Simtec boardroom. Diane walked in with a notepad and said, 'Hello. Here's one meeting I wish we didn't have to have.'

Two places to her left was Chris Jacobs. The large man sat slumped over in his chair. All of Chris's tightly wound strings appeared to have come undone, and Barry tried not to look in that direction. Instead, he glanced back over the notes on his legal pad. How had they gone so wrong? The company was at a standstill. In TechDirect, Barry, Greg, and anyone with technical know-how had been pulled into coordinating the effort to restore files. So far, they were proceeding slowly and with less than optimal results.

Mike Spakovsky was across the table between two of the other vice presidents. He'd been twisting and untwisting a paper clip until it finally broke into pieces.

Diane cleared her throat. 'I want to start with a quick briefing for those of you who are not current on all the background of our situation today. To state the obvious, someone has been tampering with our network. This started with the production line in Barry's area, when shipping addresses and configurations were scrambled over a period of days. Today's events are the second instance that we know of, but there may have been others.'

She made eye contact with each of the four men who had been excluded from the first meetings.

‘We initially tried to contain this to those directly affected. We had to act rapidly, so a few of us met and formulated a strategy. We have attempted to keep both the rumor mill and the company-wide histrionics to a minimum. Clearly, now, the issue has become of much broader concern and our approach must change.’

Barry had to admire the way she dealt with the egos of these men, like the marketing VP Randall Johnson. She didn’t apologize for not bringing them in the first time. She simply stated the facts and expected them to accept the situation. Remarkably, they seemed to be doing just that. They were now on the inside, and that was all that mattered. They were probably happy, when Barry thought about it, to have had nothing to do with the previous meetings. Those decisions had somehow led to the debacle they were now experiencing.

Diane paused.

‘The most notable event – and it is one that I suppose cannot be left out of the account, however much I would like to – is that, after the shipping errors in TechDirect, we received a request for payment in the amount of one million dollars.’

A stunned silence settled around the table. Even though he knew what was coming, hearing this stated so simply, and seeing the reaction of the four vice presidents, made Barry’s heart begin to pound.

‘That’s outrageous!’ said Jack Killebrew, the first to recover. Jack was the head of worldwide sales, and he had always been loud and opinionated.

‘Yes, we thought so, too. So we refused to pay and we now appear to be suffering the consequences.’

‘When was this? Was there a deadline for payment? Was this a specific threat?’

‘The deadline was yesterday at five P.M. Barry Shepard has been our point of contact with this person, or people.’

Barry remained facing Diane, but he felt several people appraise him with renewed interest.

‘We do not now have the time to go into further detail, to rehash our decision-making process. I also do not feel the need for prolonged discussion of the blow that has just been dealt us. I think that you are all well aware of what today has cost us, and what it may continue to cost. If you haven't read your E-mail yet, accounting is a mess and Mike has had to postpone his quarterly meeting. That, I'm sure I don't have to tell you, does not look good. I have already been in touch with the board of directors. I assured them that – even though we are suffering some adversity – we are proceeding in a controlled and orderly fashion.

'So, I now hope to present you with several alternatives. Then I will ask for your opinions and we'll take an informal vote.' She held up her thumb. 'Number one. We can still pay the money and take our chances. Because we missed the first deadline, the requested payment is now five million.'

Additional gasps from the table.

In case the point was not clear, Jim Seidler leaned forward and said, 'Five million bucks to stop a hacker.'

'It's unheard of,' said Killebrew.

'Is it?' Spakovsky said. 'We really have no way of knowing. Besides, who cares what others have or haven't done. The only thing we need to ask ourselves is, How long can we take this on the chin?'

'Barry,' Diane said. 'You have not been contacted since yesterday evening?'

'No.'

'Then I will assume this option is still available to us. If we decide we are willing to pay, then we must settle on a maximum figure that is acceptable. This may or may not be a negotiable process.'

'I'll negotiate with the bastards,' said Jack Killebrew. He was red in the face, and he had his hands out in front of him around an imaginary neck. Barry watched with some concern, because Jack had already had one stroke. He was also prone to get agitated and then suffer some sort of attack. He would first turn red, much as he was now, then clutch wildly at his shirt collar and claw for his bottle of nitroglycerine pills. The first time Barry had seen this, he thought the man was going to die right there on the floor. He learned later that, off and on, Jack had been doing more or less the same thing for years.

Diane extended her index finger. 'Option two. We can again

refuse to pay. We save the money and trust ourselves to our own wits. This was the course of action we chose on Tuesday, and in this regard the picture should now be more clear. As I'm sure you are aware, Barry, Chris, Jim, and a squadron of employees have taken extraordinary measures to secure the network. Despite our best effort over a forty-hour period, and despite considerable expense, it was not enough.

'I'd like to ask Chris if he has any reason to believe that there is more we can do? Are there steps we can take by which we will be assured of success?'

Chris was staring at the wood grain of the conference table. He shook his head without looking up.

For God's sake, Barry thought. Chris was one of the two who had been in favor of payment right from the start. He had probably seen it coming.

Diane nodded, indicating that Chris's response was both expected and satisfactory.

'We cannot be lulled into the belief that this is someone who will simply go away. We are dealing, most likely, not with one person but a sophisticated group. They have capabilities we may learn about only after they are used against us.'

'Amen,' Spakovsky said.

'And now I want you to meet and consider option three.' Diane picked up a phone on the table beside her and punched in an extension.

'We're ready,' she said. 'Please send him in.'

Diane stood and went to the door. She was reaching for the handle when the door was pushed open of its own accord. In stepped a large man wearing jeans and cowboy boots. There was no hat, but he had the kind of face – tan and weathered, with deep grooves across the forehead – that you expected to see under a hat. The hat, thought Barry, was probably outside the door in a chair.

'You must be Ms. Hughes,' the man said and stuck out his hand.

'Yes, I am. Please come in.'

He was already in, so this was a formality. Barry noticed a gold ring the size of a golf ball. He had always thought that this particular style – the gold made to look like a lump of ore – was ugly and ostentatious. But on this man it was oddly correct. The top of the thing was studded with diamonds.

'I will not take the time to introduce each person individually, but seated at this table are the top directors and vice presidents of the company.' She spun in their direction. 'To all of you, I would like to introduce William S. Dunn of Security Associates.'

Dunn nodded and said, 'Pleased to meet you all.'

'In an effort to plan for all contingencies, I arranged for this interview yesterday. As some of you may know, Mr. Dunn is president of the most highly regarded security consultancy in the country. His client list speaks for itself, including Ford Motor Company, Sysco, Royal Dutch Shell, ICI . . . let me assure you, it is a long and impressive list. He agreed to come here and speak with us on very short notice, for which I am extremely grateful.'

During this introduction, Dunn stared at the Simtec CEO with a look of modesty.

'I have briefly sketched out the nature of our circumstances for Mr. Dunn – that we have been attacked by an as-yet unknown assailant. That we refused to pay ransom. I am sure he has additional questions, as I am sure you will have for him.' She returned to her chair and nudged it sideways, offering him a space at the head of the table. 'Why don't you start by giving us an overview of the type of services you provide. Were we to bring in your company, what should we expect?'

Dunn sat and leaned forward, placing his forearms on the table. Despite the fact that he knew not a single person in the room, he appeared perfectly at home.

'You've done at least one thing right. Diane Hughes asked me this question when we first spoke, and I'll repeat exactly what I told her. The government cannot help you in this matter. The government agencies who might be called in to help do not move quickly enough and, when they do move, they will monopolize your resources. You need to act immediately and with expediency. Once the situation is under control, that's when you may choose to call in the appropriate authority. This much I know from hard-won experience.'

His eyes moved about the room, fixing each of them in turn.

'We wouldn't be sitting here right now if things hadn't reached the critical stage. A company doesn't just call me up one day because someone loses a floppy disk. Normally, by the time I get a call, every jack in the building has been scrambled. Databases are trashed. Files compromised. You are not the first company to whom this has happened, and you will certainly not be the last. But when you're in the soup, people, you've got to swim and swim fast.'

He had their complete attention.

'On the one hand, this should be comforting, because I am proof that others have fought this particular demon and won. But from now on you should know that you will forever think of your resources – your infrastructure, your personnel – differently. Once you are past this immediate concern, you will not again sleep easily at night, because you will be thinking about your data, your network, your privacy, and your ability to do business. You will never again sleep easily until you know that all of these are safe.'

He paused, then added, 'Not *think* they are safe. Know they are safe.

'When and if my team comes in, we are absolutely, ruthlessly, thorough.' He grinned. 'One company accused us of standing it on its head, but I prefer to think of us as putting that company on its feet.

'We will of course review all hardware and software configurations, but that is the easy part. That is the part that you yourself could do, given enough time. We also conduct a complete check and analysis of every employee. We examine grievances, the status of past and present contractors, any person whatsoever let go within the last five years. We conduct a one-on-one interview with each and every employee, from the housekeeping staff on up to each of you in this room. You see, my team is not comprised entirely of computer types. They are psychologists and behaviorists, people who know much more about spotting a lie than a missing data packet. We will want to determine, as quickly as possible, whether there is any internal threat.'

Dunn was no older than Barry himself. Maybe even younger. And Barry watched this performance with growing astonishment. He noticed that Spakovsky and Killebrew were staring open-mouthed.

'The single most important aspect of the investigation is my own objectivity.' He glanced at Karen Williams. 'I don't care if the culprit is you, ma'am, a janitor, or a school kid in the eighth grade. Your company is a large institution, a bureaucracy, although you may not like to think of it that way, and such institutions are rarely able to examine themselves. Who's going to do it?'

No one appeared willing to volunteer an answer.

'Who has the knowledge? Who can be trusted? I, on the other hand, have no particular interest in Simtec as a company. I do not know your internal politics. My only interest is in doing my job, and, I assure you, I step on toes equally. I have done this many times, in many settings. I can mount this kind of effort in a fraction of the time it would take you to do it alone. I am ready to begin immediately.'

He appeared to be finished.

How clever this man was, thought Barry. He had stated the case in such a way that he was sure to win. Claudia had taught him to ferret out this sort of argument, framed in a manner that altered the terms of the question. Who had asked for an analysis of their past contractors? It could very well be a big waste of time, but now it would seem remiss to suggest a smaller scale approach.

And if you accepted his terms, you accepted Dunn, because he was absolutely right: they could neither efficiently nor effectively do it themselves. It would result in a circus.

'Interview every employee—' Spakovsky said tentatively. 'This sounds expensive.'

Dunn looked to Diane Hughes.

'Mr. Dunn's fee is sixty thousand dollars per day, plus expenses,' she said. 'In addition to himself, he brings a team of some fifty specialists, so the rate is not so high as it might seem. I have spoken with references at two of the companies previously mentioned, and I also spoke with an associate at Procter & Gamble who has had occasion to work with Mr. Dunn. Let me assure you, Security Associates comes highly recommended.'

Forever doing the numbers, Spakovsky swallowed and said, ‘And how long might this be expected to take?’

‘Two weeks minimum,’ Dunn said. ‘But it has gone into months. Until I get started, I have no way of saying with certainty.’

Months. Barry multiplied it out himself. Sixty days times sixty thousand. Plus expenses. Millions of dollars, fifty specialists! To Barry it sounded like an invading army. Was this what they had come to? He considered the hundreds of people in TechDirect, and elsewhere, who had lost every file on their hard drives. He thought of the thousands of customers who had received the wrong piece of equipment, and the realization began to sink in. It came to him by looking at his company through the eyes of W. S. Dunn, an outsider who simply took one look at the Simtec peach and said, Rotten! He didn’t have to keep biting it to make sure.

Yes, thought Barry, and he suddenly felt tired. He felt more tired than on any late night he’d ever worked for Simtec. Yes, it had come to this.

8

They voted seven to two to hire Security Associates. One of the no votes came from the director of human resources, who seemed to fear a complete loss of sovereignty should Dunn begin analyzing every employee and hiring decision over the past five years. Karen Williams voted no without giving any reason. Chris Jacobs abstained. In essence, the vote was a referendum on whether Dunn would, for the foreseeable future, assume Chris's duties as the director of security.

Barry voted yes out of desperation. He didn't know anything about W. S. Dunn, sitting there at the head of the table in his blue jeans and boots right up until they took the vote. He had the credentials, and Simtec was in a bind. It was that simple. Barry preferred to pay the money to Dunn rather than hand over his wallet to a terrorist.

At 2:00 P.M. Thursday, July 20, the Simtec Computer Corporation essentially ceded control of its own computer hardware. William Dunn wasted no time in asserting his authority. His first official act was to order the file servers offline for the rest of the day. He allowed the order-entry system in TechDirect to operate, but he disconnected them from the rest of the campus network. The orders could come in, but for the time being they couldn't go out to production. Nor could stock be checked. Barry spent three exhausting hours fighting one logistical firestorm after another. By late afternoon, he had actual runners coming over from production with manual lists of what was available.

The telephone sales reps were completely out of synch, having to work from the screen and then crane around to catch a glimpse of what the technicians were scribbling up on posterboard. The part numbers in the entry system didn't directly match the product descriptions sent over from production, so some of the totals didn't mean anything. The order system sold a 37-KZS-1005, a 1 GB SCSI hard drive, but the posterboard said SCSI-2, 1 GB, Fast & Wide, Avail: 8/1. Was it the same thing? A few of the TSRs had apparently come to the decision to sell whatever the customers wanted and worry about it later.

Barry's phone rang and he scanned the LED display. It was an outside call and he picked up.

'Barry!' came a loud and easily recognizable voice. 'Jack Griffin here.'

Jack was a basketball friend. They had met playing in an adult league eight years ago, and during the emergence of Hakeem Olajuwon, they had split season tickets to the Rockets.

Barry searched for something to say. 'You get tickets this year?'

'Nah. Too expensive. We're planning a ski trip this Christmas and the wife has become a financial bloodhound. How's Caroline? Is this the year the little monster goes out for guard?'

'Still too young. She's playing in a summer baseball league. In fact, I'm supposed to pick her up tonight. I was supposed to go watch, but I don't think there's a chance in hell.'

'That's what I was calling about, old boy. That and to say hello. Word has it you had some kind of major wingding this morning. PCs going down all over the place. I thought I'd call and get the scoop.'

Barry's pencil paused in the middle of the flow chart on his desk. From the way Jack was talking, Barry knew this was only gossip, but he was shocked that word of the morning's disaster had already spread to Houston Lighting & Power.

'You know how it is,' Barry said. 'Sometimes computers crash.' He did not sound convincing.

'Our office manager has a boyfriend who works for you guys. She was talking to him this morning and he described it like a war zone over there, people running around unplugging computers, people breaking down, actually crying because they lost all their files.'

'I'm sure it depends what office you were in. The whole company was certainly not that way.' Barry realized he was not going to get off the hook without giving at least cursory details. 'This isn't going beyond our conversation, right?'

'You bet,' Jack said. 'Scout's honor.'

Barry knew better.

'We had some kind of virus get loose on the net. Frightening stuff. We got the thing isolated, but it managed to zap a few hard drives before we tied it down.'

'Unbelievable,' Jack said. He was eating it up. It would be all over his office within five minutes.

'We don't even know which virus it was, yet. Haven't had time. We've had to go back in and reconstruct files for the people who lost them.'

Don't ask how many, thought Barry.

'How many?' Jack said.

'How many what?'

'Computers. How many got zapped?'

'I really don't know, Jack.' Barry did not lie easily. 'A few. I haven't been that in touch with it.'

'This is amazing. It's the kind of thing they tell you can happen, but you never think it will. And here one of these little suckers gets in and hits, of all people, Simtec. You've got to see the irony, don't you, Barry?' Jack Griffin chuckled. 'The mighty Simtec Computer Corporation. Any idea how it started?'

Barry's knuckles had gone white on the phone. In a tight voice, he said, 'We're starting to look into that. Things are starting to calm down now.' He watched out his corner window as two people jogged down the hallway with their arms full of papers and posterboard. They were probably coming with the latest totals from production. They'd yell at the TSRs and point out how they'd just promised delivery on some item that wouldn't be available for weeks. 'I'd better get going, Jack. I've been out on the floor all day. I'm surprised you caught me.'

Barry clicked off and immediately questioned whether he'd done the right thing. He'd been forced to say something. Besides, if Jack Griffin knew about it, they were leaking like a sieve. Barry quickly sketched out an E-mail, including everyone in the group that was at the afternoon meeting. He'd received questions about the attack, he said, and apparently employees had mentioned the morning's incidents to others outside the company. His response had been to downplay the extent of the damage, and he had attributed it to a now-contained virus. They should all go with this version, he recommended, unless they had other comments. He sent the message and requested acknowledgment.

He got up and began walking the TechDirect offices. Half his employees had already left for the day. Their machines were down and they were dead in the water. A technical crew was huddled around one computer, and for twenty minutes Barry became absorbed in the attempted resuscitation. The technicians knew everything Barry did and more, and they were trying all of it. They had sent out a message saying to put a memo note in the middle of any monitor to indicate that the machine was down. They were going to work straight through the night to try to get as many people back on-line as possible.

Barry resumed his walk and began to count. Four of the analysts' machines. Six in the TechDirect support office. Three of the secretarial staff. You walked around a corner and there they were, more monitors with yellow sticky notes.

Having made the complete circuit, he circled back and took the stairs up to his floor. Claudia had left a message earlier, saying she'd be in court and wouldn't be home until late. If Caroline had to, she could catch a ride home with her friend Elizabeth, and he could pick her up there anytime before nine.

Barry checked his watch. Sure, he decided, why not stop by her game? He might catch the last innings, and he'd probably get more research done in the stands than he would by staying at the office. He forwarded the phone to voice mail and collected the two volumes he'd been wanting to read through, *Data Security 1-2-3* and *Tips, Tricks and Traps for Network Administrators.*

The mobile phone was tucked in his pocket. He stacked the tape recorder on top of the two books, went down to his car, and shed the coat and tie. Five miles from Simtec, he stopped at Cyrano's pizza-by-the-slice. He was in line behind two people when the phone rang in his pocket.

Damn! Barry glanced about the small shop: only room for the counter and three tables. Not only that, he'd left the tape recorder in the car. He exited the glass door back to the sidewalk.

The phone, now in his hand, chirped for the third time. Stall, all the executives had agreed. Lead them on, Barry. You're doing a great job.

He hit the talk button. 'Barry Shepard,' he said, striding across the parking lot toward the Jeep.

'This is Hektor here. Don't worry about the machine, Barry. I'm calling now because I don't want to be taped this time.'

Barry had his keys out. He slowed.

'Let's just chat informally, all right? Off the record. Relax, eat your pizza. Did you already order?'

Barry stopped still behind a gray Toyota. His eyes darted from side to side, but the nearby cars were empty. The parking lot served a Randall's grocery store as well as a string of shops. They could be anywhere. 'No,' he said. 'I didn't.'

'Just sit tight,' Hektor said. 'I'm not in the lot. I'm over here on a street called Muldoon, behind the center. I'm in a purple minivan. Ho ho ho. Now can we talk?'

'Go ahead. What do you want to talk about?' Barry squeezed between two cars and started walking toward the corner of the building. He stepped forward and a car's horn blared.

'Don't get yourself run over, Barry. We still need you. Once you pay off, you can jog on the freeway if you want to.'

Barry waved the driver by. A woman in a red Cadillac, shaking her head at him.

'How did Windows run this morning? I hear there's a maintenance release out. Maybe you should get it. Fix some bugs, you know.'

'We had a few kinks. We've worked them out.'

'Imagine that.' Hektor's voice was heavy with sarcasm. 'A computer company was able to find a kink in a program. I wonder how long that took?'

Barry didn't answer.

'Are you there, Barry? You've seen what I can do, and you should know that I am prepared to do more. Is noon tomorrow too early to have my check delivered?'

'No problem,' Barry said. 'You can drop it off any time.'

'Don't be a funny guy, Shepard. You haven't earned it. Confirm for me that you'll be ready for delivery instructions at noon. Then we can terminate our conversation.'

Barry made a left at the end of the building. Sure enough, the next street was residential and called Muldoon. He quickened his pace.

'Noon tomorrow is a problem. First you requested one amount, an option which we presented to our board with some difficulty. Now you want them to authorize five times that amount. We have to start the cycle all over again. You're going to have to be patient.'

'Patient is one thing I'm not. The longer you force me to wait, the more I am forced to raise my price. When you show hesitation, or duplicity, there will be punishment. Those are the only things you and your board need understand. Right now, Barry Shepard and Simtec are not demonstrating the requisite strength of will. I'm really not interested in your board, your cycles, or your explanations.'

'You should be, because I'm playing it straight. Let's suppose the board does agree to pay. I may need to get word to you. I should have a phone number or some way to contact you.'

'It doesn't work that way, Barry. You should know better. You don't call Hektor. It only works the other way around. You can give me confirmation right now for noon tomorrow, or you're wasting my time.'

'Without my board's approval, I can't confirm to you what I ate for breakfast.'

Hektor gave a mirthless chortle. 'Raisin Bran. I've gone through some of your tidy bundles left out for disposal. No eggs. No yogurt. Every few days, there's an empty box of Raisin Bran. Don't think we chose just any messenger. I own you, Barry Shepard, and don't forget it. Your wife and little daughter, too.'

Barry was dumbfounded. He squeezed the handset and felt himself losing control. 'You don't own me. And you don't own Simtec. What you've done is wasted a whole lot of time for nothing. I hope you at least learned DOS, maybe you can get a temp job somewhere.'

Barry hung up. He wanted to throw the phone against the pavement. Thank God this hadn't been captured on tape. He broke into a jog toward Muldoon. As he rounded the corner, there it was, a purple minivan parked on the curb about halfway up. He sped up, believing the car would pull away at any second. But the car stayed, and appeared not to be going anywhere at all. He came to a stop by the side window. Empty. He noticed some debris in the gutter around the wheels. This van hadn't moved in days. He could imagine Hektor somewhere laughing.

He figured they might still be watching, so Barry forced a slow walk back inside Cyrano's, where he ordered a pepperoni-and-mushroom pizza. No furtive and hurried phone calls. No tantrums on the sidewalk. With the pizza and a large iced tea beside him in the Jeep, Barry left the parking lot and headed for the YMCA baseball fields. They had obviously been through his trash. They had followed him out of the office. The more he thought about it, the more he allowed Hektor to unnerve him.

He swerved into a side street, sped for two blocks, and then pulled over. No one appeared in the rearview mirror. Apparently they only followed when they wanted to. Easy enough, they merely had to wait and pick him up leaving home or the office. He was more predictable than a dog on a leash.

The outfield clock said 6:50 when he pulled into the YMCA lot. Barry went to a pay phone, called Diane's office, and got voice mail. He took the number of her portable off a card in his wallet and tried that. When it, too, went into voice mail he gave up and left a synopsis of his conversation with Hektor: stalemate. Then he walked back to the game.

Half the kids were out in the field and the others were lined up against the fence in the dugouts. Probably only enough time left for an inning or two. He didn't know which team

Caroline was on, but he took the pizza and the *Tips, Tricks* book into the first base bleachers and sat, searching the field for her.

She was standing in the dugout, wearing a big orange jersey with a number eight on the back. The other team was in navy blue and they were at bat. Rookie League was the first year of pitch ball and it was confined to seven- and eight-year-olds. Granted the ball was pitched underhand by one of the coaches, but Barry couldn't remember playing pitch ball until the fourth or fifth grade. The kids looked outrageous out there with bats as tall as their own bodies.

The boy at the plate leaned into his crouch and made a wild, slashing strike at the ball. The next pitch bounced in the dirt about three feet short of the plate. Hoots came from the navy blue dugout. The scoreboard wasn't even turned on.

Barry wondered if Caroline had made it into the game. The rule was that everyone was supposed to play, but it didn't look like an even mix of boys and girls out on the field.

He halfheartedly took out a slice of pizza. Caroline turned and spotted him and waved with her big glove. He flapped the pizza in the air. Only a few other people were sitting in the bleachers. Whack! The kid had actually hit the ball, a slow blooper over the shortstop's head.

The chase was on. The kid tossed his bat and scampered toward first, as three different fielders charged after the ball. The second baseman got there quickest and fumbled the ball. As he regrouped and turned to throw, the runner had already passed first. No one was covering second. The third base coach was jumping up and down, gesturing wildly for one of them to get back on third.

The runner rounded second and it was a race to see who would get to third. The fielder was ahead and might have arrived in time, but the second baseman threw the ball too early. The throw was remarkably on target, and it hit the third baseman on the shoulder as he whirled around. The ball went skittering off past the foul line.

The catcher was now hollering for the ball, and the third baseman grabbed the ball and let fly. Zip, went the ball. About four feet wide, right toward the home plate umpire's head, who ducked and let the ball clang past into the backstop. In Rookie League, this was how home runs were made.

Barry laughed out loud. Professional baseball seemed so dry and polished by comparison. No fun at all. He hadn't noticed anyone else step up to the bleachers until the big body plopped down next to him.

W. S. Dunn.

'Hello, Mr. Shepard. I hope you don't mind my coming out. I wanted to talk and I'm kind of a baseball fan myself.'

'How in hell did you find me here?'

'I stopped by the office and caught your assistant . . . Gwen, I believe, on her way out.' He nodded toward the field. 'Which one is yours?'

'In the orange, number eight in the dugout.'

Caroline had turned to look over this large cowboy-looking man who was sitting next to her father. Dunn raised a meaty hand and waved at her.

She nodded gravely and turned back around to the game.

'She been in yet?' Dunn asked.

'I don't know. I just got here.'

The temperature was still in the eighties, late into the evening. Dunn pulled at his shirt collar. 'I'm glad to see it cools off around here,' he said.

'Diane said you're out of Atlanta. Ever been to Houston before?'

'I've had a few jobs here. Never in summer. There ought to be a surcharge.'

'Sixty thousand a day, I'm crying for you,' Barry said with a good deal more anger than he'd intended. He had actually felt like punching Dunn. *Get a handle.* That phone call must have gotten deep under his skin.

Dunn chuckled and waved it off. 'Most of the crew is already here. They've been flying in all afternoon, some into Intercontinental and some into Hobby. It's a mess. You know, I've thought about buying a jet. Too disorderly, everyone coming in at different times. Ridiculous, too, paying for forty or fifty seats at the last minute.'

'I would imagine we're paying for that.'

'I don't care,' Dunn said. 'It's a waste. I'd be able to do it for half. On the other hand, I hate to fly, myself. I left yesterday so I could drive over in my pickup. Jets are also expensive, and we'd only be using it a few times a year. My employees would spend the rest of the time dreaming up reasons to fly to Cancun.'

On field there was another hit. It rolled along the ground as a decent bunt, and the runner beat out the resulting mayhem for a double. Barry offered the pizza box to Dunn, who helped himself.

'That's a good read,' Dunn said, gesturing to the book on the bench between them.

'I wanted to do a little brushing up,' Barry said. He swallowed, thinking how foolish this must appear, trying to read a book on network security at the eleventh hour. What a novice.

But Dunn said, 'That's good. Even if they started in the trenches, most executives don't have a clue. Like Diane Hughes, really.'

Barry had tried to stay out of that decision, and so far he liked Diane. 'Diane was brought in for her other skills,' he said evenly.

Dunn scratched at an earlobe. 'Myself, I was surprised when Seidler didn't get the job. But that's the way it's been going. They conduct a high-profile search and then go outside the company. It's not as sexy to promote from within.'

The two men sat quietly until Dunn said, 'So, all this trouble started last week?'

'Most of the orders we shipped last Thursday, Friday, or Saturday had a good chance of going out wrong.'

'But some of the orders were still on track? And none have been changed since?'

'I've now got a team verifying every configuration. For whatever reason, some of the orders weren't changed. There's no apparent rhyme or reason. No pattern to the changes that were made, either.'

'Which tells us this wasn't some program that waited out there and then smashed the database. These changes may have been made record by record, very methodically. Would someone be able to sit there, inside the company, and do that?'

'If they wanted to, I suppose so.'

'And no verification is required? No special password?'

'Not really. Anyone on the phones has access to change an order. I know that's a lot of people, maybe it's too wide-open, but it was an efficient way for us to work.' Barry bit his lip. Then he added. 'You have to have access to the system, of course.'

Dunn took a bite of crust and seemed to be thinking that over.

Then he asked, 'This is a standard PI-type question, but I'll throw it out anyway. Do you have anyone on your short list? Your answer is just between you and me, but you'd be surprised how often people's instincts are on target.'

'I lie in bed thinking about it. I've discussed it with Jim. I brainstormed with Chris for a solid hour. I've gone through every single TechDirect employee. We've sat around and made lists.' Barry shook his head. 'It would have to be a senior programmer, an administrator. Someone can't just hop off the phone banks and pull this kind of thing. The order entry, yes, but not network log-in scripts.'

'How about someone on the outside?'

'We've stepped on toes,' Barry said. 'That's part of being in business. But I can't think of anyone who would do this to get back at us.'

Dunn was watching closely. He leaned back against the bleachers behind them. 'It was just a shot.'

Barry reached down and straightened the cuff of his pants. 'When you get down to it, and at least for the sake of argument, I should be a suspect.'

'You are,' Dunn said. 'You have to be a suspect, Mr. Shepard. Initially, everyone is.'

'That's a relief.' Here was this man, thought Barry, pulling down sixty thousand a *day,* calling him Mr. Shepard.

'Don't worry, if it's you, we'll nail you. I'll go through every disk in your office, sector by sector, and you'll have left something somewhere. They always do. You don't fit the profile, though, Mr. Shepard, so I'd be surprised.'

'You can call me Barry. What's the profile?'

'If it's coming from outside the company, I have a pretty

good idea. I'd guess the person is no younger than twenty-five, probably male. No older than thirty-five. Forty, tops. They probably have a degree in computer science from MIT, Caltech, one of the biggies. Probably worked as a contractor somewhere, sometime, and got bored. This turned out to be more fun. Maybe it's only about money – Diane briefed me on all that, by the way – but maybe it's about a grudge.' He shrugged. 'It could be an eighty-year-old woman with an Amiga. I've been wrong before.'

Dunn pointed. 'Is that the phone?'

Barry nodded, scowling. The damn thing could ring again at any moment. 'It's in my name with GTE Mobilnet.'

'Your name or a dummy name. No one's that stupid.' Dunn picked up the phone and began a slow examination. He stared at the phone from all angles, as if, with enough concentration, it might summon their adversary right there to the bleachers.

'What?' Barry said.

Dunn shook his head. 'I'm just thinking through my bag of tricks. There's a lot you can do with a cellular phone. In this case, mostly useless.'

'Tell me this, I'm sure you've seen this kind of scenario before. It's not my money, and I can't unilaterally write them a check. I don't see what they stand to gain by threatening me.'

'Have they been?'

Barry wiped his hands on a napkin. He folded it with deliberate creases. 'Nothing concrete. We know where you live, Barry Shepard. That kind of thing.'

'There are two ways they can go. They can try and be pals and, of course, that fools no one. They know you hate their guts. You're the go-between.' Dunn cocked his head thoughtfully. 'They put a little squeeze on you, maybe you try a little harder to get them their money. Someone in your position, someone influential, maybe that tips the scales.'

Barry thought back to the four-to-two vote. It might have tipped the scales at that.

'They may threaten,' Dunn said. 'But unless I miss my guess, they don't have an interest in actually doing anything about it.'

Barry took a long sip of iced tea. *Unless I miss my guess.*

The orange team finally got an out to end the inning, and they ran in toward the dugout.

'Now we'll get to see your daughter bat.'

'I guess so. I don't think there's a strict rotation.'

'In Georgia, this age group, everyone gets to bat. It doesn't matter whether you play or not. Who was that woman sitting next to you, by the way. Was she your counsel?'

It took a moment for Barry to realize that Dunn was talking about Karen Williams, sitting next to him at the meeting. Another moment before he got a read on why Dunn was asking.

'The one sitting to my left? That's Karen Williams. She's our chief counsel.'

'That's the one,' Dunn said. 'Wow.'

'She's broken a few hearts. She was going out with this guy who owns a Lexus dealership on the west side. He wanted her to be in some of his commercials, standing out in the lot doing who-knows-what, probably wearing a bikini. She refused to do it. I think that's all over now. She used to be in a new Lexus every other day and lately she's been back in her Toyota.'

Barry was a little surprised at this blatant interest in Karen. She was a knockout, he knew that, but he had never been that attracted to her himself. She'd had all her rough edges polished off long ago, and that was something Barry didn't care for. The clothes, the talk, even the smell when she walked into the room – it was all too perfect. It struck Barry as being bought off the shelf. He wondered what W. S. Dunn would think of his own wife. Dark hair, Mediterranean complexion. Barry had always thought Claudia to be attractive and sexy, while staying away from the long nails and perfume. She was probably not Dunn's type.

'You came all the way out here to ask me about Karen?'

'No,' Dunn said, all business again. 'I'm going to need to work closely with you at the start. I'll want to go in tomorrow and look at where it all started, tear apart the database, examine how security was set up.'

'Do you have a Sybase person on your staff? We use PowerBuilder as the front end.'

'I've got this one kid, he can pretty much get into anything he wants.'

Barry doubted that. He considered the months they'd spent training several of their own employees to use PowerBuilder, and even now they were only just getting it under control. If Dunn had whiz kids who could pick it up on the fly, they'd put the Simtec programmers to shame.

Caroline had moved out into the on-deck circle. She carried a purple aluminum bat that was monstrously large.

At the plate was a boy who must have missed batting practice. His limbs flew every which way and finally the bat would shoot out and chop at the ball. The coach was pitching them in soft and easy, right over the plate, but it was hopeless. Strike three.

Caroline stood up from tying a shoelace and trotted on out. 'Smack one!' Barry yelled.

'Is she a hitter?' Dunn asked.

'She's seven years old. What do you think?'

'Best time to start. You get her out in the backyard smacking tennis balls, in a couple of years, she'll clobber it.'

Yeah, Barry thought. That's what you hoped for. They'd have to see how the assessments went at school. In a couple of years, Caroline might have slipped way behind her classmates. She might get pulled away from her friends and stuck off in special classes. The thought stuck in his throat like a rock.

The first pitch came in high and Caroline watched it.

'Good eye,' yelled Barry.

The next one was perfect and she swung. The bat got around late and the ball went foul over toward the dugout.

'She needs to open up her stance,' Dunn said. 'She moves her left foot over six inches and that's a hit.'

Barry grunted. What made Dunn such an expert? Did he even have any kids of his own? Barry leaned forward, watching the next pitch sail in, right across the plate. A swing and a miss.

'She's smooth,' Dunn said. 'Opens up a little and she'll have an easier time getting the bat around.'

Another throw and another ball went foul, in the same spot as the first.

‘You got it,’ yelled Barry, and this time she did, a soft hit that expended most of its energy in the dirt. The ball rolled fair inside the first base line. When the first baseman realized it was his play, Caroline had already started running and the ball was halfway in between them. The boy reached to grab the ball and spun for the tag, but the ball slipped out of his glove and plonked down into the dirt again. Caroline kept going and stomped safely on the bag.

Barry clapped and hollered. ‘All right,’ he said.

‘You got a player,’ Dunn said. He was standing up to leave. ‘I’d better get back. Just had to stay and catch one at bat. I’ll see you tomorrow.’

‘You bet,’ Barry said. His daughter was on first, and Dunn suddenly didn’t seem so bad after all.

While Barry roared approval as his daughter advanced to third and finally got stranded with the inning over, William Sanford Dunn drove his Ford F-10 pickup slowly back toward Simtec.

It was all the little things they weren’t telling him. The way they hesitated and averted their eyes. Always the same, these companies that called you in to save their asses but made you pry to get at all the information. Did they think he hadn’t seen it all? He’d been through this more times than they had in their worst nightmares. He knew the score.

Dunn’s father had worked for the NSA, a senior technical analyst, although they’d called him something different in those days. He was a code breaker, and he had enough electronic gear sitting around in the basement that Will had pieced together a solar-powered radio at the age of eight.

Will dropped out of high school when satellite dish technology first came on the scene. He prototyped the first scramblers and was still getting six figures off the patents. He’d never been to a day of college in his life, although it was something his ex-wife Darlene had constantly pushed for: Get a degree. Be *respectable*. When she read that the Wendy’s hamburger magnate had gotten a GED and gone back to school, Darlene had become relentless. That had pretty much ended it for them, after eleven years and two children. That and a lot of other things.

He drummed his fingers on the steering wheel while waiting on a traffic light, reached over, and flipped on the radio. On the low end of the FM band he found an evening news program. Some new incident in southern Lebanon, car blown up, another seven or eight people killed. That was the world, right there. No matter what you did, there was always someone wanting to go head-to-head. The same with computer networks, Dunn thought. Once you had them, they would never be safe.

So what was really going down here at Simtec? What had gone haywire? He had seen it before, someone so wigged out that, once they pinned the man down, four police had to carry him away in restraints. This and other events had helped Dunn make the decision to start carrying a .45 in his work bag.

To be effective, he needed all the dirt – the company politics, the intercompany feuds, anything and everything. Who would be the one at Simtec he could get to open up? Not Diane Hughes; she seemed to process every word three times before it came out. Jim Seidler was just as tight-lipped. Too bad, because he probably knew more about the company than anybody. Barry was a possibility. A good possibility. Even though he was at the top of the company, he was basically still a family man trying to do his job.

What about Karen Williams? He wouldn't be too upset if Karen became his confidante, though she was a lawyer and had perhaps been kept on the periphery. He'd meet with his employees and make sure they were digging in. Then he'd stop by and see if Karen was still in her office, maybe invite her out for a drink.

9

James Murphy Dupree – Jamie D as they had called him in the Harper correctional facility – had made his first million at the age of twenty-two. He'd done that by forming a Texas corporation named Educational Systems. He wrote directly to executives of major companies located in Texas and soon had a distinguished list of sponsors including Exxon, BFI, Continental Airlines, and Texas Instruments. These companies had money to give, and in rapid order they succumbed to the energy of this exuberant young mouthpiece. Dupree preached his success, and both Tandy and JCPenney soon agreed to underwrite his fledgling minority training program. His grant proposals for remedial training and neighborhood development centers were models of do-good mumbo-jumbo, culled from the dusty stacks of the University of Texas library.

Dupree was a smart young man. He'd graduated from St. Mark's in Dallas after his parents had shunned the public school system. At a time when most people his age were drinking beer and going to football games, James had studied Latin and spent the evenings in the third-floor library of their Preston Hollow estate.

James did not play sports and he did not like music. He stayed in the library where it was safe, out of his father's way, and he read while his parents argued, their shouts echoing throughout the house. After high school, he was smart enough, and he had the proper connections, to attend any college of his choosing. If it could be true of anyone, James Dupree was too smart for his own good.

The three years it took him to graduate from SMU were a long, grueling affair. He was crushed by the tedium of his classes, as he was also crushed by the breakup of his parents, who three months after his leaving flew apart in a tempest.

At twenty-one, instead of attending the University of Texas law school as his father's twenty-thousand-dollar-a-year stipend presumed, James opened the Austin office of Educational Systems. In his first year, he made over six hundred thousand dollars. It was easy, this business of doing good for the community. There was little follow-up, little scrutiny, and even the wildest of Dupree's claims went unchallenged. Of an eighty-thousand-dollar grant to teach writing skills, seventy went into his pocket and ten was showered upon an unlikely, but nonetheless pliable, elementary school.

When the scam finally unwound, James Dupree told the court how sorry he was. He told them about his parents' divorce and about how his father, a highly successful oil broker, had failed to provide a moral center. His lawyer told the court all kinds of things. The lawyer was not being paid, as most suspected, from the wallet of the senior Dupree, but rather from one small bundle of the three hundred thousand in cash James had retained, squirreled away inside a guitar case.

James Dupree groveled in court, and then off he went for ten months of solid reading time under minimum security. He came out a man without a past. His mother was off in California somewhere, apparently drunk every day, and his father hadn't spoken to him since the day he'd made the front page of the local section in the *Dallas Morning News.* Dupree Scion Bilks Millions, said the paper, and though most readers didn't know what a scion was, the article itself made matters more than clear.

After the ten months, and given time to reflect upon Educational Systems, Dupree knew in his heart that he had never had so much fun in his life. He'd been working eighteen hours a day and it had seemed like play.

He'd only replicated that kind of sustained rush, that fix, a few times in the nine years since. Mail order, travel award programs, a legion of door-to-door sales workers – he'd tried it all. On his thirtieth birthday, Dupree took a month-long vacation to California. He rented a cottage on the ocean and spent much of the time reading about computers. There on the beach, in the middle of a chapter on dial-in access, an idea was born.

One million four hundred some-odd thousand in foreign accounts was not enough, and Dupree felt a new calling. He found that putting together an electronic assault allowed complete creativity, and he was a natural at it. Best of all, he could do most of the work with disposable, off-the-shelf workers whom he kept at arm's length. Collecting his first payment, twenty thousand from an Austin, Texas, tool manufacturer, was easy. The targets and the payments had escalated, culminating in his most ambitious undertaking, the Simtec Computer Corporation. And now Simtec was giving him the big Fuck You.

He sat up in the leather recliner and swung his legs down. Dupree had a round face, untouched by wrinkles, and a cap of smooth blond hair. The face, together with his long, gangly limbs, gave him a look he had used many times to advantage. The look of a child.

He ignored the can of soda on the end table and went for the remote. The *Nightly Business Report* was giving the day's losers, and Simtec was on top of the list. The announcer dispassionately rattled off the recap: 'Simtec Computer Corp. took a big hit today on reports of production problems and broad internal restructuring. The company issued a formal statement in which Executive Vice President Jim Seidler called the reports exaggerated. Simtec's quarterly earnings are due out next week, and the surprise postponement of Chief Financial Officer Mike Spakovsky's prerelease meeting sent jitters through the ranks of analysts and top fund managers. Simtec is down four and seven-eighths on the week. General Motors today announced . . .'

Hah! That'll shake them up, thought Dupree. Market valuation had dropped by a half billion dollars. When the stock fell five points, that five was magnified by some hundred million shares. That money wasn't out of the company coffers, but those shares were held by pension funds and by thousands upon thousands of small investors. Those shares were held by many of their own employees. Maybe he could get it to run down another five points. That would really be something. James Dupree the cause of a one-billion-dollar movement in the financial markets.

The fools should have cut him a check and considered it a lesson. Five million, compared to what they would now go through. Dupree was struck by the possibility that he'd been too cheap. Even at five million, Simtec hadn't taken him seriously. He hit the remote to switch to CNN *Headline News* and muted the sound, then picked up the phone and dialed from memory. Seven rings before the kid picked up, and by the time he did, Dupree was squeezing the arm of the chair.

'It's me,' Dupree said. 'Who the hell do you think?'

'I was in the bathroom. . . .'

'Take the goddamn phone in there, then. It's mobile, that's what it's for.'

'All right, all right.'

'I hope you saw the news. It's good, Mark, but it's not enough. We need to hit them again.'

A long sigh. 'I can't do it again, right now. I'm tired and I need to get some sleep. I've been up for thirty-six hours.'

Dupree pressed teeth into his lower lip. One of his troops was not of strong fortitude. He wanted to tell the kid, Do it or they'll find you floating in the bayou. Instead, and it took all his control, he said, 'I understand. You've been doing a great job, too. I think this is the last point we'll have to make.'

'Besides, I never wanted to wreck the company. I told you that. You said we'd only have to show our capabilities and that would be enough. We're talking about Simtec here. The Simtec Computer Corporation.'

The kid was starting to balk, and Dupree pushed a palm hard into his thigh. Oh, how he hated to depend on other people. After he wet-nursed them along, inspired them, bought any tool they asked for, it always came back to this: other people were inherently unreliable. The kid had handled his first two jobs well enough, but those had been smaller, hundred-thousand-dollar stuff. Oh, Lord, just get us through this one. Five million and Dupree would never have to cajole and wheedle again. He'd have a high-tech factory staffed with professionals. Nothing but the cream of the crop.

'I've spoken with them,' Dupree said. 'They caught what you did early on. You didn't do any damage, and they think you can't hurt them anymore.'

'Really?' There was relief in the voice, but also some curiosity and strength. Dupree knew all the buttons to push.

'Now they're bragging, saying how the bug was primitive. They're talking shit over there, Mark. They're saying the person trying to get in is not the caliber they thought. Only five or ten machines got erased, and who's going to pay on that? A hundred thousand is a lot of money.'

'Yes, it is. Only five drives were erased?' This almost made Dupree smile. Smart and gullible, that's how he liked them. Send them right over the wall with their bayonets. Gallipoli.

He flipped on the charm. 'I tell you what. I know this has been a tough one for you. I'm sending you a disk with a new tool. It's a driver that works with Simtec's top-of-the-line SCSI disk arrays. You'll find a readme file on the disk that explains exactly what to do. Now it's up to you to get me another strike. Find a way to hit them, and you've got another five coming, okay? Instead of ten we'll call it fifteen thousand. You've earned it.'

That's right, promise him anything.

'All right, Mr. Draper. That sounds good to me. I'm going to lie down and catch a few hours, then I'll see what I can do.'

'You give me a call and keep me posted. You're doing fine. Remember, we've got a great future together, but this is a real test for us. They're sharp at Simtec and they're giving you a challenge. As you know, the longer it takes, the tougher it gets.'

Dupree hung up. He sank back into the chair and reached for the drink. He punched in another phone number from memory, and the phone was answered immediately. That's why Dupree liked Wilson. Wilson had been with him for five years, and you could count on him. You needed someone to put their coat down in the mud, Wilson's was the first one off. Why not? He'd ask Dupree to buy him another one.

'I want you to keep a tighter watch on the kid,' Dupree said. 'He's expressing reluctance to go forward.'

Wilson grunted. He sounded like he had his mouth full. 'Watch the kid. Keep track of two different people. You must think I'm Superman.'

Not even close. 'Let me be clear. We will do whatever it takes to wrap this up successfully.'

'Hardheaded is what they are. If all the big shots were supposed to meet, they must have gotten together and shot us down. You're talking about a corporation with a lot of balls.'

'That's what they don't have,' Dupree snapped. 'They'll crack. It's all a matter of presentation. Then there's the whole question of Barry Shepard. Did Shepard turn out to be the right one? We need him in there pressing our case, and I don't think that's happening.'

'Could be they're not paying and that's that.' The sound of paper crinkling in the background.

'Then they're idiots, because it's going to get uglier. Every weapon we've got, I'm going to unload the barrels. What are you doing, eating?'

'A hoagie.'

'What the hell is that? What is a hoagie? That's your downfall, Wilson. You're always eating. One day you're going to miss something important.'

'I need my strength,' said Wilson. He didn't really give a shit what Dupree said. The boss was smart, and he had all the angles. More angles than Wilson would think of in a million years, but that was nothing to be afraid of.

'Make a plan for the kid. We need to keep him motivated. Also get something for Shepard to keep *him* motivated, something to guide him toward the easy way out.'

'Mmm,' Wilson said. He'd just taken another bite of hoagie. Mark Willis was twenty-six. He'd answered their ad in the newspaper and been given a careful screening. Then they'd spent all kinds of money on his toys and his training. He was the second one they'd had to develop in this way. The first had taken foolish chances and gotten himself arrested in Denver. On that fateful day, if Wilson had arrived thirty minutes earlier, he would have been in the back of a squad car himself.

'Not to worry.' Wilson said. 'I got a plan.'

'Good. And I've got that disk ready for you to take over. I'll leave it out, the usual place.'

'Give me thirty minutes. Maybe I'll take him a pizza, too. I don't know why, I've had this craving ever since I saw Shepard go into that joint. Did I tell you, after you spoke to him, he went running all the way over to the next street to see the van? Hee hee.'

Wilson had liked that, his bit with the van. It was his touch, and he laughed every time he thought about it. 'That's what I'll do. I'm going to take the whiz kid a pizza.'

'He was supposed to be going to sleep. Said he hadn't slept in thirty-six hours.'

'Then I'll wake him up.'

'Give him two hours.'

Wilson checked his watch 'Time's a-wasting,' he said. 'By that time, I'll be famished.'

Barry held the Cyrano's box, with one remaining slice, and juggled the keys to the back of the house. He flicked on the lights in the kitchen. Caroline went straight for the fridge and a pitcher of apple juice.

'What do you want for dinner?' Barry asked. 'How about soup and a grilled cheese sandwich?'

Caroline nodded from behind a glass.

On the kitchen counter, he assembled a can of Campbell's vegetable, loaf of bread, butter dish, and a block of cheddar. He went to work, and the whole thing took about four minutes.

'Hey, grubby,' he said. 'How about washing your hands?' He pointed the way to the kitchen sink.

She toweled off and started in greedily on the sandwich. 'Who was that man at the game?' she said between bites.

'We've been having some trouble with our computers, so we hired him to come out and fix them.'

'So he's a computer man.'

'He's supposed to know more about computers than just about anyone else.'

'More than you?'

'More than everybody,' Barry said, though he considered

what Dunn had said about psychologists. Maybe this was less about computer hardware than he'd thought. 'Engineers know lots more than I do about what's inside a computer. I know more about selling them.'

She'd already lost interest. 'I got a hit today. And you saw it. You'll have to tell Mom.'

'You bet. You looked like a slugger. That's what the other man said, in fact. He said you were a hitter, but that you ought to turn more toward the pitcher. Your left foot is too close to the plate.'

'Really?' she said. She jumped out of her chair and started practicing her stance.

'We'll try it in the backyard with tennis balls.'

'When?' Caroline looked up hopefully.

'Tomorrow, maybe. Soon. Maybe this weekend.'

Her gaze fell away, back to her stance. The phone rang and Barry started toward it and stopped. Let the machine answer, he decided. If it was Claudia, he'd pick up.

The voice of a strong seventy-year-old shot out of the speaker. It was his father calling from California. Three years earlier, Barry had lost his mother in a grueling, six-month battle with cancer. Ever since, his father had rediscovered his son and his family, and he called on a regular basis.

'Barry? What's with this stock of yours? I'll bet you're over there plugging holes in the dike. I hope so, because I'm losing my shirt. Bail the water, man. Bail! Unless you want your old man to have to come move in with you. Hah, hah. Hi, Claudia. Hi, Caroline. Caroline, you better not be watching that Beavis character on MTV.'

The machine clicked off and Barry shook his head. He'd always refused to discuss company information, but his dad never stopped trying to pry it out of him. It hadn't stopped his father from buying either. Over the years, he had probably made a couple of hundred thousand on Simtec stock, so Barry wasn't going to sweat it now.

'That was Grandpa,' Caroline said.

'Yeah. He said you shouldn't watch MTV. You're not, are you?' Caroline scrunched up her nose. She wasn't yet of the age where music videos were It. She slid out of her chair.

'You want anything else to eat?'

She shook her head.

'All right. I'm going to clean up in here and you're off to the showers.'

He wiped up and put everything away, then went in to check E-mail.

He hadn't logged in since 2:00 P.M., and the usual stack of messages awaited.

He read the note from Diane first:

> Barry:
> I'm going to have to fly out tomorrow at ten to attend several business meetings. Let's meet in my office at seven-thirty to go over final details. It looks more and more like Jim will need to go, too. I'd prefer him to stay and mind the fort, as I'm sure we all would, but his visits will be essential. Too much ground to cover for one person. I will be available at all times, of course, and I will be checking in on a regular basis. See you in the morning.

Unbelievable, thought Barry. The middle of a crisis, and Diane was going to take off. Not only that, it looked like she was going to take Jim with her, effectively leaving Barry as much in charge as anyone else. Barry knew how *I will be available* worked. It worked only in theory, and the one time he absolutely had to get hold of Diane, he wouldn't be able to find her.

Well, he certainly wasn't going to take orders from Spakovsky, or Randall Johnson, so they'd better all decide on some pretty explicit strategies before the two of them rode out of town.

What was so important, anyway? Diane had mentioned a pending distribution agreement, but she hadn't made a big deal over it. He hit answer and typed, 7:30, I'll be there. I left voice mail on your portable re: latest conversation. Then he punched up a message from Spakovsky.

> Barry:
> How about this Dunn character? I voted in favor because we have to do *something*. He comes into accounting this evening

and he wants to go into everything. I mean everything. In his intrusive, pedantic manner, he lectures me about employee abuses. If it's coming from inside the company, he says, we may be able to find a trail. Do I need to hear this?

His analysts are going to scrutinize purchases for the last two years. They're going to look at receivables past due. Then they're going into employee stock trades, purchases, short sales, who has exercised options – everything. Is this really what we need? Is it too late to take another vote?

Barry paused with his hand over the keyboard. He heard the shower turn on upstairs, and he remembered his promise to practice batting with Caroline. On a yellow notepad, he scribbled *batting* and stuck it off on the corner of the desk. Then he turned back to the screen.

Dunn, intrusive? That's what they'd hired him to be. He might be flashy, but not pedantic.

What's the problem with going through stock trades and financial records? Barry thought it sounded pretty good. If they were going to have a housecleaning, they ought to be thorough. Perhaps there were some skeletons in the closet after all. Barry looked at the message line, and it had not been cc:ed. Why did Spakovsky write to him, as if Barry would run to Diane and do his dirty work for him? Barry had always thought of Mike as a powerful figure in the company, but he was coming to realize Mike didn't have the clout people thought. Jim was the right-hand man, and Mike was being shoved aside. Somehow, through it all, Barry had managed to stay neutral. He had his own business unit and that gave him a lot of autonomy. Let them come into TechDirect, turn out everyone's pockets, and look in all the cupboards. He had nothing to hide.

He had started into the mail messages from his employees when he heard Claudia come in the back door. He finished a reply and walked into the kitchen.

'Caroline got a hit and she's now upstairs in the locker room. I saved you one slice from Cyrano's.'

'That's perfect,' she said, but she didn't sound like it.

'First day in court,' Barry said. He'd seen it before.

'I had a tough go and it really took me by surprise. The

man – the father – had started taping his wife on a hidden recorder. I thought it was good stuff, but the jury didn't react well. How about you?'

'We had a disaster. Seven hundred people lost all their files. We've decided to hire an outside security consultant, and I hope it takes the monkey off my back.'

'It wasn't your fault to begin with.'

'No, but it felt like it was. They got to me first. I got the letter. It begins to get a little personal.' Barry paused, but then decided to go on. 'I also find out today they've been through our trash. They know about my wife and daughter.'

'They said that? They mentioned Caroline?'

'Not by name. Just that I have a wife and daughter. They're trying to show how much they've got me on the ropes.'

'What did they say, exactly?'

'They said something to the effect of, "I own you, Shepard. Your wife and daughter, too." '

'Oh, that's great.'

'There was no specific threat. They're turning the screws on me, is all.'

'And doing a good job of it.'

'That's why I'm glad the decision to hire this security company was almost unanimous. The guy knows what he's doing, and a lot of people wanted the cover. I happen to think it's a good idea.'

'If it diverts attention away from you, I think it's a great idea. I don't like this wife and daughter business at all. Who did you hire?'

'The company's called Security Associates. It's more like an army, really. He's bringing in fifty people. Some of them are already here working. They come in and do what amounts to a complete audit – not only the computers, but financial records and personnel. The man who came to our meeting and pitched us is W. S. Dunn. He's the owner.'

'I've heard that name. I think one of our clients used the same outfit. You want me to ask about him?'

'It's a done deal, but by all means, dig up the dirt. He won't commit to a time limit. This could run us a million dollars. Maybe two.'

'For a computer consultant? I think I'm in the wrong profession.'

'We've got to have it,' Barry said. 'You have no idea.'

Claudia sat down at the kitchen table. She was holding her forehead.

'Look,' Barry said. 'They're not stupid. They know it's not Barry Shepard who's going to pay them. I'm only the messenger. Don't worry, it doesn't mean anything.'

10

Apparently, it did mean something.

Barry woke after Caroline's baseball bat rolled six inches and made a soft clunk against the barbecue on the back patio. He lay there half asleep, listening, picking up only the usual sounds. Whir of the ceiling fan. Claudia's breathing. Eerie quiet of the house.

Barry rolled onto his side and was about to slip off again when he heard a very faint, very peculiar, scratching sound. It wasn't right, and his whole body came instantly alert.

He slipped out of bed and padded barefoot in boxers and T-shirt to the closet. In the back corner rested a Sears Roebuck single-shot 20-gauge shotgun. From the toe of a hiking boot on the upper shelf, Barry fished out one shell.

The gun was a crude instrument, a relic from Barry's teens. It had no safety, no pump, no nothing. You pulled back on the hammer manually. Then you pulled the trigger. Barry cracked the barrel and inserted the shell, then slid noiselessly out into the hallway.

He passed Caroline's room and glanced inside. In the filtered moonlight, he could see her outline, asleep in a tangle of blanket. He crept to the top of the stairs, and this much Barry knew: If some fucker had come into the house, he wasn't going to hesitate. Point and shoot, and with this weapon the pointing was optional.

This whole shotgun exercise had been carried out once before, and the culprit had turned out to be a squirrel who had gotten past the screen in the chimney. If it was Mr. Squirrel this time, he had mighty bad timing.

The stairs came down in a straight line facing the front door. Barry took them in a crouching, crablike motion, and at the bottom he stopped and waited for a full thirty seconds. Which was when he heard it.

Coming from the living room, a faint scratching sound. It could have been a twig against the window or a cat on the prowl. It could have been a lot of things. The goose flesh rose along Barry's forearms, up across the back of his neck. He didn't think it was a cat.

Staying close to the wall, he edged to the doorway where he was still in shadow. Four sets of windows opened onto the backyard, and the light coming through the panes of glass made a crisscross pattern across much of the room. Square in the middle of the second window was the silhouette of a man. Barry assumed it was a man, though he couldn't see the face. The person had a knife and was trying to jimmy the lock on the sash.

The calf muscle of Barry's right leg started to jump and hop about on its own. He sank into a crouch and moved into the room, feeling his way along the ground until he came up behind the living room sofa. He pulled the hammer back on the shotgun and swung it up over the sofa back.

The man moved to window number three. He was poking and jabbing at the sash lock, and Barry heard, more than saw, the lock give a partial turn.

Ten feet away, Barry aimed toward the man's midsection. The muscle twitching seemed to be confined to Barry's legs. His hand was firm on the wooden stock, one finger edging inside the trigger guard.

As the man jimmied in past the window frame and the sash lock flipped open, Barry pulled the trigger. He was pointing the barrel in the general direction of the man's torso.

Nothing happened. No deafening shotgun blast. As though he might achieve a better result, Barry pulled the trigger again. What had he expected? a voice in his head screamed. The goddamned shells were twenty years old.

So Barry did the next best thing. He stood bolt upright and grabbed the gun by the barrel. He skirted the sofa, took a running step toward the window, and threw the shotgun like a tomahawk.

★

'Lucky for you you didn't use it,' said the police officer who was doing most of the talking. 'It would have been a mess.'

They were standing out on the back porch, surveying the debris from the broken window. Barry had slipped into gray sweatpants and tennis shoes. He glanced down at the traitorous yellow shotgun shell in his hand.

Claudia had gone back upstairs. Caroline wanted to see the police, so she was pouting in her room at an observation post by the front window.

What Barry reported was this: Someone was at the back window trying to get in. He came downstairs with the old shotgun. He saw the figure at the window. He threw the shotgun.

It was the unembellished truth. Barry saw no reason to describe how the shotgun shell had failed to discharge, how the shotgun had cut right through the window panes. The man outside must have caught a flicker of movement, because he had straightened at the last minute, right before he was broadsided by a hail of glass, wood splinters, and a rifle butt that hit him straight in the chest.

The man staggered backwards and went down hard. Then he rolled over onto his side, struggled to his feet, and took off running.

At that point, Barry went the other direction back into his study and called the police.

'No idea who it might have been?' the cop was asking. 'Neighborhood kid? Burglar?'

'I don't think it was a kid,' Barry said. He figured he knew exactly who it was, but he also figured that this police officer, standing there with his notepad and his slightly bored expression, wasn't prepared to hear the half of it.

'That's the kind of thing a dumb kid would do. Try to go into a house and steal himself a nice stereo. Make a racket and wake up the owner of the house.'

But the man hadn't made a racket. Barry was a light sleeper, and lately even more so. If not, would he have heard any of it? 'We don't have an alarm,' Barry said, thinking, I wonder if the man knew that? I wonder *how* he knew that. They'd considered an alarm system, but with a private security guard at the front gate and no history of burglary on the street, they'd always opted out. In the morning, he'd discuss it with Claudia and place the order. A nice fat motion detector in the middle of the downstairs ought to take care of something like this.

The cop pursed his lips. His eyes flicked over the house. Nice furnishings, obviously some money here, the glance seemed to say. How freaking cheap can you be?

'We haven't needed one before now,' Barry said. 'My wife's not into jewelry and there's not much else to take. No through traffic on the street, and you're not going to waltz in here with a moving van.'

The cop scribbled a few lines on a preprinted slip and handed it to Barry. 'This is your incident number. I'll punch it in with some notes on what happened. If anyone thinks they've got a match, you'll get a call.'

'But probably nothing's going to come of it.'

'You didn't see the guy. Nothing taken from the house. Unless he hits someone on the next street and gets busted, it's doubtful. I wouldn't expect him back here, though. You probably scared the hell out of him.'

I bet I did worse than scare him, Barry thought. He shook the officer's hand and took down his name, then let the two cops out the front door much to Caroline's delight.

He himself went back out on the patio. The baseball bat was lying off to one side by the window closest to the garage. That's probably what he had heard, Barry realized. The shithead had tripped over the baseball bat.

He walked in a semicircle out around the broken glass. The patio ended and became grass, and it was near here where the man would have fallen. Barry kneeled like a deer hunter and stared at the ground, looking for any sign of blood.

He didn't see any. But as he came to his feet he saw something else, a few feet further off. He walked over and stared for a moment, then reached down and picked it up. It was a three-and-a-half-inch floppy disk.

Barry walked into the office at 6:15 with the disk in his top pocket. He wanted to examine the disk and then prepare for the meeting with Diane and Jim.

Instead, as he rounded the corner into the main TechDirect offices, he found that half the desks had been pushed aside to make room for a number of rectangular folding tables. The tables looked as if they'd been brought up from the cafeteria.

Two large metal shipping cases stood open on the floor, and about ten people – none of whom looked familiar – were pulling portable computers out and setting them up on the tables.

A youngish man, mid-twenties, looked up and saw him standing there.

'Hello,' he said. 'You must be Barry Shepard.' He stretched out his hand, and after a slight hesitation, Barry took it. 'I'm Bill Dunn, Bill Junior, whatever you want to call me. I'd appreciate a chance to sit down and discuss your priority users with you. We've got about fifteen machines allocated for your area. We're doing our central distribution for your division right now. We'll be out of here in two hours.'

'Central distribution?' Barry said. His back teeth came down together hard. This Dunn looked like a tall, brown-haired college student. Almost a kid, for Christ's sake.

'Let me explain our procedure,' the junior Dunn said. 'We're issuing portables . . . our own portables . . . ' Barry had already noticed they weren't Simtecs. 'We do this for several reasons. First, you should be using your own network as little as possible until we can verify its reliability. We're also going to be pulling the net up and down all day, knocking things off-line, so just as a matter of convenience this will allow you to keep working.'

Barry rubbed his forehead. 'You realize what you're proposing? Forgive me if I'm a little short, but does Dunn – your father – honestly expect us to be able to work off a bunch of portables? What about transferring files and printing? We've got people in other buildings. What about mail and database access? We're going to have chaos with this. People running around playing tag team with floppies.'

'Oh, no,' Bill said. 'They're all connected. It's wireless, but you're on the net all right. You're on *our* net. We put pods all over the building so you can walk around and stay on-line. The signal doesn't carry outside the building.'

Barry blinked hard. A wireless network of hundreds of portables. In a box.

'We had to keep the phone reps on cable, though. Hated to do it, but there's no way to swap that out. The server is completely isolated, so unless it's already got bugs on it, we should be totally safe. We'll be getting right on the server to check it out. In the meantime, we've got file integrity programs that set off all kinds of alarms, so don't worry.'

He turned to a young woman behind him. 'Is Mr. Shepard's machine ready?'

The woman pointed to the first portable, standing at the head of the table.

'Here you go,' Bill said. 'Moved your contact manager. Latest Excel. Mail and all your front-end database apps. We took your personal files off the server and plugged them in here already. You should be all set.'

'You're telling me I can print right now from this machine? I can send E-mail?'

'You bet. Take another battery in case that one gets low. You need more, we keep a whole stack charged up and ready. Why don't you go give it a test drive? Is it all right if I stop in later and discuss your users?'

Barry checked his watch. He had to be in Diane's office in forty-five minutes. The disk was burning a hole in his pocket. He needed to call and set up an alarm installation. 'I've got a meeting,' he said. 'I'll hammer out a list before I go.'

'That'd be great,' Bill said. 'You have any problems with the portable, just holler at us for support.'

Barry nodded and Bill Dunn turned away. Then Bill looked back, as if he'd thought of another last-minute instruction, but what he said was: 'Remind me to ask you about that lawyer, Karen somebody-or-other. Put in a good word for me, if you get a chance. Tell her I know my stuff.'

Incredible, thought Barry, the father and son both.

Barry went into his office and looked at the now useless tower CPU sitting on the floor. Simtec had imported a team of complete outsiders, the outsiders set up shop overnight, and already Simtec would be calling upon them for support. He flipped up the top on the portable. It was a sleek, black case and he hit what looked like the on button. The button slid under his finger, but the computer did not turn on. He looked more closely and saw that he was moving the brightness control for the screen.

His large fingers probed the rest of the buttons and crevices of the black case without success. Was he really going to have to walk back out there and ask how to turn it on? He slapped the screen closed and flipped the thing over. A small hinge on one side indicated some kind of panel. Battery, probably, but he pried it off anyway.

The panel came away revealing a port and a button. He jabbed the button and the little portable sprang to life. Here he was, selling a million dollars of equipment every day, and he was back at square one: how to turn on the machine.

Barry knocked on the door to Diane Hughes's office at 7:31. Jim and Diane were bent over some papers, which Diane pushed back into a pile.

'Barry,' she said. 'Come in. Why don't you shut the door?'

They all sat, and though not sure why he should, Barry felt nervous.

'I've filled Jim in on the phone call you received yesterday. Anything else since then?'

Barry shook his head. 'He said noon, but that doesn't mean he'll call for sure. It's what I would expect.'

'Good. We think it's going as well as can be hoped. We're stalling. We can't expect them to be pleased about that. The important thing is, we're buying time while Security Associates is able to get in here and set up shop.'

'They're breaking out the portables on my floor as we speak,' Barry said. He noticed one of the sleek, black machines sitting over on Diane's desk. 'They're a professional operation. It's easy to see how they earn their rates.'

Jim Seidler had heavy rings under his eyes. He looked like he needed a month off sitting by the swimming pool. 'I've never seen a damn thing like it in my life,' he said. 'It's like a SWAT team handing out rifles.'

Diane adopted her get-down-to-business tone. 'Unfortunately, both Jim and I have to make several out-of-town visits. Jim will be returning late today. I won't be back until tomorrow.'

'Both of you have to go? It's horrible timing.'

Jim immediately cleared his throat. 'Diane and I have discussed the issue at length. I expressed my opinion that to cancel at the last minute would send the wrong signal, both to the industry and to the media. We're already under the magnifying glass, and we can't afford it. That's our primary concern, but this agreement is also worth seven million dollars to our bottom line.' Jim leaned forward. 'I have tried to make the case that I should be left back here to work with you, Barry.'

'Let's not open this can of worms again,' Diane said. Her sideways look at Jim shot sparks. 'We're both going and that's that.'

Barry glanced between the two of them. He opened his mouth, then closed it and nodded grim acceptance.

'These last few days have been rough,' Diane said. 'Perhaps as bad on you, Barry, as anyone. We hope we're getting this business behind us. We think Will Dunn was a good way to go, the right decision.'

'He's good,' Barry said. 'If he can't keep them out, there's no way we would have ourselves.' He'd been deciding whether to tell them about the attempted burglary at his house. It didn't feel right. They were going off on their expeditions and Barry didn't need the hollow exclamations of concern. He'd only just met the man, but he'd feel more comfortable telling W. S. Dunn about it than either Jim or Diane.

Instead, he said, 'There's something I think might be useful. I've come up with some other security ideas I'd like to implement – things Chris, Jim, and I didn't come up with on the first go-round. Dunn's going to need all kinds of access, too. We're going to need to go barging into other people's departments and pull down servers, turn off workstations, whatever is expedient. I want to be able to cut through the politics and the explanations and do whatever it is we need to do. A letter authorizing me to take whatever action is necessary in your absence might go a long way in that regard.'

Diane had a look of shrewd calculation.

'A letter, Barry?' Jim said.

Diane held up her hand. 'That's okay. At this stage of the game, Barry's decided that he doesn't trust anyone. I can't say that I blame him.'

Barry had never thought it so bluntly. Was that true? He no longer trusted anyone? He had someone breaking into his house while he was asleep. He was carrying a cellular phone so a man calling himself *Hektor* could ring and demand five million dollars.

'This isn't about trust,' he said at last.

The three of them sat quietly until Diane said, 'You'll have a letter before we go.'

11

When Barry walked back into his office, W. S. Dunn was sitting in a chair by the window. He had a stack of papers he was going through with a big yellow Hi-Liter.

'Good morning,' Dunn said. He set the papers aside but didn't bother to stand.

'Hell of a morning. Your son was after me as soon as I came in.'

'You tried that out yet?' Dunn indicated the portable.

'I turned it on and that's about it.' Barry moved around the desk. 'It's obvious you've done this before. You're very methodical. Well-organized. Jim Seidler compared your people to a SWAT team.'

Dunn gave a smile that quickly vanished. 'We may be methodical, but every case is unique. The people who rigged your log-in know what they're doing. Those were elegant traps. Simple, yet very destructive. At this point we're still playing catch-up, and much of the morning will be taken up by this bureaucratic nonsense.'

Lord help them, Barry thought, if configuring and handing out hundreds of laptops was bureaucracy.

'I understand I'll be giving my reports to you today.'

'Jim and Diane have business,' Barry said in response to Dunn's questioning look. 'I'd like you to keep me as informed as possible. I don't need every detail, but keep me posted on what you find. Certainly give me an assessment of any new trouble spots. I'll help in any way I can, or I will track down the appropriate person to get you what you need.'

'I appreciate that. You had no unauthorized log-in attempts last night. You and a few others accessed from off-site. At the moment, I have a couple of quick questions. Anything on your end, before I get started?'

'There's certainly one thing. A man tried to come in the back window of my house last night.'

'What happened?'

'A noise woke me up. I got out of bed and scared him off.' Barry considered the floppy disk and decided not to mention it. Yet.

Dunn carefully recapped the Hi-Liter. He set it on top of the papers on the table. 'That may be coincidence,' he said. 'On the other hand, you can't be too careful. All of you will have to take extra care with your person and belongings, things like briefcases, laptops, where you park your cars. We have a primer on personal security and awareness. I'll have my people circulate a copy to all top executives.'

Barry nodded. 'That sounds like a good idea.'

Dunn glanced at his notes and appeared to consider something. But then he said, 'How'd your daughter end up last night – she get a run?'

Upset because she didn't get to talk to the police, Barry thought. 'Time ran out after the next inning, so she never got to score. She was very happy with the hit.' He scribbled the word ALARM on a notepad and underlined it.

'It's a lot of fun at that age,' Dunn said. 'Win, lose, it doesn't really matter. Then, somehow, the parents infect the kids. I have a daughter who used to be an angel. Now, you wouldn't believe it. She's twenty and wants to be a stockbroker. Whoever put that idea in her head I have no idea.'

'I'm surprised she's not following the family line of business.'

'Hates computers. I gave her a Macintosh PowerBook when she went off to school. One with an active color screen, CD, a really nice machine. I don't think she's ever used it. Too much of her mother's influence. She thinks she's going to get down in the pits and make hand signals all day buying pork bellies.'

Barry smiled, but somehow this felt like a Columbo routine. The guy wanted something, but bumbled around making conversation while he had his antennae out the whole time. 'You said you had some questions?' Barry said.

'Of course. I've noticed something in your order-entry database that I wondered about. There were a number of records, thirty-seven to be exact, that have been locked out. Effectively, they are kept from placing an order. I found that curious.'

'I hadn't realized there were as many as that, but it's not hard to explain. We get all kinds placing orders in here, as you can imagine. Some of the people have a history of purchasing equipment and then returning it, purchasing and returning, over and over. Eventually, we have to tell them we can no longer accept their orders.'

Dunn pushed out his lower lip. He didn't look fully satisfied.

'There's another group who call and never order, but there's not much we can do about that. I think these people are generally older. They're just plain bored, or lonely, so they call up our reps and talk about the latest equipment, upgrades, anything. We know who they are, because they call in like clockwork. We're on a first-name basis. Five minutes on the line with them max, then we get off. Most of them settle into a routine and become very polite about it. If we kept track of the time spent on those calls, I bet we could write it off as charity.'

'The reason I ask about the thirty-seven, if you cut somebody off from ordering Simtec machines, they may have taken offense. Maybe you lit somebody's fuse. It's a long shot, but we're going to need to check them out.'

'It's hard to imagine one of those people having the know-how to get into Sybase, or to get into our servers and change batch files.'

'Like I said, it's a long shot. But someone who orders all your stuff and then returns it sounds like a tech fanatic. All they want is to check out the latest equipment. Then you go and piss them off. They think they're pretty sharp and they decide to get even. It's possible.' Dunn ran a hand along his jaw, looking pensive. Then he said, 'Anger is a good motivator. A few months ago, a construction firm called me into a site in New Orleans. They had a flipped-out foreman and one morning they went to start up, there wasn't any oil in the Caterpillars.'

'Why did you get called in?'

'Equipment in their on-site office. Accounting and payroll. CAD drawings. They had to make sure everything was square.'

'Was it?'

Dunn gave a sly smile. 'Nope.'

Barry considered this. 'Do what you have to do,' he said.

'We already are. Fourteen are off the list. We're checking the other twenty-three. I wanted to run it by you in case you had a hunch or suspicions about any specific customer.'

'Not that's been brought to my attention. I'll toss it out to the people on the phones, see if anyone ever made a specific threat about breaking into the network.'

'That would be great. The other thing I wanted to go over with you is that electrical accident you had.'

Barry sat forward stiffly.

'I wanted to get some more background.'

'One of our maintenance men, Ben Cooper, was up in the crawl space. He got hit by some live voltage. We lost a couple of breakers and it was about fifteen minutes before they found him.'

'And he was doing a wiring trace.'

'We were doing some recabling. We wanted – I wanted – to have a backup line run to each of the main areas in this building. The possibility had come up that Chris might have to shut down the backbone. Let's say a hostile virus was replicating itself across the network. I wanted to have a fallback position.'

'So Mr. Cooper was pulling new cable?'

Barry knew how this must sound. Running around haphazardly stringing cable had to appear comical to a well-oiled team that could step in and unpack a wireless network. Barry shifted uneasily in his chair.

'Ben was locating some unused cable that had been run years ago. He had worked here since the beginning. He insisted that he could locate the runs, and he went looking for them.'

'That seems like a reasonable plan,' Dunn said, but Barry could tell something about it didn't sit right. Dunn glanced at the top paper on his stack and set it down again.

'I'm going through directory dumps of the files on Horace and Wilbur,' Dunn said.

'The file servers in building ten.'

'Those two machines drive every application over there. I underline suspect files and we check them out one at a time.'

Dunn tapped the Hi-Liter pen on his knee. 'What's your theory on how that electricity got loose up there?'

'What do you mean, "What's my theory"? I don't have a *theory.* It seems to me like a tragic accident. That's what the inspectors said. How the hell would I know? If you're implying that Ben was trying to do something he shouldn't have, that's a crock. Number one, I trusted him completely, and two, he was doing what he was told.' Barry swallowed and chose his words. *The hell with it.* 'He was doing what I asked him to do.'

'That's not at all what I was implying,' Dunn said. 'In fact, quite the opposite.'

Barry had to think about that. Ben Cooper had been doing exactly as he'd been told. 'What are you getting at, Mr. Dunn? I'm not sure I understand your point.'

'Call me Will. Please. I'm clearly in no position to tell you what happened precisely. What I'm doing, and perhaps doing a bad job of it, is raising the point that getting into live electricity while doing a wiring trace . . . something about that strikes me as peculiar. By no means impossible, but odd. It's something I want to look into further.'

'You look into it all you want to.'

Dunn had cocked his head and he watched Barry for a few moments. 'I will,' he said. 'I'll let you know what I find.'

Barry started to open his mouth, but he was interrupted by a crackling sound that spat out of a small box propped against the lamp on the table next to Dunn. 'W. S.?' someone was saying. 'W. S., are you there?'

Dunn snatched up what looked like a miniature, and no doubt expensive, walkie-talkie. 'I'm here,' he said.

'We've got administrative log-in on a server called Theodore. He was also logged into Marilyn, we believe, before we picked it up.'

'What's he doing?' Dunn's voice kicked into high gear.

'Not much, so far as we can tell. Hasn't written any files. Maybe just looking around.'

'Could it be a Sysop?'

'Could be. We've been telling them all to check with us, but we had to leave voice mail to a few. Maybe they didn't get it.'

'I'll be right over,' Dunn said. He turned to Barry and said, 'Want to come?'

Marilyn and Theodore were located in the next building, Simtec 3. If any building on the campus could be called the administrative center, it was this one, home to the boardroom as well as Diane's newly renovated presidential suite.

They took the above-ground walkway that connected the two buildings, and Barry slashed his ID through the card reader. The door buzzed open.

Last Barry could remember, Theodore was a high-powered file server used by development. It had a string of SCSI hard drives attached, and some technicians had come over one day to look at Whoopi, the TechDirect machine that had the same configuration. He'd let them into the server room and watched nervously while they poked and prodded Whoopi to get at her secrets.

Marilyn, on the other hand, was a human resources machine. Simtec employees could log in to Marilyn and perform a variety of housekeeping duties, such as modify their own payroll deductions. It seemed unlikely that the same administrator would go into both Theodore and Marilyn.

Barry and W. S. Dunn swung into the conference room that had been appropriated by Security Associates. Dunn's employees were monitoring active connections all over the company, and a bank of monitors displayed server consoles from around the Simtec campus.

'What's he doing?' Dunn said.

The Security Associates employees made room for the two of them in front of one of the terminals.

'Hard to say. Utilization has gone up a few times. We've got twelve other users on at the same time, though. He may be launching programs and probing around. He hasn't copied anything over yet.'

By manipulating the server console they were able to see a number of things about each user. They could jump back and forth between a window that showed open files and another that gave a running total of the number of bytes read and written by that user. At the moment, the open files window was blank. They stared, waiting for the person to make his next move.

A bar appeared at the top of the window, highlighting a file the user had opened.

'He's looking at the menus,' Dunn said. 'Are you sure this guy's not an admin?'

The window flashed again.

'That's a text file. He's looking around.'

The window stayed blank for some time, so they checked the read/write totals. The user didn't seem to be writing anything to the server. He might be copying, or simply looking. The read totals would go up in either case.

Dunn snapped his fingers and pointed to a workstation. 'Get on that machine and give me a running count on the volume space.'

One of his men jumped to it. Dunn spun around to Barry. 'You've got backups? If we want to, we can smack him off.'

'We make incremental backups every night. We rotate the tapes and do a full backup on Friday. We keep those for a month.' Barry stared at the whirring numbers in the bytes read column.

'We'll let him stay on then. We've got directory listings from last night. He changes a file, we'll know exactly what he did.'

Several other Security Associates employees were standing there watching, transfixed by the possibility of an intrusion against Theodore.

Dunn waved a hand and set them in motion. 'You should already be checking on Marilyn,' he said. 'Get to it.'

He stepped closer to the monitor. 'Look at that. The bastard's not going to give us any clues.' Dunn indicated a section of the screen that said Ethernet Address: Unavailable.

'No good,' the man at the workstation interrupted. 'He's deleting. I've got three megabytes less than I did ten seconds ago.' His fingers flew over the keyboard as he took another reading.

'Nope. Still going down.'

'I don't like this,' Dunn said. 'I'd like to leave him on and watch, but I just don't like it.'

Barry's jaw came unclamped. 'Get him off,' he said quietly.

Dunn leaned over, tagged the user to receive a message, and wrote: *Friend or Foe? We see you. POW!* He hit send.

'That'll shake him up. He pokes his head out and here we are, waiting for him.'

There was a flurry of activity and the server utilization percentage shot up. It then went off a cliff and dropped to 2 percent. Dunn returned to the active connections screen and the user dropped off the screen, back into the black hole from which he had come.

'Got you,' Dunn said. He pointed a finger at the screen. Barry couldn't help noticing how much Dunn seemed to have enjoyed this cat-and-mouse game.

Dunn turned back toward his employees. 'Good work, ladies and gentlemen. If he logs back in, I want a sniffer here set up, ready to tell me where those packets are coming from. Now please assess the damages and we'll see what he's been up to. On the off chance he's an admin, he'll be over here screaming at us, but I doubt that.'

Barry doubted it too.

Dunn began an impromptu meeting in his war room. Barry listened to them sketch out a strategy and then walked slowly back to his own building. He stopped outside on the walkway and leaned on the railing. Below he could look out on some trees and a park area where Simtec had built an employee jogging trail. No one was jogging.

He turned to the other side and gazed across the fleet of cars in the parking lot. How had he ever come to be here, privy to what had to be the most devastating incident in Simtec's short history? What seemed like decades ago, he'd come over from EDS, young, brilliant. A problem solver, they called him. And he had proven himself, twelve hours a day ever since. The responsibility and the power came with the territory, and at $270,000, he wasn't being paid peanuts.

Still, there had always been moments where he wondered what it would be like to have his own company. First he hadn't had the capital; then had come Caroline, and there was neither time, nor energy, nor the willingness to take the risk. The company wouldn't have to be huge. Let Bill Gates have his fortune. Just a company that he owned and could run exactly the way he wanted. Like he'd tried to do with TechDirect.

What could the employees possibly think was going on? They'd sent out the memo about unauthorized log-ins. Now management was talking about a virus. He'd like to call the employees together the way Will Dunn could and say, Get to work! Save the company! Diane Hughes would have done well to stay home, bring them all over in groups to the auditorium and give them a state-of-the-company address. Tell them a large dose of the truth. If employees were involved in this, let them root each other out. He'd suggest this to Diane. Hell, he'd even volunteer to hold the sessions.

Look at the two of them, Diane and Jim. They were able to shrug this off and head out to polish up their deals. They maintained appearances, and they got to come riding back into town with their agreements, which would add a few million to the bottom line. Meanwhile, Barry stayed behind and kept house. Good old reliable Barry.

He took his foot off the lower rail and turned for the door just as one of the TechDirect secretaries burst outside. 'Mr. Shepard,' she said. 'It's Mr. Jacobs. There's apparently quite a scene over there. I think you better go.'

A large group of support specialists and office workers were clustered around the hallway leading to the office of the director of security and internal affairs. A few were peering tentatively around the corner. Barry looked, too, and saw two of the Simtec security officers lined up on either side of Jacobs' door. *Jesus Christ.* The guy had always been hot-blooded. What had he gone and done now?

Barry spotted Mike Haynes. Mike was one of Jacobs' assistants, and he had an adjacent office.

'Mike,' he called out.

Mike hurried over, and the others, seeing Barry, gave them some room.

'What's going on?' Barry said.

'I don't know. One minute I'm talking on the phone and the next, *blam!*, a gunshot goes off in the next room. I didn't know it was a gunshot at the time. I ran out to investigate and Paula's yelling, "He's got a gun." Everybody starts running out and I go with them.'

'Who had a gun? Chris?'

Mike shrugged. 'You talk to everyone out here and no one except Paula really saw anything. She says she was walking over to the printer and she heard Chris laughing. She looked in right as Chris Jacobs fired a gun into the ceiling.'

'What kind of gun, a pistol?'

'I think so. Yeah, a pistol.'

'What has security done, have they spoken to him?'

'I don't know. You can't really tell from here. They don't even have guns themselves, Mr. Shepard. Personally, I think they should get the heck out of there.'

'All right, Mike. Thanks.' He started to walk up the hallway and the guards turned to look at him. At that moment a loud crash came from inside the office. It sounded as if someone had smashed out a window. A few of the women screamed and several employees took off running in the opposite direction.

Barry stood perfectly still, and when no further sound came from inside, he approached the first guard. He recognized the man and said hello.

The guard nodded. 'Mr. Shepard,' he said, sounding shaky.

'What's the status?'

'He's in there, and we're out here. They told us he has a gun, so we're waiting.'

There was more commotion behind them, and Barry said, 'I want you to go back up there and close off the foyer. Take those people outside the building.'

The guard nodded, apparently happy to have a reason to get the hell out of there. Chris Jacobs would not be an easy man to subdue, with or without a gun.

Barry motioned for the other guard to stay put, then he

poked his head around the corner. He tried to look past the front room, with its assortment of plants and file cabinets, and thought he caught some movement in the office beyond.

'Chris?' he called out. 'It's Barry. I brought a report down for you. I think you'll find it pretty funny. All right if I come in?'

He heard what sounded like a grunt, so he took a slow breath and edged around the corner. A small alcove stood to his left, occupied by a laser printer and a fax machine. Barry took several steps forward, keeping the alcove close by.

'Chris? Where are you?'

'Where the hell do you think?'

Barry moved closer to the doorway.

Chris was sitting at his desk. His shirt and tie were disheveled, and the shards of a broken lamp were scattered across the floor against one wall. Barry ignored all that. 'Oh,' Barry said. 'There you are. I've got to tell you what just happened.'

'Yeah? What?' Chris's speech was thick, as though he'd either just woken up or he'd shut the bar down. Barry got the feeling the bar was somewhere nearby in the office, and Barry figured he knew why. The gun was another matter.

'Dunn can't keep them out,' Barry said. He gave his head a big, exaggerated shake. 'You ought to see his team up there. Thirty, forty people running around like chickens. They don't know what the hell is going on. The guy was just on Marilyn and Theodore, and they didn't even have a clue.'

'I can't keep them out. Dunn can't. What we need is an atomic bomb.'

'That'd do it,' Barry said.

'Fucking atom bomb.'

'Like I told Diane this morning, if the Security Associates army can't do it, there's no way we could have.'

Chris grunted. 'You know I bought a Ford Taurus four months ago? Backed the damn thing into a telephone pole this morning.'

'I didn't know that. That you had a Taurus.'

'Not a telephone pole. It was one of those short posts filled with concrete. They got a whole row of them protecting a trash dumpster and I go right over one. I'm sitting there with it up under the car. It nearly ripped off the back bumper.'

'Sorry to hear that. That sounds like an ugly mess.'

'Who needs to protect a dumpster, anyway? You run into it and who really cares?'

'Doesn't make sense to me,' Barry said.

Chris had a faraway look in his eyes. 'I wrapped a Mustang around a tree once. I was a kid. Lucky, too. I walked away without a scratch. You can't blame anyone for trees. They're there and you've got to drive off the road to hit one.'

'Isn't that the truth,' Barry said. 'I got run off Interstate 10 once by a drunk driver in a pickup. This was on the way to San Antonio. I went right down the embankment and crashed through a barbed-wire fence. No trees, though.'

'What happened?' Chris took a drink of whatever was in his Styrofoam cup.

'Nothing. The guy in the pickup kept going. A truck driver stopped and used his radio to call in a report. He stayed for a while and kept me company. About an hour later, a state trooper showed up.'

Chris was nodding.

'So what's this I hear about John Wayne?' Barry said. 'Someone told me you took a potshot in here.'

Chris brought up the hand that was below the desk. He was holding a very potent-looking revolver. He stared down at it, and Barry felt a prickling sensation run along his back.

'Maybe I did,' Chris said. 'I was planning something else. I ruined us, Barry. I really messed up the company. I've been sitting around here on my ass for years and there were a lot of things I could have installed. Things I even knew about – intruder detection, new encryption standards, security IDs for dial-in. We never had a problem and I'm just like everyone else who sits on their fat butt and says, It'll never happen to me.'

'You and all the rest of us.'

'But it was my *job*,' Chris said. '*Was* my job. There's not any place for me here now.'

'That's a load of crap.'

'Not a stone around here big enough for me to hide under. I was getting ready . . . you know, I was having some crazy ideas. I don't know. Stupid. But then I said, Screw the company. Screw Simtec. I'm out of here and none of it matters. Doesn't matter at all. I guess I shot a hole in the ceiling.' Chris chuckled at this.

Barry glanced up and saw where one of the acoustical tiles had been hit. Little bits of the white material were scattered across the carpet.

'The ceiling will be okay,' Barry said. 'What we ought to do now, I'll put the gun in my pocket and we'll walk out of here. We're going to go out the back. I'm going to have one of the guards drive you home. It's Friday. You go home and forget about it. Don't even think about it all weekend. Next week we're going to see where we stand.'

Chris was smiling. 'You're a good guy, Barry,' he said. 'But I won't be back. For me, it's over. You can tell Diane that.'

'Dunn is up there fucking things up left and right. That's what I'm going to tell her.'

'Whatever.'

Chris pushed the gun across the top of the desk. Barry picked it up and it was heavy. He wondered where it had come from. Had Chris always had it in his office? The two of them stood and walked out to the hallway.

'Everything all right?' the security guard said.

'We're going to need a car to pull up in back. Tell them to drive around on the grass.'

'Yes, sir,' the guard said.

'Come on,' Barry said, and pointed Chris toward the rear of the building. He could feel the eyes on them from beyond the front atrium. The gun felt like a five-pound weight in his pocket.

12

Barry went straight back up to his office, told Gwen no interruptions for ten minutes, and closed the door. He transferred Chris's gun to his bottom desk drawer and turned on the laptop. As soon as the machine was up, he popped in the disk he'd found in his backyard. What was the worst that could happen? Some kind of destructive program could trash his hard drive. The Dunn team could reformat and build him a new one in thirty minutes.

But then Barry realized, Oh God, he was also on the wireless network that Security Associates had set up. The goddamn floppy could start seeding a virus right through the air. He punched the disk out again and spent several minutes hunting for a way to drop out of the net. He found a networking icon and clicked stop, which brought up a message asking if he wanted to disconnect from network services.

Yes, he thought. Good riddance. He punched the floppy back in. The directory for drive A showed only a single file. It was a video file. Barry knew that from the file extension MOV. But he didn't have any way to play it. Shit. He punched out the disk and put it back in his pocket. Thinking who around TechDirect might be able to play it, his glance fell upon the desk.

ALARM.

Barry grabbed the phone book off the shelf and stopped at the first alarm company he saw that had a familiar name. He'd seen their sign stuck in one of the neighbor's front yards.

The woman who answered told him the first available installation was next week. Barry asked to speak to the manager, offered a two-hundred-dollar bonus for a same-day install, and he got an appointment for two hours later.

'Just wire the house,' Barry said. 'I'm not going to be there to meet you. A security guard at the front gate can let the crew in. Put a motion detector downstairs. Also do the windows and doors.'

'Most people don't do that,' the manager said. 'If you get the windows done, you can skip the motion. Or vice versa.'

'And I'm not most people. We had an attempted break-in last night and I want every window wired. I want to be twice as safe.'

'As you say. Let me fax over this form—'

'You've got the name and address. Let me give you a Visa number and let's get going.'

The manager let out a sigh. 'What do you want your initial code to be? Four digits. You can reprogram it to something else later tonight.'

'Two five two six.' The same as Barry's ATM PIN code.

'And your security word? When the alarm is triggered we call to verify in case it was you.'

'Bart,' Barry said. 'As in Bart Simpson.'

'Kids, huh?' the man said.

'Right.' Barry said, thinking it would be a cold day in hell before Caroline was allowed to watch that bunch of degenerates. He clicked off and stared out the window. The alarm was good. Right now he needed all the help he could get.

Gwen made her distinctive three-knock and poked her head in the door. 'Your wife called while you were on the phone. No emergency, but when you get a chance.'

'I'll buzz her back.'

Gwen started to close the door, but then she said, 'Mr. Jacobs going to be okay?'

'Fine,' Barry said. 'Just fine.' He caught Gwen's expression. 'Why? What did you hear?'

'I heard Mr. Jacobs had a gun. He shot it off. I heard you went in there and took it away from him.'

She was regarding him with admiration, but clearly for all the wrong reasons. Barry could see the imagination working: Sly Stallone wrestling the weapon away from a maniac and saving the innocents.

'That's a lot of bull,' Barry said. 'He had a gun and he handed it to me. He's gone home now. End of story. No harm done.'

'Lord, I'm glad about that. Could have been, though.' Gwen eased backwards.

'Wait a minute. Take this laptop. See if you can hunt down Bill Dunn Jr. Tell him I want a QuickTime video player on here. He'll know what I mean.'

He handed her the computer and eyed the mountain of interoffice mail that had mushroomed out of his in-box. This needed attention. But then he realized the call from Claudia was rather odd. She was supposed to be in court today. He picked up the phone and dialed her direct extension.

'Milford and Marks.' The receptionist.

'I was calling to see if Claudia Shepard was in the office. She apparently called a few moments ago. This is Barry, her husband.'

'Let's see . . . No, I show her as being in court all day. Did you try her extension? She must have forwarded it up here.'

Barry left a message and hung up. Apparently Claudia had called from the courthouse. No way he'd be able to get hold of her there. He turned back to his desk and the phone rang.

'This is Barry.'

'This is Claudia,' she said, making fun of him.

'I just called you.'

'I know. They didn't know I was here. Things got very emotional and we had a recess for the rest of the day. Actually, I think the judge wanted an excuse to get out of there. He looked like hell, sneezing and blowing his nose the whole time. He apologized later and said he had hay fever. The reason I called is I got some information for you on Security Associates.'

'Jim Seidler called them a SWAT team this morning, and he's absolutely right. They're unbelievable, like a bunch of commandos with computers and radios. All they need is the rifles.'

'Funny you should say that, about the rifles. They did do some work for one of our clients, Holman Distributing. Holman has an office in Houston, but this was at the corporate headquarters in Dallas. Here's the thing – apparently

Dunn shot and killed somebody out in the parking lot one day.'

'Tell me you're kidding.'

'Not at all. We got called in to do some protective work, in case it came back on Holman, but it didn't. Apparently it was an appropriate action under the circumstances, and the grand jury saw no reason to indict. Still, Holman started posturing. They called Dunn a zealot and got rid of Security Associates soon after.'

Barry tried to reconcile this new information with the impression that he had already formed. 'Which Dunn was it?' he asked.

'What do you mean?'

'There's an older Dunn, the one who started the company, and there's Bill Junior, his son, who is presently rampaging through my building.'

'I don't know. I assumed it was the one you told me about. I didn't know there were two.'

'From what I've seen, it could be either one,' Barry said. 'You're absolutely sure about this?'

'Yes. I did a search through our document database for Security Associates and that's how I came up with some of the papers. Then I talked to the partner who handled the work. I said Simtec was in the process of hiring Security Associates, and I was looking for useful information.'

Barry groaned.

'I had to tell him something. I played it down and asked if he could give me any background. I wasn't going to lie.'

'Did he say how the shooting happened?'

'There was no witness, so it's not as clear as it could be. You've basically got to rely on Dunn's version. The person was an employee who had been doing some kind of tampering with the network. Dunn confronted her in the parking lot.'

'Her?'

'Yes, a woman. She was a systems analyst who had been with the company for seven years. She had a weapon, too, and apparently she would have shot him.'

Barry leaned forward and put his elbows on the desk.

He tried to imagine one of their own analysts, for example the attractive woman down on the second floor, Carol Petit, being killed by William Dunn out in the Building 4 parking lot. It was incomprehensible. 'I wonder if Diane knew this?'

'It's probably not at the top of his résumé, but you said she discussed him with a number of people. Chances are it's a known fact.'

Barry flashed to Chris Jacobs, drunk at ten in the morning. No doubt lining up to take a shot at his own head but changing his mind and putting one up in the ceiling. 'Not that it means we shouldn't hire him. It's a crazy environment over here. You wouldn't believe the stuff that's going on. I can see where something like that could happen. It doesn't mean the man is no good.'

'Quite the contrary, the partner met with him several times and was quite impressed. He also checked with some previous clients and they had only good things to say. Dunn may be a zealot, but he has a good reputation. I just thought this was some dirt you ought to know.'

'I appreciate the scoop.'

'Will we see you for dinner?'

'I don't know. I'll call.'

'Sounds good,' she said, even though it probably wasn't what she'd wanted to hear. This was one of the reasons Barry loved his wife. They gave each other a lot of rope and didn't complain about it. With the legal battles and late-night strategy sessions that had been waged over the years, the shoe had also been worn on the other foot.

'That's all the news,' Claudia said. 'I've got a glass repair place coming out in the afternoon. The guard has a key and will take them back.'

'Good. I went ahead and ordered the alarm. The code is two five two six, and it may be armed when you get home. We'll need to change the code to something else.'

Barry hung up the phone. He had spent a lifetime dealing with people at face value, but, as he was learning, *This wasn't about trust.* He got up and nudged the door closed, then dialed a long-distance number out of his address book.

'Shepard,' said the voice on the other end. The voice had the same timbre as Barry's, but was much lower.

'Hi, Stan.' Stan was Barry's older brother by four years. As kids the two had warred and pummeled one another. Now Stan was an economist, working for a brokerage house as a market specialist. He was divorced, had no children, and for reasons Barry didn't quite understand, Caroline adored her uncle.

'Barry? I was just thinking about you yesterday. I'm finally going to get Celtics tickets. You'll have to come up for a game this fall. Pick whoever you want to see. It's not quite the Garden, but the games are still great.'

'That sounds good,' Barry said.

'So what's up? It's not like you to call in the middle of the day.'

'I have a favor to ask. Have you been watching our share price lately?'

'I recall you took a hit the other day, right? I can't say I've been watching closely. I'm strictly oil and gas.'

'It doesn't matter. I was just going to ask for an impression. Obviously we're not the talk of the shop.'

'Not the oil and gas shop. I can't speak for the other guys.'

'Like I said, it's not that important. What I'm really after is some information. I thought it might be the kind of thing you can get your hands on.'

'What's that?'

'I want to know who's been trading our stock. Let's say, over the last three months. Short sales and options, especially puts.'

Stan paused while he thought that over. 'First of all,' he said, 'you're talking about data that I don't have access to. And second, you're talking about tens of thousands of people.'

'Not every trade. Ignore anything but the big blocks. That ought to trim it down. Is there a way you might be able to . . . I don't know, call in a favor? Get someone to run a list?'

'Officers and directors? Are we talking insider trading here? You can get good reports on that.'

'Sure, that's part of it. But I'm not interested only in the insiders. Private individuals, mutual funds, whoever has been betting on a drop. This is nothing official, but I figured you could get at the information much easier than I could.'

'What's it all about?' Barry could hear his brother's interest picking up on the other end. 'You think somebody's trying to run it down?'

'I doubt it.' Barry said. He tried his best to sound indifferent. 'I'm just curious to know who's profiting from it, that's all.'

'And there's likely to be a further drop?'

'No, not at all. We could easily be up three points today. Don't go doing anything foolish.'

'Damn,' Stan said.

'So you'll try to get me a list?'

'I'll do what I can do.'

'Thanks. I appreciate it. How's . . . Brenda, is it?'

'History. I sent her packing. Actually, she had never moved in. It only seemed like it. She was into made-for-TV movies, the stupidest shit you've ever seen in your life. Then I try to watch basketball, she goes out to the couch and sleeps with a pillow over her head.'

This was the way it had been with Stan for years. Every so often he met a new woman who was the latest and greatest, and after a few months it was over.

'Too bad,' Barry said.

'Just in time, I say. Think of all those good seats I would have wasted on her. You've really got to come up for a game.'

'I'll do that. I better run, Stan. I've got a couple of fires to put out here. Thanks for your help.'

Barry pushed the hang-up button with his finger but kept the receiver to his ear. That was that piece of it. Dunn could do his part, and Barry would perform his own analysis of the stock information. They could compare notes and see if anything leapt up off the page.

He was still holding the button down, thinking about some other calls he needed to make, and he started to flip through the pile that served as his in-box. Lots of internal memos, a number of documents requiring his signature or action of some kind. He recognized the yellow flyer that reminded TechDirect employees of the monthly TSR meeting. He pulled it out and checked the time. It would be a great opportunity to bring up Dunn's question about any customer having made threats against the network.

He set the phone down and began plowing through the rest. He worked as quickly and efficiently as possible. Financial documents, budget requests that he might have deliberated over and called into question – he simply signed and moved on. The memos were scanned and went in the trash.

He'd gotten halfway through when someone knocked at the door, and Barry said, 'Come in.'

Bill Dunn Jr. poked his head in. 'Excuse me,' he said. 'W. S. radioed. He said if you were around to let you know. Marilyn and Theodore. He's found what they were after this morning.'

Barry pushed his chair back. This was a very subdued Bill Jr. and Barry immediately had a bad feeling. He had reviewed the resource list for Marilyn and Theodore. At stake was the main human resources database and some important development work. They probably shouldn't have left the intruder on there as long as they had.

'Where is he?'

'Next building, in the server room.'

Network file servers belong in an art gallery. As much time and energy goes into their creation as a painting, their status is more fragile, and they are easily as misunderstood.

A file server functions as the brain of the network and the network repository, many times holding not only commonly used applications but all user files as well. One file server can launch Lotus 1-2-3 for Janet in the next room, or one hundred people spread over ten buildings. All this while queuing print jobs, providing on-line access to CD-ROM, routing traffic on the network, handling faxes, and allowing dial-in links so that Joann and Steve can work at home. There is no end to the complexity. The only limit is processing speed and the network manager's imagination.

At Simtec, a full tape backup of each file server was performed each Friday. Incrementals – backups of only the files that had changed – were made on Monday, Tuesday, Wednesday, and Thursday. Barry walked into the server room, and he could see two Simtec system administrators bent over a machine that must have just been brought in. Dunn and one of his employees hovered nearby.

'Smart,' Dunn said. 'Bastard is smart.' He saw Barry and motioned for him to step out into the hall.

'Here's the deal,' Dunn said. He was very matter-of-fact, but underneath was a tone of thinly concealed anger. 'Today while he was on-line, and perhaps at other points over a period of days, our friend was doing quite a bit of deletion. Applications, data, system files. Theodore is in pretty bad shape. We're checking Marilyn, and we're going to check the others. There may have been damage to them, as well.'

'So while we were sitting there watching, he was deleting Theodore?'

'Perhaps,' Dunn said, making no apologies. 'Some may have been done earlier. Some may have been done with batch files. We don't know yet. He wasn't on there long enough to do it all this morning. You'd have to go through and change file attributes all over the place. I imagine that was done some other time.'

Someone in the server room uttered a loud 'Shit!'

Dunn pinched his lips together. 'We looked at the backup from yesterday to see what files had been modified. The tape is blank. What we're doing now is going back through them to see how far back it goes.'

'What do you mean the tape is blank? How far back *what* goes?'

'The tape backup software runs on the server, as I'm sure you know. There's a script that does an appropriate backup, depending on the day of the week. It also checks to see that on Wednesday, you're using Wednesday's tape. Basically, the whole thing runs on autopilot except for the person who sticks in the tape and pulls it out again.'

'And it wasn't done?' Barry swallowed.

'The script was modified. It acted like it was doing a backup, but it was formatting the tape instead. The tape operator comes in the next morning, I guess they just pulled it out and stuck it on the shelf. I'd have to see how the program works, but there was probably nothing on screen to indicate error, or failure. It did what it thought it was supposed to do.'

'Goddamnit! The backup program keeps a log file. It tells you everything that was done.' Barry reached a hand up and rubbed furiously at the back of his neck.

'Only if you look at it,' Dunn said. He added quietly, 'It was an easy mistake to make.'

Barry felt the anger welling up inside him. Surprisingly, it was directed toward Chris Jacobs. Maybe if he hadn't just heard Jacobs admit he'd been lax, hadn't been doing his job as thoroughly as he should have, somebody else would have borne the brunt of the responsibility. Someone had to be accountable and, ultimately, it was Jacobs' people who had screwed up.

The Security Associates man poked his head out and said, 'We've got files on tape last Thursday.'

'That was my guess,' Dunn said. 'He changed the script last Friday, when the last full backup was supposed to have been made. With his deleting today, you lose a week's worth of tape. Your last full backup was two weeks ago.'

'All right. What can we do?' Barry said.

'The word has already gone out to check all tape scripts. I'm going to leave John in here with your people. They'll restore whatever possible, and we'll get the server back up and running in the best shape we can.'

Dunn pulled the radio off his belt. 'Center City,' he said. He let his thumb off the button and told Barry, 'That's our name for the control room.'

'Center,' replied a female voice.

'Nobody with administrative privilege is allowed to log in anywhere. They log in, you ping them off immediately.'

'Got it.'

Dunn replaced the radio on his belt and said, 'They won't get us again that way.'

With their radios and their control rooms, Barry found it hard not to be impressed with the capabilities of Security Associates. This was a performance Simtec could never have matched internally. But Barry was also starting to see it for what it was. Security Associates was an expensive remedy, and, once swallowed, there was still no guarantee of protection.

'They may not get us that way,' Barry said. 'But they could some other way.'

'There's a period of vulnerability. I won't deny it. But we are shutting them out minute by minute.'

'Would you have caught this?'

Dunn hesitated. 'There's a good chance of it. We check files that were recently modified. Eventually we would have looked at it, yes.'

Barry was silent and Dunn stared at him hard. 'Listen. If you decide you don't want us here – at any time we're gone.'

'That's not what I'm saying. I just have to be sure where we stand. When we're discussing a problem, I don't want hopeful. I want realistic.'

'I agree one hundred percent.'

'Good,' Barry said. He turned and walked back toward TechDirect.

Halfway across the city, James Dupree was flying across the ice. He had gone to Houston's Galleria shopping complex to ice-skate, because, when he was either particularly happy or particularly upset, that's what Dupree did. In a sense, it was a treat, and this was one of the few places you could do it in the entire city.

The thing he didn't like about the Galleria was how public it all was. Today the different levels were festooned in green and red, as if the decorators wished to invoke the spirit of Christmas. The spirit of Christmas buying, Dupree thought wryly. Pack them in and let them spend. The architecture of the building was such that each level had been left open over the oval skating rink, and spectators hung over each balcony, floor after floor, all the way up. He doubted they were watching him. They were probably much more interested in that young woman who went zipping by in her blue sequined skating costume, all legs and graceful arms, dark hair pulled back out of her face. But still, they were there, and Dupree would have much preferred an old hockey rink like the one where he grew up. He used to walk there all by himself, happy to get out of the house, away from his father. He'd strap on his skates in the bleachers and circle the ice for hours. By the time he returned home, his father would usually have left on one important mission or another.

That rink had been a refuge. If he saw five other skaters, the place was having a banner day, and ever since, Dupree had valued his anonymity. So it was enormously frustrating when Mark Willis reported in with two new facts: the Simtec network was being reconfigured. He couldn't even find parts of it, which had apparently been taken out of service or otherwise diverted. Secondly, during the morning session, he had been caught on-line. The bastards had either been sitting there waiting or they'd spotted Mark through blind luck. Likewise, Wilson's attempt to put the scare on Barry Shepard had resulted in a fiasco. He hadn't even gotten inside the house. Shepard had, at best, been made to feel vulnerable, but the effect was missing. Wilson had botched it.

Dupree could sense his window of opportunity closing. He'd learned that Simtec had gone out and hired Security Associates, and concrete proof of the act had even appeared in a morning Dow Jones news bulletin. Security Associates, with that sonofabitch W. S. Dunn, was the same firm that had tripped them up in Denver. Bringing in W. S. Dunn and his sharpshooters was a desperate move, and no doubt very expensive. In effect, Simtec had opted to pay this other firm rather than pay him.

Other companies had made the choice – the proper choice – easily. Dupree had cashed their checks and moved on. They were all such novices, and Dupree gloated by sending the president of each company a list of security flaws. But he also kept his word, enumerating whatever damage might have ensued.

This time, and in spite of his excellent information – he'd just received a new batch of passwords – it appeared that Simtec needed more convincing. Dupree had reserved weapons for precisely this contingency. Weapons that went beyond what anyone – including his own contact – would ever have expected. It was the moment to roll open the bay doors. He'd be calling Barry Shepard again shortly, and with Security Associates setting up shop, time was running short.

Bumbling Simtec administrators and their hired-gun specialists would be out there, scouring the network. They'd pull people's connections like they were in a vegetable patch pulling weeds. Use of the network connection would now have to become precise and economical. Dupree spun sharply and started skating backwards. To be truly omnipotent, he would have to be able to log on and have the connection be completely invisible. That was the only way he could do his business undetected, and it was also impossible.

Dupree skated in long, smooth strides, and he thought about the little data packets speeding out across the network cabling. Just like an envelope with its address, a packet is put out on the net and sent along its way. In the beginning, Dupree had spent weeks reading about them. You would always be able to monitor packets – there was no communication without them – and therefore there was always the chance of being seen. So you planned ahead, many moves ahead, then you got on and got off the network as quickly as possible. Mark Willis had been particularly good at it.

A young boy came flailing toward the side wall, wobbling more than skating, his arms shooting ahead toward the rail in desperation. He collapsed directly in Dupree's path. Dupree skidded smartly to a stop and leaned over.

'Are you all right?' he asked, and the boy nodded sheepishly.

Dupree put out a hand and helped the boy to his feet.

'Not as easy as it looks.' Dupree said. 'You're stepping too much. It's not like walking. You've got to learn to glide over each foot.'

'Oh,' the boy said.

He allowed Dupree to steady his arm and then tried again, digging in with one skate and soon flailing again as before.

Dupree watched for a moment and then off he shot, smooth and steady over the ice.

13

William Dunn was a tall man and, when he wore it, the cowboy hat added a good four inches. He wore a hat and drove a pickup because that's the way he felt: he wasn't a suit. Never had been and never would be. Life had treated him just fine on his own terms.

The only thing that hadn't treated him well was marriage, and that's because he married the first woman he slept with, for all the wrong reasons. He was too young to know any better, and it took years for either of them to admit the mistake. One positive aspect of his marriage to Darlene, he later figured out, was the knowledge that she hadn't chosen him for his money.

Now Dunn was much wiser, and, at forty-two years old, still attractive to the majority of the female population. Women threw themselves at him in a variety of conspicuous ways. When his truck was parked in the driveway of his suburban Atlanta home, there was one neighbor – a moderately attractive divorcée – who regularly manufactured reasons to come by. Hi, Will, have you seen my cat? Will, can you help me with this Weed Eater?

He found some of these excuses humorous, but they also made him feel good. It was nice to get the attention, and there was usually enough of it that he rarely had to do much pursuing on his own.

Karen Williams was another story all together. You didn't get to be chief counsel of a major corporation based on your looks. In fact, some of the men probably resented it. He was sure most of the women did. You got to be chief counsel of Simtec because you had played the game and won, and that, in a nutshell, was what made Karen Williams so interesting.

The door to her office was open, so he walked right on in.

'Knock, knock,' he said.

She glanced up from something she was reading and said, 'More of the computer police.' Not unkindly, but the tone was hard for Dunn to read. Will Dunn was not a man easily surprised, but he glanced to his right and got quite a jolt. His son was already sitting there, looking up at him with a smirk.

Dunn's first thought was: What the hell was his son doing in there? Nonsense. He knew exactly what Bill Jr. was doing, and it was not the first time. Dunn started thinking fast. A Klaxon was going off in his head screaming Abort, Abort. He had clearly been ouflanked.

He pointed as casually as he could manage toward the stack of papers on her desk and said, 'For a case of technical vandalism, who would guess it would make so much work for legal?'

'There's always work for legal,' Karen said. 'I have to sign off on every contract that goes out of here. That's not going to stop unless they pull the plug on the lights.'

'If they can manage that, they probably will. Have you gotten one of our portables?'

Karen indicated the notebook that was perched in a side chair. 'That's what Bill was just going over with me. He was showing me how to retrieve and print documents. Like I told him, if you really want to help me out, give me a machine that knows how to read and sign. That's what I do most of the time, read and sign.'

Their eyes met and Dunn, feeling awkward, looked away. He was acutely aware of his son, sitting there like a spectator, and he found a row of diplomas on the side wall to examine.

'What were you after?' Bill said, making no effort to help out his dad. 'Were you coming to find me?'

'No.' Dunn shook off the question and forged doggedly ahead. 'I was coming to see the chief counsel.'

Karen let him stew for a few seconds and then bailed him out. 'So that's what you're calling it? Vandalism? I've always defined vandalism as much more . . . trivial.'

'An act is only trivial when it happens to somebody else. When someone spray-paints the side of your building, it's not trivial to you. Some of the things that have happened here are about the same. Some are worse.'

Karen raised a questioning eyebrow, so he went on: 'It's malicious destruction, sure enough. The difference to me is that this isn't random or spontaneous. This person has the whole thing mapped out. This is no crude spray paint. If we catch up to him, you're going to find someone with a clever mind.'

Dunn realized he was running on and clamped his mouth shut.

Karen sat up straight in her chair. '*Him*?' she said.

'Probably. I'm just going with the odds. You don't meet as many female computer professionals.'

'*If* we catch up?'

This was just like a lawyer, pick apart every goddamned word. 'I told Diane from the start that I'm not making any guarantee. Sometimes we've been able to parlay our information into an actual arrest. Other times the attacker fades off into the wiring and he never comes back.'

'Do you think it's only one person? I notice you use the singular.'

Oh, boy. 'Listen, I'd love to catch him, her, them . . . whatever. The most important thing, I think we'd all agree, is keeping them out *today*. Then we can go back and look for fingerprints.'

She nodded agreement. 'You don't mean look for fingerprints, literally?'

'No. I don't. But we've got our magnifying glass out. You don't alter programs and change code without leaving a trail of some kind. We're basically looking for the hairs and carpet fibers.'

She straightened the document in front of her and her face came up. Blonde hair pulled back, dazzling green eyes. A high-powered lawyer and a beauty besides. For a moment, Dunn felt out of his league. He didn't turn his head, but imagined his son, probably still over there smirking. He swallowed and made his decision. William Dunn hadn't gotten where he was without a healthy degree of determination.

'What I wanted to suggest—' Dunn paused, still trying to fine-tune the phrasing. 'I'd be happy to go into all this further. And I've got some questions I wanted to ask you, as well. Would you like to have dinner tonight, say around six or seven?'

Dunn waited for the reaction that said he was coming out of left field and waited for the burst of laughter from his son's direction, but Karen took his proposal in stride, as if she had seen it a mile off. Probably had, Dunn figured correctly.

'I'll be coming back here to work,' he blundered ahead. 'I think it's good to get away for a break every now and then. Get out and clear your mind.'

Bill Jr. cleared his throat. 'Is that a good idea, leaving campus while we're in the middle of a crisis?'

'I thought you'd be able to keep up with things for an hour,' Dunn said dryly. He turned a withering stare upon his son, who shifted in his chair.

Karen looked speculatively at the pile on her desk. 'Let's make it six,' she said. 'I'll be coming back here to work, too.'

W. S. nodded and strode out of the room. His eyes didn't so much as dart in the direction of the younger Dunn. They were forty-two and twenty-four, so Karen Williams was somewhere in between their two ages. And the woman had agreed to dine with the man of maturity. If he wasn't walking through a busy hall at Simtec Computer Corp., he might have kicked up his heels.

Barry motioned his senior analyst, Greg Mitchell, into one of the break rooms. The room was small, with white Formica-topped counters and one round table that seated four. Barry closed the door behind them, set the phone on the counter, and went over to pour a mug of coffee.

'You want some?' He hefted the half-empty coffeepot.

'Sure,' Greg said.

Barry poured, and the two of them went over to the table and sat. He might walk through Simtec casting a suspicious eye, but Barry also needed allies, and Greg Mitchell was one of them.

'How's the rebuild going on the hard drives?'

'It's not going so well. I've heard about five different stories, which may reflect varying states of when, or if, the person cut the machine off. A few drives have apparently been resurrected. But I also overheard support talking about salvaging raw data, which is the absolute worst case. We could spend weeks doing it, and there aren't enough people to go around. We started trying to help out internally, but support wanted it done their way. Now you've got Security Associates people running all over the place, so we got the hell out of the way.'

Barry rested elbows on his knees, hands encircling the coffee mug. 'I thought we were secure,' he said, shaking his head. 'We'd done all the right things, we had our backups. Now it turns out we were pissing into the wind. Over in the next building, some of the servers – Theodore, for one; we don't know how many more – have been making bad backups. The script that runs the backup was changed so that it does a tape format. All the guys at night do is yank the tape out and stick it on the shelf, so they never checked.'

Greg took that in and asked suspiciously, 'Why do you need the backup?'

'Someone erased the server. Chunks of it, anyway. I sat there and watched them log in. We had the server console up, and we saw the connection.'

'But then we ought to be able to nail them. If you saw the connection, you can get an address.'

Greg was referring to the unique address that was hard-coded into every single Ethernet card. 'Address unavailable,' Barry said. 'So they either come in from the outside, or somehow the address is blocked. That's one thing I wanted to ask you. Could you engineer an Ethernet card that way? So that it wouldn't give out its address?'

Greg didn't answer. He glowered and sipped coffee.

'Yeah, sure it's possible,' he finally announced. 'You'd be sending out packets with no source address. Nothing on the network would know how to talk back to you.'

'You can see the nature of our problem. Some maniac's out there on the network with high-level access. Until we stop it and discover every trap he may have left waiting for us, we're fucked.'

'Boy howdy,' Greg said.

'One other possibility that Diane mentioned, or Chris Jacobs mentioned to her, is that there could be a back door built into a server or database app, something only the original programmers would know about. What do you think of that?'

'My first inclination is to say no, but after witnessing what's happening here, I'd have to say anything's possible.'

'Then we've still got several avenues to pursue. You could log in as John Doe with some bullshit code word that opens the vault.'

'It's not impossible,' Greg said, looking more and more unhappy.

'In the meantime, we simply can't trust the servers. You should have been issued one of the portables this morning?'

'Yes, but there aren't enough for everybody.'

'I know that. Here's my thinking: First, we keep everyone off the servers, completely off the network, as much as possible. I gave my priority list to Dunn as far as who should get the portables. Other people can still use their machines as stand-alones. We can move printers and allow key people to print directly.'

Greg nodded.

'I need you to have someone go through all of our backups, tape by tape. Read a file, read a directory tree, make sure we got something on tape. At least that way we could do a selective restore. That's all they're good for – the off chance we want to pull specific files back off the tape. We can't risk a full restore because we have no idea what else may be on that tape. Any file we pull off tape goes into a secure area until we check it.'

The door clicked open and an employee started into the break room. Seeing Greg and Barry sitting there, he said, 'Excuse me,' filled his cup, and left in a hurry.

Barry waited until the door closed again. 'We need to keep in mind that we're dealing with someone who does long-range planning. Theodore was altered a week ago, maybe longer.' He considered the phone he'd been given and added, 'We have every reason to believe that they've been setting this up for weeks.'

Greg had a distracted expression. 'All the spare equipment from that meeting Wednesday, we've been doing complete on-line copies to back up the servers.'

Barry understood the question that was being raised. They had underestimated the attack. They'd started out thinking they needed to protect against data being deleted or changed, but that was no longer the point. They needed to protect against batch files, against ticking bombs that lay in wait. What a wasted effort.

'There's no way of knowing you didn't just copy over bugs that are already on there. Erase them. I'd reformat and start over. We need something we can count on as a sure, untainted server. Begin at square one and reload everything.'

Greg was sipping coffee and listening. That's what Barry appreciated so much about him. Some people, you told them your plans and they nodded and said, Yeah, yeah, yeah. But Greg was always thinking, troubleshooting it as he went.

'You'll lose all the individual setups, home directories, and so forth. We can go with several levels of users. Each level has different access, and we can add users on the fly.'

'Let's do it,' Barry said. The clock over the door showed 12:03. He pushed his chair back.

'What I want to know,' Greg said, 'is what it's all about.'

'It's about a ruthless, greedy sonofabitch.'

'And you have no idea . . .'

Barry ticked through the theories in his head. A disgruntled customer. A *fanatic,* as Dunn had said. A malicious employee. A software guru who knew a back way into the servers. Or some unknown adversary, content to do nothing more than ransom their socks off.

'At the moment, the field is still wide open,' Barry said. 'But I believe that if they keep it up, we'll nail them.'

The portable phone rang, echoing loudly in the small room.

'Greg, you're going to have to excuse me,' Barry said. The phone rang again. He snatched it up and headed out the door.

'Hello,' Barry said, walking quickly back down the hall toward his office.

'Mr. Shepard,' said the voice. 'Guess who? It's Hektor.'

Barry waved Gwen off, slipped through the door of his

office, and closed it behind him. He hit the record button on the machine and slid the phone into it.

'Listen to all that!' Hektor said. 'If I guessed I was on tape would I be right?'

'Yes, you would be right.'

'My, my. Are we actually going to be honest with one another?'

'We could try it. For instance, I believe we knocked you off-line this morning, am I correct?' Barry had been formulating a strategy for this next conversation, and he wanted to begin from a position of strength.

'Not that I know of.' The denial came too quickly, and Barry thought he detected a hint of frustration. 'Remember what I told you about stones in the pocket. I carry a pocketful, and I don't have to be on-line to use them. How are things running over there today?'

'Rocky, in places. Other places no problem.'

'Rocky, is it? Yes, I would imagine so. And worth it to make those rocky places go away, I would imagine, too.'

'Yes, it is.' Here was the gambit. He couldn't simply expect to stall indefinitely.

'Excellent decision.' Triumph in the man's voice.

'I should first of all say that any payment is authorized through the board of directors. This is not coming from me, and I have no personal authority to negotiate with you myself.' That was it, Barry thought. Give him a whiff of the money. 'I believe the board could be convinced to make the proposed payment of one million dollars, in return for certain considerations.'

Hektor cleared his throat. 'I don't think you understand me. The option for paying one million has expired.'

This was exactly as Barry expected. But at least he had put something on the table. If he could only create the illusion of progress . . . perhaps buy some time. 'I understand completely,' he said. 'But you're getting way ahead of us. You ask the board what they want for lunch and you get an answer back a day later. I can go back in and work to convince them to make the higher payment.' *I'm your friend.* 'But you must stop any further actions for the time being. It's counterproductive.'

'No. I don't think so. If there's a logjam, I must join you in freeing it. I, too, must convince the board. Convince in my own way, of course.'

'You're missing the point. The point is not that we don't believe you, or that we doubt your capabilities. The point is that these things take time.'

'Time is precious, Barry Shepard, as you well know. All this waiting makes me uncomfortable. And more expensive by the hour.'

'You shouldn't be uncomfortable. You're in a good negotiating position. You've demonstrated what you can do, and you will actually hurt your case by any further destruction. You risk pushing the board to a position where they say, All right, let's come down on this guy like a ton of bricks.'

'A whole ton, Barry? That's scary stuff. That means – what? – Simtec might pull in a second security firm in addition to the shyster you've already got?'

Damn!

'Let me tell you something – and you can play the tape back a thousand times right in their faces – those security hotshots aren't going to do you any good.'

Barry heard the sound of traffic in the background over the phone. Not loud, but unmistakably a car horn, and then the low rumble of a diesel engine. It sounded like a heavy motor, perhaps a delivery truck gearing up. One week ago, he would have found the notion comical that he would be offering to pay one million dollars to someone who might well be standing outside at a gas station phone booth. Or a car phone, Barry realized. The guy was calling him from a car phone, the same as he'd done outside of Cyrano's.

'I think we need to speak frankly, Mr. Shepard. Why don't you turn off the tape recorder and we'll go off record.'

'All right,' Barry said. The others might yell at him, but it was he who was calling the shots, and he was going to go with it. He reached over and hit the stop button, then removed the phone from its case. 'We are now officially untaped.'

'Good. I think it's important that you have a chance to consider my offer with your undivided attention. You know the extent of the damage caused by security holes I have uncovered so far. I'm sure you have a good idea of the cost of that damage. All of which, I might add, has been caused by your company's inattention to its technological infrastructure. I have a standard fee for pointing out this inattention, and that fee is currently at five million dollars. That fee is nonnegotiable; however, if you pay me today, by a mutually acceptable method that I will describe, then I am willing to give you a discount of one million dollars. That, Mr. Shepard, is quite a bargain. It is also my final offer.'

Barry didn't doubt it. But nothing guaranteed the payment would end the attack. Hektor might or might not stop the wheels that had already been set in motion. The only thing that made Barry waver was the desire to keep this lunatic away from his family. What would the others have done – Diane and Jim? Even after the shipping errors, the seven hundred hard drives, the servers, the backup tapes, he could see Jim shaking his head, no fucking way. And Diane? Barry wasn't sure, but she'd surprised the hell out of him in that first meeting with her 'Don't Pay'.

'I have no authority to negotiate,' Barry said, fighting to keep his voice calm. His heart was pounding. 'We are due to reconvene tomorrow morning, and you can be sure I will present your proposal in the most expeditious manner possible. For the reasons I've already stated, I ask you to give us that much time to consider.'

'There's no pausing to consider.' Hektor was snarling now. He'd seen the carrot, and he'd seen the carrot pulled away. 'Don't think I'm going to write you off, "Oh no, they won't pay for my services. I'll just tuck my tail between my legs and go home." Exactly the opposite, I'm going to make an example out of you. Make no mistake, I'm going to hurt you badly. It's about money, and it's also about respect.'

'You could burn our buildings to the ground and you wouldn't get my respect.' Barry felt short of breath. His voice sounded abnormal, as though it were somebody else speaking.

'I'm afraid I picked the wrong man,' Hektor said and hung up.

Barry swallowed hard. He punched the end button and set the phone down. The weight of the decision pressed firmly onto his shoulders. Whatever happened, they would now be able to turn to him and say, Barry, what were you thinking? We could have paid. We *should* have paid. He could easily have gone to Diane and Jim and made the case.

He dialed the 800 number for Diane's WorldPager and dictated a message that said, Received another call. Will be in office. Barry. Then he reached W. S. Dunn in the Security Associates control room and gave a synopsis: Expect the worst.

Gwen must have been waiting for enough silence to indicate he was done, because she buzzed to tell him Diane had phoned twenty minutes ago, when he was out of the office. 'She said everything was going well on her end, and she hoped the same here.'

'It's not,' Barry said. 'But I just left her a message. I'll stick close until she calls.'

'Your voice mailbox is full,' Gwen said. 'So they either hang up or get bumped back over to me. Your brother called, too. He said it was important and for you to get back to him. I also have the laptop with the program you wanted from Security Associates.'

'Bring in the laptop,' Barry said. A familiar knot had formed in his stomach.

While waiting for the machine to come up, he flipped through his address book to find Stan's number. He left the book open on the desk, made sure networking was still turned off on the computer, and popped in the disk.

The file was called FUNHOUSE. What the hell, it was probably something stupid. He opened the video file and it appeared on screen in a small window.

Not stupid at all. It was clearly a picture of Barry Shepard's own house. He clicked play. The video was shot from the perspective of a car going by on the street. It had been digitized from a handheld camcorder. The sound track was barely audible, until the unmistakable sound of a machine gun kicked in and covered the car engine. The muzzle of the gun appeared, too, jutting in at the bottom of the picture.

Barry watched in shock as the car drove down Willow

Creek Lane, machine gun firing away. A bullet pattern of tiny black dots traced right across the front of his house. And then it was over. An eight-second clip.

Barry played it again.

The machine gun was clearly edited in after the fact, and not very well at that. Bullets smashed the hell out of windows. They didn't make dots. But still, the effect was there.

Barry slammed the top desk drawer closed. The man had been bringing this disk to his house. To do what? Leave the disk on the coffee table? Load the file on Barry's home computer and slip back out the window? Barry considered his reaction if he had walked in and found that file on his computer in the morning. Disbelief. Fear? Certainly. But they could machine-gun his house for real; it wasn't going to get them paid.

The truth of the matter was, Barry was starting to believe Simtec should have paid at the very beginning. But they could still pay and get out before the hammer fell again. They should at least consider the option, shouldn't they?

This was the precise effect of Hektor's *squeeze,* as Dunn had called it. Barry was hesitating, and Hektor, the warrior, had him starting to flip-flop. Barry ejected the floppy disk and he wanted to tear it to pieces.

He had already ordered an alarm. What else should he do? A fence and Dobermans? He scowled and punched in his brother's number.

'Volume on your stock has gone bonkers,' Stan said. 'Our technology people are in a lather. I ran you a nice summary of insider trading, and I've gotten some scoop on the major blocks. I called a few friends and hit them up for whatever they could tell me. It's unofficial and incomplete info, so take it for what it's worth. You've got to realize it's the SEC's job to make an inquiry like that. They're the only ones who could compile a complete and accurate list.'

'I understand,' Barry said.

'Your assistant gave me a fax number, but she said you don't have a machine in your office. I didn't want this lying around on the mailroom floor.'

'No, I suppose not. There's a fax up the hall. How many pages?'

'Eighteen. And like I said, that's just the top movement at a few houses. All I could get through the back door. If you wanted to go through all the trades, you're talking about volumes of data.'

'I appreciate whatever you got, Stan.'

'Everything okay? You sound a little funny.'

'I'm okay,' Barry said quietly. 'Go ahead and send. I'll walk over and pick it up as it comes in.'

He set the laptop out of the way and put the disk back in his pocket, then went out and hovered near the fax machine until it stopped printing. He collected the sheets, closed the door to his office, and began flipping through. The first page was divided into columns, and the character formatting reminded Barry of old mainframe output.

The header at the top of each page told him the date and that the search had been performed on STC, Simtec's ticker symbol on the New York Stock Exchange. In each row he got the purchaser, quantity, price, some sort of market or transaction code, and a security number, which Barry assumed was a computer-generated ID number stamped onto every trade.

SEAN HOBARD	7500	61 1/4	01	B	123300-10-5
JOHN WITT	5000	61 3/8	01	B	670006-10-5
CA TEACHERS	20000	61 1/4	03	S	459304-90-3

He scanned down the list, made up of trades in the four- and five-digit range. On the low end, these trades represented dollar amounts between a quarter and a half million dollars. Every so often a multimillion-dollar block went through, probably a pension or mutual fund.

On the tenth page, he noticed that Jim Pearson had made another 7,500 share trade. A buy. He was sure he remembered that name from one of the earlier pages, so he had to work backwards over the ground he had already covered.

No Pearson. He disgustedly picked up the sheaf of papers

and headed up to the next floor, where TechDirect had recently installed an expensive scanner.

One of the secretaries was processing documents, but when she saw who was waiting to use the machine she quickly made it available.

'Would you like me to do that for you, Mr. Shepard?' she said, retrieving her own document and saving the file off to a disk.

'No, thank you. Although you could show me how to get started.' Not knowing how to use the equipment in his own department was a little unsettling, but it was simply impossible to keep up.

The secretary gave him a disk and showed him how to place the pages and start the scan. It was all very simple. Even working from a less than crisp fax image, this machine was able to pick up the text and place it into perfect columns. He fed in the pages and soon had a remarkably accurate file.

He returned to the office and flipped on the laptop. He opened the file and did a search on the string 'Jim Pearson'. There were numerous matches and Barry totaled the shares: twenty thousand. Not bad. Whoever Jim Pearson was, he was throwing around over a million dollars. But was Jim Pearson also calling himself Hektor? He'd have to work with Security Associates to determine that one.

He sifted through the brokerage data for twenty minutes before he came to the insider trading report. Simtec had always been liberal with the awarding of options, and many of their employees had profited handsomely. When you enabled a buy at thirty points below market, you were putting a lot of money into somebody's pocket.

It was in this context that he saw a trade registered to Karen Williams. She had apparently executed some of her options, which, as far as Barry knew, enabled her to buy at 45. She'd sold at a price of 62 7/8, so, even in a falling market that was a tidy 17 7/8 profit on each of ten thousand shares. Not bad. He made a mental note and moved on.

Then he decided to check each of the executives, in order. He chose Find and typed in 'Hughes'. The search routine got to the bottom of the file and beeped. Nothing.

He tried 'Seidler'. The cursor jumped to a line showing a sale of six thousand shares. Who knew what Jim had paid for those shares? Maybe nothing, if they were part of his compensation package. Six thousand times $60 made for a $360,000 capital gain.

He continued searching in this way, methodically going through each of the directors and VPs. Spakovsky, in spite of all his hollering about share price, had decided to exercise options himself. Or perhaps that was the cause of his concern, thought Barry. The CFO was holding a bunch of shares and he was taking a beating.

He again scanned by the Karen Williams trade.

He'd been examining the file for over thirty minutes, and closely enough to realize he wasn't going to uncover a silver bullet. The truth was, he wasn't familiar enough with this sort of data to know what was or wasn't unusual. He was growing tired of the exercise and, as an afterthought, he punched in 'Dunn' and hit Find.

Sure enough, William Dunn had sold five thousand shares the day before. Sold short, no doubt, the sonofabitch.

14

At 1:20 Mike Spakovsky called in a rage.

'They're eating us alive,' he said. 'Have you seen any of these reports?'

Barry had been fielding a constant barrage of questions from Security Associates, TechDirect administrators, and, so it seemed, just about everyone else in the company. He had no idea what Mike was talking about.

'What reports?'

'CompuServe, the Internet, Prodigy – apparently it's on all the information services.'

'What is?'

'God, Barry. It's awful. You can't imagine what they're saying in the Internet newsgroups or the forums on CompuServe. I'm going to read you some of the headlines: Major Shakeup at Simtec, Mail Troubles Tip of the Iceberg, Simtec Follies, STC Clips Employees Wings.'

He paused, and Barry could hear him flip through several pages.

'Or this one: Simtec Clueless. Listen to this, Barry. I'll read you part: "I've been told things are pretty desperate. Tech Services is struggling to run cabling on their own network to get it straight. If they managed to get that messed up with their own stuff, can you imagine what's going on inside your computer?"

'These messages are being read by thousands of people, Barry. Here's one response: "This is all absolutely predictable. I said it nine months ago when they brought in the new CEO. Just because you can push Ivory soap and cake mix doesn't mean you can put together a good computer. We all know the cause of their current troubles. The fallout is now starting, and will continue, until the company wises up and realizes an R & D approach cannot be replaced by advertising." '

Mike stopped reading, apparently waiting for Barry's response. But Barry was thinking about the unfairness of that last comment. They'd spent more on research under Diane Hughes than in any previous three quarters in Simtec's history. Barry knew that for a fact. Where did these people get their information?

'I count over a hundred postings with that subject line,' Mike said. 'From all over the country. The world, for that matter. Everything is leaking, and the news media is scooping it up. I've had four different analysts call in the last hour. The stock's been down two days in a row. They're saying these reports could lock us into a nosedive, and they want my comment. This is how it happens, Barry. Shareholders don't know what the hell's going on, so they try to bail out because no one wants to get left holding the bag. I'm talking about some of the institutions.'

'Let them bail out then. Our fundamentals are strong. Our core business expanded in Europe, and we have some bright spots domestically. There's nothing inherently wrong. We're having a decent quarter.'

'The market isn't about fundamentals. It's about confidence. And psychology. We're taking another big hit today. We could be down ten points on the week. You think there's nothing wrong with that? This is how you get a class-action lawsuit. I watched them do it to 3COM and several others. I'm telling you, the big boys take a beating and they want to get their money back one way or the other. I don't think our initial statement about the configuration errors went far enough.'

Barry had been typing a memo on the laptop. He glanced down and halfheartedly jabbed at the space bar.

'They'll get a law firm, Barry, and the firm will salivate over this. Big company with deep pockets. They'll claim we withheld information and the shareholders got duped. They don't give a shit about the shareholders, but I'm talking about thirty, forty million to settle.'

Outwardly, Barry might have looked calm, but he was furious.

The sonofabitch had nudged some rocks – what was that he said? *a pocketful of stones* – and started an avalanche. The same bastard could then call and say, Hi, this is Hektor. How's it going over there?

'You better hold a press conference,' Barry said. 'Some of this is pure rumor and we can set the record straight. There's no shakeup. Business is fine. You might even release some of our figures. Give them something concrete. Let's also consider the stock buyback fund. This seems like an appropriate time to tap into that. We voted to set that money aside and buy when the market took a dip, so let's do it.'

'Are you telling me to get with BancBoston and use the fund? Is that a go-ahead?'

No one seemed willing to make a decision around here. They were all scrambling for cover.

'No. I'm not telling you to do it. The two of us, in consultation, agreed that supporting our share price would be a wise action. I'm expecting a call from Diane, and I'll ask for her approval. Let's propose thirty percent of the fund and save the rest for another day.'

'All right,' Mike said grudgingly.

'One other thing. You exercised some of your options recently. I was wondering about the timing on that. What's that all about?'

'How did you get that information? You've been looking at my stock purchases?' Spakovsky was indignant.

'It's public knowledge. I'm only doing some checking, and I thought I'd ask.'

Spakovsky paused, then said cautiously, 'What are you implying? You hold on a minute. I'm going to be in your office in five minutes.'

And there he was, five minutes later, knocking on the door. He must have dropped what he was doing and run out of his office. Barry thought it an interesting exhibition of speed.

Spakovsky closed the door and took the same chair where Dunn had been sitting earlier. He was carrying a handful of papers, which he set on the corner of the desk. 'I brought you prints of the messages I was talking about. If you have a moment, you should give them a read.'

'I will. But I'm sitting here up to my neck in shit. How do you hear about these things? Right now, I couldn't give a flip what they're saying on CompuServe.'

'Somebody called one of my employees. She checked it out and then came to my office. She thought I should know what people were saying. And, Barry, you *should* care. Maybe you don't realize how many people read that stuff. There are over forty million people on the Internet.'

'I am well aware. And they are not all reading about us.' Barry looked right at Spakovsky and said, 'I noticed how fast you made it over here when I started talking about stock trades.'

'Where do you get off with that? That's what I want to know. So I traded some shares. That was two weeks ago, well before any of this business started. Are you saying I did something wrong?'

'Not at all.'

'Did Diane tell you to look at my trades?'

'No, and I didn't single you out. I've been looking at everyone's trades, so I thought I'd ask.'

They were silent for a moment and Spakovsky straightened up, his face toward the window. 'I decided to use some of the options now. Frankly, I wasn't quite sure how much longer I'd be on board . . .' The phrase trailed off into a question.

That's what it was! Barry took the revelation matter-of-factly, but he was inwardly shocked. He wasn't dealing with Spakovsky the hot dog, Mr. Arrogant, but a man who was worried about his job. It made sense, though, with Jim and Diane always working on this or that project. Jim and Diane going off on a trip. Hell, Mike probably didn't even know why they had gone. For all he knew, they were off interviewing new CFOs.

He'd come over to Barry's office looking for scraps because Barry Shepard played it straight, right? Maybe Barry would be the one to tell him he was getting the can.

'So you decided to cash in some options.'

'Cash in. Ha! I bought the shares and, at the time, the price was going up so I decided to hold. Now the bottom drops out and I'm stuck.'

'Ten thousand shares.'

'Down eight points so far. You do the math. I could have sold days ago. I could have stopped the hemorrhaging, but I haven't, precisely because I didn't think it would look right. Then you call with what sounds to me like bullshit innuendo.'

A flash of the old Spakovsky, thought Barry. Never too far down to be insulting. 'No innuendo,' Barry said. 'Just a question.'

'You've been looking at stock trades. You thought you might sniff somebody out.'

'That's the general idea. You told me that Security Associates was going to look at trades. My brother works for a brokerage and I was curious.'

No one was more acutely aware of market fluctuations than Spakovsky. 'What did you find?' he asked. His eyes drifted toward the documents on Barry's desk.

'Trades like yours. The institutions and pension funds are the big ones. Nothing jumped out at me.'

Spakovsky uncrossed his legs. He didn't look satisfied with that answer, but he was fully capable of conducting his own examination of the records.

'Well,' he said, standing and adjusting his tie. 'I've got a press conference to organize. Would you like to make a guest appearance before the paparazzi?'

'I've got a thousand machines to ship and we're talking to production by Sneakernet. Maybe next time.'

'Sneakernet,' Spakovsky said with a sneer. 'I'm sure the media would find that concept reassuring.'

Fifteen minutes after Spakovsky had left, Gwen buzzed and said, 'The man from Security Associates and Greg Mitchell are milling around out here eyeing your closed door.'

'Send them in,' Barry said. He'd been holed up for about as long as he could get away with.

'Gentlemen,' he said, scanning their faces. Greg wasn't wearing a jacket, and Barry noticed smudges of grey on the sleeves of his white shirt. Probably jockeying around in the wiring closet, Barry thought. You spent too much time in there and you came out looking like Pigpen.

'Status report,' Greg said. 'We've gotten a basic server configured from scratch. We're about ready to go on-line for fifty people in TechDirect.'

'Sounds good,' Barry said. 'Is it locked up tight?' He addressed this question more to Dunn than Greg Mitchell.

'I've given Greg a utility from my bag of tricks. At every workstation we configure a start-up location ID. A couple of your guys are going through the office doing that now. A file with the IDs is also maintained on the server. When someone tries to log in, the utility does two things. First, it checks the person against the allowed location IDs, then it checks the machine's address, to make sure the address corresponds to the ID we've given it. A log file tracks all activity, but if you're not on one of the machines we set up, you can't get in. Period.'

'How about administrators?'

'You can log in, but only from one of the machines we configure.'

'No way around it?'

'The routine is triggered at log-in. If you're not at a valid machine, you're denied access before you ever get in.'

'Whose utility is it?'

'Mine,' Dunn said. 'I wrote it. TechDirect has a very defined set of users, so we can get a solid implementation. When you can point to forty or fifty users who need to access a service, we can lock it down. Ten thousand potential users, that's a problem.'

'So this machine is in good shape.'

'All files off the original disks, that's good. Access comes from one of fifty users, and there's a detailed log tracking who did what from where. If something does happen, you're going to have a pretty good idea who it had to be. It's a lot better than the setup you had.'

'I agree,' Barry said. 'I thank you both. W. S., if you could stay behind for a minute and give me an update on a few other things.'

Greg took the hint and said he was going to go help finish the configuring.

'This is good progress on the server,' Barry said. 'It's good to have a set of clean files and a machine we can trust. What about the digging in human resources? I got E-mail that you're turning the place upside down, which I understand, but what are you finding? And what if the guy logs in again – how are you set up to handle that?'

Dunn stretched his neck slowly to one side, as though working out a kink. 'The personnel records are interesting. Especially the former employees. Based on the termination reports and on what the person did when they were here, we're building leads and chasing them down. If an ex-programmer is now out in California, and we can call and verify that he's sitting at his desk, then, chances are, he's not a problem.

'With this kind of information, sometimes you get lucky and turn over the right stone. The single biggest value of having us go through the records is that everybody at Simtec knows we're doing it. The guilty one starts to worry. He slows down. He makes a misstep.'

Barry liked the idea of a misstep. He wanted to do a broadcast E-mail: Watch out, asshole. Security Associates has every personnel record under a fucking microscope.

'As far as the next log-in, we're sitting there waiting with a packet sniffer. We'll get the hardware address where the person is logged in. If it's here on the Simtec campus, we'll beat the bushes and find that machine.'

'Of course, he'll know how closely you're watching. Especially after you tagged him with that message. He either won't come back or now he'll be twice as cautious.'

'If he doesn't come back – great! – we win. But I doubt it. This guy is greedy. He wants your money. He'll be back and we'll be ready. It really doesn't matter whether he's looking for us or not.'

That much was true: Hektor wasn't stupid. Barry nodded approval and picked up a pencil. He rotated it between his fingers and regarded Dunn carefully. 'You sold our stock short yesterday.'

A long count before Dunn said, 'Yes, I did.' He looked slightly repentant, but not terribly so.

'You came in here and listened to what was going on, turned right around and sold five thousand shares.'

'I'm a man who likes to place a bet every now and then. Hardly insider trading, if that's your implication. No one told me your earnings were down. No one told me what your quarterly report was going to say, or that you expected a drop. Nothing of the kind. You simply told me you were experiencing computer difficulties. It has been my experience, and I have quite a track record to back it up, that when a company has computer problems they will eventually also suffer a setback in the market. There's nothing scientific about my method, and I'm not always right, but it's a little bet I have with myself about the importance of technology.'

'Meanwhile you've been hired by us to fix those problems.' Barry squeezed the pencil tightly. 'If not illegal, it's a conflict of interest, and it's foolish.'

Dunn held up his hands in surrender. 'Foolish maybe. But not a conflict of interest. I'd rather nail the bastards any day than make a few dollars in the market.'

'You'd have a hard time convincing some people of that. It looks bad, dammit! Here's the top gun we hired to fix things and he's betting against us.'

'Don't take it too seriously,' Dunn said. 'You want me out of the market right now, I'll do it. My work comes first, and I'm pretty fanatic about that.'

Interesting choice of words, Barry thought. *Fanatic*. The way you might describe shooting someone in a parking lot at Holman Distributing.

Gwen buzzed to tell him Diane was on the line.

'I'll let you go,' Dunn said. He dropped a scrap of paper on the desk. 'That's your ID. Set a variable called LOCATION to that number.'

Barry waited until Dunn had left before he hit the button on the phone.

'Barry, hello. I'm in Boston. I got your message but I couldn't break free until now.'

'Well, since you're already there, you might call BancBoston and let them know that, subject to your approval, we'd like to initiate the stock repurchase program. Mike was pitching a fit about share price, we discussed it and thought this might be a good time to use thirty percent of the fund.'

'I have no problem with that. Mike should line it up. If I need to sign something, I'll get a number where they can fax the documents.' She sounded slightly annoyed. 'What about the phone call?'

'He called a few minutes after twelve. My feeling was, we couldn't keep telling him to wait without putting something on the table. So, I threw out a red herring and said we were in the process of getting him the million. I told him the board was slow, but they were coming around. If he wanted more money, he needed to give us time to make a case to the board. Unfortunately, he balked. He said he was going to hit us again. Hard.'

'You indicated we were willing to pay a million, and he refused it?'

'He's not taking a million anymore. He made that clear. He knows that we've hired an outside consultancy, and he did not seem impressed, as you will hear on the tape. We had some file servers deleted today, and they also managed to delete the backup tapes. Now there's an uproar in the on-line services. All sorts of stories have begun floating around out there. Mike's concerned about share price. He's going to hold a press conference and do damage control.'

'They know about Security Associates? It sounds like they're getting information straight from us. They've got to have someone inside.'

'Maybe,' Barry said. 'But remember, we've got twenty thousand employees all talking a mile a minute. The scoop on most of what we do is going to become public. Mike is more aware than I am of exactly what they're saying on the Internet.'

'I'll give him a call next.'

'If you can get him before the conference, you might give him a pep talk. I think we should release some sales numbers and calm everybody down. I know his staff lost half their files and I appreciate why he had to do it, but postponing his quarterly meeting sent the wrong message. We're not in that bad of shape.'

'The shape we're in is much more a matter of perception than reality. I'll call Mike and discuss it. Let's back up for a minute . . . How did they do that, Barry . . . delete the tapes?'

Here was the problem of dealing with a nontechnical CEO. Diane didn't understand the tape backup procedures to begin with. If he mentioned altering the script, the explanation probably wouldn't make any sense. It was no doubt much easier to envision an employee with a large magnet, somehow gaining access to the server rooms.

'It was clever,' Barry said. 'We can go over the details when you get back, but our nightly backups haven't been any good for a week now. If we hadn't needed the files off one of those tapes, we might not have caught it for who knows how long. The thought of these booby traps that can go right under our noses – including Security Associates – was part of what convinced me to make a ploy of negotiation. We need to buy some time in a big way.'

'So W. S. Dunn wouldn't have caught it either?'

You can play the tape back a thousand times right in their faces – those security hotshots aren't going to do you any good.

'He might have,' Barry said, knowing how desperately Diane wanted to hear something positive. He thought of Dunn's short sale of their own stock. Not positive.

'They're good. They've got tools and the experience for exactly the kind of thing we're facing. We've just set up a server in TechDirect that I'm confident is clean and rock solid. But it's a race, and no one can be everywhere at once.'

Diane sighed. 'I know this trip has been horrible timing, but I believe it has helped project stability. The industry sees me out doing business as usual. I've got three more cities to go to, and I'll be back tomorrow at the soonest possible moment. This is a tough deal all the way around. In the meantime, it gives me peace of mind knowing you're there to take care of things.'

That's right, pat the dog on the head, Barry thought after they hung up. If it were *his* company, he'd say, Screw the deal. Shuttle diplomacy could wait. He'd be back there on the front lines with a pickax and a shovel. But maybe that's why he wasn't CEO and probably never would be.

He hung up with Diane, reached over, and picked up the printout Spakovsky had brought over. Barry flipped through the messages with increasing ire.

Tell me about restructuring. You work for a university and you'll never know what it's like to see an entire wing of your company get lopped clean off. You want to sit there and make pronouncements from your ivory tower, but you'll never know what it's like to watch a dozen of your best friends – and good workers – walk in and get their pink slips. Furthermore, what's going on at Simtec is not restructuring, it's ineptitude. You don't mail out thousands of misconfigured machines for any other reason than a major screw-up.

The message was addressed from Mitch at IBM, of all places. Talk about ineptitude, Barry thought. He read on to see the responses, including one from the University of San Francisco:

As usual, Mitch proves that the private/public sector dichotomy is still firmly in place. Has Mitch ever worked at a university? No. Does Mitch have friends at a university? I doubt it. One might be inclined to ask, does Mitch have friends at all? ;-) But I digress.

Having worked for three universities, as well as Motorola and Digital Equipment, I can tell you that university staff and researchers routinely do more with less. A magnitude less than their private counterparts. They are also subject to exactly the same kind of pressures – time, budget cuts, race to market. As far as differences in wielding the axe, USF is currently considering the elimination of two entire departments and four programs. Does it matter that this is an egregious violation in the face of demonstrated student and community demand? Afraid not. Yeah, Mitch, we're all on the gravy train. And everyone at IBM can't wait to put in an honest day's work, right?

This had started a new thread of messages under the title Gravy Train, and Barry scanned ahead.

We were discussing why Simtec has apparently made what amounts to a last-gasp effort to reconfigure their network. Pulling down file servers in the middle of the day is not normal business. Some – we're not sure how many – employees had all their files deleted. If you want to discuss public/private, take it to the religion forum, ok?

And this one, titled Gravy Vocabulary:

> Digress? Counterparts? Egregious? I guess we know where this guy works. Sorry, my newsreader doesn't have a dictionary!

Which set off a whole string of arguments from wounded private-sector employees who felt their intelligence had been maligned.

Barry scanned the rest, which included some scathing comments about Simtec. The messages were dotted with truths about the company's state of crisis, but there was also a good deal of hysteria and falsehood. Many people were simply enjoying themselves and the prospect of watching another company take its turn in the hot seat.

Barry dropped the messages into the wastebasket. This too shall pass, he told himself. Over the last few days, he'd been telling himself that a lot.

The press was being directed into conference room B, a rectangular room that seated one hundred. Ten rows of ten with an aisle down the middle. Mike had strategically chosen the smaller of the conference rooms. He wanted to keep the event small and friendly, and he had purposefully limited the list of invitees.

The *Houston Chronicle* was there, a crew from each of the major television affiliates, CNN, and reporters from three national news magazines. The computer industry was represented by a number of columnists from the trade journals, two of whom had already been at Simtec on unrelated missions.

Mike stood at the front of the room with his hands clasped in front of him, eyeing the crowd as it assembled. He knew many of these people. They could call him for lunch when they were in town. They played golf. They got previews of Simtec's product rollouts. These were relationships Mike Spakovsky had cultivated, often feeling that he did as much PR work as he did actual number crunching.

And he had been successful. Simtec was often soft-handled by the press, when similar missteps by other companies resulted in a skewering. The company was a Houston darling and, to some extent, a national darling as well. In his right hand, Mike clutched a statement that had been faxed back with minor changes and approval from Diane Hughes not twenty minutes earlier.

Mike glanced at the head of public relations, Rhona Davison. After they had assembled the list of names, she'd been responsible for pulling them all together. She was also fully capable of giving the conference, but they agreed Mike's presence would lend credibility to the proceedings.

Something was going on at Simtec, and the interested faces gathering in the room were hot to find out what it was.

'It's time,' Mike said, and Rhona gave a cue to their own inhouse crew. They had begun the practice of taping all company events, yielding hours of footage that would later be studied and rehashed. Rhona was wearing a red power suit, and the room became quiet as she stepped to the podium.

'Welcome,' she said. 'I'm glad you were able to make it on a Friday and on such short notice. We considered giving you more time, and maybe holding this conference on Sunday, but we wanted to keep this a friendly affair.'

A few chuckles from around the room. It was true, too. Their editors and producers would just as well have hauled them in off the fishing boats and golf courses. Good, Mike thought. Anything to score a few points. His eyes moved over the video cameras and an array of people snapping photos. This was quite different from his quarterly analysts' meeting, which was usually attended by sober-looking individuals who rarely packed film.

'Many of you know our chief financial officer, Mike Spakovsky. He will be giving the conference today. We will both attempt to answer any of your questions to the best of our ability. Mike?'

She stepped away and he was on. He was immediately bathed in the glare of lights that had been set up at the back and along one side of the room. He found that he could not look beyond the second row of chairs without being blinded. Nevertheless, he tried to work the group with his eyes, moving from person to person acknowledging familiar faces, blinking and nodding at blurred visages toward the back.

'I'm going to read a short statement, which we will then discuss,' he said. 'We will be happy to field questions for as long as . . .' He glanced down at his watch, knowing full well the exact time. 'Five-thirty. Let's set that as a cutoff. I'd be surprised if we go that long.' He smiled and began to read.

'This conference has been called to deal with a number of issues that are currently being raised by the news media and others. First, the error that resulted in the misdelivery of four thousand and eleven TechDirect shipments. Second, alleged network or programming difficulties, and, third, a variety of recent stories about our financial condition that have been circulating on CompuServe, the Internet, and other information services.

'As Simtec has already acknowledged in a previous statement, an error in the TechDirect shipping program caused computers and peripherals ordered over a three-day period to be erroneously configured or to be mailed to the addresses of other customers. Simtec took immediate steps to rectify this situation, which included reverifying all order information and assuming any costs associated with the return and next-day delivery of corrected shipments. We have automatically upgraded the service agreements of any customer affected during this three-day period.

'We are conducting an ongoing investigation into how the error occurred, and we strongly suspect the possibility of deliberate tampering with the TechDirect ordering system. We have already taken, and we are continuing to take, additional steps to ensure the integrity of the ordering system. No customer was ever, at any time, billed for items that were not ordered.

'The other reports that have surfaced appear to be based largely on hype and speculation rather than fact. Over the past week, we have experienced network disruptions due to the implementation of our own internal security measures. This has spawned an amount of hearsay that is completely out of proportion with the actual events. The grain of truth has been subsumed by this hearsay, and the information services appear to be functioning as an outlet for creative license. We are reading fictions that border on the outrageous.'

Here Mike paused. He glanced to the side, ruffled through some papers, and appeared to spontaneously choose one. 'Now listen to some of this stuff.

> "SIMTEC GETS SAND IN FACE: Not only are they shipping computers to phantoms, but they are considering a major reduction in force and have already canceled contracts with several major suppliers." '

> "PINK SLIPS AHOY: My brother-in-law survived the other cutbacks at Simtec, but that was only spring cleaning. Something big must be coming. He described the mood there as incredibly somber. Sounds like purchasing better order up a truckload of Kleenex!" '

Mike shook his head. Ludicrous! And he again made eye contact around the room. 'We have canceled no contracts with suppliers. There is no reduction in force. I repeat, not one person is in danger of being laid off. We have expanded both production and hiring over the last quarter. None of what is mentioned in these so-called discussions is even on the table. I repeat, none.' He returned to the statement:

> 'As you will see in the documentation provided to you, we are now making available certain preliminary quarterly earnings estimates. Nothing is out of line with what we have projected all along. These figures are being made available on our World Wide Web site as well as our 1-800 StockInfo line.

> 'Our usual policy would have been to allow the rumor mill to run its course. By acknowledging a rumor, we lend credence that is as much undesirable as it is undeserved. However, in this case, the confluence of actual events, coupled with a drop in share price, has led us to believe that we must speak out. We abhor the spread of uninformed and malicious gossip about our company, or any other company. When that gossip is allowed to propagate unchecked, it does cause, as its result, real damage to real people.'

Mike stopped and folded the statement to one side. The hands shot up. 'Yes, John?'

John Maxwell wrote a column for *PC Week*. He was a tech at heart, and had designed a set of widely used UNIX administration tools. 'You mention a programming error and then you mention deliberate tampering. Which is it, Mike?'

'To some extent I have to say both. It's hard for me to give details before we get to the bottom of the whole thing, but let me put it this way: Even if someone deliberately altered database code or files with every intention of causing production problems, we should have been able to catch that, or prohibit it from happening in the first place. I would characterize that as a programming error, whether or not anything was done intentionally.'

'Word on the street is that you've brought in Will Dunn.'

Most in the room either knew, or knew of, W. S. Dunn. Though they hadn't all known that he had been brought in by the Simtec Computer Company. They scribbled notes.

Mike didn't flinch. 'Our strategy is that, as soon as we suspected tampering, we wanted to hire one of the best to come in and root it out. The relationships we've built with our customers are far too important to take this lightly.'

John Maxwell and Mike Spakovsky were friends, but John was working here. He tightened the screws. 'The kind of crew Dunn brought in makes it seem like more than a database foul-up.'

'That's exactly the issue. We want to know – with certainty – if anything else has been tampered with, so we are undertaking a thorough investigation. I'm not going to comment on that right now as it would be inappropriate and premature.'

They mulled over this response, until Janet Thornton from the *Chronicle* jumped in. 'What about the reduction-in-force scenario? That certainly seems a logical reason for someone to mess up your files – a disgruntled programmer, perhaps?'

'Absolutely not. There is no reduction in force. Let me give you some concrete figures. Over the past year, the number of full-time employees has increased by five hundred and thirty-seven. We now have twenty-one thousand three hundred and twelve full-time employees on this campus.' He paused, calculating everything before he said it, and added, 'The only thing I can think of that could possibly be construed as negative was the scaling back of our stock option plan. During our initial high-growth years, we had a much lower number of employees and we were extremely aggressive in the granting of stock options. We still award the options, but the exercise price has drifted higher, making them somewhat less profitable.' Take that and run with it, thought Spakovsky, a nice, fat bit of misdirection.

'All right. But what about the canceled contracts?' Thornton asked. 'Are you denying that any suppliers have been cut out of their deals?'

'Unequivocal denial,' said Mike.

Thornton waved a piece of paper in the air. 'But I have a report right here about a company called Orange Logic. This was faxed to my office today. They make some kind of circuitry, and apparently Simtec exercised an escape clause to get out of its contract seven days ago.'

Mike Spakovsky was furious. He had never even heard of Orange Logic, but he knew how this looked. He had been caught in a direct contradiction. If he was lying about this, it made all the rest of his comments suspect.

Mike stared straight at the *Chronicle* reporter. 'Orange Logic. Can you give me an address on that company?'

She rattled off a location that, like many high-tech companies, sounded like it was in the heart of Silicon Valley. The others in the room were silently watching this exchange. A few had made notes. Spakovsky turned to Rhona Davison and quietly conferred with her. She turned and left the room.

'I'll be honest with you,' Mike said. 'I've never heard of Orange Logic. I wish I could stand here and say we're giving them all kinds of business, but I simply don't know. What I can say is, our production is up over last quarter, and we are not running around canceling contracts with our suppliers. Rhona will have someone research the situation, and I'll have an answer for you before we adjourn.'

This response seemed to pacify the group for the time being.

Janet Thornton was shuffling papers again. 'There's another fax I've gotten,' she said. 'We heard your statement on the shipping errors. What's your position on the report that, let's see . . . Hundreds of Simtec employees lost their hard drives and whole file servers have been deleted?'

Mike Spakovsky could feel his brow heating up, the shirt clinging to his torso under his suit coat. Pens wiggled in all the aisles.

'I'd have to chalk that up to hyperbole.'

'Will you confirm that employees lost their hard drives? And, if so, how many?'

Mike tried to wet his lips. His mouth was a desert. 'I will confirm that we have experienced some disruption, as outlined earlier. We are currently diagnosing the exact cause, as well as the quantity of machines affected. Let me assure you that the numbers involved are far from catastrophic.'

'Just for argument's sake,' said John Maxwell, 'what's catastrophic?'

Mike saw a way to get back to safe ground and lunged for it. 'The kind of thing that's being portrayed on the Internet. Revenues cut in half. Thousands laid off. That's catastrophic. The Internet is a great system for disseminating information, and it's highly entertaining, but, as you know, there is no guarantee as to the accuracy or truthfulness of any of these messages floating around out there.'

'Does Simtec attribute their recent drop in share price to these rumors, or is the market picking up on an underlying weakness?' This came from a reporter for the local ABC affiliate. The man added, 'A lot of people are wishing they'd sold short a week ago.'

'We do not believe that this is a response to, as you say, any underlying weakness. As you all know, the market fluctuates. Sometimes according to whim. Our quarterly results will be out at the end of the month, and I am fully confident that those results will back me up.'

Mike clenched his teeth and fought through a second round of questions and denials. Then Rhona appeared in the doorway with a manila folder and a ribbon of fax paper. Spakovsky stepped down and they conferred briefly.

Spakovsky yielded the podium and Rhona stepped up and adjusted the microphone. 'I have just been in contact with our purchasing department, and I wanted to give you the facts on

Orange Logic. They are a company with whom we have had a relationship for approximately seven months. They were a supplier for a part of the drive mechanisms in certain of our JStar and PStar lines. I have been told by purchasing that this contract recently went out for bid, at which time we located an Austin-based supplier who could meet our demand at a lower cost.

'The terms of the agreement will not be made public; however, I will provide to anyone who requests it a copy of the early termination clause of the contract.'

She glanced around the room at the reporters. A few looked satisfied, some still appeared dubious. 'That's all there is. Sorry we can't give you something more sensational. I think at this point we will go ahead and adjourn. Mike and I will stick around for a little while informally.'

Mike cut a straight line toward Janet Thornton. He tried to pigeonhole her as to the origin of her information, but it soon became clear that she didn't know. The faxes had been sent anonymously to the *Chronicle* along with the subject line: Latest Simtec Info.

Thirty minutes later, the last of the reporters had left to go file their stories. Rhona went over to Mike Spakovsky and said, 'How did we do?'

Mike folded his arms and stared at the empty room. 'Rhona,' he said. 'We've done better.'

Barry was finishing up a mail message to Jim Seidler. Jim would be talking with Diane, but he would also be checking his mail. Better to keep him informed directly as well. The message was proving difficult to compose, considering the text might be read or in some way redirected the minute he hit the send button. He kept to the facts, or at least the facts according to Hektor. He had proposed the one-million-dollar payment that was being authorized by the board. The offer had been refused. Hektor had appeared intransigent and hostile. Jim would have the savvy to read between the lines.

He was reading back over the message, thinking he should add something about the backup tapes, when Dunn swept in through the outer door. Gwen started to intervene, but Dunn had the kind of manner that made it easier to acquiesce than to argue. In he came and plopped down in his usual chair.

'This is a big place,' he said. 'You walk between these buildings a few times and you've got your exercise for the day.'

Barry was unable to respond with appropriate chit-chat. 'How many different servers were hit?' he asked grimly.

'Seven. It's not as bad as you might think.'

Dunn appeared nonchalant, but Barry suspected this was only an act. He rested his elbows on the desk and studied Dunn's face. 'How much did we lose?'

'Worst case, a week's work. The deletions were spotty and, in some cases, the files can be brought back. Human resources suffered the most damage, and I've been over to speak with the woman in charge.'

'Sarah Dennis.'

'Right. She said not a lot would have changed in the last week. I assured her we'll have the database back up tonight. She can have people work on it undisturbed all day Saturday. Data re-entry, whatever they need to do. She said she can live with that.'

'Good. And you're talking to each of the other areas that lost services?'

'As quickly as we determine status and what we are likely to restore. As you said, realistic estimates.'

'Exactly.'

Dunn ran a hand through his hair. 'I also bought five thousand shares to cover my short sale. I agree with your position on that. Believe me, I hear about enough SNAFUs in the industry that there'll be plenty of other places to lay my bets.'

'I think that's a wise decision.'

'Lot of press-types hovering down there,' Dunn said. 'Did the vultures get a whiff of meat?'

'Ridiculous stories have been circulating on the Internet. Mike Spakovsky called a press conference to try to set the record straight.'

'I don't know Mike, but I've known Jim Seidler for some time. He probably doesn't remember, but I met him when he was a speaker at conferences back in the early days. This was back before the first portable and he more or less predicted the way the industry was going to go. He was right on the money. Odd, his leaving right now. Diane, too.' Dunn gave a questioning look.

And it *was* odd. Both top executives siphoned off at such a critical time. But Diane and Jim had been resolute: Her presence was mandatory, and she had appeared unwilling to leave him behind. Barry didn't like the company line, but he used it anyway. 'They're trying to make a strong show of business as usual. They had important meetings set up and didn't want to cancel. We got a finger in the eye, but we can't stop everything we're doing. I'm the one who gets to stay home and tend the fences.'

'They have a lot of confidence in you,' Dunn said.

Listen to this. He'd caught Dunn on the stock trade, and now the man was going to try and apply a sugar coating. 'We're staying in touch. I keep them as up-to-date as I can. The only problem with that is, I wonder if I'm the only one reading the E-mail.' Barry picked up a blank disk. He fingered the locking tab open and closed.

'It's possible there are holes, and we're checking it. I've not personally spent a lot of time debugging E-mail, but on some systems, if you have the right password you can read all you want to. I know of one company that got sued over reading its employees' mail. The employees claimed invasion of privacy.'

'As far as I know, we've never done anything like that. But I hate the idea of handing out information because this joker found his way into our mail system.'

Dunn settled back into the chair. His eyes narrowed, darting from side to side. 'Yes, let me think about that,' he said. 'That would work. You download, unpack it, and bingo.'

Barry didn't know what he was talking about.

Dunn lurched up out of his seat. 'I'll be right back,' he said. 'I've had an idea.'

Barry glanced at the message to Jim, but decided not to finish it until he'd heard what Dunn had in mind. He thought about W. S. Dunn and, despite his shorting Simtec stock, Barry had to admit he still liked the man. Barry recognized the air of competence, and it made him realize how infrequently he saw it, even at the upper levels of Simtec. Here it was too often rule by committee and CYA.

He fired off a message to one of Chris Jacobs' administrators requesting more information about the mail system. Then Dunn wheeled into the room carrying a floppy-disk carrying case that looked a yard wide.

'I've had an inspiration,' Dunn said. He opened the case and began flipping through the rows of disks. 'If I brought it, you may have the dubious honor of being the first person to launch a new Security Associates widget. Gotcha! Here, put this disk in and see if it's got a file called bomb.exe.'

'Bomb.exe? You're sure I want to load this disk?'

'Harmless, Barry. Like a newborn baby. Completely harmless until you go to uncompress. Then it trashes your hard drive. It acts like it's unzipping; meanwhile you get eaten alive. I figured we'd attach it to your mail message.'

Barry didn't say anything. He was busy imagining the possibilities. 'If someone's reading E-mail,' Dunn said. 'You gotta figure Shepard to Seidler is going to get read. For added insurance, you could title it something like State of the Network.'

Barry copied the file and punched out the disk. Once he sent the file, he wanted to make damn sure he remembered to get rid of it. 'Who makes these things?' he asked, holding the disk between two fingers.

'My son made that one. We tried it on our machines, but we've never used it live.'

Barry was looking at the disk label, which didn't say bomb.exe. It said MANGO in orange lettering.

'We were all sitting around in the lab one day. We had some down time and we got to talking about counteroffensive utilities. Anyway, someone was eating a mango and she got juice all over the place. We decided that if we could get that mango in there, dripping juice all over a CPU, that's about the best weapon we could think of.'

Barry could picture it, sitting around coming up with ways to trash people's computers. This was anathema to his own mission at Simtec, but he could understand the appeal. Let the creative juices flow!

'I'll rename it chart.exe and include it as an attachment.' Barry went to work at the keyboard, but then stopped mid-keystroke. 'Jim could get this before I have a chance to tell him. I can't exactly mail an explanation, or it defeats the purpose.'

'That's true,' Dunn said. 'You definitely don't want to send this before you've spoken to him.'

'Let's do it another way,' Barry suggested. 'We'll open an account for you. Then you send the file to me. Give it a juicy heading.'

'*Operation* Mango.'

Barry picked up the phone and dialed Greg. 'Okay,' he said when he hung up. 'Greg Mitchell is one floor down. Go down and get with him and he'll set you up. One thing, W. S., don't send that thing to anyone but me. We can throw a hook out there, but we can't play around with this stuff.'

'No problem,' Dunn said, grinning. 'Any mail message from me, don't open the attachment.'

15

Karen Williams suggested Pappasitos, a trendy Tex-Mex restaurant on Houston's south side. William Dunn was wishing they'd chosen someplace quieter. Waiters and waitresses hustled the large floor, squeezing between tables and dealing out enormous plates of fajitas. The bar was packed and the PA system bellowed names from the waiting list.

The two of them were sipping margaritas and waiting on their order. They'd been talking about ATM machines, which Dunn had done a lot of work on in their early stages.

'So how did you learn all these secrets?' Karen asked.

'It's simple, really. You take the machine apart – I don't care what kind of machine you're talking about – you see what it's supposed to do, then you sit back and think about ways someone is going to try to break in and pirate the thing. It's a very real-world way to work. My son, whom you met today, is extremely good at it.'

'I'll bet he is,' she said with a smile. 'And ATMs are the way you got started?'

'No. Computers. I had always dabbled in computers. That was my father's occupation, so of course there was always stuff around the house, punch cards and paper programming tapes in those days. I learned to program by using time on corporate mainframes. Back then, there was no security at all. You just dialed a number and got a tone, kind of the way fax machines are now. I was a programmer, but my company didn't take off until we got into ATMs. I hired thirty people that year. The whole year I felt like all I did was interview.'

Karen squeezed the lime and dropped it into her glass. 'I read about a case where someone made fake ATM machines,' she said. 'They set them up on street corners and people came by and stuck their cards in. Then I guess the ATM said, Out of Order. Meanwhile, they recorded the people's card numbers and PIN codes.'

Dunn was nodding. Not only was Karen Williams smart and gorgeous, she was a well-informed conversationalist. He was dealing with a grand slam. 'I thought that ATM scam was ingenious,' he said. 'I'm glad that bank wasn't one of my clients. The thieves couldn't get past the safeguards of the system itself, so they introduced a replica of the system. I always emphasize to my employees that we're no smarter than anyone else. If someone is willing to spend more time and money to break into a system than we are, they'll probably find a way. That's why, when work is slow, I've got a roomful of people who do nothing but sit around and try out hacks. We spend a lot of money on it, hammering on software, following hunches. Sometimes we find a weakness in a piece of hardware or software. I'll go in and tell the company about it and they'll pay me for the information. I've got the job every little boy playing with trucks in the driveway dreams about.'

'Maybe every girl playing with trucks in the driveway, too,' Karen countered.

'Not in my experience,' Dunn replied evenly. 'My own daughter won't have anything to do with the industry, and she didn't lack for nature or nurture.'

'There's no shortage of women on your crew, I notice.'

'There are always exceptions. It's a generalization, but women don't seem all that interested in discovering the way things work.' Karen was about to jump in, but he kept going. 'Look at you, for example. I've always thought law was more about people. The lawsuits I've been involved with were much more a matter of pride and ego. How much will you settle for? How long are you willing to pay attorney's fees? That's what it comes down to – people. Not some gear clicking around inside a box.'

Karen had been waiting to protest, but her mouth slowly closed. She rested her chin on top of one hand.

Neither had stopped for lunch during the day, so when the food arrived the two ate quickly. At one point several mariachis approached the table and Dunn waved them off. He might have liked to be a romantic couple, out for a festive dinner, but this was still business. Karen may have picked up on the same thing, and she turned the conversation back to Simtec.

'I've never seen people like Jim and Barry so worked up about anything before,' she said. 'I know we received additional threats today. Just how bad is it?'

Dunn considered his response. He had seen entire banks of corporate records completely erased by their assailants. With smaller companies, it might only be a matter of disabling one or two machines. Simtec was so large, and the resources so spread out, that it was harder to hit Simtec in that way. Nevertheless, the damage was significant.

'It may not have affected your legal operations that much,' he said. 'But you've been hit pretty hard. Barry showed me the plan that he, Jim, and Chris came up with. They're competent and it was perfectly logical, but these people were way ahead of you. You didn't realize the extent of the problem. Now I'm running around doing everything I can think of at the last minute.'

Dunn glanced over and got the distinct impression that Karen had been looking at him. Not listening so much as *looking*. 'If it's any consolation,' he said quickly. 'I have seen worse.'

'A train wreck instead of a car wreck.'

'You have a train wreck,' Dunn said. 'But at least you haven't gone off a bridge.'

The waiter appeared with the tab and Dunn dropped a credit card on the tray. 'Business expense,' he said. 'And my pleasure.'

'Thank you. I'm glad we came. There's one other thing I wanted to ask. It sounds as though I'm talking to a detective, but do you have any suspects?'

Dunn leaned forward conspiratorially. 'I believe I can say that you, yourself, are not on the short list. Though . . .' He let his words trail off and Karen straightened, looking concerned. Here was a woman who had probably heard it all, thought Dunn, but here goes. 'Though I would like the opportunity to discuss it further.' He said this deadpan, looking straight at her. Karen held his glance for a moment and then looked away.

'We better get back to work,' she said. She pushed her chair back, and in an awkward moment, her leg pressed into his under the table. She collected her purse and appeared somewhat flustered.

Good, thought Dunn. Flustered was good.

Jim Seidler arrived back in town with an abundance of bad news. Several of the companies on his leg of the junket were apparently balking at the new distribution deal. He had located Barry in the TechDirect conference room, where catering had set up trays of sandwiches and fruit. Jim ushered Barry into a small kitchen area and closed the door.

'I got your update,' Jim said. 'And I've already listened to the tape up until the time you cut it off.' His expression was stern and seemed admonishing, but he let it go at that. 'Nice try on having to go back to the board again, even if he didn't buy it. At least now we all know where we stand. We dig in, and we wait for them to make a move.'

'That sounds about right,' Barry said. 'What happened in your meetings?'

'It was wretched. Not at all a done deal. Diane made it sound like all we had to do was go through and collect the signatures. I go in there and get my ass handed to me. Some of these people aren't even on the same page. A few want assurances – monetary, legal, you name it. This may be cold feet related to the bad news we've been getting, but part of it is Simtec not doing our homework.' Jim shook his head. He had grown pouches under his eyes, and his features looked sunken.

Barry had seen the bottom drop out of countless deals before. That's the way the industry worked – you made an alliance of convenience, you made enemies, and six months later you made an alliance with your enemies. Still, it seemed odd that Diane would pursue something without the necessary groundwork.

'I don't understand,' Barry said. 'She made it sound as

though you were in favor of the trip.'

'Not at all. I said the deal was a good one, important to Simtec, but that's it. Diane pulled the trigger and she shouldn't have. Not now, with all this going on.' Jim swung his arm, palm up, indicating the building.

Barry's lips pinched together tightly.

'I'm going to get my shovel and go into the trenches,' Jim said. He started to open the door. 'By the way, do you know where Chris is?'

Barry walked over and pushed the door shut with two fingers. He gave the quick-and-dirty version of the gun incident while Jim listened with arms folded carefully across his chest.

Jim registered little reaction other than a tightening of the jaw. 'It sounds like you handled it well,' he said stiffly. 'Does Diane know this?'

Barry nodded.

'I never held Chris personally responsible. Is that what he thought?'

'He held himself responsible. I don't know what else he thought.'

Jim sighed and reopened the door. 'Well, it looks like it's you and me.'

Barry walked slowly back to the TechDirect offices. The water fountain halfway down the hall was making a pinging sound, but as Barry approached, the sound oddly stopped and then started again a few seconds later.

For no logical reason at all, Barry turned around and walked back, just to see if the sound would stop again. It didn't. Coincidence. Look at me, Barry thought, playing mind games with a busted fan in a water fountain.

So Diane had pursued a deal that was obviously not ready to be put in place. A foolish waste of time, but he couldn't allow himself to worry about that. This was his thought as he walked into his office and ran into a youngish woman carrying a clipboard.

'Oh, hello, Mr. Shepard.' She held out her hand. 'I'm Suzanne, and I was stopping by to see if we could speak for about five minutes.'

Barry indicated the door to his office. He knew who this was. This was one of Dunn's behaviorists, whatever they were. He noticed that she closed the door.

Suzanne took a seat with pen and clipboard at the ready. 'I'd like to start by talking about something of a more personal nature. This is for us to get comfortable, to get to know each other a little bit. All right?'

'Fire away.'

'I was wondering if you have any pets. Or if you ever had any.'

Pets. 'No, I don't have any. I once had a bird, a parakeet. Actually, it belonged to a girlfriend of mine. We broke up and she didn't take it. I don't think she liked the bird much.'

'What about you? Did you like it?'

Barry put his elbows on his desk and rested his forehead against three fingertips. He was thinking about Diane, about his telephone reps, about Claudia and Caroline. How did he know if he'd liked that bird? It had died after he'd had it for a year or so; he didn't know why. But not before the carpet around its cage had become filled with tiny, unvacuumable seeds.

'That was some time ago. I guess I liked it. I fed it. Sometimes it would sit on my finger.'

'I'm curious. If you liked it, why don't you have one now?'

'I've never thought about it. Maybe because my daughter Caroline is too young. If we got another bird, I'd want her to take care of it. I think it's good for kids to have a pet.'

Barry noticed how Suzanne alternately watched him and then made hash marks on the clipboard. He lifted his head, curious to see just what she was doing over there.

She was standing up. 'Well, that'll be it, Mr. Shepard. I appreciate the time.' She held out her hand.

'That's it?'

'You bet.'

'Is that what you ask everybody? About their pets?'

'Oh, no. All sorts of different things. Sports, movies, you name it.'

'Can I ask what you're doing there on your clipboard?'

'I'm making notations. I mark up a quick profile based on

your speech and gestures. How you respond. There are all sorts of telltale signs, but I really shouldn't go into that.'

Barry gave a slow nod.

'See you,' Suzanne said, and she scooted out the door.

Barry stood and stretched, massaging the back of his neck. He punched in the code for his voice mail and began weeding through. He listened, taking notes when necessary, and then deleted all twenty-seven messages. He was punching religiously at the star key when W. S. Dunn sauntered through. the doorway with what looked like a large blueprint.

Barry eyed the paper Dunn was holding. 'What have you got?'

'Some kind of wiring diagram. It's out of date, but I'm still hoping we can get some use out of it. Karen Williams turned me on to a whole file cabinet full of archived information. What this stuff is doing in legal, I have no idea.'

Barry walked over and glanced at the schematic as Dunn unfolded it. Sure enough, it purported to be a wiring trace of Simtec 4. He had never seen it before. 'Karen had this?'

'You bet. I took her out to dinner and look what I get, the mother lode.'

Not that Barry cared who was going out to dinner with whom, but it struck him as amazing that, two days in town, Dunn and Karen Williams were going out to dinner and turning up wiring diagrams of Barry's own building. Moreover, diagrams he knew nothing about.

'It looks to be a plan of the original layout,' Barry said. 'Maybe it was used by the architects for specifications. Maybe we took bids on the construction. There will have been a lot of changes since then, but if you wanted to start at ground zero, this would certainly be the place.'

Dunn nudged the door closed and said, 'What I'm trying to do is get to the bottom of this electrical *accident*.'

Barry felt the heat rising to his face. 'This is the second insinuation you've made about that. A man went up into the ceiling to trace wiring and he got into live current. It's a tragedy, but he was a maintenance man. Maybe he deliberately poked into something besides the network wiring. Or he decided to look at the electrical circuits. I have no idea.'

'Careful,' Dunn said. 'If I didn't trust you so much, I'd say you were covering something up.'

Barry pushed Dunn in the chest hard, driving Dunn back up against the wall. He jutted a finger three inches under Dunn's nose. 'I don't like that one bit. I grieved for Ben Cooper. You've got all the fucking answers, why don't you explain it to me?'

Dunn's cheek twitched, and he held up one hand. 'Whoa. It may be as you say. I just think if you weren't already up to your eyeballs, you might look at this with a little less haste. You might say, "Hey, that's curious. How does a maintenance man get himself electrocuted?" '

'What are you proposing?'

'I'm proposing to go up there and check it out myself, if need be. Something's not right about that accident. The practical matter is that I need you to update these plans. I'd like you to get with your people and try to make these as accurate as possible. I want to know about every piece of wiring in the building.' He added, 'This will help in other ways. Not only with Mr. Cooper's accident.'

Barry slowly lowered his hand to his side. The only part he could map out with any certainty was the TSR room. He'd been heavily involved with that design himself. But the years between the construction drawings and when Barry had come on board? It was anybody's guess. Greg would know parts, and a few other key people might be able to help with their areas.

'Most of us will be in tomorrow. I'll get people together and go over the drawings. Then you can do your investigation.'

'Good. I'll leave these with you, then. Tomorrow I'm bringing my jumpsuit and a flashlight. I want to look at where your man got into the current, and I may need to do some tracing. There's nothing quite like wriggling through the dust and cobwebs. If you'd like to come along, you're more than welcome.'

'Sounds like the chance of a lifetime,' Barry said. He folded the diagram and put it off on the corner of his desk. He stuck a yellow note on it: 10 A.M.? He would have to get hold of

Greg and try to schedule the time. Barry noticed the can of iced tea he had opened hours earlier. The can was now warm, but he took a sip anyway.

He sat down and turned to Dunn. 'You look at the stock trading?'

'I took what you gave me and we compared it with our own data. We both saw the same things. Lots of large institutional trades. In the past month, Karen Williams has sold. Seidler did a good chunk. Spakovsky's in the middle of a trade. It's nothing out of the norm, though, at least not all by itself. Looks like a dead end.'

Barry was disappointed. 'What about the executives? I know you've been scrutinizing us. Anything there?'

'Plenty of suspects. Jim, Diane, Mike Spakovsky, you. You're all still on the list. I will say that you're not at the top. I saw Suzanne in the hall, and she said you didn't even make her needle twitch.'

'Her?' Barry said. 'She asked me about my pets.'

'I don't care what she asked you. Suzanne is the best. She can probably talk to you about the last movie you saw. If you're hiding something, it trips off all kinds of alarms.'

'I knew from the start she was one of your shrinks. I realized right after she left, though, that what I told her was wrong. I don't like pet birds at all. I'd never get another parakeet, not even for Caroline. I'd much rather she have a hamster, fish, or even a dog. In short, I didn't tell her the truth.'

'At the time, you probably thought it was the truth. Either that, or she knew you didn't like birds all along. I'm telling you, she's pretty amazing. I get nervous talking to her myself. I hear what she tells me about other people, and I'm sitting there thinking, Oh, no, now she's doing it to me.'

Barry would think twice the next time he spoke to her, too. 'Why do you mention Diane and Jim? And Mike?'

Dunn extracted a large ring of keys from his pocket and sat down. 'Obviously, they're not all doing it, but we think that almost certainly there has been some help from the inside. Not necessarily at your level, but not at the bottom either. Someone with access, and knowledge.'

'What possible reason could Diane or Jim have? They're in

charge of the company. It would be like cutting your own throat.'

'People always have their reasons. A guy walks into a hot dog stand and shoots somebody. Maybe he got laid off the day before. Maybe he's having a bad day and he got a bad pickle. You never know. From what I hear, Diane Hughes is not well liked in certain circles here. It could be that she feels as though the company isn't behind her. She might have hired somebody to come in and cause trouble. Then she gets to rework the system the way she wants to.'

'Why would she hire you, then?'

'Probably so that an outsider comes in and does the dirty work. Let Security Associates shake things up. It's a very clever ploy, really. She sends a wake-up call to everybody. Then she gets to ride in on a white stallion.'

Barry was aghast. Was Dunn actually suggesting this? Had they found something?

Dunn was watching for the reaction. 'Maybe not,' he said finally. 'I'm just throwing out scenarios. Jim could do it for the same reason. That and he's an alcoholic with quite a thirst – enough to make him unstable. Look at Chris Jacobs. He's obviously a piece of work.

'You could have your reasons, too. Barry Shepard, family man and hard worker, thinks he's stalled on this rung of the career ladder and he wants to leapfrog. You feel like you were held back, and now you've got a grudge. We traced all the way back to your grocery store days without finding a smoking gun. On the other hand, TechDirect distribution was the first place to get hit. Why?'

Barry shifted in his chair, leaned forward, and closed the screen on the notebook. He had worked eighty hours a week to get TechDirect up and running. He met Will Dunn's stare and purposely did not respond.

'Nah, probably not,' Dunn said. 'No guilty person wants to call that much attention to himself. And then there's Spakovsky, who presents his own possibilities. . . .'

Barry frowned. He indicated that Dunn should continue.

'Homosexual, in the closet, right? How far might he go to keep that under wraps? Someone could be holding that against him, or photographs, who knows what. They might be able to get a fair bit of coercion out of that information.'

Barry chose his words carefully. 'Are you telling me this is a known fact? Mike Spakovsky is a homosexual?'

Now it was Dunn's turn to look surprised.

'I assumed that you knew. He told me that he counted you as one of his closest friends at Simtec.'

'My question is, how do *you* know that?'

'You underestimate my staff. I've got five people who do nothing but dig up dirt on you people. Spakovsky was arrested in a newsstand quite some time ago. You know the kind of newsstand I'm talking about. I don't know that he did anything wrong, but he plea-bargained. Probably didn't want a trial. He did two hundred hours of community service.'

Barry stared. 'I didn't know this.'

'He and I spoke about you,' Dunn said. 'We discussed how the trouble had started in TechDirect. He holds you in very high regard, and something he said made me almost certain you knew about that part of his past.'

Barry made a fist and tapped it against his forehead. 'Mike's always brought these different women out to company parties. I wondered about that, but I don't ask about people's private lives. I think he does a good job and the rest is his own business.'

'It's his own business unless it makes him compromise the company's security,' Dunn said and stood up. 'I'm sure you begin to see the possibilities.'

'I can see you're building some fairly dramatic scenarios. Melodramatic, might be a better word.'

'You've got to stop being such a company boy,' Dunn said. 'Being a company boy will make you blind.'

'You show me a *fact,*' Barry shot back, 'and I'll be happy to look at it.'

'Facts start with guessing. Right up until the end, we're guessing. The only fact I know is that anything is possible. You had an attempted burglary. Now you're worried about your family. TechDirect gets hit, maybe they've grabbed Barry Shepard's daughter. They've got his daughter and they're holding his feet to the fire. He'll do anything to get her back.'

Barry thought about that. He didn't like it one bit.

'Haven't grabbed her, yet? They still could. Maybe they want more leverage.'

'Leverage for what?'

'Information. Money. You wave a big chunk of money in front of someone's nose, there's no telling what they'll do. Think of those two brothers who did in their parents. I read in the paper about some guy who tried to pull an insurance scam with his yacht. He took the boat out to sea and cut a hole in it with a chain saw. The thing went down so fast, he barely got off himself. Divers for the insurance company went down and found the boat, chain saw and all. People are crazy, Shepard. People will do anything.'

Barry was staring out the window at the trees. Dunn didn't know what he was talking about, he told himself. This was about computers; it wasn't about daughters.

'I've probably said too much,' Dunn said. 'I'll come by before noon tomorrow to pick up those drawings.'

The door clicked closed behind him, and Barry sat still. So now Diane was a suspect. Because the company wasn't behind her and she might feel the need to orchestrate a coup. And Jim. Barry had known about Jim's drinking for some time. It was impossible to miss. Every time you walked in his office, the guy wanted to pull out a bottle and celebrate.

From W. S. Dunn's point of view, Mike Spakovsky was a security risk. Barry, too, was a suspect, and Dunn would have concocted theories to implicate him. The theories would look – when seen from exactly the right angle, under certain precise conditions – as plausible as any explanation he had just heard.

Dunn's crew would also have managed to dredge up some kind of dirt. Barry's thoughts drifted back over the years, selecting and discarding events until he arrived at a moment that made him wince. Not because it made him a corporate blackmailer, but because it was a painful memory. He had been a junior, playing basketball for the University of Virginia. Three of his teammates and a number of players from the football team were carousing around campus when they spotted a Buick with two students from rival

Georgetown. What happened next, happened fast. Insults were exchanged, the students were accosted and their car defiled. The words then got rougher and – in an event that appeared to surprise everyone else as much as it did Barry – the car was flipped over. One minute they were rocking the car and the next they hoisted it up and over. Four or five of them was all it took.

One of the students in the car shrieked and they all ran, leaving the capsized hulk of a car beside the road. Barry learned the next day that the kid's arm had been crushed under the Buick. When Barry thought about it now, as he had off and on ever since, he couldn't believe he had done such a thing. Two of the football players had already been involved in other incidents and they were expelled from school. Barry had not been identified as one of the primary instigators, and he was given probation. In his own mind he had never done penance, and the guilt lingered, as it probably would all his life.

Not that it made Barry a viable suspect on Dunn's list. What it did was make him ashamed. How far back did Dunn's people go? Would they know about that incident? Was Dunn meeting with the other vice presidents and saying, Shepard? Mr. Upright Barry Shepard? Let me tell you a story. . . .

Barry shook his head. He pushed the papers into a pile and grabbed the phone. He'd check in with his TSRs and check with production. He was hungry and ready to go home.

The *kid,* as Dupree liked to refer to him, was actually twenty-six years old. Mark Willis had responded to a classified ad in the Data Processing section of the Sunday *Chronicle.*

> WANTED: Intelligent young programmer to handle small projects. Familiarity with networks and connectivity desirable. Practical experience more important than degree. Send résumé or background to Box 324164, Houston, TX 77098.

Mark had been doing contract database design and writing a game called Dirt Devils that he planned to release as shareware. He was a good programmer and knowledgeable about networking issues. He was also a rebel who considered all the CNEs and SQL report specialists and mainframe programmers of the world to be sellouts.

He responded to the ad because he liked the idea of small programming projects. He liked it a lot better than sucking up to corporate yahoos who changed their database spec every third day.

Mark wrote a letter describing how he had released both a shareware game and a file-copying utility, and that he had helped found and operate the Houston bulletin board called Zorro. What the hell, he thought, and even wrote how he had once used a UNIX cracker program to break into a major corporate network. He did call and notify the system administrator, he quickly added.

He did not say that his shareware had netted him exactly $1,037, nor did he reveal that instead of a reward for notifying the company of his break-in, he received a visit and a grilling by the FBI.

Three days after he'd sent the letter, he received a call inviting him to an interview, and Mark was ecstatic. The job interview had been a strange affair, conducted in the conference room of a seemingly vacant office suite. The interviewer was a youngish man with a round, serious face. The man could easily have looked playful, even childlike with that face, but the expression he wore was screwed one turn too tight. The man's name was Mr. Draper, and he explained that his company provided network monitoring and access tools. According to Mr. Draper, Mark's experience as a teen would serve him well. The man spoke broadly of the good deeds his company performed, as well as the large fees they earned. Then he told Mark how it worked: Sometimes they got clients up front, other times they had to find and point out holes before they got a contract. After two jobs, and after receiving his first two cash payments, Mark guessed it was much more of the latter. But by that time he was hooked.

He was set up in an apartment with his own equipment, and he only need ask to get whatever he needed. 'Carte blanche, within reason,' was what the intense Mr. Draper had said. Though they remained in frequent contact, Mark had never set eyes on the man in person again. It was a different one, a big-bellied slob of a man named Wilson who was turning out to be his caretaker. Wilson had walked in one day and handed him an envelope filled with three thousand cash. 'Be careful with that,' Wilson said. 'You're a contract worker. You keep your mouth shut and you can keep it all, tax free. You start yakking to your friends, or whoever, and we're going to have to let you go. Understand?'

Mark found this *let you go* remark unsettling, meant to be taken as a threat, but he didn't push it. He understood the game, or at least thought he did. With the help of leads provided by his employer, he hacked his way into a company and made a general nuisance of himself. With the tricks he already knew, the years he'd spent programming on his own, and the variety of interesting tools and information he received from Mr. Draper, Mark was good at it. Very good. Someone – Mark guessed it was Mr. Draper – then went to the company and offered the information in exchange for a price. Loosely, if he didn't think about it too much, Mark agreed that these were valuable lessons a company should be willing to pay for. The mechanics of working that end were fortunately not his domain. He got to be a tech, and that's what he had always wanted.

Mark set his watch on the table and dialed into the Simtec network at 7:41 P.M. He gave himself nineteen minutes to work. The modem spat out a connect tone into the nearly empty room, and he flipped through a pad of paper by the computer. He picked one from a list of other log-in names: Grandpa. Grandpa had administrative access to the E-mail queues. That's what Mark was after – reports of damage, correspondence about the state of the network, password changes, countermeasures.

He dug under a pile of manuals on the desk and found a piece of paper where he kept important names and keywords. Diane Hughes, CEO, the list said. He had to get at her messages sideways, by jumping into a mail utility that allowed for compacting and archiving. One option was to copy messages to a single file and then save it off. This file could be cracked and read off-line. He grabbed the mail queue for DHughes,

JSeidler, BShepard, JWillis, and KRodriguez. He'd discovered the last two on his own by parsing through hundreds and hundreds of messages. Willis and Rodriguez had to be techs or network admins of some kind. They had both been deluged with password requests, and, waiting in their queues, they normally had revealing cries for help. The J in JWillis turned out to be Janet, and Mark thought it interesting to be reading somebody's mail who had the same last name as he did. They could be fifth cousins or something. You never knew. But if they were related, his cousin had sold out for the cushy corporate life and she deserved what she got.

Mark used sixteen minutes and bounced out of the modem connection with three minutes to spare. He noted the time on his pad of paper, while an automatic line detector in the ceiling of Simtec 4 clicked in and powered down the modem. Too easy. He broke into the composite mail file and began picking through control codes to get at the text of the messages themselves. He ran a word search on the name Hughes, scanning her messages and discarding the garbage quickly.

From: JSeidler
Subj: Status

I'm afraid the deal is headed south. I now have two out and more unsigned. They're nervous. More so than I think you realized. In an effort to keep people in, I'm saying this is tentative and we're still in the firming-up stage. Otherwise, it would be all over right now. Hope you're having better luck.

Now what was that all about? Seidler was another of the bigwigs, Mark knew that. At first he thought that *the deal* might refer to the payoff for security information, and Mark would have loved to find out how much Simtec was being asked to pay. He suspected he wasn't being told the truth, and even though he'd be happy to get his fifteen thousand, he was curious what his work was actually going to net.

What was this about two out and more unsigned? In the

context of a payment, it didn't make sense. He tried to decide if it was important enough to pull out and pass along. That would depend on whatever else he found.

From: MSpakovsky
Subj: Press Conf

The press conference went reasonably well. The rumor mill has generated tales of imminent collapse, but I believe we were able to dissuade the media from believing we are at death's door. At least one person had been faxed details of our internal disruption, but we attempted to minimize these reports as misinformation and hyperbole. We got one red herring about Simtec canceling contracts, and we dealt with it effectively.

Nevertheless, there is plenty of fodder for sensationalism of all sorts. We will make every effort to keep that kind of story-mongering in check, but it would not surprise me if we see unflattering reports in at least some outlets. We should continue to react with calmness, or even feigned surprise, to reports of internal disruptions.

Some of the claims are truly outrageous, while others are speculative, yet closer to the mark. Karen Williams has advised that, in failing to be forthcoming, she believes that we increase the risk of a lawsuit. If the whole affair can only be wrapped up quickly, we are on much more solid ground in that regard. The longer it drags on, the more shareholder losses, and the more complicit we appear.

Jackpot! thought Mark. This message was overflowing with signs of trouble and, on Simtec's part, set a tone of cover-up and deceit. He especially liked the part about acting with *feigned surprise.* Mark leaned back in his seat, a cheap, swivel chair still sporting a fifty-nine-dollar price tag. He glanced at the apartment with its dingy lighting and spare, functional furnishings. A fan in the corner arced endlessly from side to side. What a feeling of power and accomplishment that message gave him! He was winding a wheel one cog at a time at his little terminal. But, clearly, he could set even the largest of bodies in motion.

The boss – which was how Mark thought of the man whom he had met that first day – would be happy. Mark could not even picture Mr. Draper anymore, except for a vague recollection of features and his stern, unforgiving aura. Mark had been afraid of the man, sensing even then that this was the kind of man who would always get what he wanted. You instinctively knew that, but it was another thing to see it happen.

He finished with Hughes and started the Shepard queue. Perhaps he would find a message to clarify what Seidler had written earlier, about the deal heading south. His finger lifted from the arrow down key and froze in midair.

From: WSDunn
Subj: Passwords

We will be using a new random password generator to assign all passwords. No one, including administrators, should be allowed to make up their own passwords.

I have attached a copy of the generator for your convenience in a self-extracting file. There's also a readme file with more information, but it's fairly self-explanatory. Let me know if you have any questions.

Mark stifled a smile. This was W. S. Dunn's work, and Mark was interested to see how the generator worked. Did you feed in something on the front end, like your name, or social security number? If so, and he could get at the algorithm, then he could generate every password on the net.

16

At 7:49 P.M. on server Mailman, Security Associates observed access into the area where E-mail messages were stored. By the time they caught it, the user named Grandpa had been on-line for eight minutes, and Bill Dunn Jr. was right there in the war room waiting. He sat down at a terminal and started tracking Grandpa immediately. The user had administrative access, and it was possible that he was doing valid maintenance. Bill snapped his fingers and said, 'Hey, hey, hey now,' his voice escalating in volume and intensity. Several other Security Associates employees had rallied to assist, and one flipped through a fresh printout summarizing the work reports and schedules of authorized Simtec administrators.

'Grandpa . . . Grandpa . . . there it is. Craig Whalen is the guy's name. He can go into the mail utilities,' the woman said, standing to Bill's right. 'But this late on a Friday night? I don't think so.'

At 7:51, radios crackled and W. S. Dunn was advised of the probable trespass.

'What's he doing?' Will Dunn barked back at them.

'He's in the mail files. Could be reading, deleting, copying. He's supposed to be a mail admin named Craig Whalen,' Bill said. His hands were on the keyboard and the woman next to him held the radio. Bill bounced back out to another screen. 'Yeah. He's writing a file.'

'Let him run then. Anyone try to call and check with Whalen?'

'We're doing it,' Bill said. He flicked a glance over his shoulder. An employee with a phone to his ear shook his head. 'No answer. Whalen's not home.'

'Are other users connected to that server?'

'Three, at the moment.'

'Beep them that the server's going down and knock 'em all off. Set the sniffer to grab everything coming out of that machine. Our boy should be an easy target.'

A packet sniffer is a tool that allows its operator to listen to traffic over the network. It can listen to everything that's going on, which at Simtec amounts to a conversation of thousands, or it can filter packet addresses and be as selective as the operator needs, following one specific conversation between two machines. In this case, Will Dunn was interested only in the conversation between user Grandpa and the file server named Mailman.

They didn't know where Grandpa was. Yet. But they did know the address and physical location of Mailman, so they set the sniffer to record any conversation that was occurring with Mailman, and that way they were sure to find Grandpa.

The room was filled with the heightened energy surrounding a live assault. Dunn's employees pointed the sniffer at file server Mailman, and as Bill Dunn rocketed across the room to see the progress, they were already grabbing packets.

'Ha!' Bill said. He snatched up a pad of paper and scribbled down a live hardware address right off of the screen: 0000C0-02361C. 'Ha!' he said again, for emphasis. This was too damn much fun. The stupid bastard. They had him cold. It was 7:55.

Grandpa stayed on-line for two more minutes and then logged out of Mailman.

'Look around,' Bill said. 'Where's he going? Change the sniffer to follow his address.'

The Security Associates employees traced through file servers all across Simtec, but Grandpa hadn't gone anywhere else. In fact, Bill watched with disappointment as 0000C0-02361C dropped out of sight altogether.

W. S. Dunn rounded the corner. 'Okay, what's he doing?'

'He's gone,' Bill said. 'Dropped out. But we got an address.'

Dunn crossed the room in four steps. 'Bastard turned off his machine. That's the address?'

Bill nodded.

'And he's not the real admin?'

'The account belongs to Craig Whalen and no one answers his phone.'

'Call the security desk. See if Whalen signed out for the day.' Dunn took the pad of paper with the Ethernet address and stared at it. 'That's Standard Microsystems. That's an SMC Ethernet card we're looking at. We may have to personally go to every damn machine, but we need to find that card. Let's go. Bill, you run with it. I'm going to call Barry.'

Bill started firing commands. Some employees didn't carry radios, so he set up a team leader to go out and organize each building. All Security Associates employees were to stop what they were doing and start checking machines. They were to work in pairs, at least two pairs to a building. 'Don't piss anybody off,' Bill said as an afterthought. 'You're just checking Ethernet addresses, all right? Somebody doesn't like it, call in and get one of us.'

Dunn called Barry and Barry called Jim and they all met in the hallway of Simtec 3. Dunn was still carrying the paper where his son had scrawled the address.

'We were watching the guy go into the mail,' Dunn said. 'We caught him with the sniffer and got his address. He logged out right after that and apparently turned his machine off. He dropped out of the network.'

Dunn searched their faces to see if they understood the distinction. 'Just because you log out, doesn't mean you drop out of the sniffer. That means the guy turned off his machine. Maybe he was suspicious, or maybe he was all done. We don't know. We do know this much: Craig Whalen's not even here. He signed out of building seven at five-thirty-three. We just called his house and spoke to him. I strongly suspect that whoever was using that account is the guy we're after, and I took the liberty of beginning to check machines and addresses. All my people are conducting a room-to-room search. We're not going to accuse anybody of anything, we're just looking. Sound good?'

Barry nodded. It sounded great. A breakthrough.

Dunn poked the address with his finger. 'Most likely, it's an Ethernet card. The 0000C0 is the manufacturer code for SMC. Their token ring cards may use the same addressing scheme. Damn! It could also be a PCMCIA card for a laptop. I suggest you have security watch all the doors and not let anyone out of here with a laptop. Someone comes to the door with one, they take a name and we go check it out.'

Barry was nodding.

'Yeah,' Jim said. He scratched at one cheek. 'I agree. Let's do it.'

Mark spent several minutes jockeying with the attachment file from W. S. Dunn before he got what appeared to be a usable exe file. Gen.exe, it was called. He was working at the DOS prompt, so he typed GEN and leaned back in his chair to watch the file unpack.

Expanding file . . . the screen said, and the dots kept moving across in a line to the right. About thirty seconds later, he had several rows of dots, and he began to think that the operation was taking way too long. He must have slightly botched the version. He looked dubiously at the hard drive, which was still working away, but was no doubt stuck on some irregularity in the data. Could he abort out of the extraction, or would he have to reboot?

He tried Control-C, Control-Z, Control-Y, Control-Break, and Esc, all to no avail. Then the dots stopped and the screen said, Presto. Like Magic!

What was that all about? Presto? He'd never seen that message before. Surely the file had not taken that long to extract. Maybe there was some kind of sophisticated encoding built in to the process to ensure that the file hadn't been tampered with. Hard to say what a bunch of corporate programmers and a high-profile security team were going to come up with. He was anxious to inspect their work.

He typed DIR but then noticed that he was not back at the C:\> prompt. He hit return. Return again. Nothing. The computer was completely hung. Damn. He reached around and flipped the power switch momentarily off, then back on. The machine went through its memory check, but hung again when it should have entered its boot sequence.

Christ, why wasn't his hard drive being recognized? He tried the whole thing again, this time leaving the power off for a long three count. 'Dammit!' he said aloud, pushing back from the desk. He went over to the corner and knelt down by a cardboard box. Inside were a number of disks, and Mark fished through them until he found the one that said BOOT. He went back and slapped it in the machine, closing the drive door with a vicious twist.

The computer started this time and came up to the A:\> prompt. The way one might test out one's limbs after an auto accident – gingerly, and with newfound affection – Mark slowly and deliberately typed out the keys: capital C, colon. His finger hesitated and then lightly pressed down on the return key. The drive mechanism engaged and, for a moment, Mark was hopeful.

Drive not ready, the screen said, as if the C: drive was completely unreadable. Mark slumped back in his chair. His heart was pounding and he needed to think. His eyes fell on the modem, and he began to have an idea. It was an idea that he didn't like, which involved programmers who were more clever than he had given them credit. His idea revolved around a password generator that didn't generate passwords at all. In reality, who would use a password generator? Wasn't the whole idea behind passwords to allow a person to invent his own, something that he, and only he, would remember?

Maybe the so-called password generator did nothing of the kind, and instead performed a destructive function against those who were foolish enough to invoke it. Mark suddenly picked up the modem, seizing it between his hands and yanking upward against its cable. He then slammed it back down onto the desk.

'Sonofabitch!' he cried out in the empty apartment. He scratched furiously at some unseen itch on his right shoulder. Password generator. Oh, yes, he realized, looking down at the plastic box in front of him. Its red LED stared back at him like a bloodied eye. Oh, yes. He was now certain what had happened.

The 21,312 employees at Simtec used somewhere in the neighborhood of fifteen thousand different personal computers. No one had ever made an exact count, and they weren't even all Simtecs. There were also machines from Apple, Silicon Graphics, Sun, Digital Equipment, and even the odd machine from IBM.

Nonetheless, the Security Associates teams, along with the Simtec employees rounded up by Barry Shepard and Jim Seidler, were trying to check every single one of them. Small teams of two to four people would disperse into an office, booting computers as they went. Then they made a second pass, scanning for network drivers, popping in floppy disks full of diagnostics when they had to. One quick look for the needle in the haystack, a network interface card with the address 0000C0-02361C, and on to the next one. Simple.

Until one employee happened to notice that the desktop computer in front of him had two network cards, and only one of them was active. He radioed Will Dunn directly. Dunn was in the thick of things in Simtec 3, brandishing his screwdriver like a baton.

'Dunn here.'

'I've got two cards here in a JStar desktop model. We could easily skate right by this.'

'How do you mean?'

'One card isn't active because they switched over to a second card. We'd miss it.'

Dunn stopped still in the middle of the bedlam around him. He was standing in a maze of cubicles on the second floor, and he stared across the tops of the dividers.

'Hold it,' he barked into the radio. 'All my team leaders need to stop and listen to this. You need to check each machine for multiple network cards. If they've got cards stacked up in there, open the box on the computer and do a visual check. Have someone go back and verify the ones you've already done.'

The searchers backtracked. They dug in. The hunt would continue for two long and ultimately unsuccessful hours. Many Simtec employees had left long ago and didn't witness any of it. Others watched with curiosity the clearly frantic procedure that was being called a mandatory equipment inspection. The Simtec security officers would observe three people try to leave campus with laptops, but all three would check out.

At 10:15 P.M., Barry Shepard met up with Dunn in the

third-floor hallway of TechDirect. Barry had just sent Diane an E-mail message detailing the latest events.

'Barry,' Dunn gave a clipped greeting. His eyes were expressionless.

'I'm still sending out E-mail,' Barry said. 'We need to have one of your people watching that no one goes into the mail directories. Let's deny access to any mail admins, and no one else gets in there for any reason whatsoever.'

'Good.'

Barry made a sweeping gesture to indicate what he would later think of as *the search.* 'Now what about all this?'

'Can't find the machine. I'm betting it's a laptop, and it's now hidden.'

'All right, so we're not likely to find it. At least we've got the address. They can't touch us again that way.'

'Sure they can. They slap in a new card with a different address.'

'Ah,' Barry said. How stupid. An Ethernet card was a disposable item. Knowing that a certain address had been used in the past provided little protection. 'How about filtering addresses? It's exactly what you were doing here in TechDirect by locking down machines with a location ID.'

'On a companywide scale, filtering won't work. You'd have to build, in essence, a hundred different internal firewalls. You'd have different rules for each and every server. You've got multiple protocols, widely varying sets of users – it's just impossible. What you'd wind up with is a nightmare the likes of which you can't imagine.'

Barry allowed that to sink in. *A nightmare the likes of which you can't imagine.* It was exactly what he had now.

Mark dreaded making the call, but he knew it had to be done. The boss had to be informed.

Dupree answered on the second ring.

'Hello. It's Mark. I had a little problem when I was on-line not long ago.'

'They saw you?'

'Not that I know of. All I did was grab E-mail. I was on and off in sixteen minutes.'

'So what is it?'

'I downloaded a mail message with an attachment. The attachment was supposed to be a password generator, but when I tried to get at it, I'm afraid it corrupted the hard drive on my computer.'

'You're *afraid* it did, or you know it did?'

'I know I can't get to my hard drive, and I think it was a deliberate trap. They put the mail message out there hoping I would download it. I shouldn't have trusted it. It was a mistake.'

Dupree closed his eyes. This was no time to get knocked out of commission. Friday night, and not only was Simtec refusing to pay, they were giving him a slap in the face.

'Tell me about this mail message,' Dupree said softly.

'It was a message to Barry Shepard. I copied all his mail to scan for anything interesting. They were talking about how no one should make up their own passwords. Everyone was supposed to use this new password generator.' Mark paused. 'The message was from W. S. Dunn.'

'Ahhh . . .' It was a death gasp. As though James Dupree had been run through with a sword. He could sense the doors being slammed closed and locked all over Simtec. It was the only time James Dupree had ever lost, and here he was, back in Denver, with Dunn sticking it to him all over again.

Dupree's head tilted back, eyes closed in terrible calculation. He would have to respond immediately.

'Do what you need to do to get back up and running,' he said in a flat voice, his thoughts elsewhere, charging ahead. 'I'll call you soon to discuss the next step.'

He hung up the phone on Mark Willis and, in his mind, he severed a second connection as well. How odd it now seemed, that first day his contact had surfaced with offers of information. It was the only time such a thing had ever happened, such a sure, sweet deal. Dupree got a down payment up front in order to conduct his attack, and he also received a raft of information. More resources than he could ever have mustered on his own. The arrangement was simple: if Dupree got Simtec to pay, he kept the money.

Seemingly, all he had to do was step up and do the work. Then he'd collect his much larger bounty and move on. A plum, ripe, and hanging on a low branch, or so it had appeared. Only now, the unthinkable had happened: the plum was drawing higher, receding from his grasp, and his perch grew wobbly. Dupree was forming a suspicion about this – that it was the outcome his contact had expected all along.

If this was the case – if their goals did not, in fact, coincide – then he was simply being held on a tether. He ground his hands together fiercely. He would not be kept on a leash, and he did not need someone to hand him information. Not anymore. Instead, he must be free to react decisively. Angrily. Quick, ruthless steps must be taken.

Certainly, there was a cost. No further information would be forthcoming. But that no longer mattered. Dupree stood and began pacing the floor. What it all came down to was the same advice given to the most lowly employee in search of job security: *Make yourself indispensable.* When what you knew was important enough, valuable enough, that was when you became truly independent.

He would be unrelenting, as Simtec rallied against his assault, and he would force an escalation. Should his contact attempt to retaliate, he would have to be all the more cautious. This introduced an element of risk for which Dupree had long prepared. He had been so tirelessly careful – never using his real name, never even reusing the same false names, as he signed up phones, cars, and all his accounts – that he was sure no single item would ever be linked to any other item. Truly, none of it could ever be linked together at all.

Dupree pivoted on one heel, marching with growing conviction. If he could not be tracked, he could not possibly be caught.

17

It was 10:43 when Barry made the final turn toward his house. Even though the entrance gate was open, and security knew his Jeep, he pulled up at the guardhouse and stopped.

The guard had a small portable television and was watching a baseball game.

'Something I can do for you, Mr. Shepard?' the guard said, leaning out of the sliding-glass door.

'I just wanted to reiterate that I don't want any visitors coming to our house. No repairmen, no deliveries, nobody at all. Not unless you call and check with us. Okay?'

'No problem,' the guard said. He cocked his head. 'Something going on I ought to know about?'

'Not really. We've had some strange things happening at work, and I want to make sure they stay at work.'

The guard nodded knowingly, as if he heard this sort of thing all the time. 'No problem,' he said again.

Barry waved and drove on through. Probably figures I'm a paranoid fool, Barry thought. Somebody hid Shepard's pencils at the office and now he's convinced they're all out to get him.

He pulled into the driveway and the garage floodlight flicked on. He'd been toying with the idea of calling Chris Jacobs and still intended to squeeze in a call before 11:00. He'd make it a friendly call to check in and keep Chris informed, but perhaps also a chance to pump Chris for information.

Claudia was in the kitchen reading. 'Hi there,' she said. 'You look tired.'

He could hear the television in the living room, so he didn't have to ask where Caroline was. He put his suit coat over a chair. A casserole half full of meat loaf stood on the counter, and there were mashed potatoes in a saucepan on the stovetop. He got out a plate and served up a double portion, then stuck it in the microwave. 'What a day,' he said. 'How about you?'

'No court, so I had it easy. We're replanning our strategy and we're not going to use the tapes at all. I left the office early and came home. The alarm guys were still here and they gave me a tour. You ought to see all the gear up in the attic.'

'Okay,' Barry said, distracted. 'Damn.'

'What?'

'I forgot something at the office.' He shook his head. 'I'm supposed to trace out some computer wiring tomorrow. I wanted to look over the diagrams.'

The microwave beeped and he collected his plate.

'I saw the news report,' Claudia said. 'It was pretty much a whitewash, but I've been getting needled all day for behind-the-scene stories.'

'I hope you're not giving out details. We've got enough leaks without me being part of the problem.'

Claudia made a zipping motion across her lips.

Barry sat. He had been tense the entire day, and only now did he relax slightly. 'We may have lost Chris Jacobs today. You've met Chris. He's director of security and internal affairs.'

Claudia closed the *Time* magazine and frowned. 'What do you mean *lost*?'

'Chris has always been hot-blooded, and he's been taking this hard. Rightly or wrongly, he holds himself responsible, and today he snapped. He fired a gun up into the ceiling.'

'He had a gun in the office?'

'He must have. It was the first I knew of it, but he's the director of security. The fact that he had a gun, or had access to one, is not in itself that surprising.'

'What was he doing with it?'

'You mean why did he shoot the ceiling? I think because he decided that was a better target than his own head.'

Claudia slapped the magazine down on the table. 'You people are self-destructing over there. An employee can't just fire a gun into the ceiling. You bet you lost Chris Jacobs.'

It was curious to see his wife react so angrily when to Barry the event had become no more important than any one of a series: erased file servers, empty backup tapes, the emergency press conference, or even W. S. Dunn shorting Simtec stock. To top it off had been their wild, ill-fated search for the suspect computer. For long stretches of the day, Barry had forgotten all about Chris Jacobs.

'Claudia,' he said. 'I think leaving Simtec was exactly what Chris had in mind. He told me straight-up that he was through.'

She stared at Barry and appeared to realize that this was not the paramount matter of the day. 'Then I guess you have your sacrificial lamb,' she said. 'Though they normally don't volunteer for it. You remember right when I joined Milford? We were caught up in that scandal with Danbury's staff in Austin. That bit of infamy forced out two partners.'

'I remember reading about it on the front page, thinking, I can't believe this is where my wife is going to work.'

'Well, after they left, most of the furor subsided. Maybe Chris is doing the same thing for Simtec. Is he that close to Diane? Would he be willing to take a fall?'

'Chris is just trying to do a good job. He thinks he screwed up and he's accepting responsibility. I don't know whether I agree with that or not.' Barry remembered the erased backup tapes. 'There are certainly some areas that weren't being handled properly.'

She paused. 'They're not coming after you, are they?'

Barry made a sound like a snort. 'Who is *they*? All day long I was the only one running the place. If that hurts anybody, it's not me.'

'Where's Diane?'

'She's off wheeling and dealing. I don't want to go into all of it, but things are so ugly at the company – I'm talking about a state of chaos – and there she is MIA. If it all got out, she'd have a lot of explaining to do, herself. I don't think he wanted to say it, but Jim was upset. He went almost so far to say she was being negligent.'

'What do you think?'

'After I spoke to Jim I gave it some thought. It's not as

though we can't contact Diane. I talked to her on the phone. She reviewed a press statement by fax. We send E-mail. As a practical matter, what it does is introduce a delay into everything you do. Both Jim and Diane were gone today, and I have no doubt plenty of things got put off. People who are bringing something to Jim may not feel comfortable bringing it to me, or they may not be able to find me. So they decide to wait. Other decisions you'd expect to take care of on the spot don't get made. When you've got key people out-of-pocket, it's a hindrance. Whether it's negligent is not for me to say.'

'That kind of determination would be up to the board.'

'And the board is going to hear about this. They've already talked to Diane and she soft-pedaled. She tries to play it cool and keep as much as possible under wraps. But the board will be on her again after today. They'll be putting the pieces together and asking questions.'

'What does your hired gun, Security Associates, have to say for itself?'

'They're not perfect, but they're doing more than we could have, and they're doing it faster. For the most part I've been impressed.' Barry got up from the table and carried his plate to the sink. He turned around and said, 'Did you know Mike Spakovsky was a homosexual?'

Claudia blinked. 'I'd never thought about it. Why do you ask?'

It was at this moment that Caroline chose to take a break from television and come into the kitchen for a snack. Most of Caroline's TV time was spent with videos, but she was also allowed unsupervised viewing of the local PBS station.

'Hi, Dad,' she said. 'I'm watching a show on channel eight. You said it was good to watch channel eight, but this show is *weird.*'

'I said that in general I think their programs are better, but that doesn't mean every single show is good. You've still got to be choosy.'

'Hmmm,' she said, digging around in the refrigerator.

'How was school?'

She opened the other door and pulled out a frozen pop. 'Vomit,' she said.

'So . . . it was a good day?'

'No! They're rebuilding the roof and it smells awful. I thought I was going to be sick.'

'I see.' Barry glanced at his wife, who was watching with a bemused expression. She had probably already gotten the vomit story. 'Maybe they'll have it done by Monday.'

'I hope so,' Caroline said. She pointed toward the living room. 'I gotta get back to my show. It's weird but it's good. People are living in a space colony and they're fighting an alien.'

'That doesn't sound like PBS. Are you sure you've got the right channel?'

'Yes,' Caroline said over her shoulder. 'And it's weird. I like it.'

'You better get finished up,' he called after her. 'It's *way* past your bedtime.'

Claudia allowed a few seconds to pass and said, 'She was acting moody earlier. I said it was okay if she stayed up until you got home.'

'Was that moody?' Barry jutted a thumb toward the living room. 'She seemed fine.'

'Maybe that's because you're home now. I don't know. What's this business about Mike Spakovsky?'

'Dunn pointed out that Mike is a homosexual, and that someone could be using that to blackmail him. That was the idea, in essence.'

Claudia scowled. 'You better not start spreading that one, or you're going to wind up in court. Not unless you have actual evidence to back it up.'

'I'm not saying I believe it. I was just curious.'

'Watch out who you're curious with, saying crap like that. He's saying that all homosexuals are a security risk, and that it's easier to bring pressure to bear upon them than it is you or me, which is a highly dubious statement. Unless he's got something to back it up, it sounds to me like a load of garbage.'

'Dunn's got a theory to implicate almost everyone at the

company in one way or another,' Barry said defensively. He felt unduly chastised.

'Well, he better keep it to himself until he gets proof. He's going to land you in a world of trouble.'

'He also pointed out that Jim Seidler is a drunk, which I already knew, and that Diane might be orchestrating the whole deal in order to solidify her position.'

'I'm not sure I follow.'

'His sources tell him that Diane is not well liked in certain parts of the company. To some extent that's true, although I think she's won quite a few converts. The idea is that by fabricating an attack from the outside, she could use the turmoil as cover to do whatever she wants. I was thinking about that in the car and it's true. We're in a crisis and, right now, she could hire, fire, reorganize whole departments – whatever she wants – and we'd probably let her do it. Her actions wouldn't get nearly as much scrutiny as they would under normal conditions.'

Claudia was wearing a pensive expression. She cocked her head to one side and said, 'That's pretty clever,' she said. 'Far-fetched, but clever.'

'I don't buy it. Number one, she's not making any changes. If she had her own agenda, the orders would be flying already. Number two, I've spoken to this guy on the phone myself. He's dead serious about getting his money or taking Simtec down with him.' Barry pictured the Cyrano's parking lot, when he had run over to the next street to check the van. The guy had been toying with him and enjoying it. 'Call it intuition,' Barry said. 'This doesn't feel like part of a script written by Diane.'

'Sounds to me like Security Associates is throwing out a bunch of hooks and waiting to see what bites.'

'Absolutely. Dunn so much as told me they'd traced back through EDS and even my grocery store days. They hadn't found anything, but I'm still on the list. He told me that, too. What's amazing to me is the speed with which they get their information.'

'That's their job,' Claudia said. 'And sixty thousand a day isn't peanuts. At Milford we sometimes use a man named

Richard Green. He's a PI and he gets a thousand a day. You wouldn't believe the stuff he can come up with. You give him a day and he can read back your financial history, credit balances, loans outstanding. He'll also tell you where you buy your gas and what kind of toilet paper you use. I guess it's not illegal, in the sense that a mortgage company can find out most of the same histories, but he must have strings he can pull in all the right places.'

Barry's view of the pristine world of a large legal partnership had been under constant revision ever since his wife had taken the job. 'I didn't know you used people like that,' he said thoughtfully.

She shrugged. 'He's a lawyer actually. He used to be called DeeWee, for all the DWI cases he handled. He was always schlepping around the court building, making two hundred-fifty bucks a pop to go in and conference your case with the DA. He was somehow in with the police, because he had clients lined up out the door. He was making a killing, but I imagine the clients finally got to him and he decided to go the PI route.'

Barry looked skeptical.

'He's a nice guy. Sharp and good at what he does. Sometimes we need that kind of information and, frankly, I don't know where we'd get it without him. Our lawyers certainly wouldn't know where to start.'

Barry had shifted in his chair and he smoothed one trouser leg over the top of his thigh. He then propped his chin on one hand and stared at the kitchen cabinets. Thirty seconds later he turned back to his wife. 'This guy . . . Richard Green,' he said. 'Do you have his number?'

Barry walked through the living room, heading toward his study. He saw that Caroline's program was ending and said, 'It's time for you to hit the bed.' He leaned over and gave her a goodnight kiss. Was it his imagination, or did she grab him around the neck and squeeze a little bit tighter than normal?

'Sleep tight,' he said, and gave her another kiss. Then he went into his study, closed the door, and called Chris Jacobs.

Chris was awake and sounded perfectly sober.

'Sorry to call so late,' Barry said. 'I just got in.'

'Not to worry. We went out for pizza, and then we rented *Apollo 13.* Everything is quite all right. I'll tell you, Barry, there's something about knowing exactly where you stand. It's liberating.'

Barry fidgeted with a rubber band. 'That's good to hear. I wanted to at least check in with you. If you've got five minutes, I'll toss some questions out on the table, too.'

'Absolutely.'

'Did you know Jim and Diane were going out of town today? I'm wondering what's going on there. Yesterday was the first I heard about it.'

'Same here, I believe. Maybe they told me Wednesday.'

'What do you think about both of them going?'

'Probably foolish. But I think they got caught up and started posturing. The funny thing about it is, if Jim stays behind to mind the fort, and the fort burns down, Jim loses. On the other hand, if he saves the fort while Diane's off signing contracts, then he looks like the hero. I imagine that's risky for Diane.'

'We had a meeting this morning,' Barry said. 'I got the distinct impression that Jim wanted to stay behind but Diane wasn't about to let him.'

'Probably didn't want to let him mind the fort. She'll allow you to do it because you're not as threatening.'

'Well, Jim's back now, and he says the whole trip was premature. They're still figuring out the groundwork.'

'I don't know much about it. You can always ask Diane point-blank, Why wasn't this put off?'

'That's not my place, but the board may ask her that exact question. The board may also want to know why, when a story hits the news, they don't know the half of it.'

'No doubt.' Chris's tone made it clear that he no longer cared about the board.

'I also wanted to give you an update on Security Associates. I believe we came very close to a breakthrough tonight. Dunn caught someone going into the mail files, and he got an Ethernet address with a sniffer. Between his people and our people, we turned the place upside down looking for that machine, but so far we didn't find it. Dunn thinks it was a laptop and the person stashed it away.'

'That sounds reasonable. What makes you so sure they were somewhere on campus?'

'We talked about that. It's the way they were logged in one minute, the next minute they dropped out and the machine disappeared. The person got finished, or thought he was being watched, and he hit the off switch on his computer. With a dial-up device, the Ethernet address is the address of the machine they're coming in through, or in some cases the actual modem. The person logs out off-site, back at their house, wherever, but we've still got this piece of equipment out there on the network at Simtec. We should be able to see it. We should have found it.'

Chris Jacobs didn't answer for some time. At last he said, 'Maybe.'

'How so?'

'Maybe you can see it on the network. Maybe you can't. I'm thinking about how you could engineer a modem. I remember reading about the Berferd case at AT&T. They actually cut the transmit wire on a machine so that it couldn't talk on the network.'

'Yeah, but if you cut the transmit wire, then when you dial in you're screwed, too. You can't talk on the network either.'

Chris thought for a moment. 'That's true. Scratch that idea. I'm not doubting Dunn. Turning off the machine is the simplest, most logical explanation for it to disappear off the network. Keep it simple. Most of the time that's the right way to go. I'm only saying there are other possibilities.'

Weren't there always, Barry thought. *And too goddamned many.*

Much more by chance than by design, late on the night of Friday, July 22, W. S. Dunn found himself kissing Karen Williams on the neck.

The two of them had chosen to pack up and leave Simtec at the same time, from two different directions, and Dunn was walking across the parking lot with his head down, thinking about where some sonofabitch might have hidden a laptop in any one of a dozen buildings chock-full of filing cabinets, trash bins, closets, and crawl spaces. The ease with which you could hide a portable computer was mind-boggling. If it was a laptop – and Dunn was convinced that it was – neither Shepard or Seidler nor even Security Associates would find it in a million years.

Karen had to get right in his path before he looked up, and when she asked what had him in such a trance, that was exactly what he told her. 'There are too many damn places to hide a laptop in these buildings. I'm probably going to think about it all night long.' He then went into a diatribe about all the places they *had* checked, and how they had wasted a good two hundred man-hours doing it. Finally, he turned to Karen and demanded where she, under the circumstances, would hide a laptop and expect to get away with it.

'I'll tell you,' Karen said. 'But there's a local pub around the corner, and I'll feel a lot better doing the telling if I had a cold Corona in my hand.'

This proposal came as a complete surprise, and Dunn said the first thing that came to mind. He said, 'You don't strike me as the type who hangs out in pubs.'

'Well, you would be wrong,' Karen said. 'Because I'm a regular.'

And it was clear that she was. When they drove over to the place called McNally's, walked across the dirt parking lot, and pulled up at a couple of barstools, half the people in the place waved to Karen with familiarity and friendliness. This courtesy did not extend to her newfound acquaintance.

The surprises with Karen Williams did not stop there. After what became a series of Coronas and several games of fifty-cent pool – every one of which was won by Karen Williams – Dunn found himself at Karen's townhome, and he found himself getting all the signs.

Actually, he'd gotten some of the signs earlier, at dinner, but the thing he was learning about Karen was, she wasn't in the business of *allowing* or *permitting*. She was doing exactly what she wanted to do, and she had a way of letting you know that.

He kissed her on the lips, the throat, and she made a series of erotic sounds, goading him on. This went on for two minutes and might have become a wild scene indeed had Dunn not stopped still, suddenly realizing that the sounds had given way to silence and that Karen's neck had become stiff and intractable.

He pulled away and stared off over her shoulder, directly into a large piece of artwork. The piece was a collage of torn paper dominated by reds and oranges. Nice enough work, with an elaborate frame that had probably cost more than the art itself.

'What?' Karen said.

He was trying to think it all through. Get invited over. Get the big green go signal right there in the living room. Get the stop signal right before takeoff. It was another one of those unfathomable puzzles.

'What is it?' she prodded.

'It's this,' Dunn said. His eyes didn't leave the deep orange color into which he was sinking. 'There's nothing better to stop a bear cold in its tracks than lack of interest. Or even *perceived* lack of interest.'

Karen looked him over with a funny little smile. 'Is that what you are, a bear?'

And then she did something he hadn't had happen in a good many years. She reached around behind him, took one of his buttocks in her hand, and pulled him forcefully in toward her.

William Dunn found that he liked that very much.

Another hand – there seemed several to keep track of – moved up his back. He felt a set of nails rake over his neck and up into his hair. Dunn forgot all about the painting and leaned into the task at hand.

Karen's mouth came up alongside his ear and a soft, firm voice said, 'How about right here on the sofa?'

It sounded like a very good idea.

W. S. Dunn rolled over and scratched his chest. He couldn't see the clock, but he could hear its numbers flipping down into place every sixty seconds. He'd been hearing them for twenty or thirty minutes now, and he knew that, whatever time it happened to be, his night of sleep was over.

Nevertheless, he could feel the warmth of Karen Williams in the bed beside him, he could hear her quiet exhalations, and he thought about staying. It would be nice to wake up here in the morning, make coffee, and perhaps linger in bed during the early-morning hours. Perhaps they would make love again, not with the fire and intensity they had exhibited the night before, but with a slow, deliberate enjoyment of one another. An enjoyment that he had not found for some time.

He turned onto his side and put his arm across her body. Karen stirred and then settled without opening her eyes.

Several more numbers flipped on the clock. Dunn pushed the covers back and sat up on the edge of the bed.

'You're getting up?' Karen said, in a voice more asleep than awake. 'What time is it?'

'I have no idea. I was going to shower and go back into the office. I'm awake, and there's a lot that needs to be done.'

She rested a hand against his back. 'In the beginning, you know, I voted against you. But I was wrong. This is tearing the company apart and I'm glad you're here. We probably should have paid the money from day one.'

He reached over and smoothed the hair back out of her face. 'Five million is too much,' he said. 'And I'm going to nail them.' He leaned over and kissed her, and her arms came up and encircled his neck.

Karen pulled him back onto the bed toward her. Dunn could feel himself coming alive again, as one of her hands played down across his back. He could feel the nails, applying pressure in all the right places. His whole body was beginning to tingle, and the other hand ran up along his thigh. Perhaps the office was going to wait.

After fifteen minutes they lay together in a now-quiet tangle. Karen turned her neck toward the nightstand. 'It's four-thirty and I'm not getting up yet. You can shower and help yourself to the kitchen. The coffee's ready to go if you turn on the pot. I'll be in to work later. Stop by and see me.'

'Perhaps I'll have good news,' Dunn said. 'I've had people working straight through the night. You never know when you'll get a breakthrough.' He slid out of bed, went to the kitchen, and flipped on the coffee. Then he showered and left the town house by the back gate, walking around to the street where he had parked the truck.

He heard another car start, further up the street to his left, and Dunn thought of all those men and women, all over the city, who were leaving the homes of people they had spent the night with. It was its own subculture – that world of dating and searching and generally being in the fray for companionship.

The other early-morning traveler had swung the car out into the street and the headlights popped on as Dunn fished in his pocket for the car keys. Other side, he realized, and transferred a mug of coffee from one hand to the other. It was at that moment that he heard the roar of the engine behind him.

He turned his head and saw that the car was accelerating in his direction. It was out in the middle of the road and due to miss him by a good three feet. Still, they were going way too fast. Teenagers, he thought, and he was still a little too happy, and feeling a little too good about the world, to have his instincts sharpened the way they might have been. He pushed one hand into his pocket and glanced up again at the approaching headlights.

The vehicle was now only a car length away and Dunn watched in horror as the driver cut the wheel toward him. The headlights pinned him, and he had nowhere to go. Too far to make it to the front of the truck and too late to go back. He sprang sideways, up against the side of the pickup, even as the driver turned in more sharply. The other car's bumper grazed the bed of the pickup with a screech of metal and ricocheted forward, not even an inch between the two vehicles. In the fraction of a second that remained, Dunn tried to grab the roof of the pickup and haul himself up out of the way.

It wasn't enough. The bumper caught Dunn at thigh level, knocking him up into the air like a bowling pin. He yelled a shocked mixture of fear and anger and pain, and he dropped to the pavement with a broken leg and a shattered hip. Still quite conscious.

'Oh, Jesus,' Dunn said, pushing himself up onto his forearms. He tried to move his legs and got nothing. What had just happened? The numbness and shock made it difficult to understand. He looked down the street and saw that the car had slowed, its taillights red as it sat idling in the middle of the road.

'Motherfucker,' he panted. His breath came in ragged gasps. 'You did that on purpose, didn't you?' He lay forward onto his chest and reached for the set of keys that had flown out of his hand. If he could get the keys, and somehow get the door open, Dunn had an automatic under the driver's seat. Let this punk come back and see him, then.

He dragged himself forward, trying to block out the agony of his lower body. Get the keys, he told himself. Get the keys. Get the gun. In the periphery, he was aware that the car had begun to back up. Then the driver spun the wheel and swerved diagonally across the street. He was turning around.

Dunn was able to reach out and grab the keys and work his body back toward the truck. The pain in his side was so overwhelming that he was not thinking clearly. He pushed off with one arm, stretching up toward the door. He opened his fingers to grasp the handle and dropped the keys.

He kept his grip on the door handle, though, and swung forward, the weight of his upper body suspended from that one handhold. His eyes were half closed in the glare of the headlight and his other hand scrabbled along the ground after the set of keys. There wasn't time. Some part of his brain knew that. There would be no weapon pulled from beneath the seat. No real way to fight back at all.

Even now he could sense the car approaching. He could hear its engine, as his vision registered only a bright light growing brighter. He released his grip on the door handle and fell back to the pavement. The ground's impact was a dagger straight into Dunn's spine, and it came close to paralyzing him completely.

He flopped over sideways, going under the edge of the truck just as the car tires squealed past, twelve inches from his head.

This time the car kept going, but W. S. Dunn was through. His body lay there on the ground in a broken heap.

It would be twenty-eight minutes before another motorist would slow to examine the pile of garbage in the road. The driver would roll down his window and look out, only to realize that he was looking at a human arm. The driver would gag, stomp down on the gas pedal, and four blocks away call 911 on his mobile phone.

18

Barry Shepard was alone in his kitchen at 6:30 Saturday morning. The microwave hummed, warming a slab of yesterday's meat loaf, and he sat hunched over a coffee mug, staring blankly at the newspaper. He had no interest whatsoever.

A bell sounded and he glanced over toward the counter, then realized it wasn't the microwave at all but the telephone. He shuffled to the wall and picked up.

'Barry?' A woman's voice.

'Speaking.'

'This is Karen.' Hesitant. 'Bill got hit by a car early this morning outside my apartment. He's been rushed to the hospital.' Her voice disintegrated. 'He lay out in the street for almost an hour.'

It took Barry several seconds to realize that Karen meant Karen Williams. And Bill? He was having difficulty placing the name. Bill who? It hardly seemed an appropriate question to ask.

He searched through the names and faces with which he associated Karen Williams. The microwave went off beside him. Beep. Beep. He jabbed at the cancel button. 'Karen? This Bill . . .'

'Dunn,' she said. 'William Dunn.'

'Hit by a car?'

'Yes. The police are here right now.'

Barry smacked the countertop with his palm. 'I'll come over. I'm not dressed. Give me ten or fifteen minutes.'

'Thank you,' Karen said. Barry hung up and slumped against the kitchen wall. His hand was balled into a fist at his side, and he stared out the back window of the house. You woke up in the morning, mustering whatever hope and strength and optimism you could for the day ahead, and, just like that, it was all taken away.

He dressed quickly and casually and left the house carrying only the mobile phone. And the phone proved useful. After driving a few miles in the direction of Karen's town house, he realized he didn't remember exactly where she lived. He'd only been there once, to attend a birthday party for the number two man in legal.

He dialed information and got the number, then called Karen and got instructions. When he pulled up in front, the street was still blocked off and an HPD officer was diverting traffic down a side street.

Barry rolled down his window. 'Excuse me, Officer. I'm a friend of the man who was hit.' The cop signaled him through, and Barry parked on the opposite curb.

It was obvious where the accident had occurred. A dark stain had spread over the concrete, and the roadway was littered with paint chips and bits of plastic from a shattered taillight.

'Good morning,' Barry said, approaching a second officer who was scribbling notes on his clipboard.

'Help you?' the officer said, glancing back at his partner. Who had let this guy through?

'I believe a friend of mine was involved in this accident, a William Dunn.'

'That's him, I'm afraid. William S. Dunn. The lady inside call you?'

'Yes, she did. I haven't been in to see her yet, but I wanted to ask you what happened first.'

The cop gestured to the street. 'No skid marks. The person either didn't see him or didn't even try to stop. Probably drunk.' He had to look down and reference the clipboard. 'According to Ms. Williams, this must have been about four-thirty in the morning. She didn't hear a thing.'

Barry prodded a piece of plastic with the toe of his shoe.

'Ms. Williams says this was the first time he came over,' the officer said. 'They got here around eleven o'clock, and he left between four-thirty and five.' The officer waited for a reaction. His face was inscrutable.

'That sounds accurate. We've all been working late at Simtec. They must have come back here to blow off steam.'

'So, everyone's an employee of Simtec. Do you know William Dunn well?'

'Not very. He's worked for us the past few days.'

'Can I get your name, please? We may need to get in touch.'

Barry gave him the information mechanically. *If only Dunn had kept his pants on . . .* No, that kind of sentiment was wrong-headed. This could have happened anywhere, at any time.

'How bad is it?'

'Mr. Dunn was not conscious.' As a substitute for more information, the officer tapped his pen on the clipboard.

Barry contemplated the debris in the street.

'You'd do best to talk to the hospital, Mr. Shepard. Would you have any information about his family and how to contact them?'

'His son is also doing some work for us. I have no idea about the rest of his family.'

The officer took out a card and handed it to Barry. 'Would you ask the son to call us?'

Barry accepted the card and looked it over. He was supposed to walk in and hand this to Will Dunn's son? 'Okay,' Barry said, thinking exactly the opposite. The cop nodded and went back to his notes.

Barry turned around at the sidewalk. 'Do me a favor. You've got my number. If you find out anything else about the accident, would you give me a call?'

The officer gave him a curious look, but said he would.

Barry took the steps up the front door and rang the bell. He gave Karen a comforting hug, and they took a seat in the living room. Her town house was furnished with expensive, ultramodern furniture, much of which Barry had admired at the birthday party. At the moment, it all went unnoticed. 'The police say the driver didn't see him at all, didn't even try to stop,' he said. 'May well have been drunk.'

'The cops think everyone is drunk. They wanted to know had Will and I been drinking.'

The question had entered Barry's mind, too, but he didn't say so.

'I told them we had one margarita with dinner at six o'clock. We had a couple of beers after we left the office. It wasn't like he was wandering around out in the street drunk.'

'No. I wouldn't imagine he was.'

'A couple hours' sleep,' Karen said, 'and he was going back to the office. All he wanted to do was work on the computers. He'd say something and you could tell that's all he really cared about. It's not the money.'

Karen was half dressed for work in a blue skirt with a hastily thrown-on sweatshirt up top. Her hair was tangled and still damp. She smelled fruity, but she didn't look that way.

'What do you think, Barry? I can't help imagining this has something to do with Simtec. We worked late and happened to leave at the same time, so we went to McNally's. Then we came back here. Anybody could have followed us.'

Barry shifted uncomfortably. 'Let's not jump to conclusions. The police are calling it a hit-and-run accident and we don't have any evidence to the contrary.' He didn't know if he was saying what he truly believed or what he thought she wanted to hear.

'That's too coincidental. Here he comes to work for us, walks out in the street, and gets hit. It could make the difference between whether or not we pay.'

'I don't think so,' Barry said, but he did not elaborate. He didn't say how appealing the idea sounded – just pay and have it all over with.

'I don't want to sound cold,' he said, 'but I need you to wear your professional hat for a minute. I consider it far-fetched, but, if it turned out that this accident was related to Dunn's work for us – in other words, if it wasn't an accident at all – would Simtec be liable in any way? I hate to ask the question. I'm going to go meet with Jim and I'm sure the question of our own liability is going to come up.'

Karen gave him an icy look. 'I don't think Will Dunn is the type. You can tell that to Jim.' She pulled at the sleeve of her sweatshirt. 'We should have paid the money from the beginning.'

'I still think we made the right decision,' Barry said, a statement which he wasn't sure he believed one bit.

★

Still early, and the ice was almost empty. James Dupree turned sharply and began skating backwards. His turns were precise and quick and, this morning even more than usual, appeared to come easily.

How easily he had dueled with Simtec's hired gun and won. Who was this W. S. Dunn, anyway? A nobody. Dupree might have lost the first game, in Denver, when his forces had suffered one arrest and he'd had to pack up his operation, but in the end he had won the match. He had already been informed of the successful action at 6:00 A.M., and this did not so much make him happy as it made him confident. The law of the jungle prevailed, and Simtec had to be taught that if they were going to deliver a slap, they were going to get punched in the teeth. A company full of bean counters would never have the fortitude.

Dupree stopped by the railing of the ice rink and rested. He considered one of his favorite stories – Homer's *Iliad.* He had read it during high school, sitting in the library of his father's mansion. He rarely thought of that house anymore, but, when he did, he always thought of it as his father's house. Never his own childhood home. Not even his mother's. The book told the epic battle of the siege of Troy. The Trojans and the Argives. As one of their great warriors was slain in battle, the two sides had paused for an agreed-upon period of time. There was an element of decency and respect to the proceedings, so unlike modern warfare.

Yes, as a show of respect, he would let a few hours pass before reiterating his demands. Demands he was sure would now be met. For he had one further trump card to be played, and he gauged that now was the time to expose that card. When your opponent was down, reeling in the dirt from a particularly well-placed blow, when your opponent's neck was bared, it was usually enough to show the sword. Only when the opponent was obstinate – foolish, really – did you have to use it.

Caroline Elizabeth Shepard, age seven years two months, knew that something was wrong. On a normal Saturday, her mother or father would come into the bedroom and wake her up, talking about what they might do that day. The house would already smell like pancakes, or waffles, or some other wonderful thing that they never ate during the week. Downstairs her dad would be playing one of his jazz CDs, which Caroline liked, but which would have to be turned down once she'd eaten and wanted to get started on cartoons.

But this morning was nothing like that. She lay in bed for thirty minutes, waiting, until she realized no one was coming to wake her up. No music was drifting up the staircase, and there was no aroma of a special breakfast. When she went downstairs to look around, she found her mother sitting at the kitchen table, staring out the window into the backyard. She'd noticed Mom doing this the day before, too, but now it went straight to Caroline's heart.

Dad was gone again. She could tell by the stillness in the house. It seemed like he was never home anymore, and Caroline knew that the event she'd been looking forward to – practicing baseball in the backyard – wasn't going to happen. He'd forgotten. Or he'd left early on purpose – that was probably it.

'Good morning,' her mom said, seeing her come into the kitchen. 'I was just about to come up and get you.'

Sure you were. Caroline glanced toward the stove and the kitchen counters, but everything was bare. 'What would you like for breakfast? There's cereal, or I can whip up some eggs.'

Her mom didn't really mean it, about the eggs. 'Cereal's good,' Caroline said. She went over to the fridge and got out the carton of milk herself. Her mom came over to help with the box.

Caroline carried her bowl to the table, and she noticed how her mom had stayed standing by the sink, now looking out that window at the side yard, just as she'd been staring out back. It was as though there were a dog or something out there, and he'd run around the house. Except Caroline knew there wasn't any dog.

'Can I rollerblade today?' Caroline said.

The quick frown on her mother's face gave away the answer even before she said it. She should stay inside today, her mom explained. She could rollerblade on another day.

Caroline took a bite of cereal and it tasted like cold mush. Her mom and dad were upset. Dad had left, and now she wasn't going to be allowed outside. It was even worse than she'd expected, and Caroline knew exactly what the problem was. It was as plain as could be. *She* was the problem. She wasn't doing the right things in school. She wasn't any good, and her parents were mad about it.

The last few days at school, they'd been playing a game where the teacher would hold up a word. Everyone was supposed to say the word out loud and then write it down. For Caroline this wasn't a game at all. It was torture. The word flashed up and seemed to hang in the air for only a second before being yanked away. No time to tell what the word was. It looked like *talk,* but then it turned out to be something completely different, like *tick,* or even *cat.* Caroline had stopped saying the word out loud because too often she said the wrong thing. When she went to write the word down, several conflicting versions floated inside her head. She couldn't figure out where to begin.

She stirred her spoon in the cereal bowl. She was trying to be a good girl, she really was, but maybe she was a retard just like that boy had said. And now her parents knew it, too.

Barry checked his watch: 8:36. There wasn't time to go to the office and then make it back to the restaurant where he had agreed to meet the private investigator at nine.

He used the mobile phone to call Jim Seidler's office. Voice mail picked up after the second ring, and Barry left a message saying he'd be in late. Something had come up that they urgently needed to discuss. Nine-thirty and I'll be in your office, Barry said. This Richard Green had better be on time.

And he was. From the Jeep, Barry picked him out. Green was strolling across the parking lot, well dressed, even on Saturday, but something unmistakable about the look: mirrored sunglasses over a square, unsmiling jaw.

'Richard Green?' Barry said out the window. The man gave no sign of recognition but veered in Barry's direction.

'Mr. Shepard.'

'Yes. I'm afraid I'm going to have to skip breakfast, but if you'd like to get in the car we can probably go over the details in about five minutes.'

Green stepped around to the passenger door and climbed in. 'You have a lovely wife,' he said.

'Thank you,' Barry said. 'I also have an enormous problem.'

'Most people don't come to me unless they do.' Green smiled. He removed the sunglasses and slid them into his top pocket.

Barry unfolded a piece of paper and said, 'I made the list you requested.' On it, he had written the names Jim Seidler, Diane Hughes, Mike Spakovsky, William Dunn, as well as the names of several other Simtec VPs. Beside most of the names, he had written date of birth and Social Security number.

Barry scanned the list again and fished in the console for a pen. He drew a line through the name William Dunn. 'This man was struck by a car this morning in a hit-and-run accident,' he said. At the bottom of the list, he added the name Karen Williams.

'Hit-and-run accident?' Green said. His nose gave an inquisitive twitch. 'What exactly is this all about?'

Barry nodded. His mouth was dry. 'I suspect that somebody's peddling company information. The employee's name may or may not be on this list. I may be altogether incorrect, but I've got to start somewhere. I'd like you to look at anything you can, but especially finances. Any odd financial dealings. Large cash inflows or outflows. Problems. Anything that indicates one of these people might need, or has recently received, a large sum of money.'

'I'm sure some of these folks pull in quite a salary,' Green said, staring at the list. 'I recognize the names. Ten or twenty thousand won't even look like a blip going through these accounts.'

'If it's one of these, it'll be a lot more than ten thousand.'

'Fair enough.' Green folded the piece of paper and put it in with the sunglasses. 'Looks like several days' work. I like to get a retainer up front.'

Barry handed him a personal check made out for three thousand dollars. Claudia had told him about the retainer, and he was glad to have made the check out beforehand. The whole meeting made Barry uneasy, as if he were doing something illegal.

Green pointed at the phone between the seats. 'Why don't you give me your mobile number?'

Barry glanced at the phone. How could you even begin to explain such a thing?

'It's not mine,' Barry said. 'You've got my work number, or call me at home.'

Whenever Barry walked into Jim Seidler's office, he couldn't help but be impressed. Unlike his own working office, complete with stacks of paperwork and the obligatory file cabinets, Jim's office maintained an aura of regality. The carpets were a plush burgundy and the furnishings must have cost a fortune. Jim did an enormous amount of work – he was still very much a hands-on manager – and yet the office maintained a minimum of clutter. The office had a feel that said: This is where the deals are made.

Jim was sitting at his desk waiting. 'Where's Dunn?' he said. The circles under his eyes were deep and dark. He was becoming a raccoon. 'Can't find Dunn. No one knows where Barry is. What the hell's going on around here? Last I heard, we were getting our ass grilled over an open flame.'

'I called. Did you get my message?'

'That's why I'm here. Otherwise I'm sure I could find something else to do, like check with production on the day's build. I'm not sure anyone's paying attention anymore. Let's hear what you got.'

'William Dunn was struck last night, more accurately, early this morning, in an auto-pedestrian accident. The driver didn't stop, so that's about all we know. Dunn's in the hospital, and he most certainly won't be helping us. I wanted to come by and tell you, and, before he hears it from somebody else, I need to find his son.'

Jim drew in a long breath. He watched Barry, perhaps hoping for some indication that this was a joke. But it was not, and he saw that. He leaned forward onto his elbows and rested his fingertips at each temple.

'An accident?' Jim's voice came out tight and angry. 'How?'

'Early this morning outside of Karen Williams' town house. The police have nothing to indicate how the accident occurred. Karen was inside at the time, and, so far, no other witnesses have come forward. Late on a Friday night, the common thinking seems to favor a drunk driver.'

'Karen's house? I don't understand.'

'They went for a drink after work. Apparently they hit it off. Karen's upset, and I told her to stay home and not worry about the office today. I'm most worried about the other Security Associates people. I'd like to walk you through all the changes they've implemented. They've been doing a good job. After this, who knows?'

Jim rose from his chair and crossed over to a mahogany cabinet on the side wall. 'We've hired someone the board knows nothing about, a major contract awarded to stop a major security breach, and now it, too, becomes a debacle.'

Without any pretense, he opened one door and pulled out a bottle of Scotch. He poured himself a heavy portion and drank it in three gulps. 'You know who sits on our board. They're rich, powerful people. Five of them make you and me look like paupers. I'll tell you this, Barry, there's one thing powerful people hate, and that's secrecy. They hate to think something's going on behind their backs.'

Jim poured again, but this time held the glass without drinking. 'They've constantly got their noses in the air. Sniff. Sniff. Trying to smell out a plot before it gets them. Where's the guy who's going to take my wallet? Where's the one who's after my company? That's the way they live, and they're going to get hold of all this – the man getting electrocuted, Security Associates, this accident – and they're going to have Diane's hide, God bless her.' Now he drank.

This time he didn't refill. He held the glass and wiped his lips on the back of one hand. 'All we can do is go back out there, do our jobs, and hope a ten-ton weight doesn't land on our heads. It's got so we can't even go out and get in our cars without causing a disaster around here.'

Barry felt like going over and getting a glass himself. He noticed a bunch of white specks, almost like crumbs, on the carpet near where Jim was standing. Bits and pieces of ceiling tile. He'd seen the exact same thing in Chris Jacobs' office, after he'd fired the shot into the ceiling. Jim must have had his office recabled, probably with known, safe wiring. Something else Barry needed to do that, right now, just didn't seem to be a priority.

'You better find his son,' Jim said. He didn't look up from the bottom of his glass.

Bill Dunn Jr. took the news quietly. His face was a rock.

Barry didn't know what to say. 'I drove there myself, this morning, as soon as I heard. I thought about trying to find you, but there was . . . nothing there. No reason for you to come. They'd already taken your father to the hospital. One of the cops gave me his card and asked me to have you call.'

Bill's jaw was set and he looked a good deal older than his twenty-four years.

'We understand if you can't keep working. Take off, do whatever you need to do. We'd appreciate it if you would leave your people on the job and allow them to continue. I'm very sorry.'

Bill held out his hand for the card.

'I'll let you use the office,' Barry said, getting up. 'Take as long as you need.' He walked around the corner into the break room. He stared at the TechDirect Quality Achievement awards lining the wall. He poured coffee he didn't want, then dumped it down the drain. Bill would no doubt have to go down to the police station, the hospital – Barry sent up a prayer – hopefully not the morgue.

The mobile phone rang while Barry was walking toward the rest room. He changed course and headed outside the building to the second-floor walkway. Three rings. He drew in a breath and hit answer.

'It's Hektor,' the voice said, hitting Barry like a blow to the chest. 'I waited what felt like a proper period for you to collect your dead and wounded. I am a man of honor.'

'What?'

'I understand you suffered an accident this morning. Your heroic defender no longer carries the shield.'

How could the man know this? He'd told Jim only thirty minutes earlier. The two of them, Karen, the police, Bill Jr., these were the only people who knew, unless . . .

'You think you're smart,' Barry said. 'But you're a fucking idiot.'

Silence, now, on the other end. Then, 'Do you ever watch *The McLaughlin Group*? I think our little debate has gone on long enough. We need an exit question, a decisive way to conclude our discussion. I want to provide a small demo for you that will provide you that exit question. Be at the deli next to the place where you like to buy pizza. Go there at twelve o'clock, sit, order a salad.' The man hung up.

Barry threw the phone off the second-floor walkway. It arced past the jogging track and landed in the woods.

He'd been back in the office fifteen minutes when the phone buzzed and Gwen said that Claudia was on the line.

'Hi there,' Barry said when he picked up. He was unprepared for the broken pinched-off sound of Claudia's voice.

'I can't find Caroline,' she choked out. 'I've searched the whole house. She's hiding or she's not here.'

Barry snapped upright in his chair. 'Why would she be hiding?'

'I don't know. She doesn't answer. Something's happened.'

'All right, I'm on my way. I'm leaving right now.'

'Gotta go,' he called to Gwen, already on his way by. He was down the stairs and out to the car in under a minute.

Barry didn't clock himself, but if he had he would have discovered that it was possible to go door-to-door, with the benefit of an empty Saturday freeway, in fourteen minutes. He lurched to a stop in the driveway, jumped out, and bolted to the front door.

Claudia was inside, her eyes puffy, pushing things around in a downstairs closet. 'Caroline?' she called. She got down on her hands and knees and searched an unlikely set of shelves. She pushed a seldom-used golf bag aside and examined the corner behind it. She came out of the closet and said to her husband, 'She's not anywhere. I've searched the house twice.' A statement that made the tears start flowing all over again.

Barry took his wife in his arms, and she struggled to get out the story.

'She had her colors out and she was doing a drawing. I went back to the bedroom and made a phone call. Twenty minutes, at the most. When I came out she was gone. I didn't think about it at first. But then I realized I couldn't hear her anywhere. Not in the bathroom. Not upstairs. I checked her bedroom. I looked all over, even out in the yard. That's when I called you.'

'Did she say anything about going out to play? About doing anything else at all?'

'Earlier, she said she wanted to go rollerblading. I said no, we should stay inside today. I even had all the doors locked.'

She'd gone rollerblading. Barry pulled away in the direction of the back door, but Claudia held on to his hand. 'I already looked. The Rollerblades are in the garage.'

'I'm going to search the house again. Or maybe she's somewhere outside. Were the doors all still locked?'

Claudia nodded, wiping her eyes.

'Well, she may have locked the door behind her. She knows how to do that. You could start calling the neighbors. Maybe one of them has seen her.'

Claudia looked doubtful.

'If no one has seen her, if she's not here or out in the yard, we're calling the police, okay?' Barry said. 'Let's give it a good solid search first.'

'Caroline?' he bellowed, heading for the stairs. 'If you hear me, you better come out right this minute.'

While Claudia thumbed through the subdivision telephone directory and started dialing neighbors, Barry moved through the upstairs of the house in a fury. He didn't get down on his knees and peer under the bed. He grabbed the whole bed frame and hoisted it up into the air. He hauled open closets and raked clothing aside. Medicine chest, linen cabinet, dirty clothes hamper – everything was dumped out, thrown open, whatever it took to ensure that there wasn't a little girl hiding inside.

In Caroline's room, Barry walked to the front window. He

had a good view out onto the street, the very same street where some lunatic had seen fit to manufacture a drive-by shooting and send it to him on disk. Oh, yes, they'd given him plenty of warning, hadn't they? He closed his eyes for a long three count. Then he went back to the search.

He paused at her night table and picked up one of her drawings. It was a beach scene, and sitting right on the beach were what looked like a glass of chocolate milk and a plate of peas. They were small green things, and Caroline liked peas, so that's probably what they were. She must have brought the drawing upstairs with her, which implied she hadn't simply run out the door the minute Claudia's back was turned. Barry walked back into the hallway, turned, and looked at the doors to the other rooms he had already gone over. Was Caroline that clever? Yes. He imagined she was. If she was hiding – and he wanted to be absolutely sure that she wasn't before calling in the police – she could very well have slipped back into one of the rooms after he had searched it. He thought for a minute and went back into Caroline's room. Grabbed a piece of her drawing paper.

He went back to the first room and gave it another check. Then, as he left the room, he closed the door, tore off a scrap of paper, and slipped it in the crack. He reworked the upstairs quickly and then scanned the hallway.

Every door was still closed. Every piece of paper was still there.

He descended the staircase trying to puzzle it through. His wife had searched the house. Twice. There weren't very many hiding places downstairs. It was doubtful they were going to find her inside. He glanced at the items spilling out of the downstairs closet onto the floor. But the doors had been *locked*.

Claudia came barreling out of the bedroom. 'Frank Kline saw her down there about thirty minutes ago.' She headed straight for the front door with Barry right behind her. The Klines lived four houses down, and the two of them hit the street in a jog.

'Wow. That was fast,' Frank Kline said when he opened the door. He was a retired commercial pilot, and he scanned their faces. 'What's wrong?'

'We just didn't know where she was,' Claudia said. 'We've been looking and looking and we started to get worried. You say she was in the backyard?'

'Still is, as far as I know.' He opened the door and gestured them inside. 'Come on in. Calm down. We've got that side gate into the backyard. I saw her come on through about thirty minutes ago. I started to go out and say hello, but I saw that she wanted to climb up into my son's old treehouse. She's done it before, and she was already halfway up, so I thought better to leave well enough alone. My son never liked it when I'd go out and talk to him while he was in his fort. I'm sorry. I figured you knew she was down here playing.'

'No need to be sorry,' Barry said. 'We had an attempted burglary at our house, and we've been on edge lately. She's still out in the treehouse?'

Frank Kline raised his eyebrows at the mention of a burglary. 'I haven't seen her come down.'

'We better go out and have a talk with her.' Barry stuck out his hand. 'Thanks, Frank. She can come down here and play all she wants to, but she needs to let us know first.'

'You go right on ahead. The sliding-glass door opens onto the back patio. I'll stay behind and finish watching my ball game.'

'Thank you,' Claudia said.

'I wouldn't try and climb up there,' he called after them. 'Those steps will take a kid, but you're liable to come falling down on your head.'

They marched straight across to the fort that was perched up in the arms of an unlikely mimosa tree. The fort itself was a small plywood box about twelve feet up, with a dark, rectangular hole for a doorway.

'Caroline?' Claudia called up. 'Caroline. Are you in there?'

No answer.

Barry gave it a try. 'Mr. Kline told us he saw you go up there. Don't make us go get a ladder. You're not in trouble. We only want to know where you are.'

Silence. But then Barry thought he heard a faint scraping sound, and Caroline's face peered down at them from up on the platform. 'I am too in trouble,' she said. 'You're mad at me.' Her eyes were red and, even from six feet away, Barry could tell that she, too, had been crying. What was going on around here?

'Why don't you come down and tell us why you think you're in trouble? Then we'll tell you why you're not in trouble at all. Okay? I promise.'

Caroline thought about that, and she regarded her mother and father fearfully before easing one foot and then the other out onto the first step that had been nailed into the trunk of the tree.

'What's that you've got?' Barry said. 'Why don't you drop it to me so you can use both hands?'

Caroline's expression shifted into a little frown of determination and she continued on down with the object still clutched in her right hand. As she came closer, Barry could see it was a sleeve of Ritz crackers.

They let her make it all the way to the ground, and then Claudia pounced and enveloped her daughter in an enormous hug. 'What makes you think you're in trouble?' she said. 'Why are we supposed to be mad?'

'Because of school. I couldn't play this game that everyone else was playing. And then someone said I was stupid.' She had tears running down her cheeks. 'And Daddy left and wouldn't play baseball like we were going to. And no one made breakfast and no one woke me up and no one even wants to talk to me.'

'Oh, Caroline,' Claudia said, her own eyes welling up as she knelt there on the grass.

Barry watched his wife and daughter and bit down on his lower lip. He waited for Claudia to let go. Then he leaned over and hoisted both Caroline and her crackers up into his arms.

19

Barry didn't make it back to Simtec, and he didn't retrieve the phone out of the woods where he'd thrown it, until 11:45. He picked up the phone, brushed off a clod of dirt, and hit the power button. The damn thing still appeared to be intact. He carried it out to his car and slung it on the passenger floorboard.

At the last minute, he phoned Jim and told him about Hektor's call – that Hektor had already known about Dunn and may well have been responsible. Jim did not seem surprised. Barry then told him about the twelve o'clock meeting.

'What do you mean, a demo?' Jim wasn't slurring his words, but after the shots Barry had seen him putting away, he wouldn't have been surprised.

'I don't know. That's all he said. He wanted to give me a demo. He acts like this is going to settle it, once and for all.'

'Are you sure you want to go alone? Why don't we send someone with you? For safety. They can sit in the parking lot and keep an eye on things.'

'Jim, I don't want to meet these people. You think I'm not nervous about it? But let's be honest. If they want to do something to me, or you, or anyone else in this building, they have all the opportunities in the world without telling us to go to a deli and order a salad.'

Jim was silent.

'I'm going to go and do as directed. If someone shows up and gives me a pitch, I'll nod and say, 'Very interesting, let me take it back to the board.'

'Which is the truth. Saturday morning and I've already fielded two phone calls from Jenkins and another from Fitzhugh. They're very concerned about the news and the financials.' He added, with a trace of sarcasm, 'I bet half of it's that they're losing their own money. Most of them waive all compensation in order to get stock options. They wind up sitting on top of all these options and right now it looks like a leaky boatload. They want someone to start plugging holes.'

The board members weren't the only ones making a profit off stock options, Barry thought. Jim Seidler had done well for himself, lately, too – $360,000 well.

Jim continued. 'A few of them – I think you know the names – were dead set against Diane from the beginning. They're going to use this to flush her out and it's going to be all I can do to cover my own ass. Have you seen the preliminaries from Mike? The two-week totals are out.'

'And?'

Jim clicked his tongue. 'You should see for yourself.'

Barry knew what that meant. He'd been convinced that Diane was doing a good job, but now, with poor earnings, jittery markets, and an internal security nightmare, he wasn't as sure. It certainly wasn't TechDirect's fault that things had been allowed to get so screwed up.

'I talked with Bill Dunn,' Barry said. 'His dad's in surgery, and he'll be at the hospital. He's leaving the rest of the Security Associates team in place. They're getting the network more and more locked down, and I still believe time is working in our favor.' Barry glanced at his car clock. 'I need to run to this meeting. I'll call you when I get back.'

'Be careful,' Jim said, and that's exactly what Barry planned to be. Careful and smart, both. He waited for a spot and parked directly in front of the deli. He backed the Jeep in and left his door unlocked. Then he went in and chose a table well back from the front glass. He ordered a Caesar salad, though he wasn't at all hungry, and stirred sugar into an iced tea.

Every person who walked in, Barry examined the face and hands. There was an emergency exit to his right, and if he didn't like what he saw, he could be out the door in half a second.

The Caesar salad came and Barry stared at it. He ate a piece of bread and drank tea. After about five minutes, a kid in an apron came out from behind the counter.

'Are you Barry Shepard?'

Barry nodded. He saw that the kid was holding an envelope in one hand.

'The guy said you'd order a salad and you did. He told me to watch for you and give you this when you came in. He said you'd give me five bucks.'

Barry took out his wallet and handed over a bill. The kid disappeared back behind the counter. Barry glanced around the restaurant, but no one was paying even the slightest attention. He tore open the envelope and inside was a map, one page of a detailed city of Houston street guide. The page had been photocopied and a path marked out in red pen.

The path led to Dorfman Park, which was circled, and the note said, 'Meet us at the park where we can conduct our demo. No calls, please. We only want to see you.'

Barry looked out the front of the restaurant. He was sure they were there, watching to make sure he didn't call. They'd probably watch him all the way in the car, too. And if he did call, what then? They probably wouldn't show.

He refolded the map and went out to the car. Dorfman Park wasn't far, only three turns to get him through a residential neighborhood and he'd drive straight into it. He already had the route memorized.

He drove out of the parking lot slowly, carefully. He let them see he was going to play by the rules. His heart was pounding. He made a left and headed into the neighborhood, wishing he had taken Jim's offer to have someone follow along. But then he'd get to the park and find nobody there.

It was hot outside. Typical July in Houston. Ninety-five degrees. He had the air-conditioning on high, but it was hot in the car, too. He was approaching a stop sign, and the car in front of him came to a dead stop. The passenger door opened and a man got out. He held up two dark objects, one in each hand. Even from that distance, Barry could tell they were Simtec NoteStar notebook computers. The man nodded at Barry, then started shuffling toward the passenger side of the Jeep.

The man looked dumpy and unthreatening, and Barry watched him waddle over and transfer both computers to the same hand so that he could open the door. Was this the man who had been playing havoc with their entire company? Was this the man who had shunned Barry's offer to pay one million dollars?

The man answered Barry's question as soon as he had the door open. 'Don't shoot me,' the man said. 'I'm only the errand boy.' He set one computer down on the seat and climbed laboriously up after it.

'This shouldn't take five minutes,' the man said. 'You better pull over to the curb. I'm not a computer person, so you may have to help me out.'

Barry did as he was told, and he left the motor running.

'The boss wanted you to see this. I don't know why he couldn't just tell you on the phone. It's not enough to *tell* them, he said. They've got to *see* it. So here I am.'

'Why didn't the boss come himself?'

The man reacted as if Barry had told a joke. 'You ought to know that. What do bosses do? They like to delegate.'

Barry noticed that the rotund errand boy had a phone wedged into his pants pocket, the same type of phone Barry had been given. The pants looked extremely tight even with the pockets empty, and the man extracted the phone and dropped it on the seat, then hauled one of the NoteStars up into his lap.

He hit the on button. Then he did the same for the second NoteStar. 'That much I know how to do,' he said. They waited for the notebook to boot up. The man watched the screen, so Barry watched the man. He was wearing some kind of stretch slacks, blue, and a soiled short-sleeved shirt. His brown loafers looked about fifteen years old.

Barry tipped his head up and examined the car in front. It, also, was blue. A Buick. The license plate read LLC 946, and Barry repeated the number to himself twice. Without glancing up, the other man said, 'Don't worry about the car. It was borrowed an hour ago.'

Borrowed. The computer screen was now up, and Barry turned his attention toward it. 'I'm not sure I remember how to do this,' the man said. 'You see, you only get to do it once per computer, then it's all over. I didn't get a lot of practice. I have to go in here to change the date. . . .' The man acted like he was telling Barry something he didn't already know, using only one pudgy index finger to work the keyboard.

'What I'm trying to demonstrate here is something very simple. This is what will happen on July twenty-fifth.' He tried to add a flourish by allowing his finger to pause over the enter key. Then he tapped the key lightly.

Changing the date on a computer is a simple feat that takes only a fraction of a second. In this case, however, the hard drive appeared to activate and Barry could hear the mechanism working away. What was the man trying to prove? They'd written some kind of program so that, if you changed the date to a certain day, your hard drive got copied, or trashed, or whatever it was doing? A message indicating drive access failure appeared on-screen.

'Damn. I forgot.' The man slapped the seat, and his phone bounced off onto the floor. A set of keys and some pennies had also fallen out of his pocket. 'I was supposed to show you what was on here. There were a bunch of programs, factory loaded. You're going to have to take my word for it.'

'I believe you,' Barry said. If they could modify server scripts and batch files, they could load programs onto a notebook computer.

'And now it's gone.'

'I believe that, too.'

'Oh. Well, maybe I'm not doing a very good job explaining. The point here is that your machines do this all by themselves. You get to July twenty-fifth and kablowie, good-bye everything.'

'No, our machine doesn't do that. A *modified* machine might, but only if you could get your hands on the computer before the customer did.'

The man waved a dismissive hand in the air. 'Bingo. I believe we modified them. All of them. July twenty-fifth they all blank themselves out, unless we tell you how to fix it.'

'Bullshit.'

Unperturbed, the man reached for the other notebook. 'Here, you do this one. I'm told this is untouched, exactly as it comes from the factory.'

He handed over the machine and Barry set it in his lap.

He brought it up and quickly scanned the directory structure. It looked like a standard, Simtec-installed set of files. He checked to make sure no rogue program had been loaded at start-up.

Then he changed the date to July 25. After a short delay, the drive kicked in and Barry grimaced, tracing his finger along the edge of the case. The code had either been loaded as part of the original system, or it had been added after the fact, in some other way. He'd have to take a machine back and go over it.

'Now you've seen,' the man said. 'I better go.'

'Can I keep this?' Barry asked in a subdued voice. He was already thinking ahead to his arrival at the office when he could grill the Simtec engineers.

'You don't need it. Just go into your warehouse, pick any machine. They're all the same.'

The fat man was enjoying himself too much, and Barry wanted to punch him.

'Any NoteStar? Any particular configuration? What?'

'The way I understand it . . .' the man said, opening the door, grabbing keys, scooping up change, snagging the phone on the floor, '. . . any machine at all. It'd be a sin to let all those people out there lose their files. They'd hate you, I'm sure.' He stared at Barry, allowing the words to sink in.

Barry had a hundred questions, he knew none of which would be answered. Here was one of the perpetrators, right beside him. He had to try. 'It's so obvious,' he said. 'If you were able to modify our master files, you've got someone in production. You've had help from the inside.'

The man shook his head. 'I wouldn't know about that. Inside, outside, like I said, I'm the errand boy.' He waddled sideways clutching the computers, trying to stuff the phone back into his pocket. Then he remembered a folded piece of paper in his top pocket, which he extracted and tossed back in onto the seat. 'We'll be in touch,' he said, just before he slammed the door with his butt.

Barry pulled out and swung sharply into a U-turn. He made several corners, checking the rearview to be sure there was no one behind. Then he pulled over and snatched up the piece of paper. He unfolded it and read.

> We are angry, and our dealings have taken a violent turn. Alas, it did not have to be so. But you still have the ability to get these circumstances under control. This demonstration previews the kind of development Simtec should expect if our negotiations fail. Except that the next will come as a complete surprise. No warnings and no prior alarms. Be advised, this is the last show of force that we are prepared to reveal. There will be no more counterproposals. You will receive one phone call and, should you refuse to pay our fees, should you equivocate in any way, you will be left to meet the calamity that awaits you. The wheels are in motion, so only foolish people would choose to win the battle over a few dollars when the war is already lost.

When he finished, Barry's whole body had stiffened. One hand was clamped onto the steering wheel.

The mobile phone rang and Barry snatched it up. 'Barry Shepard,' he said, the same way he answered in the office, but a whole lot less friendly.

Silence. The other party clicked off.

Barry stared at the phone; then he used it to call Jim Seidler. Voice mail picked up instead. The car was hot. Barry could feel sweat running down the back of his shirt. He dialed the extension of Jim's assistant and, miraculously, got a live body.

'This is Barry. Is Jim in his office?'

'No, he's not. I believe he's gone downstairs to meet with Security Associates.'

'Find Jim. Page him, track him down. Tell him we'll meet in his office in fifteen minutes. Tell him Barry said he has to be there, it's that important, okay?'

'Okay,' the assistant said, no doubt wondering when the head of TechDirect began ordering around the executive vice president.

Barry refolded the note and pushed it into his pocket. He tested the speed limits all the way back to the office.

★

He had been waiting for ten minutes when Jim walked in and said, 'I'm glad you're here.' He crossed to the phone and dialed an extension, then punched it up on speaker.

'Spakovsky.'

'The board of directors has reacted strongly,' Jim said. 'Several members are very upset, and they've called a special meeting for one P.M. tomorrow. If you haven't already heard, they're making an official request for a complete set of records. They have every right to do it, and they will fax you notification. You'll have to get a copy of the financials hand-delivered to Fitzhugh and Jenkins.'

'I hadn't heard yet,' Spakovsky said, and he sounded more surprised at that fact than he did at the request itself. He exhaled slowly, the air whistling right out of the speaker-phone. 'Besides the records, is there anything else I can do?'

'Why don't you call Fitzhugh and offer to get together off the record? Convey to him the current state of our offices and the disarray in our operations. Let him seed this out to the board before we meet. We need to be forthcoming. If we get caught trying to hide things, we'll get skewered.'

Silence from the other end.

'We have to minimize the surprise factor, Mike. You play it as you think best. I've got Barry here and he looks anxious, so I'd better go.' Jim clicked off and pointed in Barry's direction.

Barry said, 'One o'clock tomorrow isn't soon enough.'

'Why? What is it?'

'I have the latest target. On July twenty-fifth, a number of our hard drives will corrupt themselves. I called Greg Mitchell and he's bringing us several machines direct from production.'

'What do you mean, *corrupt themselves*?'

'You'll get a chance to see for yourself. You change the date ahead to the twenty-fifth, the drive kicks in and starts zapping. I've seen it happen.'

'That's what the demo was about?'

'That and this note.' He handed it over and started pacing the office. It was a short note, but Jim kept staring long enough to have read it through five times. Jim didn't look up until his assistant buzzed and said Greg Mitchell was at the door with the equipment.

Several employees from TechDirect trooped in, carrying monitors, keyboards, notebook computers, and a variety of desktop CPUs. These they spread over every available piece of real estate on Jim's bureau, a side table, and a low coffee table by the wall. Barry dismissed all but Greg.

'Jim, you know Greg Mitchell. He's our senior analyst. I'd like him to sit in and maybe offer us some insights on this.'

'Sure,' Jim said. 'Let's see what we've got.'

Barry nodded and Greg took the cue. 'These are all brand-new machines. We requisitioned them fifteen minutes ago.

A few have been configured with end-user software; two shouldn't have any apps yet at all.'

'You went to production and got them?' Barry said.

'Absolutely. Right off the line.'

'Is it safe to say these are a representative sample of the machines we are shipping out today, July twenty-second?'

'Absolutely. That NoteStar was in the box already. I stole it from bench seven. I told them if they had a problem to call you.'

'Okay,' Barry said. 'These are our machines, coming off our own production line.'

Jim had adopted a skeptical look, as though he were being given a sales pitch. He indicated that they should continue.

'I want to simulate what will happen the first time one of these computers is powered up, on or after July twenty-fifth. I'll go to the DOS prompt and use the DATE command to make that one change.' Barry walked to one of the desktop machines. It was a JStar Pentium in a low-profile cabinet. His fingers tapped over the keyboard, and just as someone had performed for him an hour earlier, he paused before hitting the enter key.

Jim and Greg were watching every move.

Barry drew in his breath and stared straight ahead. He tapped the key. Almost immediately, the hard drive started to work. Barry typed keys at random. Nothing. He clicked the mouse, but now the screen appeared to be frozen.

A short time later it was all over. When he snapped the machine off and back on again, it was as if the disk drive, or the record of what was on it, was completely gone. Barry had suspected it would happen, but he'd been holding on to a sliver of hope: It was a hoax, the code had been found, never planted, or it affected only an isolated corner of Simtec's line. But now he'd seen it on the notebooks and the desktop units. There was no reason to believe the others would be any different. When a mail order box went out via Federal Express, when a trailer truck pulled up at CompUSA, this was what they were shipping: ticking time bombs.

Greg walked up to the machine and prodded the keyboard tentatively. Jim's head hung down and he was kneading his forehead.

'What do you think, Greg?' Barry said.

'I want to take it back and tear it apart, then we'll know for sure.'

'What do you *think*?'

'What it would have to be is some kind of process that gets loaded at bootup. The code sits out there – maybe it patches an interrupt, like a virus – and every so often checks the date. When the date equals such and such, the code kicks in and does whatever it does. Probably trashes the partition, the FAT, something of that nature.'

'Is that what it looks like to you, Jim?'

Jim nodded without looking up.

'All right, then. We're convinced.'

'How long?' Greg asked.

Barry's eyebrows notched upward.

'Do we know how long this has been going on?'

Barry shook his head. 'I assume this was planted the same time as the rest. The backup batch files and the shipping addresses were hit a week ago. Seven days, ten days, it's a hell of a lot of machines either way.'

'All models?'

'If you can change the master files, you can hit every machine that comes through production.'

The same went for applications, Barry realized. The config center had the apps on servers, and a worker could pull a custom configuration in a fraction of the time it would have taken an end user.

Barry picked up the phone on Jim's desk and punched in an extension. Jim, himself, was still frozen with his forehead cupped in one hand.

'Gwen? You know the new computers we got for the training room? I want you to transfer the call in there and go pick up by one of the machines.'

They waited while Gwen walked down to the brand-new TechDirect training room. Over the past two months, they'd outfitted the room with an assortment of Simtec models used for teaching both the telephone sales reps and the technicians. Barry tapped his index finger on the desk until Gwen came back on the line.

'Okay, turn on any one in the first row by the door. Any one of the Star series. It's already on. Fine. We want to change the date to July twenty-five. No, I don't care about the year. Leave it at this year. We can experiment with that later. What's it doing?'

Greg moved closer, as though he might be able to hear what Gwen was saying.

'I see. No, that's what I suspected might happen.' Barry frowned and covered the mouthpiece with one hand. 'Chewed it up. We brought those machines in three weeks ago. Beginning of the month.'

He removed the hand. 'Gwen? Try one of the Comets at the back. Do the same thing with the date.'

She did and reported that the Comet's hard drive was again doing something odd. When she tapped the keyboard, nothing happened.

'Try another one.' Barry's voice betrayed a growing alarm. 'Try the one connected to the overhead.' The desktop machine they were using to drive the LCD presentation panel had been there for over a month. Barry's finger maintained its rapid beat on the desk.

'Shit! No, that's fine. Don't worry about it. Just leave the machines. Thanks.'

He hung up the phone. Jim Seidler was staring at the wall.

'All of them?' Greg said. 'Then this has been going on a long time.'

Barry couldn't answer. His throat was tight and dry. He walked over and stood in front of the now lifeless monitor. *We can't* go *through this.* His heart was pounding. *We can't.* But as he worked frantically through the options, he was already discarding them, one by one.

20

A complete operating system was preloaded onto virtually every server, desktop computer, and notebook leaving production. A few people would simply delete the Simtec files, repartition the drive, and start over with some alternative OS, but that was the exception.

After a painful search during which he erased seventeen hard drives, Barry was able to determine that the master configuration files had been altered on June 21. At least, that was the date they had been switched out on the configuration center's main file server. Today was July 22.

Greg Mitchell was dispatched to assemble a group of programmers to tear apart the bad files. Barry and Jim began constructing and issuing database queries to total up the affected machines by type and shipping destination. Barry ordered two of his staff members to begin pulling a list of customer names with TechDirect purchases since June 21. Construct a list with machine type, customer name, address, and any available phone numbers, he told them. Home and work number. He didn't tell them why.

Barry also knew that, even with a list of known end users, the bulk of Simtec's shipments had gone through resellers and superstores to customers who had never, or had not yet, registered their products. The database queries were excruciatingly slow and the whole network was sluggish. Traffic was being bottlenecked as segments of the backbone were being brought down by Security Associates and rerouted.

Little by little, working together, Barry and Jim tallied the scope of the damage. Jim's breathing was short and troubled. He looked like a ghost: 431,606 computers had already been sent out with corrupt operating systems.

He snatched up the phone and began flipping Rolodex cards with his thumb. Then he spent ten minutes searching three different corporate headquarters until he located Diane Hughes. She was in conference, the person said; perhaps he would like to call back.

'Right now,' Jim said, and his tone said that he meant it.

'Couldn't this have waited a few minutes?' Diane snapped when she came on the line.

'No, it could not. I'm putting you on speaker. I've got Barry here with me.'

'Hello, Barry. Couldn't I get finished with the meeting? This looks like hell, dragging me out of a meeting like that.'

'I'm afraid not. We've got quite a situation here. I'm going to suggest you return to Houston.'

'What kind of a situation?'

'Well, now. Where to begin?' Jim's voice was heavily laced with sarcasm. Where indeed? Barry thought.

'William Dunn was hit by an automobile this morning, and now we've got several hundred thousand machines that are going to expire three days from now. How many is it exactly, Barry?'

'Four hundred thirty-one thousand, six hundred six.' He didn't even have to look down.

'W. S. hit by a car? Is he all right?'

'He's in surgery,' Jim said. 'He may have died. We don't really know.'

'Died?' Her voice kicked up an octave. Jim didn't answer. He was being merciless.

'What's this about machines expiring?'

'They destroy their own hard drives. Four hundred thousand of them.'

A long silence, then a quiet, 'Oh, dear. It sounds as though I should come back. I had two more stops . . . I'm going to have to call and tell them something.'

'Tell them whatever you want. Barry's gotten a note that states we'll get one more opportunity to buy our way out of this. I've begun to waver on paying, Diane. I'm telling Barry not to answer the phone until you get back and we think through our position. By the way, Jenkins and Fitzhugh are red hot. They want to know why CNN knows more than our own board of directors. They've called for a special meeting tomorrow at one, and they requested a set of records. Mike is going to be swamped trying to comply. I'm sure you'll be a required guest of honor at the meeting. See you soon.'

Barry watched in amazement as Jim hung up the phone, cutting off any rebuttal. He turned to Barry and said, 'Who needs to listen to all that? To hell with cutting a deal. This ship needs a captain.'

That it does, Barry thought. Jim had been directly confrontational, even insubordinate, but it was good to see some decisiveness. Why had the board ever gone outside to begin with? Why hire Diane Hughes, Barry found himself wondering, someone who had little grasp of what went on inside a computer, much less a computer company, when Jim would have had a firm grasp on almost every aspect of their operations?

'I need to go talk to production,' Barry said. 'We have to go through the master files and reload good stock.'

As if he'd been reading Barry's thoughts, Jim reached over and put a hand on Barry's arm. 'You stick with me and we're going to get through this. We're going to make it.'

Barry nodded. He let himself out of the office and began the walk to production. The air felt good. It was hot, the sun sharp in his face, but things were happening again. Working alone, it had been hard to keep up with Security Associates and their myriad demands. But, working with Jim, they could become more proactive. They could target whatever changes they wanted and push them along. They'd pay the money, five million dollars, so what? The 430,000 computers Simtec had shipped, including the 80,000 sold by his TSRs in TechDirect and put together by the config center, would not come to a screaming halt. They would not be confronted by a mob of angry customers and swarming journalists. The public relations debacle would not materialize. There would be no attacks. And no more threats against his wife and daughter.

Barry slowed his walk, taking a deep breath and glancing out at the woods behind Simtec. He heard the steps of a jogger behind him and moved over to the right.

At the last second, he realized that the steps were too close and coming too fast. He started to turn his head and caught sight of a blue blur, then a powerful body slammed into him. It might have been a classic football tackle, except that Barry wasn't wearing pads. A vicious shoulder caught him in the midsection of his back. He was spun sideways and went down hard, flat out against the concrete walkway.

Barry had had his wind knocked out before. He knew that you had to lie there, wanting to gasp in huge mouthfuls of air but unable to control your lungs. He rolled onto one side as the man swung his foot into Barry's forearm. The kick sent fire up into his elbow and shoulder, and Barry rolled the other way, dazed and trying to shield himself. He managed to squeeze in a first tentative breath, anticipating the next blow. Both of his hands were up around his head, offering scant protection against a swinging foot. He heard a shuffling sound in the grass, a rustling of grass and leaves. The rustling grew softer, then stopped. The man could be standing there, right behind him. Barry sucked in a ragged breath, pulled his arms down, and came over onto his knees. The man was gone.

Someone shouted from the direction of the building.

'Hey!' the voice called again, closer. 'Are you all right?'

It was a familiar face from Simtec's accounting department. Barry tried to push off and sit up, but a sharp pain spiked into his side. He groaned and fought to get air into his lungs.

'Stay still,' the man said. 'We'll get someone in medical out here.'

Several other employees were now gathering outside, and the man issued instructions to one of them, who took off back into the building. Simtec had an in-house doctor as well as several staffers trained in first aid.

Barry had managed to sit up, and he glared at the group of gawkers. Some of them got the message and began moving on. 'Who hit me?' he asked the man from accounting.

'I didn't see. I happened to be walking by in the lobby. I looked out and saw you lying here. You say somebody hit you? It must have happened before I walked by.'

'Someone blindsided me. I heard him coming and thought

he was a jogger.' Barry steadied himself with one hand and got slowly to his feet. Again the spike of pain in his side.

A woman who Barry knew only as Debra had come out and was standing beside them. 'I saw the whole thing,' she said tentatively. 'I was up on the third floor and, from where I sit, you can see this whole area.'

'Then you saw what happened,' Barry said. He kept one arm tucked carefully against his ribs.

'Yes, I did. First you were walking along, and I looked down and thought, That looks like Mr. Shepard. Then this big guy comes jogging along behind you. He looked normal enough, only I thought, It's too hot to be jogging. Everyone jogs in the morning, not in the heat of the day. So the man got closer and he slammed right into you. I let out a shriek, I'm telling you, I was so surprised. You fell down, Mr. Shepard, and I'm up there yelling, "Oh, my God! Oh, my God!" '

'What did the man do?'

She squinted, as though being asked to recall something that had happened weeks ago. 'He came up alongside you, I'm not sure what happened, like he was jumping. Maybe he was looking for something. He bent down in the grass for a second and then took off running. I had to leave the window to call security.'

'I appreciate your doing that,' Barry said, but he was mystified by her account. 'You say the man was looking for something?'

'Maybe. It seemed that way. It all happened so fast.'

One of the first-aid people came trotting around the corner with her kit, and Barry could also see four security guards coming out from the lobby of the building.

'It's Debra, right?' Barry said.

She nodded.

'Debra, did the man look like anyone who works for this company? Anyone you've ever seen before?'

She shook her head.

'Would you be able to give a fairly accurate description of the man you saw?'

She looked doubtful.

'I'd like you to try to give these guards a description.'

Barry knew the man was probably long gone, but he ordered the guards to search the woods and the parking lots, then talk to security at the front gates.

He thanked the man from accounting and got his name. He thanked Debra again. Then he went inside with the woman from first aid.

Greg Mitchell twirled a pen between his fingers. He'd pulled out a dozen manuals and had them spread out three deep across his desk. Barry and Jim were asking him to sort through the operating system files. Where was the bad code loaded? Was it a virus? How did it function? How could it be undone? Use a debugger to trap the instructions, they said. Disassemble it. Do whatever you have to do. Fast.

And while I'm at it, thought Greg, I'll bring you the moon and the stars. He'd been a programmer for several years, but then he'd moved up, becoming an analyst, then a manager who supervised other people's code but rarely wrote much of his own. He had no idea where to begin.

They could run a suspect file through a disassembler, which would take them back to the raw instructions. Then, as Greg recalled from work years earlier, they'd be looking at statements like:

```
pop   cx
mov   di,ax
xor   ax,ax
push  ds
```

It would take Greg days to sort through this. Some people, very few, could simply read down the page and tell you what was going on. He called Mitch Ryder's extension and got voice mail. He tried Mitch at home and left a message. Sue Baker was good, but he was almost sure she was out on loan to Simtec Europe. He called her house anyway, and her husband said she'd be gone for another month.

There was another guy Greg remembered. A Czech or Russian they'd hired recently to do assembly and source-level code work. Vadim was his name. Greg looked for him in the directory, but the guy was too new to be included. He called personnel and got a name and home phone number.

The woman who answered at Vadim's number spoke a thick soup of English.

'Vadim?' Greg said, trying to enunciate his words carefully. 'Is Vadim there?'

'Not here,' came the reply, followed by a string of words that sounded like, 'Here day not nick tennis.'

Greg tried it again. 'Is Vadim there? This is Greg at Simtec.'

'Not here. No go Simtec . . . Vadim . . . bolen!'

Was that bowling? It sounded like bowling.

'Has Vadim gone bowling?'

'Da. On bolen.'

Greg pulled at his hair. 'I need you to do me a favor.'

'What is favor?'

Greg plunged ahead blindly. 'Find Vadim. Tell him to call Greg.' He gave his phone number and made the woman repeat it.

She uttered something unintelligible, followed by a series of clucks.

Greg hung up. He was going to call every fifteen minutes until he got Vadim. If the woman didn't produce him in two more calls, he'd drive over there and find Vadim himself. Greg closed his eyes and crushed one palm against the knuckles of his left hand. *Pop. Pop. Pop.*

Three Tylenols later, Barry sat at his desk. Probably a bruised rib, the woman had told him. He ought to get it checked out. Instead, he'd gone out to the production center and straightened out the files that were being loaded onto each new machine. They were the wrong files, he told the line manager. They'd been loading an operating system with a bug in it. Take the files off the servers and reload from the originals. The workers looked at him like he was crazy but did as they were told.

On the way out, the manager cornered him.

'First Greg's over here grabbing machines, then you come over and tell us to reload all our OS files. Is this tied in with the shipping problems? Do you mind telling me what the hell it's all about?'

Barry could see the manager was worried. He worked hard and ran a tight shop, and now the big cheese comes over and acts like he's not cutting it.

'You're doing a fine job. We're digging into a new . . . issue. That's about all I can say right this minute.'

'If we're having a problem, don't you think I ought to know about it?'

'We've uncovered a bug in the files and we're working to pin it down. You'll get a full explanation ASAP.' Barry turned and walked on, and he could feel the man eyeing him suspiciously, all the way out.

Back in his office, Barry swiveled in the desk chair and stared at his shelves, frowning. Something looked different, but he couldn't place it. The books were too neat, or maybe they had been moved. He glanced at the door and went to the other end of the bookshelves, where he bent down in front of an aging set of three-ring manuals. He had decided against storing the password list in his desk. A locked desk seemed like an invitation, especially with a flimsy lock you could pop with a paper clip. The third manual from the left, at page 101, held a copy of the list Jim had given him as well as the additions compiled by Greg Mitchell. Barry eased the binder out and flipped pages. Still there. He pushed the manual back into place and examined the rest of the shelves: books, pictures, a chess set he never used, a special set of bicentennial beer cans. Wasting time. He returned to the desk, picked up the phone, and dialed home. Claudia answered on the second ring.

'Hi. How's everything?' He tried to sound cheerful.

'I'm fine and Caroline's fine. She's been getting lots of attention.'

He hesitated, and Claudia was immediately on the alert.

'What's wrong?'

'I was thinking about hiring a bodyguard to stay at the house. Someone to go around with you if you need to go out. Maybe for the next couple of days.'

There was a long silence. 'Do you think that's necessary?'

'I don't know. I also thought about asking Jack Griffin to go over there and watch his weekend sports at our house.

He's an NRA freak, you know. If I asked him to, he'd bring over enough weapons for an army. He's also a nosy blabbermouth, and he'll tell everyone he knows he spent the weekend protecting Barry Shepard's wife and daughter.'

'Can we do neither? Can we discuss it tonight and make a decision? I promise to keep the doors locked. We've got the alarm system and a security guard at the front gate. I won't go on any errands, okay?'

'Okay,' Barry said. 'But if we don't resolve this over the weekend, we may have to make arrangements for Monday. You and Caroline may have to stay home, or you could spend a few nights with a friend.'

'We'll talk about it,' Claudia said unhappily.

He hung up, but found that the phone call had not resolved the matter. His thoughts were not on Simtec but drifted instead to W. S. Dunn, to the frenzied search for a missing Caroline. To getting slammed down onto the concrete on the grounds of his own company.

In spite of what they'd just agreed, Barry flipped open the yellow pages. He studied several pages and dialed Titan Protective Services. They had a big ad that said Security Officers, Armed & Unarmed. Complete Protection. Immediate Response. Barry called and hired two men to go out to his house and sit by the curb, a block away from his house.

He hung up, feeling a slight improvement in peace of mind, and logged into the network. The mail messages were piling up in his account. Two of his staff members had written fierce notes complaining of the treatment they'd gotten by Security Associates interrogators. Barry ignored these messages. He plowed through normally important messages like a buzz saw. Mike Spakovsky requested a meeting with him to discuss matters regarding Jim and Diane. Sure, Barry shot back. Let's meet. He didn't suggest a time. He had taken the phone offline, so he knew that, if it rang, it was Gwen and the call had been screened. It was ringing now.

He swiveled sideways and winced when he reached for the phone.

'A man named Richard Green. He insists you'll talk to him.'

'I will.' Barry switched the phone to his other hand, pulling the one arm in close to nurse his side.

'Barry! Glad to catch you in the office. I wanted to give you a report because I've found a few items of interest. Is this a good time?'

'Sure,' Barry said, but he wasn't at all sure. His side hurt like hell, and he was about to have to notify eighty thousand TechDirect customers that their machines were equipped with a self-destructing operating system. It wasn't a good time and Barry didn't care. In fact, he'd be happy to tell Jim, Diane, and anyone else that he was having each and every one of them checked out.

'I like to call as soon and as often as I get anything. I've come up with some data on Seidler, Williams, and Hughes. Seidler recently sold off his house. Right now he's renting a furnished apartment. One account that had a big balance has been almost depleted. I'm drawing a question mark.'

'Jim has been going through a divorce. Did you know that? He doesn't say much about it, but I take it it hasn't been pleasant.'

'I know about the divorce. I can't get a copy of the actual settlement, but usually one or the other person gets the house. Sometimes, if nobody wants the house, they'll sell it off and divide the cash. The curious thing is, the house went for four hundred thousand. If he'd been willing to wait, he might have been able to get five. To me, that's odd. What's the big hurry? Put it on the market, wait, then you both get an extra fifty thousand. The other question is, what did he do with his half of the money? He ought to have two hundred thousand sitting out there in an account, and I didn't see it. You asked me to find suspicious. All I'm saying is, there's a pattern to these things. Where people put their money. How they do things. Jim doesn't follow the pattern, and my eyebrows went up.'

Barry tried to picture the selling off and dividing of his own house. He wasn't sure, but he figured the house might bring as much as three hundred thousand. Three hundred fifty, three hundred, taken in the context of a divorce, would he really care?

'All right, keep Jim on the list. What about the others?'

'The preliminaries on all of them are being checked out. I've got a lot more digging to do, but was this Hughes woman related to Howard, by any chance? She's loaded, but I suppose you know that.'

'How loaded?'

'Twenty million.'

'That's more than I thought, but I'm not surprised.'

'She's kind of a wheeler-dealer. Not the tax-free municipal type. She's heavily into Canadian oil-and-gas stocks, speculative bonds, that kind of thing. Definitely willing to take risks. It seems on the up-and-up, though. She's losing her ass on the Canadian stuff.'

Barry was amazed, just as Claudia had predicted. Green had gotten this information in four hours. On a Saturday. 'How do you know all this? Am I allowed to ask that?'

'No, you're not. But in this case, I know her brokers. I do some work for them. They're not giving me anything I couldn't get on my own.'

Barry wasn't sure about that, but he let it go. This was about results, not Green's research methods.

'The last one you added to the list, Williams.'

'Karen Williams.'

'Her taxes have been audited for the past three years. That's unusual, because the IRS can find easier targets than lawyers. I think it has something to do with an ex-boyfriend who happens to be a sleazeball. You get within arm's length of this guy, the feds probably put you on the list. Nothing more there yet, but I wanted you to know about the boyfriend. That's it for now.'

Gwen had appeared in the doorway, pushing open the door and waving her arms. 'Okay,' Barry said. 'I better let you go.'

'I'll be in touch,' Richard said.

'Your father,' Gwen hissed, hopping up and down in the doorway. Barry sighed. His father was one of the few who made Gwen do that. 'I've got him parked on the line and he's been holding for five minutes. He refused to let me take a message.'

Barry took a moment to absorb everything he had just been

told. So Diane was a gambler. It didn't really surprise him. As far as where the money had gone from Jim's house sale, he was willing to bet Jim had found something clever to do with it. Clever and probably nontaxable. Roll it into another house after a while. That was probably the story. He remembered Jim's black Ford Explorer, sitting down in the parking lot with a mashed fender that looked ready to fall off at any moment. Two hundred thousand from the house and substantial profits in the stock market. Jim had quite a cash flow, yet he wouldn't even fix his car. The man definitely had his quirks.

He punched the blinking button on the telephone. 'You're driving my assistant crazy,' he said. 'Don't you have anything better to do?'

'Well he *is* there,' his father's voice boomed. 'Too busy to save his father from losing a bundle, but he's there.'

'Listen, Dad, I'm up to my eyeballs here and it's not really a good time for me to talk.'

'You don't have time to talk to your old man. I can handle that. You don't want to hear how I met Arnold Palmer the other day, that's okay.'

'I'll hear it later.'

'Arnold Palmer, son.'

'Later.'

'You kids probably want to meet Michael Jordan, but when you get to be an old geezer, the one you want to meet is Arnold Palmer.'

'I'm glad. Glad for you, glad for Arnold. Is that why you called? To tell me you met Arnold Palmer?'

'Answer me this one question: Is my portfolio going to keep going down? Do you have any idea how much of a beating I'm taking? I'm black and blue over here. I'm a punching bag.'

'It's temporary.'

'I was looking at boats, did you know that? I was thinking about maybe a little cruiser. That way I could do my fishing. I could putter up and down the coast. You know what I'll be able to afford now? A flat-bottomed skiff. A dinghy. I might as well fish off the pier. Is that what you want?'

Barry stole a line from Jim Seidler. 'Stocks go up, stocks go down. I've seen it happen before.'

'That's it? For your own father?'

'That's all I can tell you. I wouldn't run out and sell. That's more than I'm saying to anyone else, because no one else would be talking to me right now. They'd be letting me work.'

'Don't sell? You mean, I may still get my boat?'

'If that's what you want.'

'In that case, I'm going to do it. I've had my eye on this wooden beauty, an Alaskan. You ought to see the pilothouse on this baby. If I buy the big one, I'll take her all the way down the coast and I'm going to come through the canal. I'll go straight across the Gulf and I'll dock in Galveston. Then I'm going to sell it to you at a reduced price.'

Barry thought of the fiberglass bubble that already dominated his garage. 'I don't want the boat I have,' he said. 'Much less yours.'

'It's not for you. It's for Claudia and Caroline. They need a boat. I can take a plane back home. No, I'll take Amtrak. Does Amtrak go through Houston? Sure it does.'

Gwen appeared in the doorway and Barry nodded vigorously. She cleared her throat and said in a loud voice, 'Mr. Shepard? The camera crew is ready. They need you right now.'

'Gotta go, Dad. I'm already late.'

'What's that about a camera crew? Why didn't you tell me about it? What's going on over there . . . ?'

'I'll tell you soon. Gotta go.' His father was still talking when Barry put the phone back in its cradle.

It was two o'clock in the afternoon before Jon Tomfohrde in Conoco's Information Technology Center opened the latest Simtec mailer. Oh, joy. Why did they keep doing this to him? Every other week it seemed like another goddamn update. Look at the cover letter. It was a half-assed printing job done on an ink-jet printer. Some shithead had put a finger right in the blue ink before the page had dried.

Half the time they made you jump through hoops to load stuff that didn't even appear to do anything. Your end users wouldn't notice. Your boss didn't know you stayed late on a

Saturday to get it done. Nobody knew or even cared that you loaded patch STC135.EXE.

This system of having to keep up with patches and updates put network administrators in a terrible bind. Software was released before it was ready and fixed after the fact. With a network operating system, there was always some kind of tweaking going on. The process was endless. But if you didn't do the updates and then suffered an avoidable crash, you might get your ass handed to you along with a permanent vacation.

No time like the present, so Jon glanced at the install notes and tossed them in the trash. Simple. You had to down the server and swap out the SCSI disk driver on any Simtec SmartStar superserver. The letter claimed 20 percent increased disk throughput with this new driver.

Bullshit, thought Jon.

But he swapped out the file anyway, notifying three users that they would be down for five minutes and could then log back in. Tough, Jon thought, you work on Saturday you've got to be prepared for this shit.

He brought the first of several servers down, copied the new driver over, and then brought the server back up.

No problem. The server came right back on-line and he went on to the next one. He did the five servers that carried all the traffic in the corporate headquarters. Then he took the elevator to the comm center and did each of the servers that tied into Conoco regional offices. In about thirty minutes, Jon Tomfohrde touched vital parts of a vast network that connected almost every user in Conoco's workforce.

He didn't know it, but technicians at AT&T and Boeing were doing exactly the same thing.

At 4:10 P.M., Peter Jenkins punched an angry Michael Gaines into a three-way conference call. Peter was a seven-year Simtec board member and chairman of the board for the past two.

'So what the hell is going on?' Gaines barked. 'I'm ready to sail. I'm headed for Milos, and I get hunted down and ordered back to the hotel. I've been waiting for hours now.

Do you know what time it is here? This is the conference call from hell. There goes the vacation, not to mention two thousand bucks a day for that sailboat. I'm telling you right now, Simtec's going to have to pick up the tab—'

'Shut up, Michael.' The high-pitched, reedy voice belonged to Roland Fitzhugh. Fitzhugh was a member of the audit committee, and he held the powerful chair of the nominating committee. 'The share price is going to hell and Simtec is having some major problems. We've called a meeting for tomorrow and there may be a vote on Diane's stewardship.'

Silence, except for a muffled croak from Michael Gaines. Fitzhugh grinned. He hated Gaines and couldn't be happier the do-nothing sonofabitch was out of the country. Even Greece was too close.

'Peter, you were saying?'

Peter Jenkins also served on the board of Pennzoil. He'd never been in a situation quite like this, and ever since a friend, a founding partner in the powerful law firm Emerson, Wells, Johnson, had called to discuss what he termed the 'Simtec situation'. Peter Jenkins had become frightened.

'I've just spoken to Spakovsky,' Jenkins said. 'He's going to fax out a preliminary copy of the figures tonight. He knows about the meeting and I tried to sound him out about Diane. Apparently Jim was right, she hasn't been there in two days.'

'Spakovsky was her main supporter in-house,' Fitzhugh protested. 'He's scared to death of Jim Seidler. Now he's trying to duck and run.'

'Mike's interested in self-preservation. He's trying to cut his losses,' Jenkins said. 'She's obviously not going to get any help from Seidler, and Chris Jacobs is apparently MIA.'

'Has anyone spoken to Rowster? He's going to love this. Since day one he's wanted to lead Diane out to the wall and put a hood over her head.'

'Rowster will be at the meeting. So will Cummings. I've also spoken to Coopers and Lybrand, and they will be represented.'

Michael Gaines had gotten up the nerve to speak again. 'Would somebody please fill me in on what's going on?'

'Don't you read a newspaper?' snapped Fitzhugh 'Even the *International Herald Tribune* ran a story on Simtec. Shipping and distribution was the first thing to go, computers getting sent all over hell and back with the wrong configurations. Apparently internal corporate operations are completely out of whack. Share price has dropped ten points and the PR department is jacking off. Quarterly results are due out in a week, and the word is that sales are taking a big hit. They'll try to hide it in the overall figures, but it's going to show anyway. There, now you can sound like you've been doing your job.'

'I'm on *vacation*,' Gaines whined.

'That will sound great when you get sued for dereliction of oversight duties.'

'That's not funny.'

Peter Jenkins cut them off. 'Listen. We've all gotten caught pretty much with our pants down. I don't think we were properly informed, that's the damnedest thing. It's as if this was hidden from the board.'

'That's improper,' Gaines said indignantly. 'She misled us.'

'We called and asked,' Jenkins said. 'We exchanged several faxes. I spoke to Diane twice personally. Nothing. Zero.'

The woman who was sitting on the other side of Barry's desk, looking none too happy to be there, was named Sheila Thibodeaux. During his absence, Bill Dunn Jr. had placed her in command.

'What's the latest you've heard about W. S.?' Barry asked.

'He was in surgery for six hours. They did lots of reconstructive work on the hip. Bill wants to stay at the hospital until he comes to, which could be anytime or could be hours from now. Bill's going stir crazy and says he's coming back over after that.'

'He is under no pressure from us. I told him to do whatever he needs to,' Barry said, but he secretly hoped Bill *did* come back. It felt more secure having one of the Dunns there, and he'd take either one.

'As I was explaining,' Sheila said, and she had managed to make it clear that she was wasting valuable time. 'We'll reload the post office and the mail servers and then we'll transfer all the messages from the old server. The message files will be the only carryover.'

'I'm not sure we ought to be focusing on the mail servers right now,' Barry said. 'I don't think that's a priority.'

'I've got three people allocated to mail. I can reassign them somewhere else, but that won't make an appreciable difference. Every task has an appropriate level of personnel.'

Barry swallowed and stared across at her. Sheila was about thirty-five. She was wearing jeans and a T-shirt that said Coors Invitational Volleyball. Her people were putting the scalpel to Simtec in over a dozen different places. At that moment, she might well hold more power than anyone in his entire company.

'We're going to need to do the mail sooner or later,' she said.

Barry knew what she wanted to say. She wanted to say, I was only keeping you *informed,* you big dumbass. I wasn't looking for input. He knew what W. S. Dunn would have said. He would have said, Shut up, Shepard! We're doing the mail.

The phone rang and Gwen informed him that Claudia was on the line.

Barry put his hand across the receiver. 'Fine,' he said to Sheila. 'Do the mail.'

He waited until she'd left.

'Hi.'

'Who are the goons?' She was not amused.

'They're already there? I meant to call and let you know.'

'I thought we were going to discuss this. Can you imagine what I'm thinking here? I get off the phone and you're telling me to be careful, stay inside. Then I look outside and see two men sitting in a car in front of our house. I was about three seconds from dialing nine-one-one, but I called the gate and they assured me you had given authorization.'

'They weren't supposed to do that. They were supposed to watch from up the street.'

'Well, they're blocking the mailbox, so they might as well come in and have tea.'

'That won't be necessary. They're going to sit there and keep an eye on things.'

'Great.'

Barry looked across the desk and frowned. Where was the cellular phone? He scanned the shelves and the side table: no phone. He tried to remember the last place he had had it. Jim's office? Yes. Production? He wasn't sure. Had he taken the phone with him? That's when he was knocked down. He pushed back from the desk. 'That's it! They wanted the phone back.'

'What are you talking about?'

'Nothing. I've lost the mobile phone and I need to go. I'm sorry about the men out front. I just wanted to be sure. I was worried.'

'I'm worried, too. We'll talk about it tonight.'

He got up and walked outside to the hallway. Hektor should have simply called and asked for the phone back. Why would Barry want to keep it? He would have held it out and said, Take it. Gladly.

He took the outside stairway back down to the sidewalk and began to retrace his steps. He'd been carrying the phone in one hand, enjoying the sunshine. He could remember that part, turning his face up and thinking how nice it was to be outside. Then he'd heard the jogger, and the next minute he was lying on the ground. The man had kicked his arm, probably to jar his grip. He must have held on to the phone even after the fall, although he had no recollection of doing so.

He recreated the entire sequence in his mind, seeing it now with clarity, how it must have happened. He goes down, phone still in his hand. The man kicks his arm and the phone gets tossed off into the grass. Debra had said that the man bent over, like he was looking for something.

He stopped on the walkway, lining himself up with the back door of the building. This was where he had fallen, the phone would have flown out of his hand and should be over in the grass. A three-foot band of St. Augustine gave way to weeds and brambles, then a pine carpet under the trees.

He had to step off the sidewalk in order to search closely. He made one pass and then stepped further away from the sidewalk.

If it was here, this is where it would be. He walked slowly forward without seeing anything but grass and weeds. A few more feet and he'd be at the edge of the woods where the pine needles started. He paused and his eyes swept the ground back toward the sidewalk. Another step and his foot hit something solid, half-buried in the weeds. He reached down and felt for it, and, even though he didn't want it to be, there was the phone.

Wilson and Dupree stood in conference just inside the entrance to the Galleria. One of Wilson's hired thugs waited out in the car. That's the way Wilson thought of them, too. Thugs. Dupree might be the brain, but he, Terry Wilson, was not a thug. He might be a slob, he might dress like he shopped at the Goodwill, but he was smart and he had freedom. He had sixty-seven thousand dollars squirreled away in a bank account. A thug had nothing. A thug had to do what he was told.

'We got the phone back,' Wilson said. He was unable to meet Dupree's eye. 'I had already made one call, so we swapped it out and got him on a phone that's brand new. It's completely clean. No need to worry.'

'How the hell can I not worry? You do something so goddamned stupid. You get in the car with him and you take the wrong phone. I'm calling on our private number and who do I get? Barry Shepard!'

'We're okay, boss. Take it easy.' Anything to calm the man down. That was it, call him boss. He liked that.

'Besides,' Wilson said proudly, 'the kid has been working with that last disk I dropped off. I made a point of checking on it and he sounded excited. He said he had come up with a neutron bomb.'

Dupree's scowl became a measure lighter. 'What did he say?'

'He didn't go into detail. He found an upgrade letter, something like that, and he was all pumped up. He said the important thing is, it involves other companies. You told him to hit Simtec, but this hits others and it's Simtec's fault. He says this is worse.'

'I'm not sure I understand. You need to go out there and find out exactly what he's done. Then call and I'll decide how to proceed. After that, we're through with him.'

'Are you sure you want to do that, boss? He's pretty good.' In truth, Wilson had started to *like* the kid a little.

'I know the personality,' Dupree said. 'We're having to push him and he's no longer trustworthy. If he knew the *truth* about that disk, he probably wouldn't even have used it. I'm spending too much time coaxing him along, and that makes me nervous. It should make you nervous, too. Clear?'

Wilson nodded. Ordinarily, he might have complained, letting Dupree know it was going to cost him. But Wilson knew he had fucked up with the phone and now was not the time to be pushy.

'I'll call you later with an update.' Wilson motioned with his head toward the street. 'The man's going to need a thousand. He says he popped Shepard good.'

Dupree wrinkled his nose. He was like a bank teller, sniffing every withdrawal. He knew that Wilson had probably promised five hundred. Five hundred would go to the guy out in the car, five hundred Wilson would keep for himself. Dupree knew about Wilson's little bank account. He had once found a First Interstate transaction slip in one of the cars, and he called regularly to check Wilson's balance. The idiot had never changed his PIN code from the last four digits of his Social Security number.

Sixty-four thousand, as of Dupree's last call. It was laughable. Over the years and the different ventures, Dupree, himself, had socked away seven digits. He would have been willing to give Wilson more than the sixty-four thousand had he asked. Had Wilson put it forth as a business proposal. But that's what happened when you were caught in the mentality of a small-timer, like the ones they'd seen by the dozen in Harper. The only difference was that Wilson was loyal, stole very little, and up until today he had never made a mistake.

Dupree turned away from the plate-glass entrance and dug into his pocket. He pulled out a small pack of bills, secured with a rubber band. He quickly peeled off ten hundreds and handed them to Wilson. Then he peeled off five more.

'Get yourself a hamburger,' he said. 'Get it later. After.'

Wilson pushed the bills into his own pocket. He owed the guy in the car four hundred. Six for him, plus five more. Eleven hundred in one day wasn't shabby. Suddenly he wasn't feeling so bad anymore.

Dupree grabbed Wilson by the shoulders, and even though Dupree was neither large nor imposing, he stared Wilson down.

'What's up?' Wilson said. His voice warbled slightly.

'Be careful and do it right,' Dupree said. He released Wilson's shoulders and tapped one temple. 'Be smart.'

The room shifted in and out of focus and William Dunn didn't fight it. His eyelids were too heavy, the room too uninteresting. What bed was this? What day? What city?

An insistent throb was emanating from somewhere in his lower extremities, but it wasn't painful. His eyes slid closed and he considered the throb. He considered moving to try to eliminate it, but that would certainly be too much work.

'Dad?' came a voice at his side, and Dunn's eyes opened again. He knew this face, and the face was full of worry and concern.

'Dad, how you doing? It's good to see you coming around.'

How was he doing? Dunn didn't feel qualified to answer. He'd like to close his eyes again, take some time and think about it.

'I've been sitting here for hours. It's about time you opened your eyes. I've been bored out of my skull.'

This was just like his son, Dunn thought. Start blabbering away at you, even if it didn't make any sense.

'You want some water? They said you'd want water.'

Dunn had to admit, water sounded pretty good. He nodded and he heard the sound of pouring off to his right. It seemed to take minutes.

And much in this way, in small incremental steps, a yes or a no, or a long ponderous thought that ended nowhere, William Dunn came back to who he was, and where, and why.

Barry slumped in his chair. How desperately he had wanted to *not* find the phone. To understand why he'd been knocked down. But apparently Hektor had other reasons. Simple intimidation? Perhaps. He flexed one wrist, sprained from the fall, and pulled one of the papers from the pile on his desk.

He'd been working on the emergency notification procedure they would use to contact Simtec customers. He calculated that every TSR could get hold of and explain the defective OS problem to at most one person every ten minutes. If they commandeered additional office space and phone lines, he might be able to get 150 people all dialing at once. Smiling and dialing. Or at least, trying to smile.

That meant they could contact a theoretical nine hundred customers per hour, a number Barry knew was wide of the mark. Part of the telephone corps would be put on hold, reach voice mail and be forced to play phone tag, or miraculously reach the person they were calling but spend more than ten minutes giving the explanation. Highly likely that calls would run long. People would be curious. People would be hesitant. People would be angry.

Even if they started today, this very hour, even if they reached one thousand customers an hour and worked straight through the night, they would contact twenty-four thousand per day. Were they really going to call people at home, in the middle of the night? They had more than 80,000 TechDirect customers, as well as the 110,000 retail customers who had mailed in registrations – 190,000 ten-minute phone calls. They would never make it.

He considered sending telegrams. They could be dispatched in huge batches, but there was no verification that they had been received and acted upon. If the telegram requested a callback, he still had to have someone there to answer the phone, which looped back to the same problem he already faced. And what, exactly, would the telegram say? What would the phone reps say, for that matter? The last thing they needed was 150 people each giving his or her own version of what had gone wrong. There needed to be a standard script to work from, and Barry had already wasted an hour trying to hammer one out. He read it through and scowled. The muscles at the back of his neck had tightened into walnuts. He looked up and saw Spakovsky hovering in the doorway.

'What do we need to talk about?' he barked, surprised at the tone of his own voice.

Spakovsky closed the door. Then he turned and said, 'Whether or not we're going to keep Diane.'

Barry's mouth twitched. 'Go ahead. I'm listening.'

'I'm going to be here all night preparing documents for the board. Recent sales figures have been a disaster. Between that and the press and the internal chaos, there could be a vote. The board may want something to save face.'

Barry knew Spakovsky was close to one of the board members, so this was more than hearsay.

'Jim has withdrawn all support, not that he was ever a supporter. At the time, though, he wasn't able to toss in a negative. This time around he will be consulted. Chris is . . . well, Chris is gone, I suppose. You and I could offer a measure of approval. Not that we'll be present, but there may be inquiries.'

Obviously, there had already been inquiries. 'So what am I supposed to do?' Barry said. 'I'm going to get a phone call? I'm supposed to vote yea or nay, is that it?'

Spakovsky paced, hands fidgeting against one another. 'I don't think it would be put so bluntly. Or, perhaps you will express your intention through me.'

The arrogant sonofabitch. His relationship with the board was the last bit of real power Spakovsky had. This was just like him, too, a bit of backroom dealing with a wink and a nod.

'I'm not voting,' Barry said. He wondered if Spakovsky had been briefed, and if he comprehended the problem with over four hundred thousand Simtec computers. Probably not. He wondered how much the board members knew of events over the past week. Probably only a fraction. But that was how important decisions were made all the time, by people who were familiar with only a piece of the puzzle. They were like the blind men feeling the elephant, except that when these people felt a leg and said it was a tree, by God they had the power to make it a tree.

'Let the board do whatever they want,' Barry said. 'I want no part of it. We've got our own decisions to make. I spoke briefly with Jim, and he's now in favor of payment. I'm leaning in that direction, myself. Diane should be here within the hour, and that will be the first order of business.'

'You won't get any argument from me,' Spakovsky said. Then he added, 'I've been there all along.'

'It's not that we made a wrong decision, Mike. Given what we knew at the time, we made a choice.' Barry thought about going further but decided it wasn't worth it.

'So, neutral, then?' Spakovsky said. 'On the board's vote?'

'I'm not neutral. I choose for my opinion to remain private. It is not my job to make this decision, and I'm not going to masquerade as if it is.'

'I can respect that,' Spakovsky said without sincerity.

Barry returned back to the work on his desk, but Spakovsky lingered, as though expecting Barry to change his mind. Barry looked up and said, 'Good luck with your reports.'

21

The decision to pay five million dollars came without meetings or fanfare. Diane had a long conversation with Jim, a shorter one with Mike, and then she called Barry from a phone in the backseat of her chauffeur-driven Cadillac. She was on her way in from the airport, and she requested that she and Barry meet in her office at 6:00.

Still nothing from Greg Mitchell. Dammit, they needed to know about that code. How did you fight this thing? Simtec could issue a disk, if need be, a kind of 'fix-it' file that could be express-mailed out to customers and dealers. The solution could be as simple as booting from an emergency floppy and clicking a button.

Barry glanced over the contingency plan he'd been working on for three hours. Might as well finish it up and have Diane sign off. He had already taken the text of the message through a dozen revisions.

'We at Simtec believe in the highest standards of customer service, and we regret to inform you that . . .'

He had drawn an *X* through that one almost immediately. It seemed contradictory. How did you have the highest standards of service and allow a factory-installed death trap to slip onto your machines?

'We regret to inform you that . . .'

No, the tone wasn't right. Too somber.

'It has been brought to our attention that . . .'

Too passive. Who brought it to their attention? Was Simtec so inept that they could ship bad files and not even notice it themselves?

This wording would be read by hundreds of thousands of Simtec customers. These were proven customers who would hopefully remain loyal. The message would be scrutinized by the media, then relayed to millions more. It would be second-guessed by computer column pundits across the nation. He knew that they were walking a tightrope.

'Simtec engineers have discovered that some of our products sold over the past three months may have been subjected to tampering.'

Here was a statement that set the right tone. Simtec had discovered the flaw. Machines had been tampered with. They, Simtec and the customer both, had been victimized. Victims, yes, but they were going to overcome the assault. Now he had to convey the gravity of the situation without sounding hysterical.

'A destructive piece of computer code that waits until July 25 to initiate may have been placed on your hard drive, and we want to ensure that you take the necessary steps to eliminate it.'

Accentuate the positive: We're all in this together, and we're going to get you out of it. He finished scribbling out the letter by hand, borrowing and transcribing segments from his earlier attempts. When he finished, he read the letter straight through. It sounded forthcoming, proactive – without revealing too much. A well-worded bombshell.

Mark Willis was lying on his back on the sofa, waiting for the oscillating fan to swing back his way. He was sick of the computer. He was sick of the invisible man who was directing his life. He was young, sharp, and a better programmer than anyone he knew. Sometimes a nine-to-five job began to sound better and better. All you did was go in and punch a clock. He could see how it happened.

Maybe he could go to work for an interesting company. He could do computer work for the Sierra Club or Greenpeace, someplace like that. Those Greenpeace people were always raising hell in their inflatable boats. Maybe they needed computers to keep track of it all. Mark would like that. He could make something special out of his talents without becoming a sellout. Then he could walk away from this whole questionable deal.

A black-and-white TV over on the countertop spewed out the latest in simulated true crime, but Mark ignored it. He'd been ignoring the subject of crime a lot lately. At first the work had been fun, designing hacks and testing them out against real people, and he had gotten better and better at it.

But now he was constantly pressured to take it further, do more damage, and he was trapped in a spiral. If he were caught now, he might even go to prison. No prior arrests, save for the one hacking incident that he doubted was on his police record, but he was past the age and well beyond the innocent tricks that could be chalked up to youthful indiscretion. This was willful and had become, even if the target was a bunch of corporate yuppies, more malicious than he'd anticipated. He'd make sure they paid, but this would be the last time. Fifteen thousand was a lot of money. He was going to take it and split.

Mark thought about going outside, maybe walking up the street to one of a dozen restaurants that clustered around Richmond Avenue, but this was southwest Houston. It would be growing dark, and he wasn't all that confident of his prospects out walking alone. It wasn't that he was small, or particularly timid, but he'd heard about gangs in the area, Hispanic gangs, and he'd seen the graffiti. To them, he'd come walking along like a whitebread snack.

He heard the sound of footsteps on the stairs outside. Great, the neighbors were back. Now he'd get to hear them argue and shout at one another and, if last night was any indication, end up having furious sex. The sound of it came right through the walls, and the woman, a small brown-haired clerk at the local Blockbuster, didn't seem to hold anything back.

Mark was startled to hear the knock at his own door.

He swung his feet down and said, 'Who is it?'

'It's Wilson.'

'Oh,' Mark said. 'Just a minute.' Wilson had taken to stopping by more often, and Mark suspected it was to keep tabs on him. The man would come into the apartment, sniffing around at nothing in particular. His visits were usually brief, his communications terse, except for one time he had arrived when Mark was playing the game Tetris. That had interested

Wilson, the various blocks descending while Mark jockeyed them into place. Mark was a master, and he made it look easy. Wilson tried it one time. He hadn't even figured out how to rotate the blocks before the whole screen had filled up.

Before going to answer the door, Mark walked over and flipped on the computer. Even if he'd run out of ideas and energy, appearances had to be maintained.

He took a quick glance about the apartment and unchained the door.

'Hey,' he said. He went back and sat down on the sofa.

Wilson stepped into the room. 'Doing anything good?' he said. He glanced about and his eyes went to the TV, where a woman was being held up at gunpoint. A subtitle at the bottom of the screen read DRAMATIZATION. The acting was awful, with two beady-eyed punks staring hungrily at a tearful, melodramatic actress.

'You're watching a load of crap, is what you're doing.'

Mark shrugged. 'I'm not watching. I just keep it on.'

'You got any beer in the fridge?' It was an honest question, because Wilson would have liked one. But if the cupboards were bare, that was reason enough to get out and drive to the store.

'I've got milk, peanut butter, coffee. One slice of old pizza. I was thinking about walking over to pick up some things, but this neighborhood is something else. I was walking the other night and this car comes by real slow, checking me out. I didn't look over and they left me alone.'

'Bunch of punks,' Wilson said, but the fact was, Wilson rarely left his car, and when he did, he usually carried a gun and a knife. It was a jungle out there.

'I spoke with the boss. I told him how hard you were working and he wants to give you a raise.'

'Yeah?' Mark sat up straighter.

'He was impressed that you were able to come up with this other thing, the way you were talking about you could hit Simtec—'

'It doesn't hit Simtec. It hits their customers. I downloaded a list of their major corporate accounts, so I've got mailing addresses and the contact people.'

'So what's it do?'

'You know the SmartStar, Simtec's top-of-the-line file server?'

Wilson shook his head. Never heard of it.

'Well, it's an expensive machine. You can easily spend twenty thousand on one, and all the major companies buy them because they're the best. SmartStars run maybe seventy percent of the corporate networks in the United States. Exxon, General Motors, Bank of America, look at that mailing list on the table.'

Wilson glanced at the list, and what the kid was saying was true. The printout was a laundry list of the biggest companies in the United States and the world.

'I'm with you so far,' he said.

'So I've got the addresses of the network people at all of those companies. Really, I found them by accident. I thought it was a list of user accounts in Simtec, but it turned out to be this. Right there in the same directory was official Simtec letterhead. So I realized that I could put that SCSI driver on an update disk and mail them out just as easily as Simtec can. They're always doing that, revising drivers and mailing them out. Sometimes it's to fix bugs, sometimes it's an improvement. The companies on the list pay for this service. They want the best and the latest as soon as it comes out. Nothing stops me from mailing to the exact same list of people. If the package looks good enough, the people on the receiving end won't suspect a thing. Why should they?'

Wilson couldn't think of a reason.

'I logged back in and found a template for making Simtec disk labels. I had to go out and buy an eight-hundred-dollar color printer, but the labels came out nice. They look close to the real thing. The letterhead does too.'

A piece of the letterhead lay on the kitchen table, and Wilson picked it up and read the copy. The letter sounded as corporate as could be.

'I copied what they said in their last mailing,' Mark said. 'It asks them to swap out a file on their SmartStars. It's a simple process. Mr. Draper explained how, on July twenty-fifth, the file goes active and causes the network to freeze for one minute. I figured, if we're going to freeze Simtec, why not freeze some others as well? I thought sending the disks out was a pretty neat idea, so I mailed two dozen letters yesterday with Airborne Express just like Simtec does. Actually, I used Simtec's account number.'

Wilson stared at the letter in his hand. It was addressed to a Mr. Bob Stuart at a division of The Coca-Cola Company. The paper had a crinkle in it, and Mark had written a note on one corner: *reprint*. Wilson had picked up the disk from a faculty mailbox at Rice University, and he knew that the file on the disk was designed to do much more than freeze the network for one minute. It rampaged through files and deleted whole disk drives. It tried to spread into files going down the wiring to everyone on the network. It went after the personal computers sitting on everybody's desks, as well as those machines that Wilson didn't quite understand, the servers. The SmartStars.

And Wilson was beginning to understand the possibilities here: Exxon, General Motors, Bank of America. He had confined his thinking to Simtec, but the kid was a fucking genius. A natural. You hit companies all over the place – hundreds of them – and it was all Simtec's liability. It was Simtec's product and appeared to be one of their own mailers. By the time everyone sorted it out, Simtec's credibility, the faith of their largest corporate accounts, would be ashes. It *was* a neutron bomb.

'Which companies?'

'The first twenty or so. A through C. I mail-merged the address file so I've got the letters for all the other companies, but I thought twenty was enough.'

'I'm amazed, Mark I really am. You're one smart guy. I want to go down to the car and get you the cash for that printer. Eight hundred, you said?'

Mark was beaming. 'Plus labels and paper and extra ink cartridges. And blank disks. Sales tax. I spent about a thousand in all.'

'I don't think that'll be a problem,' Wilson said. 'You hold on a minute and I'll be right back.'

Wilson went back down to the parking lot and called

Dupree. He explained the situation, and five minutes later he was back in the apartment peeling off hundreds. He handed over ten of them and watched with interest as Mark folded them together and pushed them into his front pocket.

'Just like I told you,' Wilson said. 'No problem. We're all impressed as hell with you. I mean that.'

Mark grinned and his eyes dropped to the floor.

'Here's the deal. We need all the leverage we can get. He wants us to go ahead and mail the rest of the letters. What've you got, a couple hundred?'

'Two hundred eighty-two, less the ones I already sent.'

'I'll help you stuff envelopes. Whatever you need. We're going to take them to a drop box so they'll go out tonight. We'll go FedEx, UPS, whatever we need to do. And . . .' Wilson was trying to measure how this was going over. 'You're going to get a ten thousand dollar bonus. Tonight.'

That was what Dupree had said, Promise him anything. It didn't really matter.

'Wow,' Mark said. He looked around the room, unconsciously pulling at his lower lip. Ten thousand dollars for doing a simple direct mail. He turned back and gave Wilson an appraisal. 'You're going to have to learn how to print labels.'

They missed the last local pickup, so Wilson was forced to drive all the way to Intercontinental airport to get the letters mailed.

The woman working the counter gave him a funny look, coming in on a Saturday night with five grocery sacks full of express mail.

'I'm the manager of mailings,' Wilson said. 'We got hung up today and couldn't get these out on time. You're sure they'll go out tonight?'

Slob that he was, somehow manager of mailings seemed to fit Wilson. The woman had never heard of such a position. 'Simtec, huh?' she said importantly. 'We'll get them out. You can count on it. We don't deliver on Sunday, but they'll be there first thing Monday morning.'

'You're an angel,' Wilson said. 'That's what I want. That's perfect.'

He trotted out to the car and thought about what he had to do next. Then he drove back into town, tapping his finger along with an Aerosmith oldie on the radio.

He went right through the door into Mark's apartment and said, 'Come on, I'll buy you a beer.' Wilson looked over the apartment again, as though he were searching for someone else to invite. 'Then we'll get you paid.'

Ordinarily, Mark would have declined. He didn't really know this man, undoubtedly his watchdog, but tonight a beer sounded good. He'd been working nonstop for days. Even watchdogs got bored, and perhaps Wilson was trying to break the ice.

'All right, let me get some shoes on. And a ten spot.' Mark motioned with his head toward the kitchen.

'It's on me,' Wilson said, thinking, Good, cash in the kitchen. Hopefully whatever was left of his five thousand from the last job. That would make a nice deposit in Wilson's account.

Mark pulled on some tennis shoes, and the two left by the front door. Wilson was driving a white Isuzu pickup. He rotated between three cars that Dupree had provided, but the one he'd used to hit William Dunn was now mothballed. The little truck was his least favorite. He had to hunch down to get in, and when he hit a bump, his head smacked into the ceiling.

'You got a truck,' Mark said. 'Cool.'

'Can't stand it. Damn thing runs better than any car I've had, but I hate it.'

'You buy it new?'

Stupid question, thought Wilson; the body of the truck was beat to hell, but the kid was trying to make conversation. 'No,' he said. 'It's a hand-me-down.'

'So,' Mark said. 'Do you think we're going to get paid? By Simtec, I mean?'

'I have no idea.' Wilson stared out the windshield. He didn't want to discuss work. He didn't want to discuss anything. He turned off onto a side street that cut through some apartments and then past a baseball field. His left hand moved down beside the seat and found the knife he had positioned there. He folded open the blade, coughing once to cover the sound.

'There's a Circle K up here past the apartments,' Mark said. 'Turn left at the stop sign.'

Wilson went straight instead. He had that tingling sensation up across his forehead, and he hoped his voice didn't betray him. 'I want to find a liquor store,' he said. 'I think there's one up here, and we can make it just before closing.'

'Oh.' Mark tapped his fingers on the dashboard.

Wilson moved the knife up beside his left leg. He set it there and then took the wheel with his left hand. He'd driven this stretch of road twice already today, working through his moves. He reached down with his right hand, as though he were putting the hand in his lap, and grabbed the handle, blade down, the way you hold an ice pick.

They were coming to the stretch of road by the ball field, two blocks with only a single streetlight and nobody around.

'You ever play any baseball?' Wilson said. He gestured toward the field out to the right and Mark turned his head.

The knife came up fast, Wilson bringing it up to his chest level. This part was exactly as he'd practiced it, slapping his empty hand across into the passenger seat. This time he whipped his arm around and caught the kid right in the chest.

Mark might have seen something coming. He started to turn back right at the last second, but far too late to make any difference. The knife went straight in. Mark's head turned toward Wilson and one hand fought up toward the door handle.

Wilson didn't let up. He held the knife there until the hand stopped fighting. He had pulled off into a parking lot beside the road, and he watched in the mirror for headlights. Finally he withdrew the blade and wiped it on Mark's blue jeans.

Then he took out a large plastic trash bag from under the seat. He opened it and slipped it over the kid's head and shoulders, maneuvered it down to his waist. He pushed the whole bundle down onto the floorboards.

Damn, he muttered to himself, and wiped his hand on a small towel. He grunted and leaned his bulk across the seat. Then he pawed his way past the plastic and found the kid's blue jeans. He had to probe the pockets with two pudgy fingers until he came up with the apartment keys and wallet.

Then he went back in and poked around some more until he found the little packet of hundred dollar bills.

Wilson repositioned the bag distastefully. A five-minute drive and he'd be rid of this ugly parcel. He already had a place picked out.

Barry spent another hour finalizing the notification. At eleven o'clock, he headed wearily out through the empty TechDirect administrative offices and out to the parking lot. Four or five hours' sleep and he'd be back. Right now, he was becoming useless, reading the same sentence five times before it registered.

Claudia had waited up, watching an old movie on a portable TV in the kitchen. Barry warmed some leftovers and carried them to the table. He motioned for her to leave it on, but after four minutes of Cary Grant, the phone rang. Barry went over and answered the extension by the refrigerator.

'Barry? I didn't catch you at work and I wanted to let you know how it's coming.'

Fortunately, it was Greg Mitchell. Barry couldn't bear another call from Seidler or Spakovsky or, for that matter, Diane Hughes, every statement full of political jockeying and not-so-subtle undertones.

'I was about to call you several times but then I got caught up in other things,' Barry said, and he thought: like discovering that the executive vice president and the CEO are involved in a clash of the Titans. So what if four hundred thousand computers blew up? Let them all go kaboom with Diane and Jim holding on.

'I've got to tell you, first of all, that I'm really in over my head with this code and I'm having to rely on other people. Whoever I can pull in, really.'

'I understand.' The refrigerator motor kicked on and started its periodic clanging. Barry moved down the counter.

'The Security Associates people have been a big help. We've picked through the instructions that check the date. We see how that works. We're going through what happens when it activates. That's where we are right now. We've made progress, but it's slow. We've had to fight through tunneling code. It's got encryption. This thing is a hairy bastard.'

'Does it go after the file allocation table? Is that what it's doing?'

'You get writes into the FAT and it hits the partition table. That's why you get the hard drive failure. What I've been hoping for, in my own mind, is something like a switch that will turn off the code. You know, something they built in to deactivate the segment.'

'That would be clever.' And it would probably cost them five million dollars to find it with any expediency. Greg had been fighting with this ever since he left Jim's office ten hours ago, and this was how far they'd gotten. 'Get people in there to work on it all night. Go home, grab some sleep if you need to, but I think you know the importance of nailing this down.'

'Jim's been by. He had some suggestions and gave us a pep talk.' Barry stared balefully at the side of the refrigerator. He'd been focusing exclusively on the notification plan. 'If Jim has ideas, you should pay attention to them. He's a much better engineer than I am.'

'I'm afraid the debugging is just slow.' Greg Mitchell sounded exhausted. 'It's not like pulling apart our own work, you can imagine, with documentation and folks who can look at it and recognize the game plan.'

'I should tell you this, Greg. We've been offered the opportunity to buy our way out, and we're going to take it. If there is a built-in keyword, we may get it that way. On the other hand,' Barry said, thinking aloud, 'we could pay and get nothing. We need to keep working on our own, both on the fix and what to do for machines that go down.'

'We'll keep on it,' Greg said. And then, as though waiting to hear his death sentence, he quietly added, 'How many machines?'

'Four hundred thirty-one thousand, six hundred six.'

'Oh, my God.'

'You see? None of us will be able to sleep tonight anyway.'

Barry hung up the phone and turned to find Claudia staring at him.

'I'm surprised you told him.'

'Told him what?'

'About paying the money.'

Barry still had half his meal on the table, but he wasn't hungry. He went to the refrigerator and poured tonic water. Straight. He pounded the side of the refrigerator until the clanging stopped.

'I also said it was important for him to keep working, which it is. But I don't think it's right to have Greg in there busting his brains, thinking it's do-or-die, meanwhile we go out and buy a solution. I think he deserves to know that the possibility exists.'

'Won't that take the edge off?'

Why was she fighting him on this? 'I don't think so. Just because you're going to court, and you think the opposition might settle, you don't stop preparing, do you? In fact, the more work you do, the more likely you don't have to go to trial. You should have heard his voice when I told him the number of machines.'

'Maybe so,' she said thoughtfully. 'When did you decide to pay?'

'That was Diane's call, but Jim and Mike both supported the decision. I did, too. The damage we're confronting—' Barry shook his head. 'Not only that, the board of directors is apparently at a boiling point, and Diane has to provide some answers. The two of us met this evening and she seemed completely out of it. I think she never expected the magnitude of what these people were capable of – none of us did. I was talking about how to notify our customers, and it was going right by her. In nine months, Claudia, I had never seen that woman lose focus once.'

Claudia considered this. Then she said, 'I'm glad you're going to pay.'

'Part of me is glad, too. Part isn't.'

'Could it happen tonight?'

'I'm not going anywhere tonight.'

Barry craned his neck to see out to where the car sat by the front curb. 'What about those two outside, what do they do all day?'

'They sit in the car. Sometimes they smoke. I spoke to them once, when I got the mail. He noticed me coming down the walk, so he rolled down his window. I guess he thought I was coming to speak to him. "Howdy," he said. When he saw I was getting the mail, he rolled the window back up.'

'Do they eat? Where do they go to the bathroom?'

'I don't know,' Claudia said. 'It's their job. I'm sure they have some kind of routine. At first it was disconcerting, thinking there were two men out in front watching over the house. I can tell you this, I've grown used to the idea and now I kind of like it.'

'Good. I like it, too. Have the neighbors called to see what the hell is going on?'

'I called the Richards, the Klines, and the Burtons. I said we'd gotten some threatening phone calls, so we'd hired the security patrol for a couple of days.'

'Because of phone calls? What did they say about that?'

'I got mostly answering machines. I did speak to Rick. He thought it was unnecessary. He said if anyone comes into his yard, Coney will tear them to pieces. He said we could borrow him if we want to.'

'A dachshund?'

They both laughed, but then Barry winced and put a hand to his side.

'What's that all about?'

'You wouldn't believe it. I fell down today at the office.' Barry sipped tonic to hide his guilty expression. Claudia watched suspiciously.

'You fell down.'

'Yes.'

She gave him a hard stare.

Oh, what the hell! He capitulated. She would eventually get it out of him anyway. 'Someone pushed me down on the jogging track behind the buildings. I was going over to the production center, and I heard someone coming behind me. Next thing you know, I'm lying on the ground.'

'Deliberately? You're saying the person knocked you down on purpose?'

'Of course he did. He kept on running and was long gone by the time we got our act together.'

'Why? Why would somebody do that?'

'Intimidation. At first, I was convinced they did it to get

the phone back. A woman who was inside the building said she thought the man was looking for something in the grass. I didn't have the phone, so I thought they must have taken it back.'

'But you still have it.' She glanced toward where the phone sat on the kitchen table.

'I know. Now I've decided it was a little reminder. We can find you anywhere, at any time, even at your own building. There's no other explanation. The man didn't say a word.'

Claudia was perched on the edge of her chair, fitting the pieces together. Barry gets knocked down. He hires two guards to sit in front of the house.

This last move was sounding totally reasonable.

Terry Wilson parked on the opposite side of the Westwood apartments. He was now in a blue Cutlass. He strolled back through the grounds, past the scrappy bean-shaped swimming pool and started up the stairwell to Mark's apartment.

Halfway up, he heard something, a metal crunching sound. His eyes darted to the right. Shit, some punk and his girlfriend were sitting out on the landing. They had already looked over toward him, so Wilson did what he always did in such situations – act normal, like you know exactly what you're doing. The technique had saved him more than once.

There were only two keys, and the first one he tried went right in. At the last second, he turned his head toward the punks. They were watching him, more out of curiosity than anything else. He nodded in their direction and went inside.

He had to feel around for the light switch and, in the process, knocked his knee into a chair. His teeth came together hard. The knee still hurt from when he'd fallen down outside Shepard's house. The fucking guy had taken a swing at him with a baseball bat, Wilson had decided. A second bat had been outside on the ground, so that had to be what it was.

At first he'd been furious, but later, after finding himself all in one piece, he'd decided that was a pretty cool thing for Shepard to do. It was the kind of thing he himself would have done, finding someone trying to come in through his window. You stepped up to the plate and wham, smacked a home run right through the glass.

He flexed the knee and shook it off. Dupree had better pay him well for this. Then he made a wolf-grin and began his search.

The search lasted three minutes. There wasn't much in the kitchen to search, and when he hefted a box of Rice Krispies, the weight didn't feel right. Inside was an envelope, which Wilson dumped greedily onto the counter. He made a quick count: thirty-four hundred dollars. Where had the other sixteen gone? How did you spend sixteen hundred dollars, living in a dump like this with all expenses paid?

The printer, that's how. He remembered the kid had paid for that out of his own pocket. Wilson stuffed the envelope into his pants and began going over the apartment. He examined the commode, the bathroom cabinets, the sofa cushions; he checked the living-room carpet for loose places. Until he came, at last, to the computer.

It was still on, and he glared at it with mistrust. Dupree had given him explicit instructions about this. All information, every disk – anything to do with the computer – was to be eliminated. But with those two punks out there, Wilson would be damned if he was going to walk out the front door carrying a computer. He was going to have to erase the thing.

He approached the desk dubiously. They were screwing Simtec for a hundred thousand dollars – he suspected Dupree might be lying and asking twice that – the least they could do was use one of Simtec's own computers. To Wilson these no-name brands didn't seem classy; it was like smoking generic cigarettes. Dupree had called the computer a *clone,* whatever that meant. It was a perfect example of these computer words that had formed their own cryptic language. Clone? it sounded like the damn thing had come in on a spaceship. What it really meant, Wilson had decoded, was *copy,* maybe even, *cheap copy.* In the same spirit, he figured he could look at someone's wrist and say, 'That's not a Rolex, that's a clone.'

'Let the kid buy a clone, software, whatever he wants,' Dupree had said, sending Wilson to the store with five thousand cash. Dupree asked for the receipts, too, which was a pisser because Wilson had wanted the chance to skim.

Wilson sat down and tapped the keyboard. His heart was beating. Here was the chance to show what he'd learned, because he *had* been learning. He prided himself on staying a step ahead, and he'd managed to pick up more computer skills than Dupree, or even himself, would have ever imagined.

He knew how to navigate his way into different directories, and he knew how to delete what he found there. That seemed to be enough to get the job done, and for the next twenty minutes, Wilson fought his way through the directory tree. When he got through, he was sweating.

Lastly, he used a towel to wipe down everything he'd touched. Not that he expected trouble. The body wouldn't be found for some time, and even if it was, the apartment had not been rented in the kid's name. Still, the cops could be clever sometimes, and he didn't want to take any chances.

Barry woke up in the middle of the night, thinking about the cellular phone. The phone hadn't been taken back from him. Was it possible something had been done to it? Why else would the man be bent over in the grass, searching? That would explain why Barry had found it again. He'd found the phone, but perhaps it had been altered.

He lay there, half-asleep, going over it a dozen times. His mind drifted to Jim and Diane. Mike Spakovsky. Jockeying for position between themselves and with the Simtec directors.

Barry had met the directors on numerous occasions. But he didn't court their attention, and he had never spent time with any of them outside of business. The board was a distraction, a necessary by-product of any corporation, but not always a welcome or efficient one. Barry Shepard's company would remain private, he decided, and in those early-morning hours he again began to think it through: he wanted to manufacture, to produce something tangible. There were plenty of widgets that Simtec was too preoccupied to produce themselves. With his knowledge of production and marketing, not to mention his contacts in the company, he ought to be able to land one of those contracts. And once he got it, he'd never lose it, because Barry Shepard's widgets would be the best.

He would reward quality work and performance. He'd establish the kind of corporate culture where, if you tried to stab someone in the back, you'd be out the door.

He rolled over and stared groggily at the alarm: 4:15. The cellular phone. If there were more than one phone, no doubt the others would be registered in his name also. He hadn't checked at the time, but there were probably a raft of phones registered to Shepard. Jay Starns would be able to look them up, just as he had the last one.

Barry remembered speaking to Jay and jotting down the fax number in his day planner. Had he not also taken down the serial number of the phone? He sat straight up in bed. Claudia stirred and rolled over. He picked up the cellular from the bedside table, turned off the motion alarm and padded downstairs.

The day planner lay on the desk. He flipped through the pages to a section even more chaotic than the rest. Starns, he had scribbled in the upper left corner, beside a fax number and what appeared to be a serial number: 0034LD2598. As he recalled, there had been several numbers, and at first he had not given the correct one. He shook the phone out of its sleeve and flipped it over. Pried off the back cover. He read off the numbers: 3153G, next line 13459D12.

The first line, 3153G, sounded like the model number. The other would be a unique serial number. It really didn't matter, because neither one matched the number written in his day planner. He turned to a fresh page and transcribed the new serial number from the plate in the battery compartment.

He sat still for a moment, turning the phone carefully in his hand. This cellular might look exactly the same, but it *was* a different phone. A ceiling fan ticked overhead. They had gone to great difficulty to get that phone back, which meant somebody must have made a mistake. What that mistake might be, he would have to discover, but the thought made him feel good. Simtec had already made far too many of its own.

22

The 431,606 computers started going off early on Sunday morning. The first call came in at 2:00 A.M. to Simtec's twenty-four-hour technical support.

'I'm afraid something's gone wrong with my hard drive,' the caller said, sounding fearful, but still confident the Simtec gurus could bail him out.

'What's the problem?' the tech support specialist asked, rapidly punching keywords into a search field on-screen. The first suggestion out of the database was 'Reinitialized with conflicting OS version,' and the two worked through a series of steps designed to identify the problem, all to no avail.

Next was 'Missing command interpreter,' and an increasingly distraught customer jumped through several more hoops with an equal lack of success.

After forty minutes, tech support finally said, 'This sounds like a new one,' but by that time, someone else was calling on another line with exactly the same description. Before the night was out, the problem would not be new at all.

Barry Shepard was called at 5:15 A.M., as he was stepping out of the shower, by the manager of the TechDirect Customer Assurance Center. He grabbed a towel and made a dash for the phone, got it on the fourth ring, and stood dripping on the carpet. The manager apologized profusely for calling on a Sunday, but he thought it might be important to get the jump on an assessment. He described what they had encountered and that it appeared to be more than an isolated occurrence.

Barry hung up and smashed his fist against the dresser. Forgetting cellular phones and their vagaries, he dressed hurriedly in slacks and a sport shirt. Claudia slipped out of bed and pulled on a robe. 'What is it?' she said, appearing in the doorway behind him.

'That was Ed Roberts. He's the manager of technical support. The problem I told you about last night? The hard drives are already going. They haven't gotten their money, and it sounds like they're hitting the drives.' He began furiously pushing an electric razor across his jaw and neck. Twenty seconds and he clicked it off.

'How would they push up the date? You said the computers were shipped a month ago.'

'They've found a way to do plenty of other things,' Barry said between his teeth. 'I need to get in and take a look at it, then get with Jim and Diane and plan how we're going to respond. There is also an emergency board meeting today, and Diane is in the hot seat. It's going to be a zoo.'

Claudia came over and raised a hand to his cheek. She ran it down his jaw. 'There's that look again,' she said.

His eyes flared a mixture of anger and defeat. 'I'll call you later in the day.' He slipped on loafers and was out the door.

While driving in, he talked to both the CEO and the executive vice president. Barry didn't want to undercut anyone's authority, and so he decided to play it straight and keep them both informed. Let the board of directors speak on such matters.

He found the Technical Support Center in chaos. The center was organized as a series of cubicles down each side, where the technicians took calls. A work area in the middle held a dozen Simtec models, set up in a test bed. Concern about overtime and a considerate manager made for a lower staff count on Sundays. The few technicians on duty scampered back and forth across the floor while the no-longer-benevolent manager barked orders.

The whole scene made Barry feel desperate. Furious. The ground was yawning beneath them, twitching and preparing to open a giant mouth that could swallow them all. Why now? Why had Hektor jumped his deadline? There were other explanations – perhaps a few people had inadvertently set the system clocks on their computers ahead – but that seemed like wishful thinking. From the reports of Tech Manager Ed Roberts, they were dealing with dozens of machines.

If all four hundred thousand were starting to drop, Simtec would be forced to issue radio and TV announcements and go live with a press conference. Diane had charged Barry with verifying the problem and determining its scope. Then they would discuss the next step.

As soon as Ed Roberts saw him, he cut a path toward Barry.

'This is impossible,' Ed said. 'A nightmare.'

'When did you get the first report?'

'Between two and three A.M. this morning. I wasn't beeped until four. I got here at four-thirty. After I got a sense of what was going on, I called you.'

'I'd like to look at the reports and go over what you've tried so far. I've been in touch with both Jim and Diane, and I need to give them an assessment. We're going to meet on this as soon as possible.'

Ed's lips set into a firm, straight line. He'd called his boss to report a highly unusual set of errors, but he hadn't expected it to shoot to the top of the company within the hour. 'They're going to meet with you?' he asked warily. 'What do they want to know?'

'We're all extremely interested in this. The problem may be related to a file . . . something that was introduced to a number of our machines. Kind of like a virus.'

Barry saw the look on Ed Roberts' face and knew what he was thinking. 'Yes,' Barry said. 'Whoever did it is the same person responsible for our other problems.'

'Give me a print of those logs,' Ed said to one of the technicians, all of whom seemed to be eyeing Barry's arrival with interest. Barry made it to the Tech Center a couple of times a month, but never on a Sunday morning.

A sheaf of paper was handed to the tech manager and he began flipping through.

'One of these was running Norton AntiVirus. Another one claims to have had a McAfee boot scan. You say a virus was introduced to our machines. Do you mean a new virus? Why haven't I heard about it?'

'I don't have the details,' Barry dissimulated. 'We've got a team working on it, and I'll let you know as soon as we have anything concrete.'

Barry looked down and began leafing through the call reports. Along with the customer profile, he got the abbreviated shorthand of the tech support reps:

>2:08/097145 Cust rpts crashed HD. Comet SN JC08114AZ3

Tried cold boot. RAM chk: OK, then nothing. Acts like no partition. Chk CMOS: OK. Had cust boot from floppy. No HD. Cust says all normal as of yesterday. No backup.

>2:26/097146 Misc HD prob. JStar SN JS3575QBAA

Cust gets nothing on bootup.
Has no originals. No avail system disk. Requested overnight mail repl. OS

There were eleven reports in all. None exactly the same in the way the problem had been described, but close enough. Half the calls had come in between 2:00 and 3:00 A.M., probably late-nighters, then another half dozen after 4:00 A.M., the early birds on the East Coast.

'They can't see the hard drive at all,' Barry said. 'Is there anything you can think of that hasn't been tried?'

'We're working on it. You see that group over there?' Ed Roberts indicated a cluster of three techs who were hovering around a telephone and a hastily set-up Comet. 'They've got some kind of Sysop on-line. The guy is very knowledgeable. They're walking him through everything they can think of.'

'Okay,' Barry said. He had seen enough. 'Keep doing all you can. Mail out disks if they want them. If they're in the support program, we'll send out a technician.'

Neither of which would do any good, but at least it would help keep people pacified. Barry lowered his voice. 'Instruct everyone *not* to reveal that this is a known problem. We don't need technicians telling anyone that this has been going on all morning. We need to get a handle on it first.'

Ed nodded agreement. Nothing would be worse than telling a customer his hard drive had crashed – that he might have lost everything on it – due to a known and as yet unsolved problem.

Barry held up the call reports. 'I need to hold on to these. We'll be back in touch, hopefully within an hour.' At the door to the room, Barry took one last look. The fax machine was spewing paper onto the floor. A phone was ringing unanswered at somebody's desk. The tech crew looked like a small, ragtag army that was rapidly depleting its ammunition.

Barry grabbed coffee on the way to his office. Someone had left the morning *Chronicle* on the countertop, open to the front page of the business section. SIMTEC HIT AGAIN.

He scanned what he already knew. The stock had dropped ten points due to shipping errors, a slew of bad marks from the analysts, and, most recently, rumors of in-house turmoil and a possible shake-up. The article was succinct but deadly, pointing ominously to the threat of further losses. Mercifully, Barry's name was not mentioned once. The mistakes of his own unit had been subsumed by the larger and more recent morass of blunders.

He went to his desk and dialed Jim Seidler at home. Ever since the divorce, Jim had been secretive. *Quiet* might be a better word, but after what Richard Green had said about the house sale, the whole episode struck Barry as secretive. Jim answered after three rings but said he was on the other line.

Barry waited, fingering the printout of calls reporting the bad hard drives. If the stock market analysts and the newspaper columnists read what he held in his hand, the stock would go into a free fall.

Jim clicked back on. 'Barry, are you still there?'

'Yes.'

'Sorry, that was Richard Rowster. He's had his ear to the ground and he's in a frenzy. Apparently, he spoke with his lawyer and they want me to fax the documentation on our director's liability policy. I told him to call Karen Williams.'

With four years on the board, Richard Rowster was Simtec's good old boy. He'd been brought in for his military contacts, and Barry had heard that in those circles the man was known as *Rooster*. He was colorful all right, and his practical experience from the boards of Raytheon and McDonnell

Douglas had occasionally been useful, but he was also a loose cannon, as unbridled before the media as he was unpolished.

'I don't know Karen's schedule,' Barry said. 'You might try to reach her at home.'

'No. Let Rowster wait. He already insisted I meet him at the airport. I'll go out there, hold his hand and get him calmed down. You know Spakovsky's giving a report at the meeting. Coopers and Lybrand will make a statement. You better hang loose this afternoon, in case they want to drag you in, too.'

'What would they ask?'

'They might want to know about your area. You've had a good track record, and they may want to ask your opinion. It's only a possibility.'

'My opinion on what?'

'They might want another perspective on our current operations, our leadership. More of a background assessment.'

'I'd like to have time to prepare for that.'

'And I'd rather walk naked through downtown than talk to them at all. You're going to see a bunch of idiots swinging a sword in there. They're just as likely to whack off a head and have three grow back in its place. Let's hope they only swing once.'

After taking aim at Diane Hughes, thought Barry. Then the executive vice president would be sitting pretty. 'I've seen the tech reports,' he said.

'What does it look like?'

'At least eleven machines have cratered. It sounds to me like the date kicked in early. We won't know for sure until we get one of the actual machines. Of course the techs didn't ask about the system date, but I think it's too coincidental to believe eleven computers had the date set to the twenty-fifth.'

'Eleven is not enough to pull the trigger on this press package,' Jim said. 'Not while we've still got solutions out there.'

'I don't know about solutions, but the package isn't ready anyway. Did you see the morning paper? The stock will go through the floor. I showed a draft press release to Diane, but she seemed distracted. She barely read it. I think we need to change the tone. We need something that says exactly what was done, how they did it, and then describes the steps we've taken to correct the situation. We need to lay this out in plain English – one, two, three.'

'And what should those steps be?'

Barry's voice elevated. 'We're working on that. As you know, we've had people on it all night. You need to get over here. Then we can sit down and iron it out.'

'Whatever we do, we don't drop this bombshell yet. That's what I say.' Jim paused, and with apparent satisfaction added, 'You can call Diane and get her reaction. It may be the last big decision she makes.'

William Dunn lay in bed, feeling where they'd put the pin into his femur. They called it a pin, which sounded dainty and less intrusive than the reality of a goddamned stainless steel rod the width of a pencil. They drilled the rod right into your bone, tied it with a rope attached to a twelve-pound weight, and slung the weight up and over a pulley at the foot of the bed. A torture chamber should be so pretty.

He was picking up twinges from the general area in his leg, but he also knew that he wasn't feeling the half of it. There was a trade-off you made between pain medication and clear thinking, and Dunn knew you couldn't have both. He would fight that battle as much as he could, and he'd hit the button on the morphine pump when he had to.

Karen Williams had called last night. He could remember that. And he'd received calls from several of his longtime employees. Perhaps it was only morning energy that would soon dissipate, but right now his twenty-eight hours in bed seemed to stretch into days. Will Dunn was restless.

He rotated his head and glanced around the room. After his son had left, another keeper appeared in his place. It was a young guy, an Internet connectivity and UNIX specialist. Poor kid. His expertise didn't place him in the thick of things at Simtec, so they must have foisted this duty on him. Sick bay, way out of the action. The guy was sitting in an armchair reading a novel, unaware that Will Dunn was now awake.

Dunn cleared his throat and punctured the silence of the room. 'Hey there,' he said. 'How about getting me a laptop?'

The young man sat up and the novel fumbled out of his hands onto the floor. He snatched it up and stood at attention.

'And make sure I've got a phone line in here. I'm not going to be able to connect to that hospital thing.'

The young man looked from Dunn to the phone on the bedside stand.

'What's your name?' Dunn said.

'Tony Martoli.'

'Tony, get us a fax also. If we're going to do any work around here, we're going to need to fax.'

Tony dropped the paperback novel onto the chair behind him. He was back in business.

Greg Mitchell drank his second Diet Coke of the morning. The drink was sweet and bubbly and he didn't really want it, but it was the only thing to be had, so he drank it anyway.

He and two other Simtec programmers, Vadim and Marty Simon, had set up shop in a conference room on the second floor. They were also getting indispensable help from two Security Associates employees. One was a debugger and the other had good Intel background.

As his mother had tried to explain on the phone, Vadim had the flu. He was pale, and he left for the bathroom on a regular basis, but little by little they were picking through every piece of the disassembled code. They'd brought in two computers, telephones, and they had the chalkboards covered with chicken scratch.

Greg rubbed his eyes and yawned. His mind was drifting. SONIC would be a good name for this project, he decided. Jim Seidler had stopped by late last night and made the statement that 'If they couldn't stop them, these machines were going to go off around the country like a sonic boom.'

They usually named their projects at Simtec, just as they did at most hardware and software manufacturers. That way an employee might say, 'Hey, what are those guys working on in the conference room?'

'Oh, that's SONIC in there.'

And even though you might not have a clue what the SONIC project was, you could now refer to it in the concrete. He got put on SONIC. The SONIC team is behind schedule. Who the hell does he think he is? You'd think he was working on SONIC.

The whole project took on a life of its own, grew a reputation and a personality and became a focal point its human appendages could rally around. Except that now, Greg Mitchell was hoping that no one would ever know he worked on the project. SONIC? No, I never heard of that one. Couldn't tell you who was involved.

SONIC? They were too fucking slow. All their machines cratered.

'You did what?' Dupree said, gaping at Wilson.

'There were some kids on the landing. I couldn't carry the computer out the front door, so I erased the hard drive. I went through every directory and deleted the files.' Wilson felt proud of himself. The boss was probably shocked to discover how much he knew about computers.

Dupree stared in disbelief. His mouth worked open into a half-yawn that was not a yawn at all. He waited long enough for Wilson to take it back, to tell him that it was all a joke, and then he said three words: 'You dumb sonofabitch.'

This was not the praise Wilson had expected. His teeth came together hard.

'Did anyone tell you to delete files? Did anyone say, That's okay. We don't need the computer back?'

Wilson was trying to work it through. Where had he screwed up? 'Did you want the files?'

'No, I didn't want the files. The problem is, every PC utility in the book has a command that allows you to retrieve deleted files. You didn't delete anything. All the files are still sitting there.'

'How's that?'

A reddish flush crept up from Dupree's neckline. 'They're there. They haven't been erased. If I had a computer right here I'd show you.'

Wilson looked away suspiciously, as though he were being

tricked. 'Screw that,' he said finally, but the tone was an admission of failure.

'You're going to have to go back and do what I told you. Get the computer.'

Wilson frowned. Those people might be outside again, and something about the place had given him a bad feeling. His very ignorance about computers was making him timid. If it were a television set, he could carry it out onto the landing and spin any number of yarns. He was fixing the antenna for his nephew. He was swapping it out for one that was cable-ready. But Wilson didn't know about computers, didn't even know how to talk about them. Look at the only thing he'd tried to do – delete files. Here he was thinking he was smart, and he'd fucked up.

'They got a good look at me once already. It was like they were used to seeing the kid come in and out, but who the hell was I? If I come walking out with a computer, there may be questions. They might call security, the cops, whatever.'

Dupree squinted, sizing up his alternatives. 'You want to play computer technician, here's what you do. Take a screwdriver with you. Take the case off the computer and take out the hard drive. You can put it in your pocket. I don't care about the rest. Do you know which one the hard drive is?'

Wilson nodded vigorously. He *thought* he knew which one it was. He'd figure it out.

'There will be two cables connected to it. One is power and the other is a flat gray ribbon cable. Unplug those and unscrew the drive. It'll take five minutes. You got it?'

Sure, Wilson thought. No problem.

The cellular phone rang just as Barry was getting up to go back to the Tech Center. He dragged out the taping device and stuffed the phone into it.

'This is Barry,' he said. He kicked the door closed with the heel of one shoe.

'Hello, Barry,' came the now familiar voice. It was a cocky, singsong voice that made Barry furious.

'I'm taping,' Barry warned. He was expecting to get

payment instructions, and he wanted to have them unambiguous and on record.

'I don't care if you want to tape me or not. I should think the picture is pretty clear to you by now.'

'The picture is not at all clear.'

'Then let me clarify. You have researched the status of your computers? I suspect you are aware of our recent demonstration.'

'Yes. I believe so.'

'You *believe*?'

'What do you mean by demonstration?'

'Don't be coy. A sample of what will be happening two days from now. A minuscule sample, really. A few computers were primed for action two days early. I'm sure it has been an eye-opener for everyone involved.'

'How many is a few?'

'I really can't say. A couple of hours' worth. How many go through production in that time? You would know better than I.'

So, that was it. They set the activation date differently, to July 23, and a couple of hours later, swapped out the files again. Depending on the meaning of *a couple of hours,* the time of day, and the volume of orders on that day, the files would have been downloaded to anywhere from a dozen to several hundred computers. Not yet an eruption of catastrophic proportions.

'The important thing is that you now take me seriously. We are capable of doing more than erase a few files. Much more. You have only seen the tip of the iceberg.'

'We have taken you seriously from the beginning.'

'Not true, Mr. Barry Shepard. Not true. You took me only one-fifth as seriously as I wished to be taken. Now you're going to make me wait until the very last day, and I believe you should pay a penalty for that. Yes, I believe that you should. You will pay double. Ten million. It's like landing on Boardwalk when someone has a hotel. It's expensive.'

Barry had no bargaining position, and they both knew it. He pressed his palms into the desk and rocked forward. 'I'm sitting here trying to pay you. I'm talking in good faith. You've already set your price. You can't just change it.'

'I can do whatever I want. I can ask for whatever I want. You have no idea what's going to happen at midnight on Monday. Not in your wildest dreams. I've been saving this one, Barry. I'd like to tell you to see the look on your face, but I'm afraid I've got to wait. Unless I'm paid, truth be known, I'm going to just let it happen.'

'We want to give you a check today. Five million. And in return we will require certain assurances.' Unenforceable assurances, but they'd ask all the same.

'You want to pay today? Wrong, Barry Shepard. Hektor doesn't take checks on a Sunday.'

'You won't take it?'

'How am I going to deposit it? How am I going to know if it clears? You'll pay me first thing Monday morning, and you will pay by a wire transfer. You need to get all your authorizations in order for first thing Monday morning. Ten million, Shepard. Go preach it to your handlers.'

'A wire transfer.'

'Exactly. We'll plan on Monday morning at nine-thirty. I'll call at that time and make arrangements. You and I will do the transfer. You need to make sure that, given an account and a routing number, you can make the transfer happen immediately and without error. I won't release a scrap of information until it clears the account.'

'What if we can do that today?'

'On a Sunday? Do you know any bankers, Barry Shepard? Do you think bankers are going to worry about your problems *today*? One tiny little Simtec transfer. Do you think the Federal Reserve gives a hoot? I don't think so.'

'Give me some time to work on it.'

'Time! First I get snubbed, they tell me to get lost. Take a hike, Jack. Now they can't slip me a check fast enough. Isn't that the way of the world? Ten million, Barry Shepard. Get busy.'

There was something about the tone, the confidence of Hektor's voice, that made Barry absolutely certain of what he was hearing. Hektor had a weapon – something in addition to what they had already seen – and he was going to use it. *Tomorrow.*

And now Barry Shepard was simply afraid.

He picked up the phone and made a conference call to Jim and Diane. Diane was in her car and Jim didn't pick up. He recounted the details of the conversation to Diane. A wire transfer for ten million dollars, tomorrow morning. He also explained Hektor's threat, and his own fear, of additional damage.

'We're backed against a wall and he knows it,' Diane said.

Barry agreed. He could feel the wall hitting right up against his spine. As soon as he hung up, Barry called Ed Roberts in Tech Support. 'Ed, it's at most a hundred machines. Greg Mitchell has a team working on a fix.'

'So you've known about—'

'For one day,' Barry cut him off. 'Here's Greg's number in the conference room. You need to get with Greg and call me back.'

Barry returned the phone to its cradle and stared at the Simtec Excellence Award, framed and hanging on the opposite wall. He'd been voted to receive it by the rank-and-file employees, his own workers as well as others he didn't even know. 'For Superior Performance,' the piece of paper said. 'With Appreciation from all of your Fellow Employees.' The award meant a lot to Barry, and he wondered if he hadn't let those employees down in some way.

He got up to walk the hallway and found Bill Dunn sitting outside in the coffee room by himself, staring at the floor. Bill's shoulders were hunched. His young face looked worn and unshaven.

Bill glanced up and said, 'I was on my way to see you.'

'How's your dad? I've been checking off and on with your people.'

'The hip socket, the thigh – they patched him back together. The doctors give you the clinical description, but they don't really say anything. I asked one of them point-blank, How bad is it? Will he walk okay? The guy wouldn't answer. I guess they're afraid to pass judgment, but when it comes to describing how he drilled a metal rod through his leg, he had no problem with that.'

'We don't really expect you to be here. We understand if you'd rather not be.'

Bill gave a dismissive shake of the head. 'One of our guys is over there in the room with him. Apparently my dad woke up this morning, looked around and said, "Get me a laptop. I need a fax machine." But I phoned fifteen minutes ago, and he was resting. He sounded tired again. We'll send over some equipment anyway.'

It was exactly what Barry would expect from W. S. Dunn. They'd be throwing dirt on the grave and a bony arm would push its way out, searching around for a laptop. It was an image he decided not to share with Bill.

Barry started to disclose his latest phone conversation with Hektor, but then he held back. Five million, ten million – did it really make any difference to Bill Dunn? Could Security Associates do anything they weren't already doing? Barry took the seat opposite. 'Sheila gave me several updates yesterday. As far as the network, I know we've accomplished a lot.'

'That's not the weak point anymore. Sheila's tough. She's been with Security Associates for eight years. Much longer than I have, really. All of our plans have moved forward without interruption.'

'I appreciate that. We all do.'

'When a company hires us on, it's to come in and fix the problem. Period. I keep thinking about all those corrupted machines out there, all over the country, and it makes me sick. I feel responsible. I think about my dad, I think about those machines, and I think what a shitty job this turned out to be.'

It was the kind of blunt assessment that you got from a twenty-four-year-old, and Barry knew it was right on target. 'The machines were done a month ago,' he said. 'It's hardly your mistake.'

Bill stared off into space, then turned his head abruptly, 'I think we need to level with one another.'

'Okay.'

'We'll probably never know who hit my dad. Probably never

catch them. I've resigned myself to that. But he told me last night the pieces he could remember, and that car came straight at him. It wasn't an accident and the driver wasn't drunk. The police can call it whatever they want to.'

Barry swallowed hard. The two sat quietly for a moment, Barry watching this younger version of a man he had come to respect.

'Someone in Simtec is channeling information,' Bill said. 'They'd have to be in order to get the kind of access they've had and the familiarity with the way you do business. We've got to find who's working this on the inside. Otherwise, we close one hole and they'll find a way to open another. We've got to end this permanently, and we need some leads.'

Barry could feel Bill Dunn's eyes staring at him, reading him. His own glance went from the countertop to the floor. Back to the counter.

'I've got a few ideas,' Barry said. 'Funny you should mention leads, because yesterday I hired a private investigator.'

'You hired a PI?'

'What happened was, I got tired of not having any reliable information. Your dad, Diane, Jim, everyone seemed to have a finger on the pulse. Or so it seemed to me, so I decided to gather some of my own data. All I've learned so far is how much money everyone seems to have, or be hiding, or playing around with.'

His eyes rested on the object he had been carrying, which he then reached out and picked up.

'This telephone was given to me in order to communicate with the man who has been pressuring us for payment. Yesterday, I was walking outside Simtec three and somebody knocked me down. I'm almost certain they swapped out the first phone I had with a new one. I've got the two serial numbers, but I haven't had time to look into what might be behind all that. I'd be willing to bet there's something there.'

Bill sat up, looking suddenly alert. 'Let me get this straight. This is the phone they've given you to communicate with?'

Barry nodded.

'Yesterday, they knocked you down and switched the phones, and you've got both serial numbers?'

'I had written the first number down in my day planner.'

Bill Dunn Jr. came out of his chair. He picked up his own phone and punched in a number, then re-explained everything Barry had just said. He waited, listening, and then clicked off.

'Mr. Shepard, you need to give me those serial numbers. We need to get on this. You can bet there's something there.'

23

Jim Seidler sat in the back seat of the limo at Intercontinental airport, waiting for Richard Rowster to appear outside of Terminal B. Rowster treated Jim like a toady, but the executive vice president put up with it because Rowster was Jim's ace in the hole.

The electronic doors whooshed open, and Rowster stepped dramatically out to the sidewalk. His white hair was cropped in its usual crew cut. He wore khakis and a navy sport shirt.

The driver bolted from the car to help with his garment bag while Rowster sauntered around and slid in beside Jim.

They shook hands. Rowster pointed at the rack of glasses. 'What are we drinking?'

'Nothing,' Jim said.

'Wow. This must be serious. I bet that means nix on the golf this afternoon. You look worried, Jim.'

'I do and I should. We're in a pickle.'

'Why don't you tell me about it.'

The car got rolling, and Jim stared out the window for a moment. He scratched his head with practiced disgust. 'I think we got set up, Richard.'

'How so?'

'It goes without saying, you didn't hear any of this from me.' He waited for Rowster to nod, and then he continued. 'I'll start at the beginning. You know about some of the problems we've been having – the shipping errors, the reports of internal disruption. That's the tip of the iceberg. There's all kinds of shit flying around that hasn't yet gotten out. We're getting hit from the outside, and we're being blackmailed to buy our way out.'

The only time he'd lived in the South was when he'd been

stationed there, yet Rowster had a southern drawl that he could switch on or off at will. He often used it to hide his voice in moments of excitement or nervousness. 'My, oh my. Ah see you all have been hidin' a big secret. Does Jenkins know this? He's the one who called me, and he thinks it's an internal problem.'

'Nobody on the board knows. Diane wanted to keep it in-house.'

'Well, the cat's going to claw its way out of the bag, Ah can tell you that. You've got some folks who are going to walk into this meeting and unload. The first Ah heard was the computers getting shipped out wrong. That's part of the blackmail?'

'That was the first strike. Although we had some other problems in production the week before, problems on the line with the robots. We haven't determined if that was sabotage or not. Believe me, we've had our hands full trying to keep the lid on.'

'What else besides the shipments?'

'Besides that? You name it. File servers were erased. Backup tapes destroyed. Hundreds of employees' files were lost. There's no guarantee half the data in the company hasn't been compromised. We've been getting hit left and right.'

Rowster gave a grunt of surprise.

'It's been terrible,' Jim said. 'And we became aware of the worst part only yesterday. The files we load onto each of our new computers were tampered with. Instead we've loaded a piece of destructive code into the boot record of every machine. The very code that starts our computers has been made into what's called a Trojan horse – code that acts like it's doing one thing but at the same time does something harmful. We're already working on a press conference.'

Richard Rowster was eating this up. His eyes sparkled. 'And what measures has Diane taken?'

'Well, that's the worst thing. She left town for two days on business, until I finally called and told her she absolutely had to get back here. She went off and left us hamstrung.'

'Not good.' Rowster stroked his jaw. 'Not sound management. Her failure to inform the board is a further miscalculation.'

'I'm sure that will all come out in your meeting. All you have to do is ask where she was on Friday and Saturday while all hell was breaking loose. And—' Jim paused. He appeared hesitant.

'There's more?'

'The other thing is, I've been wondering how this blackmailer got all the dirt on our operations. He must have had passwords, phone numbers, account privileges, all kinds of access.'

'I reckon you have a theory.'

'Nothing I can prove. Two months ago Diane commissioned a security study of our entire corporate campus. The project even had a code name, Caspar. We assembled passwords and potential trouble spots, and all the information was summarized and handed over to Diane. That one document would have made a hell of a template.'

'How many people had hands on it? We had a case like that at Raytheon. Any one of them might have sold out—'

Seidler waved him off. 'Possible. But the odd thing to me, the thing you've got to ask yourself, Why do this whole study and then nothing comes of it? She has yet to do anything with the information.'

'Let's say she gathered intelligence and passed it along. Why?'

'Crisis. She could use it to shake things up. Maybe chop a few heads. All I'm saying, we didn't overhaul policy. After an extensive security review, we weren't even asked to change our passwords. The study was a waste.'

'You're suggesting the bitch stuck it to you,' Rowster said. He reached over and got out a small can of grapefruit juice. 'We've got the security problems themselves. Then there's Diane leaving town and her failure to inform the board. The way I count 'em she's had three strikes.'

He snapped off the pull tab and raised the can of juice to his lips. When he was done, he glanced at his watch and back at Jim. 'Where do you have me staying tonight, anyway?'

'The Doubletree. I'm going to drop you and go straight to the office. I'll send the car back.'

Rowster settled back in his seat. He had already heard

plenty. He'd get the rest on his own or it wouldn't be any fun.

Wilson sat still, watching the apartment complex. His stomach barked for attention, but he wasn't going to eat until he got the hard drive.

He had come by once the night before, but the two neighbors were still out on the balcony. Not only that, as Wilson stood in the shadows by the swimming pool, he had seen that they were talking to a security guard.

That spooked Wilson. The guard was a flunky earning six dollars an hour, but he had a badge and he might have a gun. Wilson couldn't tell. In any case, the guard had the law on his side, and Wilson was not going to risk his freedom over some kid's computer. That was one thing he had learned from Dupree: caution.

So he'd come back in the morning. Sunday. People should be sleeping late, or in church. He went upstairs, unlocked the door, and slipped inside. He eased open the blinds and went to work.

'Bring a screwdriver,' Dupree had said, and that's what Wilson had done. Only he'd brought a flat screwdriver, and he immediately saw that he would need a Phillips. He quietly cursed his boss and made a second trip to the car. A little dog started yapping from somebody's terrace. Wilson could see its snout jutting through a gap in the wooden fence. Yap, yap, yap.

He retrieved the Phillips from a tool bag under the front seat and took a different route back from the parking lot. A young Hispanic woman was carrying two large bags of groceries up the sidewalk, and Wilson stepped off to let her pass. Instead of appearing grateful, offering a 'Thank you,' she turned and appeared to glare at him, as though he were the source of her current travail. Wilson hurried on. This place was giving him the creeps.

He made it back to the apartment and went to work on the case of the computer. *Five minutes,* Dupree had said, but it took ten just to get the screws out and figure how to lift the case off. He pulled and he pried and, at last, the cover came loose with a loud clang that made Wilson cringe. By that time, sweat was running down his forehead. It was morning, but the apartment was a furnace.

He could hear some kids downstairs in the swimming pool. Probably had parents with them, too. He should have carried the whole damn thing out while he had the chance. He mopped his face with a shirtsleeve and peered blindly into the tangle of cards and wires inside the box.

Barry rarely rode in sports cars and, after the Cherokee, this Miata made him feel like a bug in the middle of the road. It had two doors and no backseat, and the floor and space between the front seats was piled full of clothes and manuals and what looked like boxes of disks and technical gear.

They had called the GTE Mobilnet twenty-four-hour service number, and Barry had requested a copy of his call report. As he had suspected, the two serial numbers belonged to two different phones. Even though they were being billed to his account, none of the incoming calls made to either number could be tracked. Her hands were tied, a cheerful GTE service rep told him. When a call is made to a cellular, no record is kept of the calling party.

She rattled off the outgoing calls he had made from the phone – the only ones where numbers were logged – and they were all calls he remembered. The call to Karen Williams' house yesterday morning, when he hadn't been able to remember directions. Two calls to his home number. Several to Simtec extensions.

'That's it?' he said, his initial excitement giving way to disappointment. He had jotted down the Simtec numbers, but he already recognized Gwen's extension, Jim Seidler and Jim's assistant, and another where he had likely been trying Greg Mitchell.

'Yes, sir,' the woman said. Then, 'Just a minute, what's this one here? Oh, this is the one you had taken off due to a poor connection.'

'I don't remember that,' Barry said.

More punching of keys. 'You must have called customer

service, because we removed it from your billing statement. The charge for that call has been deleted, and we're showing an oh-seven code for bad connection.'

Barry tried to keep his voice even. 'Could you give me that number again please? From the call that's a no-charge?'

She read it off, and the number didn't sound at all familiar. Perhaps the phone *had* been used. He didn't know how it had happened, but someone had made a call on his phone, and the number had found its way into the system. He scribbled the number on a small pad of paper, tore off the page, and waved it at Bill Dunn.

Ten minutes later, Bill had an address. The number was registered in an apartment complex. Bill Dunn turned to Barry and said, 'Are you coming?'

So now here they were, Bill steering the car with one hand as they shot through traffic. He hit the brakes and Barry lurched into the shoulder strap as a red Datsun swung out onto the road directly in front of them.

'Idiot!' Dunn yelled in the general direction of the offending driver.

The way Barry saw it, riding in a tiny death trap you were in no position to be starting trouble. But Bill Dunn said, 'People don't like small cars. I don't know. I've punched out of a lot of tight spots where it's the only way I would have made it.'

Just what Barry liked to hear, that the driver *punched out* of tight spots. He glanced down to the side mirror again. He'd been checking it regularly ever since they'd left Simtec.

'No one back there,' Bill said.

'It's happened before. They called me on the phone while I was standing in line to get pizza. They were right there in the parking lot.'

'The pizza at the ballpark.'

Barry was surprised. 'Yes, I think it was.'

'My dad told me about that. He said you'd lost your appetite, then your daughter got into the play and you got hungry all of a sudden. I guess kids are good that way,' Bill said and then shrugged. 'I wouldn't know.'

'That's what he told you about our conversation?'

'And that he knew you were being blackmailed, but you weren't comfortable talking about it. You had your guard up.'

It was remarkable, suddenly seeing yourself through the eyes of another person. How transparent he'd been – not wanting to trust anyone, not even the man they'd hired to bail them out. And how naive he was, at that baseball game three days ago with his network *Tips, Tricks* book, unable to recognize how bad it could get.

'This looks like the spot,' Bill said. A large brick entrance held a sign proclaiming Westwood. He drove past the leasing office and several clusters of buildings. They were looking for number 212 and Bill parked near a rack of mailboxes.

'We need a plan.' Barry said, pushing open the passenger door.

'I really don't expect anyone to be here. They swap out your phone for some new phone, they've got to worry you might figure it out.' Bill reached back into the car and grabbed a gray carrying case. 'Just in case, computer repair.'

Computer repair, thought Barry. Not much of a plan, but it was certainly something Hektor could appreciate. They went into the courtyard of the building that housed units 210-229. A small swimming pool in the middle of the courtyard played host to a couple of kids and a woman who eyed them over the top of a *People* magazine.

They climbed the steps to the second level and found number 212 right at the head of the stairwell. There was one window with a cheap curtain.

'You stand over there,' Bill said. 'On the off chance someone is here, we don't want you getting recognized.'

Barry moved to the side, wondering if they really should have come, if this wasn't something for the police to look into. Hektor could be in there. A bunch of them could be.

Bill Dunn rapped heavily on the door.

They waited. No sound from inside the apartment.

He reached out and rapped again.

Nothing.

In a movement so deft that Barry, who was standing right there, almost missed what had happened, a metal shim appeared in Bill's hand, poked in past the doorjamb, and the front door slid open.

'Hello? Computer repair,' he called into the open door. He moved directly inside. Barry checked both directions on the second-floor landing and stepped in behind.

The light was on, but the front room was empty. There was a sofa on the front wall, and over on a table in the dining area stood a computer. The funny thing was, the case was off and some of the cables were sticking up into the air.

'Computer repair,' Bill called out again. He went quickly through the apartment, checked the kitchen, the back bedroom, the bath. No one was home. He turned back to the computer on the table. 'This looks like our patient.'

Barry glanced back outside. Nothing except for the sound from the swimming pool. He gently pushed the door closed and joined Bill by the table.

The machine was partly dismantled. Cables were unplugged, and a small pile of screws was spread out on a piece of paper. Could this one scrawny machine in this equally scrawny apartment be the cause of all Simtec's problems? The prospect seemed unbelievable.

Barry had been trying not to touch anything, but as soon as he got his hands on the computer, he became eager, hurriedly snapping the cables back into place. 'One of these bays is empty,' he said. 'Looks like it might have had a tape backup or CD in there. Maybe a second floppy drive.'

Bill had moved off into the kitchen. He looked into the pantry and the oven. He opened the fridge and peered inside. 'I don't think anyone's coming back,' he said.

'Why not?'

'Milk out on the counter. It's warm. The oven's on low and there's a pot pie in there baked hard as a rock.'

'If they forgot the oven,' Barry said, 'maybe they left something here, too.' He pushed the power cord back in and snapped on the switch. The machine sprang into life and ticked through its memory check; then it bombed out with the message, Bad or missing command interpreter.

'Can't boot,' Barry said. He picked up a screwdriver and tapped it on the table in frustration. But the message he was getting here was not the same as the July 25 torpedo that destroyed vital drive information. This hard drive appeared to be intact and, if they were lucky, accessible. 'We need a boot disk,' he said, already scanning the room doubtfully.

Dunn had come up beside him and was staring at the message. 'I've got a case full of diagnostics in the car. I could go get them. Or, we could just take it.'

'Take the computer?'

'You bet. After what they've done? It's the least you can do.'

Barry pinched his lips together. He'd like it far better if they could be in and out, leaving the apartment the way they found it. He leaned forward over the machine, stared at the empty bay, and said, 'Go get the disks.'

Wilson had heard the sound of someone coming up the stairwell outside the apartment, and he stopped to listen. He was hunched over the disassembled computer, with one piece out already and a couple of others in varying states of de-installation. He didn't know what was what. There was a mass of cables and wires that ran every which way, and in order to get the thing apart, he'd unscrewed every screw he came to, unplugged every wire he could pull on.

When the footsteps stopped on the landing outside the door, he backed soundlessly away from the table. The knock was loud and startling. Who could it be? He slipped further away, back into the bedroom, at the sound of more forceful knocking.

When he heard the door click open, he lay down on the ground and squeezed himself into a slot behind the bed. The carpet was damp and moldy where condensation dripped off an old window air-conditioner. Wilson felt the wetness soaking into his left shirtsleeve, and a scowl of distaste formed on his face.

There were two of them. He could hear them talking in the next room. They were discussing the computer, and damned if they weren't going to try to put it back together. Had Dupree not trusted him and sent somebody else? That was probably the answer. The hell with Dupree.

He heard the door to the apartment open and close. It sounded as if one of the men had left, and Wilson slowly eased himself up, forcing his large frame to move quietly. He extracted a knife from his pants pocket and slid the blade open. He edged into the doorway and peered out past the doorframe.

Barry Shepard was sitting right there at the table, and Wilson was stunned. What a blunder he'd made, taking the wrong phone when he got out of Shepard's car! But it was an honest mistake. The phones all looked exactly the same. Wilson had promised he'd take care of it, and he did.

It was the stupid kid's fault. Mark didn't keep his mobile phone charged, and Wilson had been forced to call on the apartment line. And now this. It was fucking unbelievable. One call to the apartment on Shepard's phone, and the Simtec people had figured it out.

He measured the distance between himself and Shepard. He could cross the ten feet in one second and take him down. Get him with the knife and then hit the door. Do it now, before the other man came back. Get out of there.

The only problem was, it might ruin their chances to get paid. One of their head honchos gets whacked, there was no telling how Simtec might react. Dupree would explode and tell him he messed up the whole deal.

He looked back into the bedroom for something to use as a club. He'd smash him over the head and leave it at that. Could have been a burglar. Could have been anybody. Then he'd get the hard drive and get out of there – which reminded him, he'd left it back on the floor by the bed. A metal box with a button on the front. He was sure he'd gotten the right part. The floppy drive was still in the computer. It had the big wide opening with a little lever you slid into place.

A quick search of the bedroom yielded nothing. A cheap lamp stood on top of a set of shelves, but it had a bulky shade and would make a racket. The hell with it, he'd use his fist. Wait until Shepard turned away and then rush him.

He moved into the doorway, as catlike as Terry Wilson was able to move. Shepard had his side to the bedroom, intent upon what he was doing. If Shepard reacted quickly enough,

Wilson knew he'd have a fight on his hands. But these corporate types were as soft as they come. He'd take the guy with one punch.

He reached down and eased the knife blade closed, turned the knife sideways in his hand, and clenched it into a fist. His muscles poised for the rush, when Barry pushed back and came upright at the table. 'They took out the three-and-a-half. Now why the hell would they do that?'

The sound froze Wilson. Who was Shepard talking to? Wilson was sure he had heard the other man leave, but maybe there was another one in there. He tried to lean out and get a peek at the rest of the room.

Nobody. Time to move. Footsteps rang out on the stairwell. Damn! The front door swung open, and Wilson eased backward.

'I've got a boot disk and utilities, boys,' said the man who had just returned. 'Let's see what we've got.'

Shepard slapped in a disk and rebooted. 'Why would someone take out the three-and-a-half?' he said. 'I went into the setup and this machine was configured for both floppies.'

'You got me. Maybe it broke, or they needed it in another machine.'

Both men stared at the screen as Shepard typed in a series of commands. 'Everything's erased, but the drive seems fine and the partition is intact. There may still be something on here.'

Shepard hit several more keys, and the other man said, 'I wouldn't copy anything over yet. You're liable to go over the top of the other files.'

'You brought some disk utilities?'

'Norton is on the disk. I've got others in the box.'

Wilson had his ear up near the door. He had no idea what Norton was, but he didn't like the sound of it.

He had spent thirty minutes removing that drive, apparently for no good reason. It wasn't logical. From what they were saying, it sounded like the files were still on the computer. He deleted files and it turned out they weren't really gone. Now the damn machine hadn't stored the information where he thought it was going to. He could hate a machine like that, a machine that made him feel stupid every time he tried to make a move.

'There they are,' Barry said, looking at a list of deleted files from the root of the hard drive. He'd have to work through each of the subdirectories, recovering what he could, file by file. It was going to be a tedious process.

Bill Dunn was already pacing. 'This could take forever,' he said. 'We don't know what we're looking for. We ought to just take it.'

Barry felt the young man hovering just off his right shoulder as he resurrected the autoexec file and used the TYPE command to display it.

'What a bunch of bozos,' Bill said. 'To think you've got to fork over money to them.'

Barry gave him a sharp look. 'The way I see it, we've got no choice.'

And, much to everyone's surprise, Barry then said, 'Ten million dollars. It's only a matter of working out the details.'

Wilson had been craning his neck to listen, but he was wholly unprepared to hear this particular figure. When he heard that James Dupree was about to collect ten million dollars, the combined surprise – at the amount, and at his own stupidity – caused Wilson's head to pop back so sharply that it snapped into the door behind him. He stood for a moment as though stunned, which he was, not from hitting the door, but from the enormity of the dollar amount from which he had been excluded.

He was a fool.

Barry heard the thud in the next room. It sounded as though someone had hit a wall with his fist. He turned to look, and Dunn took a step sideways, making a pushing motion with his hand: quiet.

He took a first step toward the bedroom when a man came charging out with his head down.

He was a large man, and he hit Bill full in the chest. Bill went down hard and landed on his side, up against the sofa.

One arm flailed as he tried to grab the sofa and get back to his feet. The man swung again, catching Bill in the side of the head. His neck snapped back from the blow and his legs buckled.

The man's face instantly registered, even as Barry leapt from the chair. It was the same man who had brought the NoteStars. The two of them had sat side by side in the Jeep.

In his rush to get up, Barry knocked into the table and took a faltering step forward. He cocked his arm and punched from the side, delivering a glancing blow.

The man was overweight, but he had a thick, strong upper body. He smacked Barry aside and made a run for the door.

Barry charged and punched again, this time a short jab that connected with the man's side. The man shrugged it off and swung a large forearm that knocked Barry against the wall. The man whirled around to face him, which was when Barry saw the knife.

'Stay still,' the man said, reaching behind himself for the door handle. There was four feet of space between the two of them, and no one made a move.

Without looking down, the man fumbled into his pocket and came up with a small gun. 'You come outside in the next five minutes, you get a bullet.' The man hauled open the door and backed out.

Barry's jaw tightened as he watched the door swing closed. He heard footsteps on the stairwell. Bill Dunn rose unsteadily to his feet, rubbing a hand against the side of his face.

When they did open the door again – at first standing out of the way as it swung back on its hinges – they emerged silently out onto the balcony. The man was long gone. The kids were splashing about in the swimming pool down below, and Barry dried his palm against the side of his pants.

Bill Dunn moved up alongside him. 'My father and I have fought with these people for years. Most of the time you never get closer than the files themselves. You find a rigged file somebody planted and you think, That was lucky. I'd sure like to get the bastard who put this here. Well, here we are, and we blew it.'

'We've got the machine,' Barry said. 'Let's take it and get out of here.' He walked back into the apartment, went and checked out the back bedroom where the man had been hiding. He opened a drawer and saw a few items of clothing: socks, a Miami Dolphins T-shirt. A pair of blue jeans hung over a chair. On top of the dresser was a four-inch statue of a skeleton. It seemed to Barry the kind of stuff you might see in a teenager's room.

He looked down beside the bed and saw something else. And when he walked back into the front room, he extended his hand, palm up, and said to Bill Dunn, 'We also got a set of keys.'

24

Peter Jenkins began motioning the emergency board meeting to order. There had been no pre-meeting meal and very little of the usual pre-meeting banter as the men drifted in and took their seats around the rectangular table. A few of the members, like Richard Rowster and Paul Cummings, a veteran of the Apollo program and avid venture capitalist, were walking tall. Others, like Fitzhugh, looked ready to duck and run.

A technician was doing a sound check toward a box in the middle of the table. He eyed the people filing into the room apprehensively. 'That's better,' came the voice of Michael Gaines. 'Can you hear me?'

'Just sit tight, Michael,' Jenkins said. 'We can hear you fine.' He thanked the technician and waved him off. When Peter Jenkins took his chair and began speaking, it was as though he had rapped a gavel.

'By virtue of a two-thirds majority vote, we have requested this meeting,' he said. 'According to the bylaws, and due to the nature of my responsibilities as chairman, I am called upon to preside. However, we have no formal agenda, nor is it spelled out how to proceed in such matters. If someone else would like to propose a structure, or even conduct the meeting, I am open to suggestions. . . .'

He let the offer float and glanced furtively in Diane's direction. She quickly leaned forward and dusted a hand in the air, trying to retain as much of the old protocol as possible.

No one else said anything. Diane cleared her throat and began speaking. 'We have a financial report due to be given jointly by Mike Spakovsky and Wade Warner of Coopers and Lybrand, but I understand that they are making copies and will be joining us shortly.' Actually, they were up the hall redoing their comments after Diane slashed through them with a red pen.

Jenkins nodded. 'I will therefore open the floor to preliminary discussion.'

Rowster was ready to jump out of his seat, but he bit his tongue and kept quiet. Let the moderates and the peacemakers have their say.

Peter Jenkins was an oil-and-gas man who had spent many years on the board of Pennzoil. His experience and moderation had earned him the position as Simtec chairman. He had a neatly typed document in front of him and, without looking up, he said, 'I think we all know the reason we are here. Anyone who reads the daily newspaper could tell you. Misshipments numbering into the thousands. Reports of turmoil inside the company. Analysts downgrading the company's stock. Accusations that Simtec has begun canceling contracts.' He paused and made eye contact around the room. 'We need to get to the root of these reports. We need to separate fact from fiction, and we need to decide if action on the part of the board needs to be taken.'

'Hear, hear,' Cummings blurted, as though he were in the British Parliament.

Diane looked around the heavily polished table. Someone had set out ice water, but none of the other standard amenities were present. She glanced from face to face at the men circling her covered wagon.

'Is there more to add to the list?' she said. 'Or does that cover it?'

'That'll be a start,' grumbled Rowster.

'Then let's begin at the top.' Diane recognized her advantages: she had her fingers on the precise numbers involved; she knew the personnel; she could trace the decision-making process. To some extent, she could portray events with some latitude. There was an outline, but she was free to color as she chose.

'We did, in fact, have a number of machines misdelivered,' she conceded. 'Either the machines went out to erroneous addresses, or customers who had placed orders received the wrong software configuration. In some cases, a customer received the wrong computer model altogether. We have taken steps to redress any inconvenience experienced by those customers, and this is a topic we could discuss at great length, weighing the costs, the steps taken, the public relations advantages—'

This was too much for Rowster. 'It's hard to imagine any of this being a public relations *advantage*,' he said nastily.

'If you'd let me finish, please. I was going to say, the public relations advantages of choosing one tactic over another.' She turned from Rowster to the group as a whole. 'Free replacement of any equipment, discounts, extended service agreements. You must also weigh the advantages versus the possible negative effects of publicizing our response. I'm not sure how much and which of these considerations concern you, gentlemen. We've had database tampering. Hard drives have been erased. So have backup tapes and data that resides on file servers. If we are going to go into the details of each and every one of these circumstances, then I hope you are prepared for a long afternoon.'

She was excellent at reading an audience, and she noticed several of the men shift uncomfortably in their chairs. They didn't know all the details, and they didn't want to know. The element of surprise is a powerful tool, and Diane was going to enjoy this next part.

'The errors of which I speak have been caused by an extremely well-planned and well-executed attack on our corporate computer network, most likely by some kind of outside organization. We now face a dire threat on July twenty-fifth. That's two short days, gentlemen. We have hired the best network security firm in the business, Security Associates, to assist us in combating this evil, and I am sure you will agree that this was, and is, a situation we could not broadcast to the heavens.'

She examined the faces. Several registered astonishment at this last revelation. Not Fitzhugh, whose expression was made of stone. Spakovsky might have already told him, she guessed. And Rowster still wore a smirk, damn him.

'Let me hear this again,' Peter Jenkins said, his fingers agitating a pencil in front of him. 'You say that an outside *orga-*

nization was responsible for the shipping errors on those computers?'

'Probably some kind of terrorist group,' she said. That was it, strike some fear in them.

Rowster guffawed. 'You mean a hacker, don't you?'

Diane's eyes narrowed. She could learn to hate this man.

'I mean a highly organized, highly intelligent group, working to create havoc in our computer network and blackmail us into paying money to support whatever cause is on their current roster. To me, that is terrorism.'

'No, Ms. Hughes, that is blackmail. It is not terrorism. When someone drives through the plate-glass window downstairs with a car bomb, then we'll have terrorism. I make this distinction in order to avoid hysteria. Someone has broken into your network and apparently they have also demanded money. I suspected something of the sort. The oversight duties of the board should be to assess the response of the management team to that threat. Wouldn't you agree?'

Diane fought to remain calm. She wanted to scream, Bastard! Stuff your oversight duties, but instead she said, 'I think that is precisely your role.'

Jenkins was looking desperately around the table. He had assumed the position of de facto mediator, but he had been completely blindsided by this revelation about a hacker. *Terrorism.* He coughed. 'I think we should take a break,' he said. 'Can we get some coffee in here? Is that possible? Let's meet back after a brief recess.'

No one objected. They broke and bolted in all directions.

Barry parked the Miata and glanced at the limos parked in the circular drive in front of Simtec 3. The board members would already be in session, casting straws to determine the leadership of the company. Bill Dunn had decided to stay behind at the apartment complex, working his way through the cars with the ring of keys they had found.

On the seat beside Barry was the CPU, a standard desktop clone with a tag that said Big Byte. He hoisted it out of the car and carried it upstairs. Gwen was immediately at his side, scrutinizing Barry as well as the Big Byte.

'I've been trying to find you for forty-five minutes,' she said. 'Didn't know where to find you. What's that, a clone?'

Barry made room for the machine on his desk. 'Gwen, I need some time. I need to look at this machine. If anyone asks, I'm not here.'

Her eyes narrowed, and she again regarded the Big Byte. 'Okay,' she said. 'You're not here.'

Barry locked the door to the office. He transferred cables from his own computer and, while the Big Byte was coming up, he left an identical voice message for both Diane and Jim. He told them about the machine he had recovered, that he had it in his office and was starting an examination.

Then he sat down and went to work. Starting in the root directory, he began recovering files. The obvious files were retrieved under their correct names; on others, he had to guess. The directory structure appeared to be standard Windows-Apps. Applications were in directories off the root, and he located a few more apps in a branch off the WINDOWS directory.

Barry worked cleanly and efficiently, but, even so, there were hundreds of files to sort through. After fifteen minutes, he abandoned his original objective of reconstructing the hard drive. It would simply take too long and be too involved to try to return the drive to its original state. He didn't care about the applications anyway.

Microsoft Word was Microsoft Word. It was user files Barry was after and, so far, he wasn't finding any.

Peter Jenkins, twelve-year veteran of the Pennzoil board, considered himself to be unflappable. A class act. He and his wife Judy could go anywhere, anytime, and they did. Embassy parties. Socialite fund-raisers. Celebrity balls.

You didn't get this far by burning bridges, and he was already uncomfortable with the idea of participating in the ouster of one of Houston's corporate icons. Diane hadn't been elected long, but the position of Simtec CEO was such that the person filling it became known in a hurry.

He dawdled by the water fountain until he saw Rowster

come out of the rest room. Jenkins cut a beeline and stopped just short of pulling Rowster aside by the collar.

'You knew, didn't you?' Jenkins said.

Rowster looked amused. 'Knew what?'

'About the blackmail, the hacker. It was obvious you knew exactly what was coming in there.'

'I'd heard some of it, yes. But you never know the spin you're going to get until it comes straight from the horse's mouth. I was anxious to hear her confirmation.'

'So? You might have mentioned it. Here we are talking about a competency vote and it turns out some of these problems have been brought on from outside. From what it sounds like, truly extraordinary circumstances. It seems to me this changes everything.'

'Does it? You must have missed what I said. Hacker or no hacker, you still have to gauge how management reacted. This is a production problem, a management issue no less than striking workers or government compliance. In this case, you'll find the shit hit the fan and Diane bolted. She left town. Not only that, she sent Jim off on a wild-goose chase, too. Until he came back and told her to get her little rear end back to Dodge.'

'But why would she do that?'

'She could use the crisis to clean house. Apparently, Jacobs is out already. Diane wanted to sack a few people, only it's gone too far. Much further than she expected. It's very clear, Peter. She walked off and left the wheel of the ship. Now look what you've got. I'll bet the stock sheds another ten points next week. I've spoken to some media friends, and we're going to see a lot of ink on this. They smell something rotten, and you can bet they're rushing to break the story.'

Jenkins stared into the dark eyes of this man whom he'd been told was the most troublesome general the army ever had. Wasn't even a full general, some kind of pre-general, a man caught between ranks and retired before he could do any more damage. The only reason he wasn't kicked out on his rear was that he was in tight with so many congressmen that he had all the full generals by the balls.

'I see,' Jenkins said, knowing without a doubt that Rowster would be the one to deliver that wet ink. He'd call the papers, all his editorial and broadcasting buddies, just to give them the story himself. He'd get his fifteen minutes in the fame chair, as well as the chance to punch Diane in the gut. Diane and anyone who stood with her.

'The hacker stuff, that's going to be in the stories, too?'

'You can count on it. The board can either sit here like a bunch of swinging dicks, or we can make a statement,' Rowster said, staring him down. 'The entire incident was mishandled by Simtec leadership, and we are making a move to restore confidence.'

'Damn it, Rowster. You've already made up your mind. I think we should listen to what steps she's taken and go from there.'

'You sit here and listen all you want. Everybody in the country is going to know that Simtec's been taking it up the ass. It's a great story, the company's pocket got picked while the chief executive officer was asleep.'

Jenkins looked like he was about to cry. 'We need to at least hear her out,' he said weakly.

'I'll hear her out.' Rowster's tanned face spread into a grin. He borrowed a line from an earlier conversation: 'Just ask her what she was doing on Friday and Saturday.'

Jenkins would spend the next ten minutes furtively conferencing this latest information, one at a time, with the other members of the board. It would be some time before they would all find their way back to the table.

Bill Dunn tried to be inconspicuous, moving up alongside each car to peer in through the side window. He knew he had a car key, but it was a generic brass copy and could belong to many of the cars in the lot. It could also belong to none of them. He had already set off one car alarm and been forced to abandon that side of the apartment building.

Therefore, it was with some degree of surprise when he finally slid the key into a lock, tensed for an ear-splitting wail, and felt the door of the car open.

It was a blue Cutlass, and he was standing on the passenger side. He scanned the area and saw no one, ducked his head, and took a quick survey inside. Some crumpled paper napkins on the floorboards and a McDonald's french fry container.

Better make it fast. He used one of the napkins to open the glove box. The treasures inside included a battered owner's manual, two pennies, a Q-Tip, and a large rubber band that had melted and was in the process of fusing with the car itself.

Poking out from under the seat, though, Bill spied the end of a canvas bag. He hooked the fabric with one finger and pulled it out. Then he prodded the mouth of the bag open: wrenches, pliers, several sockets, and a small socket wrench. Crap.

He got down on one knee and peered under the seat. No gun. No telephone. No Simtec Attack Manual. Directly under his nose, however, was another crumpled ball of paper. This one, at least, did not appear to be a McDonald's napkin.

He picked up and gently uncrumpled the paper. At the top, it said Rice University Parking Citation. There was a ticket number, a violation code, initials of the ticketing officer, and instructions for payment. The ticket was dated three days earlier.

That was odd, Bill thought. A Rice parking ticket. It didn't amount to much, but so far it was the best he'd come up with and he tucked the paper into his pocket.

He gave the rest of the car a quick toss and found no swift link to the identity and whereabouts of its owner. Of course, he might have missed something. And the idea that something crucial might still be in there, undiscovered, made Bill decide: What the hell. He'd just take the whole car.

A trickle of sweat made its way down Barry Shepard's back, but he was staring too intently at the screen to notice. He bounced back out to the root of the C: drive and into another directory called UTILS. Here he found directories named TOOLS, HACK, and NETMOD. He went into each of these and spent more time trying to piece together what had been there. TOOLS held a commercial disk utility program. HACK held what Barry guessed were hacking and security widgets.

One was called Hotwire, and he vaguely recalled it as a program used for testing system security.

Barry jabbed at the keyboard. So far, there was no silver bullet here. He had found the applications, but where were the letters and memos? The diaries and log files? The utilities themselves were only partially useful. Perhaps a network administrator who knew more than he did could go back and pin down some of Hektor's techniques. That was really a job for Security Associates.

He was interrupted by a loud knocking at the door. 'Barry? It's Jim. I got your message.' The doorknob jiggled.

Barry opened the door and went back around his desk. Jim Seidler stepped inside and closed the door behind him. He leaned back against it, taking huge breaths. He looked haggard and terribly out of shape.

'Just got your message,' he panted. 'I ran over here. That's it?' He pointed at the computer on the desk. 'What's on it?'

Barry shook his head grimly. 'Not a whole lot in the way of user files. I've got security tools and a few utilities. They may give us some insight, but no breakthrough evidence. No names and addresses.'

'There's got to be more than that. No notes? What about E-mail messages?'

Barry's lips pressed together. He shook his head.

'I don't believe it,' Jim said. He straightened and stepped over right in front of the Big Byte and tapped its case. 'I don't want to offend you, Barry, but I've got a suggestion. I want to take this machine to the techs and have them go over it. You said the files were erased and you're restoring them? You could miss something. Worst case, you could mess it up. We shouldn't take that chance for the sake of expediency.'

Barry throttled the defensive statement that jumped to his lips. What Jim was saying was true: he was no expert on disk recovery. But it was also clear that to delay worked in Jim's favor. If Barry made a discovery, and if it somehow lessened the crisis, that worked to Diane's advantage.

Jim said, 'There's something else. This could make you look bad. The board members are discussing this right now. How do you think it sounds, I go in there and say, "Barry confiscated a machine." They'll all be on the edge of their seats. Then I say, "He took it back to his office, locked the door, and worked on it in private. Unfortunately, he didn't find anything." '

This was exactly what Barry had never been good at, seeing how one of his actions could become politicized. Even turned back around against him. But he fully understood the implications of what Jim was saying. 'I agree we need to be more methodical,' he said stiffly. 'We should take our time and examine every byte on it.'

'Good. I've got to get back. I may get called into the meeting. I'll send someone over from Chris's office to pick this up and handle it. We'll quarantine the machine and do it right.'

James Dupree sat smoking a cigarette in a midtown coffee bar. He rarely smoked, but he considered this something of a celebration. A victory smoke.

This had been a tough fight, with Simtec resisting beyond all reasonable expectation. Now, finally, he had his opponent out in the open, staggering, unable to heft a sword. It had all come about – he could not help but think that it had *only* come about – through his own training and preparation. His own initiative. He had laid the proper groundwork all along, and, when the time came, he cut loose and named his own stakes. The siege had proven irresistible.

Dupree swizzled the foam on top of a cappuccino and glanced about the bar. The place had a bohemian look, and was no doubt favored by midtown artsy types. He could not consider that crowd without a measure of scorn. What a business he was in! Here he could sit, in complete anonymity, and no one had the slightest hint that he was about to receive ten million dollars from one of Houston's corporate darlings.

If only his father could see him now! His father was a wealthy man, but James was sure *he* had never clinched ten million in one fell swoop. He'd like to rub the news in Allen Dupree's face. Here, take this, chump!

He ground one foot into the tile floor and stared at a framed Miró print on the opposite wall. Of course, there were other possible angles. Simtec might have given no more than a hollow offer to pay, a diversionary tactic. More delaying.

But what had Simtec to gain from that? The 25th would come regardless. They could have no way of knowing what he had or hadn't done.

No, when they paid, it was because they wanted an end to their troubles. The cost of fighting him, James Dupree, was greater than the cost of a simple cash outlay. When you threw a problem to the bean counters, this was what it always came down to.

Simtec would have to transfer the money to one of his accounts, a number he would give them at the last minute. From there, Dupree would whisk it off through several other accounts. Banks that were known to be discreet. Numbers incremented on one side of the balance sheet and decremented on the other. It was not a process that could be undone.

With this payment, he would go on a trip out of the country. He would place himself out of harm's way, beyond the reach of any possible reprisal. It would be difficult, but he would take a stab at a vacation.

25

During the recess, Diane had photocopied and distributed the original one-million-dollar demand letter around the table. She spent the next twenty minutes giving the board members an overview of the escalating damages and demands.

Paul Cummings scratched at the top of his balding head and consulted a pad of paper. Ever since the meeting had reconvened, he'd begun taking copious notes. 'I want to revisit the timing,' he said. 'Let's run through the decision making and how it all fits together. In response to the bad configurations, you offered immediate replacement with the proper equipment, and you upgraded each customer's service agreement.'

'Three years on-site,' Diane said. 'Barry Shepard has an excellent track record of customer service. He tells me this offer has unruffled a lot of feathers.'

Before the meeting was allowed to begin, Michael Gaines had insisted that Roland Fitzhugh read the demand letter to him twice. Gaines now bleated from the speakerphone: 'What's the cost on that? All those upgrades?'

Diane knew that the other board members had little use for Gaines, and even less, she figured, with him away on vacation, participating by telephone. With an expression of contempt, she said, 'We have an extremely low three-year failure rate. The service cost is not significant.'

Gaines was silent.

'Going back to the timetable,' Cummings said, in his deliberate, methodical way. 'At this point, the requested payment was still one million dollars?'

'Call it *ransom*, Paul. That's what it is,' Rowster said.

'You are correct,' Diane said. 'At the time we became aware

of the shipping errors – this would have been around one P.M. Tuesday, July eighteenth – the top executives voted not to pay. We had no knowledge of the other potential targets, nor how additional attacks might be carried out. No specific threats were made in the letter, as you can see.'

'Then the destruction of employee hard drives. And the various—' Cummings flapped a hand in the air for help. He didn't understand file servers, and he didn't want to talk about them. He settled for: 'The departmental data was compromised.'

Diane nodded. 'By that time the ransom was five million, and we voted to take the immediate step of bringing in W. S. Dunn and a full team from Security Associates.'

Rowster drummed fingers on the table. 'Obviously, an inadequate countermeasure.'

Diane responded quickly. 'After an incident like this, you begin to think about vulnerability in an altogether different manner. We did well to bring in Security Associates even if we *had* paid.'

A hoarse, rasping sound emanated from the back of Richard Rowster's throat.

Cummings examined his notes. 'You are now asked to pay ten million dollars. On July twenty-fifth – in two days – you face widespread damage, and you have agreed to pay.'

'By wire transfer, nine-thirty tomorrow morning. That, in a nutshell, is the progression,' Diane said. 'I won't tell you I'm proud of how this has all worked out. We have sustained damage. No doubt about it. As I've briefed you, the threat of further destruction has become entirely convincing. Nonetheless, I do defend our decision making. When you examine our choices in context, you will not find them to be imprudent.'

Cummings rallied himself and his notes into position. The pen finally came to rest. 'Here's how it appears to me,' he said. 'At each point, you've been slightly behind the eight ball. If you could pay a million and not have the employees lose information, with hindsight, you would do it. If you could pay five million and not face the current damage, you would also do that. Each time you refused payment only to have the refusal rammed down your throat. Until now, when you're dragged kicking and screaming to the table, and you have little other choice.'

Diane listened to this pronouncement with her eyes averted. Paul Cummings was the most universally well-liked and respected member of the board. If she was going to get in a dogfight, she'd rather it develop with somebody else.

Jenkins glanced sternly about the table. With no other comments forthcoming, he said, 'All right, let's hear the financials.'

The registered owner of the blue Cutlass came back as Pat Dapor. Bill Dunn scribbled down the name and address, thanked Sheila, and hung up. He made sure the Cutlass was locked away on the Simtec grounds. Then he picked up the Miata and drove out to the address listed. He found himself staring at a vacant lot. On one corner of the lot was a large pile of gravel, and the surrounding weeds and dirt were criss-crossed by heavy tread marks.

He used his mobile phone to call Barry and exchange notes on what they had each found. 'So, nothing on the hard drive,' Bill said, disappointed.

'I didn't see anything of value. Jim's going to have the techs go over it with a microscope.'

'Dead end here, too. I drive over and it's a bunch of weeds. I'm not surprised, but I wanted to come check it out. You never know.'

'That means they did what, bought the car somewhere and made up an address?'

'There are lots of ways to do it. Even a legit dealer will take the address off a utility bill. For all they know, you just dug the bill out of somebody's trash. They don't know and don't ask. You wind up with a legal registration, inspection sticker, maybe you've even got insurance, though I didn't see a stub in the glove box.'

Barry considered that. He pictured Hektor, or probably somebody working for him, digging through the trash to come up with a utility bill. 'So, the name's no good either.'

'Not likely. I checked the phone book for Pat Dapor. There aren't any Dapors in the city. I'm going to drive over to Rice University and poke around. I found a Rice parking ticket and my dad thought it was worth looking into. I'll check faculty and alumni. Current students. Probably nothing there, but it'll make him happy.'

'Good luck,' Barry said. 'I also called the investigator I hired, Richard Green. I gave him the apartment number and asked him to find out anything he could. I'll keep you posted.'

Barry hung up and thought, Pat Dapor. A Rice University parking ticket. Bill was right: there was nothing there.

The numbers, as presented to the board by Mike Spakovsky and backed up by a smiling and nodding independent auditor, appeared respectable. Some product lines were showing strong sales, others were lagging. When had this not been the scenario? the CFO asked good-naturedly.

'You're being disingenuous,' Paul Cummings said. 'All you have to do is look at the weeklies over the past month.' Cummings was referring to sales data gathered from the largest superstores in the country, and he began flipping pages. 'Compare the Comet line, July eighth with July twenty-second. That's a sixty-seven percent drop. We're talking about a nightmare at the cash register.'

Spakovsky glanced at Diane and forged ahead. 'If you examine the estimates I've provided, we've got quarterly gross up for the fifth straight quarter. That's what investors will see far more than daily fluctuation.'

'Investors are skittish,' Cummings challenged. 'They're out there worrying, watching the shares drop, wondering if this is long term.'

'It's not rocket science,' Richard Rowster cut in. 'When you're drowning in bad ink, no one buys your stuff.'

Spakovsky grimaced.

'Meanwhile, Simtec is talking out both sides of its mouth. The consumers are confused. The dealers are confused. How big a drop do you need to see before you send up a red flag?'

Spakovsky continued to make his case, but the board was having nothing of it. Rowster, Cummings, even Jenkins, all poked at the monthlies until the stuffing fell out. Which was the way Rowster finally put it. He said, 'All right, we've dug through the fluff and when it comes down to it, we're holding a turd.'

Spakovsky paled and said nothing.

'The month of July will go down as one of the worst months in the history of this company. August may be even worse if we don't make a move and make it now.'

Spakovsky and the auditor were excused. The others scowled, each waiting for someone else to speak.

Peter Jenkins cleared his throat. He did not look at Diane, but rather at the portrait of John Sims, who peered down from the wall opposite where Jenkins was sitting. 'I understand the delicacy of the situation. With the way documents have of turning up in the wrong hands, I even understand why you might refrain from discussing these matters in writing. However, with the problems you've been having, it does seem you might have been more forthcoming in private conversation.'

Diane sat stiffly in her chair. Jenkins wouldn't look at her, so she addressed the others. 'All of our actions have been governed by two critical issues. First, to minimize our response time and, second, whether through documents or private conversation, we have tried not to feed the fires of rumor. Do not forget that we were dealing with, and continue to deal with, a crisis situation, in which one is forced to make decisions on the fly. I feel confident that we have made the right decisions.'

Roland Fitzhugh's hand chopped the air. He was the chairman of the nominating committee, and Diane's approval had come straight through him. He now gazed across at her with all the scorn he could muster. 'The president has it backwards, and she needs to understand that an uninformed board, a board neglected and kept completely in the dark, is much more apt – to borrow your phrase – to feed the fires of rumor.'

Rowster was tired of pussyfooting. He jumped in with all the southern intonation he could muster. 'Ah'm glad you bring up that point, about this being such a crisis sitee-ation.

Maybe you can inform us now about your actions these past few days, you know, describe how you were all caught up in the heat of battle.'

Jenkins fought to regain control of what was on the verge of becoming an inquisition. Justifiable, certainly – look at her, acting as if the board was irrelevant – but an inquisition nonetheless. 'What Mr. Rowster is referring to is reports that you have been absent for several days and less than an active participant in the decision making during this critical time.'

Diane blinked once and hesitated for only a beat. 'Both Jim and I were away on business this past Friday. I was also out of town most of Saturday. We were conducting timely and important negotiations on behalf of the company.' Recalling all too vividly the outcome of those negotiations, she dug a fingernail into the fleshy pad of her right hand.

'Out o' town . . .' Rowster said, allowing the words to hang there like a curse.

'I accept full responsibility for my absence. The timing of the meetings and my schedule in general were regrettable. I chose to pursue a course of action that at the time appeared to offer Simtec a competitive advantage.'

It sounded as if, somewhere in Greece, Michael Gaines dropped the handset of his phone. Then he was back, clearing his throat from across the Atlantic. He spoke as though he were delivering one of the Ten Commandments. 'There comes a moment when you cancel trips. You reschedule meetings, Ms. Hughes. When your stock drops ten points, I suggest you have come upon one of those moments. Business dictates that you wake up and get your hands dirty.'

Diane considered Michael Gaines a buffoon who knew nothing about running a major corporation. When he could make pronouncements with the tacit approval of the other board members, she knew the meeting had turned squarely against her. She was powerless to stop it. Her trump card had always been her confidence and the conviction that she could project out into a room. Normally that conviction was contagious, but this time her prime character trait had become her undoing. Her own confidence was being turned into a negative and echoed back at her. But she knew no other way.

Rowster interlocked and flexed his fingers. 'Tell us about Caspah,' he said. Eyebrows went up around the table.

Diane had also misunderstood the breadth and nature of the board's inquiry. It was far less about Simtec's numbers, and much more a personal interrogation. She was still pinching her hand under the table, and she bore down with the thumbnail. She would not raise her voice, tell them Caspar was none of their damn business.

'Caspar was the name of a security study we conducted recently.'

Jenkins stared at Rowster with an open mouth. He had scooped them all again.

'How would you characterize that study?'

'I'm not sure I follow.'

'You know, Ms. Hughes, was it worth it? Did you learn anything?'

'We had a comprehensive survey, part of which was a confidential questionnaire given to all those in supervisory positions. We also had one-on-one interviews. All of the results and recommendations were compiled into a report which was to be implemented as soon as it came out of the revision process.'

Rowster smiled at this. 'Is it safe to say this report contained passwords, access codes, and a mother lode of privileged network information?'

'A mother lode, Mr. Rowster? Are we gold mining?'

'Somebody obviously has been. You help compile a hacker's bible and then you have all these security problems. Quite a coincidence, wouldn't you say?'

'I find it tragic. If a thorough analysis had been done some time ago, we might not be sitting where we are now. That is why we are doing a top-to-bottom rewrite of the policy and procedures manual.' She bit her lip, wanting to say more, that the study was supported by both Jim Seidler and Chris Jacobs, but to bring that up now would sound defensive. Weak.

'Ah think you miss mah point. Is it possible this report found its way to the wrong hands? Here it is, one pretty little document with all the necessary information to make exactly the trouble you now have. Ah think, personally, that this report was not handled in an appropriate manner.'

How dare the sonofabitch! Diane could feel the blood rush to her cheeks. 'You are not in a position to make that statement.'

'Maybe. Maybe not. Ah find it highly likely that the report got loose. My brethren here can come to their own conclusions. I also find it reprehensible, Ms. Hughes, that the study was conducted, the results were compiled and delivered to you, but nothing was ever done with them.'

The other board members were following this exchange intently.

'Our goal is to have the new procedures manual in place by the end of the fiscal year. This is a realistic time frame, given the scope of the project.'

It was a weak response. Fitzhugh shook his head and Cummings scribbled a note.

Diane had not anticipated this line of questioning, nor such an open frontal attack. She showed a hint of desperation as she plunged ahead. 'You act as if nothing had been done, but that is not the case. We were in the process of analyzing what was in place. I suspect, sir, that running a company may be different from running a military operation. We do not have the luxury of handing down unquestionable mandates. We have a board to answer to, shareholders, and we have to consider our own employees. Every decision and policy is the result of a process. We cannot manage by decree.'

'If there is a lack of will and commitment to get the job done, the enemy will always find himself in a favorable position.' Having fought the good fight, Rowster leaned back in his chair, beaming militarily. 'Fellow board members,' he said. 'We need to get on with this.'

Diane turned away in disgust.

Fitzhugh remained stoic, and Jenkins eyed the room furtively.

'I've heard enough,' Cummings said. He pulled at one earlobe.

'Me too,' Gaines said. 'More than enough.'

Jenkins swayed forward, leaning into his role. 'Something

has to be done to reassure the analysts and investors, that much is obvious. The markets cannot withstand more bad news, and I am of the opinion that they cannot bear more of the status quo. This company needs to show that it has taken decisive action in the face of extreme adversity. It is for this reason that we have come directly to you, Diane. We don't want an ugly fight. We'd like to lessen the embarrassment for everybody. We think it would be best if you chose to resign your position as chief executive officer.'

'Second.' Rowster followed on cue.

'I don't think this is coming as a great surprise to you,' Jenkins continued. 'It can't be, after all that has transpired. But what I am about to say you may find shocking. This board, in return for your cooperation, is ready to extend a similar severance agreement as the one given to your predecessor. Given your short tenure, we believe that offer extremely generous.'

'Generous?' Diane said, standing up, already telling herself that this might be her last time in the boardroom. Telling herself that it didn't matter, that she would never speak to any of these men again, ever. 'Gentlemen.' She drew herself up proudly. 'You can all go fuck yourselves.'

26

In his west Houston hospital room, W. S. Dunn now had a live modem connection to his laptop. He was propped up against three enormous white pillows, browsing the Simtec tech support logs.

On its toll-free number for home and small business users, Simtec received, on average, two hundred calls an hour. The logs flowed down the screen in an endless tale of woe. Customer added multimedia kit. Now computer doesn't boot. Customer bought memory upgrade through mail order. Won't work. Advised to return and order Simtec part no. 12-561101. Person claims cockroach crawled inside drive bay. Now drive gives intermittent problems.

Most of the reports Dunn scanned and discarded. He knew exactly what the technicians were going through. Call the store where you bought the CD-ROM, baby. Tell it to the mail order house that sold you the memory. Call Orkin!

But Simtec personnel were charged with being prompt, knowledgeable, and courteous. There it was, right in their mission statement. Which was why the majority of them only lasted six months. The others learned how to survive.

Dunn moved down the list, hunting for that hidden anomaly, the call that might be a harbinger of damage they were yet to uncover. And he intended to go through the text of both the consumer log and the corporate log, which promised to be no less a tale of woe, though occurring at perhaps a higher level.

A nurse pushed through the door carrying a clear plastic cup. No doubt it was something else for him to drink, and Dunn eyed the yellowish fluid distastefully. The nurse stopped cold, surveying the room. The patient had a computer gadget up on his belly. What looked like a fax machine was standing where his food tray was supposed to go. Occupying the rest of the electrical outlets around the room were a variety of other nonstandard items. There wasn't a flower in sight.

'Just what are you doing in here?' the nurse said.

Dunn offered what he hoped was a winning smile. 'Judging by your tone,' he said. 'Your name tag must read Nurse Nice.'

A line like that either works or it doesn't, and the nurse had to decide which one it was going to be. She eyed the cord that came out the back of the laptop, ran up and over the top of the wall. Tony Martoli had succeeded in locating an outside line down the hall at a supply station. Liberties had been taken.

The nurse broadened her stance. 'I'm not sure you can have all this in here,' she said. 'This looks like some kind of a violation. This isn't a Radio Shack, this is a hospital.'

'I know it's a hospital,' Dunn said. He turned his head to the right, eyes closing slowly while his face pronounced a deepening concentration. Dunn's left hand appeared to struggle up into the air, hovering over the keyboard. When he opened his eyes, the hand dropped back to his chest. 'You see? I'm administering therapy here. The arm is almost one hundred percent.'

The woman's mouth puckered and her eyes flared. Then she spun on her heel and went back out the door. The little plastic cup was no longer important.

'Martoli?' Tony was sitting in a side chair during all this, not saying a word. 'You better get out there and find us an authority figure. Explain the situation and request his or her assistance. Be gracious. Otherwise, in about five minutes that nurse will be back in here pulling wires.'

When Barry came to the phone, Jim said, 'Well, you might as well hear it from me: Diane's out.' No joy, no regret. This was Jim delivering a fact.

'I see,' Barry said after a few moments. He had known it was coming. He'd gotten all the signs. But it was still a shock.

'And I've been named interim president.' Jim sounded exhausted. 'The board has already given me an earful. Until they deem we have regained control of the situation, they wish to be brought in on all decisions. We're on a break, but then I'm going to start giving them background. I'll try to bring them up to speed, and I'd like you to come over and sit in.'

Interesting choice of words. You might be called to give a report. You were usually not asked to *sit in*. 'I'll do whatever I can,' Barry said.

'The board thinks highly of you. This is a good chance for you to show you're on top of things. You, more than anybody, have been rowing the boat, and don't be shy about it.'

'When do you reconvene?'

'Twenty minutes. I also wanted to make sure you got all the press releases together, the ones you've been working on for customer notification.'

'They're sitting right here on my desk.'

'I want you to get the whole bundle together and ship it over to Mike Spakovsky.'

Barry swallowed. His eyes darted to a stack of papers. 'To Mike?'

'He's putting a team together to coordinate our efforts. I've charged Mike and Karen with responding to this. You've made a good start, but we feel you've already got a full plate. We need you out from under this.'

Silence. Who, Barry wondered, was the *we*?

'It's a PR issue, and a legal issue, Barry. I believe it prudent to have them look things over. The whole concern is becoming more complicated by the minute. I've had it pointed out that this may not be an open-and-shut case of Simtec notifying its own customers. The possibility exists that other machines have been similarly afflicted. Non-Simtec machines. By accepting responsibility, the way your first announcement is worded, are we also taking responsibility for those other manufacturers?'

Barry knew his answer would be unacceptable. He had tried to make Simtec sound forthright. They were a company that would stand behind their products and make good on their mistakes. If the problem cropped up in Dells, or IBMs? No, they didn't want responsibility for other manufacturers' problems, but that possibility seemed remote.

'I believe you've been led off into hypotheticals,' Barry said as evenly as he could manage.

Jim Seidler chuckled. 'Ah, Barry. Always the realist. Get the stuff to Mike. Then we'll have you talk sense to this board.'

It was 4:20 P.M. by the time Bill Dunn parked at Rice University in a parking slot marked for visitors. The campus was much larger than he had expected, the buildings impressive, full of marble and columns.

A young man was doing a pre-run stretch over at the edge of the parking lot, so Bill got directions to the library, which squatted at the end of the main quadrangle. He walked over and pushed through the heavy front door, signed in, and hunted down the reference desk.

'I have a name and I'm trying to find out if that person might be a student or faculty member here,' he said.

The young woman working the desk handed him a book with current faculty and staff listings, as well as a copy of the latest student directory.

'How about alumni?'

She shook her head. 'We don't keep a directory of alumni. The alumni office might be able to help you. They're not open now, but you could check with them tomorrow.'

'What about yearbooks?'

'Sure, you could do that. They're in the stacks on the third floor.' She jotted down a call number.

'Thanks,' Bill said. He stood at the counter and flipped through the current listings. No Pat Dapor. He left the directories on the counter, took the stairs to the third floor, and hunted down the yearbooks. The library had copies of the *Campanile* dating back to 1916, the cloth covers battered and fraying. Bill did some quick math and started checking in the 1950s. The student body was small and he worked quickly. In the *D* pages of the 1975 book, a prankster had adorned several of the men and women with devil's horns. Bill kept going, right up through the 90s without success. Horns or no, there was not a Dapor who had ever attended Rice University.

His dad had said that people often used names that gave

something away, that the name, and the connection to Rice University, was worth looking into. But Bill wasn't even sure what he was looking for. The only thing these names gave off was the smell of old, slowly yellowing paper.

He reshelved the books, walked down, and checked out of the library. On a whim, Bill asked for directions to the computer science department. He crossed over and entered one end of the building beside a bank of vending machines. Bill had taken a few computer courses at Georgia Tech, and he had to admit, this school had a different feel to it. It was smaller and had an air of privilege, as though there were stores of knowledge here, and the knowledge was passed from individual to individual like a baton. Fine for history and English literature, Bill thought, but it didn't fit the field of computers very well at all. With computers, all too often you went to class and listened and held your hand out there for the baton, and when you pulled your hand back in, you found it was empty. Many computer science faculty weren't in the race themselves, and they couldn't prepare you from the sidelines.

He walked the hallway slowly, taking in the bulletin boards, reading the notices that hung on faculty doors. In a small room with a sink and a coffee machine, he found several rows of mailboxes. Too many for faculty, so the grad students must get boxes as well.

From the looks of things, most everyone was gone for the summer. Each box had accumulated the same stack of memos, and Bill flipped through them, all the way back to May.

He scanned through the names on the boxes: Albert, Anderson, Chang, Cionski. No Dapor. He finished examining the names, walked the hallway again, and left. If the old man thought this was a hot lead, let him get out of the hospital bed and find it himself.

James Dupree skidded to a sharp stop and heard a spray of ice pelt the wooden baseboard. It was a gratifying sound and one that brought the admiration of several nearby youths. Dupree tromped over to a nearby bench and unlaced his skates.

He then took out a handkerchief and wiped down each

blade. He tied the laces together in a bow and slipped on the leather blade guards. He stepped into his loafers, hooked the laces with two fingers, and swung the size ten and a half Bauer skates over his shoulder.

The round clock by the rental counter showed a quarter to six, and Dupree scanned the surrounding shops. No, better to have dinner somewhere else. Somewhere more private. He moved onto the concourse, which on this level was always full of people: tourists, wealthy shoppers from Mexico and South America, young couples out for a stroll, well-dressed women clutching their parcels. He scanned the faces, then cut through a gap in the traffic toward the hallway leading out to the lower-level parking garage.

Dupree had done so much groundwork and, in the case of the Simtec Computer Corporation, he'd been given so much information to begin with that he had considered the battle a no contest. That had been a gross underestimation. He'd watched his first blows go unheeded and felt his confidence falter. Go away, Simtec had said. *We refuse to pay.*

Which they had said for quite some time, but were saying no longer. Dupree's ability to recover from his initial setbacks, to snatch a victory, made this fact all the more gratifying. Dinner, he decided, should be in celebration of his upcoming trip to Europe. A nice pasta and red wine, and he thought of just the place. He pushed through the glass doors and stepped back into the Houston heat, so tedious compared to the cool air over the ice.

He was driving a nondescript Corolla sedan, and he'd had to park far from the entrance. He began picking his way through the automobiles, rows upon rows of them, full of people who came to this mecca to shop and gawk and while away their few leisure hours.

Dupree was feeling a little too comfortable with his position. On this, the last day before the largest payoff of his career, James Dupree had allowed himself to grow self-satisfed. He didn't notice that a man several rows ahead had folded a newspaper and tucked it in under his arm. If Dupree had been paying closer attention, he might have thought, What an odd place to read the newspaper, a hot parking garage filled with exhaust fumes, and Dupree might have paused. He might have turned aside.

But he kept going, and he could see the maroon Corolla just ahead, when the man appeared at his elbow.

'James Dupree, we're going to get in the car. We're going to sit. We'll talk.'

Dupree tipped his head and saw that there was not only a newspaper. There was a gun in the newspaper. The fact that the gun wasn't immediately being used told Dupree much. So he said the first neutral thing he could think of, 'And who are you?'

'I'm the one who needs a list. I need you to make me a list of what you've done and where. I am prepared to make you give me this information. How many ways do I have to say *it*?'

Dupree immediately knew what this was, and he knew who had sent this man. What did you do to a renegade? You punished him. Dupree would have done the same thing, and he knew that, somehow, he had been tracked. The enormity of that fact briefly fogged Dupree's quick responses.

He glanced back to the newspaper, and his next thoughts were several: that this was a hired gun, albeit a very cool, very professional one, and that Dupree could probably tell him whatever he felt like. Dupree could sit there and spew information about networks and rigged files right off the top of his head – whatever came to mind – and this guy wouldn't know the difference. But he also realized that his strongest card, his only card at the moment, really, was that he was the one who possessed that information. He had been trailed or in some other way sniffed out, psychologically and athletically profiled and pinned down at his one watering hole. Somehow they had managed to do that, pick him up at the only place where he regularly went, but this person beside him was still a drone, and drones had orders. This drone was supposed to return with information.

'My car?' Dupree said, gesturing toward the Corolla.

'Sure,' the man said, and his eyes flicked in that direction.

Which was when Dupree swung the ice skates. He didn't go for the man; he went for the newspaper. The man looked back a moment too late. The skates slashed down into his hand, taking the newspaper and gun with them.

Everyone's a fighter when they have to be, which made James Dupree the worst kind: smart and unorthodox. While the man was off balance, instead of stepping back to prepare a punch, thereby entering a battle Dupree surely would have lost, he gave the man a body blow with his shoulder, knocking him onto the ground between two cars.

Dupree dropped the skates, kicked the gun under a Volkswagen, and took off running. After the first row of cars, he started to zigzag, keeping low and darting through the gaps. Another few seconds and Dupree heard a popping sound behind him. The car to his right lost its rear window.

Fine, stand back there and fire away. He'd already put a good distance between them, and he wasn't presenting much of a target. Another fifty yards and he'd be back inside the mall.

Everything was happening with such speed, but also with such clarity of purpose, that Dupree was able to make choices as he ran. Hit the glass doors running? Veer right and take the ramp up to the next level?

Dupree did not expect the woman. Short brown hair. Pants. Jacket. Macy's bag held at waist level. As soon as he saw her, much in the same way he had understood everything else, he understood this, too. A female, working the perimeter. Even he could admire the touch. You hired it out, and you hired well. The woman wasn't screaming. She wasn't dropping to the pavement. She was calmly walking up the middle of the drive between this row of cars and the next. Long before she turned toward him, Dupree knew what was coming.

As the woman stepped in front and started to pivot, Dupree jumped. He launched himself up over the hood of a car. This was an unexpected maneuver, and it bought him a few more moments. Maybe longer, only he landed horribly. One arm caught under him in such a way that the elbow bent back at a grotesque angle. His shoulder hit the concrete and popped. He lay on the ground, his body contorted, the pain only starting to register.

James Dupree gasped for breath. It had all come down to

this. Sonofabitch. Fucking whore. A person came to you – sought you out with great difficulty, in fact – and dropped a sweet deal in your lap. Come do your damage at my house, they said. Too sweet a deal, it turned out, because they came back at you and took it away.

Out of the corner of his eye, Dupree saw the woman come into view. He watched her raise the Macy's bag.

Now they'd never know what he'd done. All that Hektor had planted and planned. No one could tell them. Obviously, that didn't matter.

His last thought was of Hektor, the Warrior, felled in battle. Here there would be no grieving Priam, come to collect his son's body.

Dupree hoped they all suffered.

27

By 7:00 P.M., the board members looked as haggard and tense as the Simtec executives. And they'd only been at it for one day. As they went into details of the malicious piece of code, embedded on every machine since June 21, the board absorbed each new revelation with uniform horror.

Greg Mitchell had been called in to report on his progress in stopping and repairing the damage, and he was being peppered with questions.

'Go over that again,' Peter Jenkins was saying. 'That part about the antivirus software.' Jenkins didn't know computers at all. He'd had something installed at his house, though he wasn't quite sure what it was, and he understood even less about a computer's inner workings. Throughout Greg's discussion, Jenkins was lucky to follow half of what was being said.

Greg backtracked and tried it again. 'Most antivirus software uses the same set of techniques. When you talk about a virus signature, that's because the virus is nothing more than a set of computer instructions. For a known virus, those instructions can be spotted. That's what the antivirus program is doing when it's scanning for virus signatures. It's looking for known viruses. Now, there's another set of viruses that change their instructions. They *mutate*, as it's called, in order to avoid detection. The mutation may, for example, randomly intersperse do-nothing statements so that no two infections are exactly alike. I think that's what you were getting at, Mr. Cummings, when you were asking about programs detecting unknown viruses, and shouldn't they be able to stop what we've got on our machines. Antivirus programs handle unknown code differently, with widely varying degrees of success.'

Roland Fitzhugh gave a quick shake of the head. 'I'm not sure I got all that. Can we just cut to the chase? There's a bug. It's on an estimated four hundred thousand machines. We asked about antivirus software, and wouldn't that protect some percentage of the customers?'

Under the table, Greg pressed his hands against one another. 'It's not really a bug,' he said. 'We should make that distinction clear. A bug is a flaw in a program. More of an oversight, if you will. For that matter, I wouldn't call it a virus, either. The operational definition of a virus is that it replicates. You know, people carry it around on floppy disks and it gets on other machines, and other floppies, and so on. This code doesn't do that. More accurately it's a Trojan horse. To be precise in the wording of an announcement, you really shouldn't call it a virus, because it doesn't replicate.'

'Bug, virus . . . who cares?' Richard Rowster cut in. 'When it's on four hundred thousand machines, it doesn't *have* to replicate.'

Barry Shepard had been trying not to interrupt. Let the board ask their questions. Let them try to get up to speed, all of which was wasting an inordinate amount of time. He caught Greg's attention and made a rotating motion with his finger: Move on.

'We tested seven popular antivirus tools to see what would happen, whether they'd give some kind of alert when the code went active. We found that one of the seven programs did in fact lock it out and prevent damage.'

'One?'

'If the software is configured for maximum protection.'

'So that might help what percentage of the customers?'

Greg hesitated. He looked at Barry. 'We also haven't taken into account those machines that might have been reconfigured for another operating system. The customer may have deleted the files that we ship on the drive. They may have started over from scratch.'

'We're going in circles,' Rowster said. For several hours Rowster had been a dynamo, virtually seizing control of the meeting. But now he had run out of gas and he wanted a drink. He thought longingly of the liquor cabinet in Jim

Seidler's office. 'Lump all that stuff together and give us a percentage.'

'Well . . . my best guess would be that ninety percent of the people out there are going to get hit. Between ninety and ninety-five.'

Richard Rowster was indignant. He slammed his shoulders back against his chair. 'That's no good,' he said. 'A ninety percent kill. That's just unacceptable.'

Barry excused himself during what the board insisted was the final break in their marathon meeting. They had gotten into rehashing the financials and arguing over nuances of profit and loss. Barry was no longer providing input, and he had had enough. He walked to his office and made phone calls. Then he drove to the hospital to see W. S. Dunn.

'When Hektor calls at nine-thirty tomorrow morning, we're sticking with the plan to pay the money. The board's opinion is, What else can we do?'

Dunn's lips pressed together and he said nothing.

'Of course, the board's real opinion is that if we had paid earlier, we might not be sitting where we are now. They're great on hindsight.'

'And the machines? I spoke to my people who are working with Greg. They've got a fix ready.'

'Close to ready,' Barry corrected. 'They're still working through all the last-minute possibilities. If the user loaded a third-party disk manager, the boot record may not be what we think it is. We've got to be able to handle that gracefully, without error. They'll go straight through the night, working it up, and the file will be available for download as soon as we go public. I don't have to tell you, when we make this announcement it has to stick. No backtracking and no misinformation. I'm sure we'll be tweaking both the file and the wording of the announcement right up until the last minute.'

'And Diane?'

Barry shrugged. 'I haven't seen her since it happened.'

'What's your opinion?'

'I wasn't present in the meeting, so I don't know what reasons were given. I can't speak to that. I do think Simtec shouldn't be where it is right now. No company should be. I know in my heart a lot of it isn't Diane's fault. But the board wants to save face. If not her, who should it have been?'

'Could have been a lot of people,' Dunn said slowly. 'But none quite so dramatic.'

Barry shifted over his feet. Dunn reached down and started to close the lid on the laptop that was lying next to him on the bed.

Then he said, 'Look at this. You want to see the amusing bastard we're dealing with?' He turned the laptop toward Barry. 'This is code from the Trojan horse. I guess Greg has told you how it operates. Greg copied the boot record, the boot sector, and the FAT into files for me to download. Right here in this chunk—' Dunn arrowed up. 'You see that copyright symbol? It's not the real symbol, but that's the way some programmers do it, with parentheses. Look right next to that. What do you want to bet the egomaniac put his initials in there? M. M. I called Sheila and let her know, so we could cross-check with the profiles on your employees. No match, but I bet that's what it is.'

Barry leaned closer and stared at the hexadecimal code.

20	20	20	20	20	
28	63	29	20	20	(c)
31	39	39	37	20	1997
4D	2E	4D	2E	20	M.M.

'This shows you the kind of person you're dealing with,' Dunn said. 'Someone who writes a Trojan that's not even that good, yet they still want to carve their name in the tree trunk.'

It was the first time Barry had seen the actual code, and he couldn't take his eyes off it. On screen, it didn't look like much of anything at all, but Simtec had allowed this particular horse inside the walls. Now the soldiers were spilling out into the night and they were poised to bring down the city.

'What do you mean it's not good?'

'I mean there's nothing revolutionary here. Some recycled virus code that's been floating around. All techniques that are well known. The standard attempt at encryption.'

Barry was surprised at this disparaging assessment. The weapon had proved its potency, but W. S. Dunn was considering matters of *style*.

Dunn sank back against the pillows. His face was gaunt and pale. 'I'm not feeling so hot,' he said. 'I'm going to use that pump on the stand and fall asleep. I'll be awake in the morning, though. When that call comes in, you keep in touch.'

Barry himself slept for three hours, woke up at 4:30 A.M., and stared at the ceiling. He stayed that way until 5:00 before accepting that his sleep was over: today was the day. He showered and dressed with economical motions. Then he sat on the edge of the bed next to Claudia, who stretched, rolled on her side, and rested a hand on his thigh. 'I was thinking about it last night, before I fell asleep,' she said. 'It's not the end of the world, paying the money.'

'No, it's not.'

'You can look at it like this, it's the cost of doing business.'

Barry didn't say anything.

'Bee? It *is* the cost of doing business. Juries award that kind of money sometimes. Right or wrong, you pay and keep going. You can't beat yourself up over it.'

It still surprised Barry, sometimes, that his wife knew him so well. For a moment, his hand found Claudia's. 'It's said and done in a few hours,' he said, then stood up. 'See you tonight.'

He glanced in at Caroline, a little bundle in the middle of the bed. No, it wouldn't be the end of the world, he repeated to himself. He headed downstairs and out to the car. But it sure felt like it.

Mike Spakovsky was in the boardroom directing traffic. A technician had brought in Mike's laptop and had it hooked to an LCD projection panel. Whatever the chief financial officer did on the laptop was thus replicated in a huge ten-foot image at the head of the table. Right now, the screen was blank.

'I'm going to need a phone line in here,' Spakovsky said, in a tense voice. He pointed to a number of jacks along the baseboard of one wall. 'Is one of those a phone line?'

'We're getting that, Mr. Spakovsky. We'll have that all hooked up for you.'

Spakovsky turned and found Peter Jenkins surveying the proceedings from the doorway. Spakovsky caught the chairman's eye and shook his head, as if to say how hard it was to get anything done right.

But Jenkins was watching Spakovsky and thinking how the man was going to be out in the street within a month. Jim Seidler had already pulled Jenkins aside and expressed his interest in finding a replacement. For the time being, Jenkins had convinced him to hold off. Too much change, too fast. Too much up in the air right now. But Jim wouldn't hold off indefinitely. And once they put him at the helm for good, he would get his way.

Perhaps Spakovsky sensed some of this, because he turned and snapped, 'I need it all set up and ready to do a dry run. I'm going to transfer some money and I want it up on that wall. You tell me the minute it's ready.'

With half a bagel in one hand and a towel around his neck, Bill Dunn phoned his dad. He was staying in a hotel near Simtec and, if Simtec was going to buy information, he planned to be right there when the information came through.

'Dunn,' his father said.

'Good morning,' Bill said. 'How are you doing?'

'Still in the hospital.'

'Right. I'm getting dressed now. I'm going to head over to Simtec and be there when they get the call.' His father hated to be out of the loop, so Bill added, 'I can have you on the line when it comes in, if you want.'

'They're not going to get anything.'

'You never know.'

'Someone's going to get ten million dollars, and Simtec's going to get squat. I hope I'm wrong. I hope they get a whole list of fixes, but I don't think so. That's my prediction.'

Bill sat down on the edge of the bed. 'I talked to Barry. He made it sound like a corporate decision. The board wants to pay and hope for the best.'

'That's exactly what it is, a corporate decision. The board's got a monkey by the tail and they don't know what to do with it. Throw money away, I guess that's something.'

'It's their money, Dad.'

'I had a dream about the sonofabitch The guy was wearing an outfit, like a superhero. Muscular guy. Looked like he could leap over buildings in a single bound. The outfit had an *M* on it. *M* on the front. *M* on the back. M. M.'

'What's that all about I wonder?'

'That's the initials in the code. Did you ever look at the hex? There's a copyright symbol in there along with the initials M. M.'

'Dad?' Bill said. He dropped the bagel onto a nightstand. 'I saw an M. M. at Rice University. I'm going to call you back.'

Rice was much more active on a Monday morning, and Bill Dunn had to park in a big lot by the stadium and walk. He went straight to the computer science department and began working the hallway, certain he had seen it – seen something – in here somewhere. The initials came as a sharp tug at his memory, which he was determined to hunt down. He again read the bulletin boards: half-price texts for sale, roommates wanted, a rider to share gas to California. The doors to the faculty offices held an assortment of comic strips and grade reports, and Bill moved quickly from door to door.

Halfway up the hall, he found it. A short memo that looked as though it had been typed on a typewriter.

ALL STUDENTS:

COSC 3201 Wed, July 19 and Fri, July 21 will be rescheduled.
COSC 6410 Thu, July 20 will be rescheduled.

If you have an appointment to meet with an advisor, see Dr. Cionski M-F 10-2 in Rm. 114.

The brief note was signed with the initials M. M.

Could it be possible? No, Bill told himself, even though his heart had leapt into high gear. Think of all the people who must have these same initials. Hundreds of them. Thousands. But only one was a computer science teacher at Rice.

He examined the rest of the door for further clues. A large poster of Vienna covered the bottom half of the door, and just above that a photograph was held by a thumbtack. In the photo, two men stood in the foreground by what appeared to be a guardrail. Behind them was a series of snowcapped mountains. One man was short, with dark, unkempt hair and a pouchy face. The other man had a long wisp of gray beard, which, at the moment of the picture, the wind was lifting horizontally. It looked like the two had stopped at a scenic turnout, and Bill was willing to bet that one of the two was M. M.

A second notice gave the standard posting of office hours. Presuming he was the inhabitant of this office, M. M. declared his intention to be available between the hours of 1:00 and 3:00 P.M., Tuesdays.

Bill knocked on the door and listened carefully. No soft footfall, no telltale rustling of papers from inside. He checked the hallway, took out his driver's license, and tried it in the door. The license slid in a quarter inch before hitting a solid, unyielding bolt of metal. Judging by the iron on the outside of the door, the bolt would extend a good inch or two into the doorjamb. No easy jimmy.

The sound of two voices echoed down the hallway and Bill took a quick step back. The voices were coming from an open doorway, and Bill moved closer.

They sounded like students, discussing something about linked lists. It was computer talk, and Bill looked inside and saw the students were in a small lab. A half dozen machines were set up on tables around the room.

'Excuse me,' Bill said, and the two glanced up. 'I was wondering if either of you have had, or know anything about, this Dr. M. M. up the hall?' Bill did his best to look like a prospective student.

'That's Dr. Milstead.'

'Milstead. What does he teach?'

'In the summer, one intro class and one seminar. Right now it's advanced algorithms. Dr. Morose, we call him. I've been here three years and I've never seen him smile. Not once.'

Bill wrinkled his nose. 'Not too good, eh?'

'There's plenty worse. You could get Hines—' The two found something about this idea very funny, and they burst into laughter.

'Milstead's pretty sharp,' the other one said. 'He's just too damn serious.'

Bill Dunn was moving back and forth over his feet. 'Hey, you wouldn't happen to know where he lives, would you? I need to put something in his mailbox, something I want him to look at.'

One student shook his head. The other one thought about it, then said, 'No idea. There's a department directory in the top drawer of that desk. You can have a look in there.'

'Thanks,' Bill said. He opened the drawer and pulled out the listing. It consisted of several pages someone had printed on a dot-matrix printer and stapled together. Bill flipped through to the faculty section, traced a finger down the page until he came to the entry for Dr. Martin Milstead.

By 8:50 A.M. everyone had gravitated toward the boardroom. The board members were present, along with Seidler, Spakovsky, Barry Shepard, and Karen Williams. It wasn't a formal meeting and they had dispensed with Michael Gaines, yet everyone had arrived early and they were milling around, grazing over the pastries and coffee the catering people had set up on a side table.

Richard Rowster had cornered Barry and was pumping him for information about the man he and Bill Dunn surprised in the apartment.

'So, he was right in there with you the whole time?'

'He was hiding in the back bedroom. We checked the place when we went in. Obviously, we didn't see him.'

Rowster was incredulous. 'Sounds to me like you were damn lucky. The fucker could have blown your heads off.'

'I'm sure he could have.'

'So he comes running out of the room and knocks you on your keister.'

'No, he knocked Bill down. I tried to jump in, he pulled a knife, and that ended it. He got away.'

'Unbelievable.' Rowster's hands were twitching with excitement. 'But nothing useful on the computer?'

'Afraid not. I gave it a quick going over. Jim took the machine to have the hard drive gone through sector by sector. I just asked about it. Nothing there.'

'That's damn unfortunate. And what about this car? No leads there either?'

'It's a blue Cutlass. Bill Dunn had the car towed here. In order to preserve whatever prints might be inside, he decided not to drive it. That's not an avenue we've pursued yet.'

'So, you've got the actual car?'

'It's parked in a bay at the production stage.'

Rowster could barely contain himself. He unleashed a large smile. 'Barry Shepard,' he said. 'You've become quite a thief.'

It had been two days since the last detected intruder log-in. Ten Security Associates employees were doing nothing but monitoring different segments of the Simtec network. The rank-and-file employees were completely locked down as far as what they could run, and where and when they could do it.

Teams of technicians had pored over file and application servers, mail accounts and post offices, and database apps on all manner of different platforms. They had scrutinized the links to the Internet, the modem pool, and they had dismantled an experimental wireless net in Simtec 7. Security Associates personnel had conducted over four thousand interviews and drawn up psychological profiles and a watch-list. All this hardware, software, and employee documentation would ultimately make up a report of some 970 single-spaced pages.

Whoever had been getting into the network wasn't doing it anymore, and the sense among Security Associates staff was that they had it down cold.

At 9:31 A.M., the Ethernet address that hadn't been used in two days – the address Security Associates thought would never be used again – went live. Three alerts immediately went off on monitor stations around the central control room.

Sheila Thibodeaux immediately got hold of Jim Seidler in the boardroom.

Jim listened for a moment and said, 'I understand. For now, let it go.' Out the side of his mouth, he said, 'They're into the network again.' He punched the call up on speaker and set the phone down.

'Okay.' Sheila's voice. 'Not logging in anywhere. We're following . . .'

Everyone around the table was motionless.

Sheila, now yelling at somebody. 'Damn it, find out what segment that's coming from.'

More yelling in the background, a jumble of shouted instructions. Then Sheila's voice again, loud, though not directed at them. 'Pull out the connection to building ten and see if it drops. Whoa, here it comes—'

Barry had seized the edge of the table.

'It's mail. He's sending mail in.'

Two different machines started grabbing packets. It was a brief transmission and then it was over. Just like that. The machine snapped off like a light, taking its address and location with it. The technicians immediately punched up the packets. Therefore, they were the first to know, and then convey the information to Sheila, who in turn conveyed it to those in the boardroom, that Barry Shepard had received a piece of mail.

Bill Dunn found Hibury Street about five miles from Rice. The neighborhood was residential, full of older, one-story homes set back from the street on wooded lots. He left the car on the curb in front of the house numbered 7312. No car in the driveway, but Bill could see a light on in the back part of the house.

He carried two things with him to the front door: a page of computer code bearing the copyright M. M. and a phone, his dad jawing at him all the way up the sidewalk.

'Now don't confront him with it. You don't want to go too far. Give him a taste and let him run with the hook. Let's see what he says. Don't go inside the house, either. Right now, you're just asking questions. We'll be able to tell if he's the man, and then—'

'Dad?' Bill said. 'I could hand him the phone and you could talk to him, if that's what you want.'

Silence. 'Oh,' W. S. Dunn said. 'I guess so. You do it your way. Leave the phone on, though. I want to hear.'

Bill rang the doorbell and waited. The door had a knocker, so he used that, too. Five good raps. More waiting, shifting his weight from side to side, thinking about what he was going to say. He retreated a few steps so that he could look through a bay window into the dining room. The light was coming in from the kitchen, the edge of a countertop visible through the doorway.

'Not answering,' Bill said. 'I'm going to walk up the driveway and see what I see.'

'Careful,' Dunn said.

Halfway up the drive, Bill could get a good look inside the kitchen. From there, an archway opened onto what appeared to be a sitting room. No sign of anyone. He walked up to the garage door and looked through a pane of glass. Inside was a hodgepodge of yard equipment and a red Mustang convertible.

'You won't get a warrant,' W. S. said in Bill's ear. 'Afraid not. You know how many people have the initials M. M.? Initials and a parking ticket found in somebody else's vehicle. They'll laugh you out into the street.'

Bill Dunn went back and got in his car. He stared out the windshield. The fucker was home, though. Bill knew it.

The mail message was titled: Instructions. And they were concise. There was an account number and a routing code for Simtec to wire the money. As soon as positive indication of the transfer was received, important details about Simtec's current and future vulnerability would be faxed to the following number.

'That's TechDirect's administrative fax,' Barry said. He had used Spakovsky's laptop to project the message up for everyone to see.

'Okay, let's do it,' the chief financial officer said. 'This is our phone call.'

'I wonder why he didn't call?' Barry asked. He stood up to allow Spakovsky back to the laptop.

'It's a clean transaction,' Jim Seidler said, still looking at the message. 'Very orderly. Businesslike. No room for a last-second shouting match.'

Richard Rowster was pacing up and down the length of the table. He had spoken briefly with the Security Associates people and hung up the phone. 'They were on-line for all of thirty-six seconds,' he said. 'That's not enough time to track anything down. They used mail just to show they're still on the network. To give us a poke in the ribs, the bastards.'

The appearance of a blue, character-based screen with the heading Electronic Funds Menu pulled everyone's attention to the image being projected on the wall.

Spakovsky said, 'This is the screen into our accounts at Southern Bank of Texas. I spoke with the bank first thing this morning to let them know this was time critical. They're waiting on the transfer, and the money will go out as soon as we put this through.'

Spakovsky chose 3, Payments, and waited a moment while a new screen loaded across the modem connection. 'Jim, I'll need you over here to key in a second PIN.'

In his years with venture capital, Paul Cummings had witnessed some tenuous deals. Even so, this morning he'd been unusually quiet, and he now held his head in his hands. 'I don't believe I'm watching this,' Paul said to nobody in particular. 'I voted for it, but I still don't believe it.'

'There it is,' Spakovsky said, tipping his head to examine the various fields as they appeared in large lettering on the wall. At the bottom of the screen was a horizontal listing of keyboard commands: F1 Enter F2 Cancel F3 Menu F10 Help.

Mike Spakovsky filled out the electronic transfer form and punched in the first Simtec access code. Twenty minutes earlier, Barry Shepard had eaten a cream-cheese Danish. It now tasted like sour mucus at the back of his throat. No one said anything while Jim Seidler leaned over and typed a sequence of keys.

'Everything in order?' Spakovsky asked no one in particular. He straightened in his chair. Then his finger came down and stabbed the F1 key. The screen blanked and regenerated. 'There it goes,' he said. His head bobbed once in the direction of the screen.

28

'They sent the money,' W. S. Dunn said.

'Yeah,' Bill replied. 'It's the eleventh hour. That's what they would do.' The both of them were working their way into evil moods.

'I'm lying here on my ass, going over the corporate support logs. It's been a total waste of time. Meanwhile you're sitting out in the street.'

'I've got someone coming out to take my place. We're going to stay here and wait for Milstead. I'll go back to Simtec, and I'll be there when they get something.'

'*If* they get something,' his father corrected. 'Which I doubt. But it's a good idea for you to be over there. When the press releases drop, it's going to be like a bomb going off.'

'I'll call you from the office,' Bill said and clicked off.

W. S. looked around the room that had become his cage. 'Martoli,' he barked. 'What do you see in those logs?'

'Nothing that sticks out, sir. It's the usual stuff you'd expect from corporate clients: questions about upgrades, networking, backup. It all looks routine to me.'

'Me, too,' Dunn said. He tried to reposition his lower body, and a sharp pain shot up from his right side. He eased his weight slowly back down. Dunn hooked the tray table that held his own laptop and pulled it closer. He jabbed half-heartedly at the arrow key.

'Look at this joker. He's calling in to gripe about Simtec's latest disk driver patch. The guy says he ran a benchmark against the new driver and it's not any faster. He's even got the numbers in here, quoting chapter and verse. You work for Simtec, you've got to sit there and listen to this crap.'

Martoli shook his head. 'Some people got too much time.'
Will Dunn hit page down.

Bill Dunn decided to try one thing before leaving Hibury Street. He started the Miata, drove down the street and around the corner. Then he pulled over and cut back across the corner yard on foot, staying out of sight behind a row of bushes.

It was all of four minutes before the rabbit poked his head out of the burrow. The diminutive Dr. Martin Milstead, his hair in a perpetual tangle, scurried out the back door of his house to unlock the garage. Same man in the photograph on the office door, and Bill Dunn started running. He crossed the street and was out of view as he came at Milstead.

As he rounded the corner into the driveway, the man had the door to the Mustang open and he was getting inside. Bill put on a burst of speed, reached out a hand, and caught the driver's side window.

Dr. Milstead screamed.

It was a low-pitched, throaty scream, that sounded more like the man had dropped a brick on his foot, and it was accompanied by a physical jump of several inches. A taller man would have smacked his head into the roof.

The whole reaction somewhat rattled Bill, who realized he had no gun, no weapon of any kind, in the event Milstead had one. He hadn't even brought the phone. He reached into his back pocket and pulled out the folded piece of paper with the computer code.

'Dr. Milstead? I wanted to ask you about this.'

Milstead frowned. His face screwed up in consternation. What was this? Was this merely a student who had been staking out the front of his house? Was this another complaint about an assignment, a request for due-date extension? While keeping one watchful eye on Bill Dunn, the man gingerly accepted the paper.

As soon as Milstead saw it, his eyes went wide. 'I don't know anything about this,' he immediately protested. 'What is this you're showing me? I must go. I'm in a hurry.' He gave a sharp tug at the door handle.

Bill watched this performance with incredulity. 'Of course it's yours. Look. You put your initials right there.'

'No. You're mistaken.'

'I'll make a bet with you. You won't be allowed in either your house or your office while we exercise a warrant and seize your equipment. Any printouts we can find. What do you want to bet we find traces of this program?'

Bill watched Dr. Milstead's face as he heard this news, and Bill realized for the first time that this man was truly afraid. He was trembling.

'A warrant.' Milstead was thinking that one over. 'Then . . . who are you with?'

'My name is Bill Dunn. I'm with a company called Security Associates.'

'Ah,' Milstead said. His shoulders fell and he watched Bill to see if this wasn't some kind of prevarication. Slowly, he turned back and stared at the sheet of paper in his hand. 'I did this under contract. That's all I can tell you. Don't know anything else about it. Got the specs. Did the work. That's it.'

The light and warmth of discovery filtered through Bill's limbs. He sank to his haunches, squatting in the car doorway, his eyes on a level with Milstead's.

'You did this under contract for *whom*?'

Now it was Milstead's turn to show surprise. 'You mean, you don't know?'

Bill shook his head.

Milstead reached over to the passenger seat, where he had tossed an armload of books and papers. He retrieved a folded section of the newspaper and extended it to Bill.

'That article right there. That's the man who hired me. He was killed yesterday.'

When Barry picked up the phone, W. S. Dunn said, 'I think you just wired ten million dollars to a dead man.'

Barry said, 'Come again?'

And so Dunn told him, or started to, before Barry interrupted.

'Let me get this straight. The guy who wrote the code is a professor at Rice University?'

'Bill is sitting in his house right now. He claims he did the work as a contract. Didn't know anything about how the program was going to be used. It wouldn't surprise me.'

'Who the hell takes a contract to write a Trojan horse?'

'A lot of people,' Dunn said. 'The next part is this: the individual who hired this professor was shot dead in a Galleria parking garage yesterday evening. According to the ID on him, his name was Patrick Draper. The police are looking at it as a failed robbery attempt, but I think we now know otherwise.'

Patrick Draper, Barry thought. The name on the car from the apartment was Pat Dapor. Sonofabitch.

Barry wasn't sure why – after all, he should be happy to hear that the man had been shot – but he was furious.

'Well, we damn sure wired that money to *somebody*.'

'I'm sure you did,' Dunn said. More quietly, he added, 'Barry, I wouldn't sit there too long waiting for something to come in on that fax machine.'

Barry spit a blast of air between his lips. Was that it? Anger, because they weren't likely to get anything for their money? But they'd known that risk to begin with. More than anything, Barry realized, it was the sure knowledge that they had been beaten. Ruthlessly and efficiently. Now someone was out there already covering up tracks.

'I'm going to call Greg Mitchell,' Dunn said. 'I'll compare his notes with what we learn from this professor. We'll nail down this end of it. If you can give me an hour before your announcement, I'll call the boardroom and give my opinion. You can take it from there and run with it.'

'An hour it is,' Barry said. He hung up the phone, locked his fingers behind his head, and squeezed. Then he called Jim Seidler.

Martin Milstead was sitting with head bowed. He'd been in the same position ever since Bill Dunn Jr. told him what his program had been used for, and that it was due to go off in one day and affect 430,000 machines.

'You're going to be infamous,' Bill said. 'I hope you have tenure. Although, I doubt tenure will protect you from something like this.'

At this, Milstead glanced up. He was sitting at his own kitchen table, but his gaze was that of a lost man. He looked like a bomb had gone off in his hands.

'But I had no idea—'

'Save it,' Bill said. 'We've already been working on a fix, but I want the source code so that we can check it. I also need to know if there's anything else you've worked on.'

'Okay, I can do that. We'll have to go to my office.'

'Then let's move,' Bill ordered. He clapped his hands together twice.

For the enormity of the operation that was going on around him – mobilizing every available employee, bringing in temp workers, stringing up dozens of additional phone lines and equipment – Barry found that the building seemed oddly quiet.

A little pile of computer screws stood off to one side of his desk, and he prodded them with one finger. They were the screws from the Big Byte computer they had found in the apartment. When the crew had taken the machine off, they must have left the screws behind.

Part of what was so infuriating, you surprised and fought with a man in an apartment, you seized his car, you got a computer science professor who had been hired to write the code being used by your enemy, you now had the man who had *hired* the guy to write the code, you even had an actual computer taken from them – and it all led to naught. The ball had unraveled, and that thing you'd been hoping to find at its center simply wasn't there.

Barry thought back to the machine he had taken from the apartment. Jim reported the technicians had found nothing. No more than he, himself, had seen. WINDOWS, HACK, UTILS, NETMOD. He allowed the word *netmod* to form on his lips and realized that it could well be an abbreviation for *net modem*. A net modem was a small box that didn't have to be attached to a computer's serial port, like a regular modem. A net modem could be hidden off in the most unlikely of corners, allowing someone off-site to connect to your network via a regular phone line. Yes, that would make perfect sense:

no PC ANYWHERE. No remote access server. A net modem would allow instant access to the network at any time.

Barry remembered all too well their frantic search through the Simtec campus. They'd been convinced the intruder was on-site because of the way the machine, or its Ethernet address, appeared to simply snap off, as though someone had cut power. Could a modem be made to do that? Probably.

If the person was coming in by modem, they had all been wasting their time. And if the modem had been used to send E-mail that very morning, the damn thing was still out there. Barry stared up at the ceiling in his office. He listened to the air whooshing out of the air-conditioning vent, and he began to form a suspicion. An ugly suspicion, because the evidence had been there all along for him to see.

Why had Ben Cooper been electrocuted while performing a routine wiring trace? Why, indeed? Dunn had considered it peculiar from the very start, but Barry had resisted. He had preferred to wear blinders, to convince himself that Ben Cooper had made a mistake and brought it upon himself.

Barry got up from the desk and went out to the main corridor. A man was pushing a canvas mail cart filled with telephone gear. Barry glanced at it and passed by. He walked the length of the third floor, looking up at the ceiling and thinking it through. The last time Dunn had brought up the Cooper incident, they had almost come to blows. He could remember Dunn's retort, that he would go up there and check it out himself if he had to. But then Dunn had been hit by the car, and he'd never done it.

Reaching one end of the building, Barry turned and started back. Access to the ceiling area was through an opening in a locked maintenance closet at either end of the building. The opening stood at the top of a metal ladder, and, up in the ceiling, the metal service walkway ran the length of the building.

Of course, with a step ladder in the right place, Barry imagined that you could move a few of the acoustical ceiling tiles and simply hoist yourself up. Girders and support beams crisscrossed the ceiling area, and, once up there, it might be possible to work your way over to the catwalk. For that matter, you could put the ladder in a back office, rest room, mop closet – anything was possible. Everywhere except for the center of the building, where he now came to a stop. Here a section of the second and third floors was missing, allowing for an expansive atrium and open-air cafeteria down on the ground level. The catwalk passed somewhere overhead. No one would be putting any ladders out here.

'What are you doing?' came a voice behind Barry's left shoulder. He turned to find Mike Spakovsky, standing there in an immaculate suit and tie. 'You look like you're checking light bulbs.'

'I'm checking the ceiling. I need to go up and follow some wiring.'

'Wiring, Barry? Can't we have someone else do that?'

'I want to do it,' Barry said, and Spakovsky, who had started to say something else, closed his mouth.

'Whatever,' Spakovsky said. He glanced at his watch. 'I broadcast live in the pressroom in an hour. It would be nice if you were there.'

'Sure,' Barry said. He turned back to study the ceiling. He stared at the white tiles with their fluorescent lights spaced evenly down the entire length of the building, and he thought about Ben Cooper.

29

'All right, so you didn't put the code anywhere else? It's not in any other file?' Bill Dunn stood in Milstead's office, flipping through a printout and notes that the professor had retrieved from a locked cabinet.

'What do you mean? What would be the advantage?'

Bill folded his arms across his chest. 'You understand the way this was done? The master files on a central server were replaced, and your Trojan got loaded on every machine coming through production. But we don't know if that's all that was done. Let's say you modified other files, like EMM386. Maybe you hit a mouse driver. It gets swapped out on the central file server, but only for a day or two. All of a sudden we've got another variable floating around out there. We've tried to go back and check a variety of machines, but we can't be sure we've gotten them all. That's what we're afraid of, missing something like that.'

'Oh, no,' Milstead said. 'Nothing like that.'

'No EMM386.'

'No.'

'No executables or COM files.'

'No.'

Bill's eyes narrowed into a hard stare.

'Well, maybe one thing . . . but it was so recent. It can't have been used yet. I'm sure it shouldn't concern you.'

Bill Dunn was only twenty-four years old, but he had experience enough under his belt to consider Dr. Martin Milstead the worst kind of computer vermin. Self-righteous, even while they used their skills to stab you in the back. Bill wasn't small, and he reached across the desk and seized Milstead by the collar.

'What can't have been used yet?'

Milstead gulped. 'A recent file. Like I told you, I thought it was for the military—'

Bill could feel the man's Adam's apple pressing up against the knot of his hand. He pushed harder and Milstead's eyes began to water.

'I'll show it to you. It has nothing to do with PCs. It's for file servers. An SCSI disk driver. Please,' Milstead croaked. 'I can't breathe.'

Barry opened the maintenance room with his master key. He ran his hand against the cinder-block wall until he found a light switch. Then he stepped inside and closed the door. On the opposite wall, a steel rung ladder climbed up into the ceiling.

He gripped the metal rungs and started up, tasting the stale air, cool but unventilated. At the top of the walkway, he squatted underneath a knot of ductwork. This would be what Ben Cooper had seen, Barry thought. A gray powder of dust covered every available surface. A series of light bulbs spaced at fifteen-foot intervals cast a dull glow down onto the catwalk. The report said a number of light bulbs had been burned out, so Ben would have seen even less. Wires and pipes stretched off into the darkness on either side. Where did you begin?

Barry pulled out an amp probe borrowed from the technicians' office. Unwrapping two wires, one red and one black, he spun the selector so that it would measure up to six-hundred-volt current. If there was more loose electricity up here, he wasn't going to blunder into it. He could thank Ben Cooper for that.

He shuffled forward, paused, and positioned the voltmeter. He used the electrical probes to touch all possible combinations of the metal infrastructure around him – walkway, ductwork, U-bolts and braces – his eyes darting from the wire leads to the needle on the voltmeter. The needle remained motionless. Sitting down in the back of the Jeep were a pair of Nike running shoes. Nice, fat rubber soles, if only he had remembered them earlier. He glanced up at the catwalk, stretching out in front of him until it ran out of sight. No indication of the opposite end of the building.

★

W. S. Dunn picked up the phone and his son said, 'This guy has also been working on a malicious SCSI driver. He started the project last week. Now what do you think that's all about?'

W. S. had the TV turned to a news station and he was waiting for the announcement from Simtec. He waved a hand at Martoli, who hit the mute button.

'What kind of SCSI driver?'

'Disk driver for file servers, not stand-alone PCs. Milstead says he only just got it done. So, it can't possibly have been used yet. I called Sheila and had her check three machines. He appears to be telling the truth.'

W. S. cocked his head, scanning back through his own memory banks in search of a reference. The past two days had produced so much flotsam that he was unable to locate it. Was it something at Simtec, or something he'd seen while working from the hospital? Perhaps it was a bit of trivia he'd picked up from Barry Shepard, or Greg Mitchell, or Sheila.

'Martoli,' he said. 'SCSI driver. What have we seen?'

Tony Martoli was sitting in a chair with papers spread out on the floor. He rested his elbows on his knees. 'About a zillion configuration problems. Bought CD-ROM drive, doesn't have SCSI card. Driver won't load. Driver won't support a multichanger. You name it.'

Dunn had been discarding each of these with a wave of the hand. 'Not PC stuff. How about servers?'

'Well . . . there was the company that put in a new drive. Hewlett Packard two gig, I think. Hooked it up and the driver won't recognize it. There was that guy complaining about the update. Said he ran a benchmark and the driver didn't do anything.'

'That one. Who was that?'

'I don't have the slightest idea. I can pull up the file and go back through till I find it.'

'Let's do that,' Dunn said. 'Bill? We're going to check it out. We've got a few references to SCSI drivers we want to nail down. I'll call you back.'

Mike Spakovsky straightened his tie before stepping into the hall. Broadcast and print journalists were already beginning to accumulate in the hallway, and he knew they would be sizing him up and snapping photos.

He gave a wave in their direction, but did not advance far enough to encourage Q & A. Instead, he forked off into a side room where a huddled conference was still in session.

'Barry's over there doing God knows what,' Spakovsky said. 'Trying to trace wiring.'

Karen Williams frowned. 'He'll be here, right? He'll make it for the conference?'

Spakovsky gave a broad shrug. 'I assume so. It's not like he's reading any of this, anyway.'

'But he needs to be here,' Jim Seidler said. His face looked angry and forbidding. He looked back to the paper they'd all been going over, and he jabbed it with his index finger. 'I don't like the word *tendered.* She didn't tender her resignation. The board gave her the boot and you can't soft-pedal it. For all you know, she's with her lawyers right now and we'll see a lawsuit by the end of the day. What's that going to do for *tendered*?'

'I have to read this,' Peter Jenkins said. 'And I'm going to say it in a way that I feel comfortable with.'

Jim scowled at the group, shaking his head. 'Karen, you go over that and make sure that it's airtight. I want to see a finalized copy in five minutes. We'll be meeting in the boardroom.'

Sweat ran freely down Barry Shepard's forearms as he stooped to crawl under one of the structural supports. He had to go down on hands and knees in order to pass underneath the three-foot clearance between support and catwalk. He first tested with the probe, holding a small flashlight between his lips and using his hands on the wire leads. He read the gauge and advanced slowly, wincing as the metal grid dug into his knees.

A generator clicked on, filling the hollow, above-ceiling cavity with a soft, high-pitched hum. Six feet on the other side of the support, he paused to examine the cable tray.

Little by little, he was making sense of the tangle of wires. Several bundles of twisted-pair cabling ran the length of the tray, carrying signals from the wiring closet directly to jacks all over the building. The jacks in turn served telephones, fax machines, printers, and computers.

Every so often along the cable tray, a group of wires fanned out into the darkness. Along their individual runs, each wire had been secured with cable ties before diving at a wall joint toward somebody's wall jack.

Later installations had not been so tidy. He found cable runs where the wire was simply tossed over pipes and light fixtures in the most expedient manner possible. Some of the wiring was run directly over the top of fluorescent lighting, and it was easy to marvel, as he did now, that the network ran at all.

These added, maverick wiring runs were the hardest to track. He dutifully tried, as he came upon them, snapping the wire up and down while he trained the flashlight to find where the cable ended. He used this technique now and heard a clattering sound, as though something had fallen onto the ceiling below. His tug on the cable might have pulled loose a connection, and Barry wouldn't have been surprised to hear a yelp from below, as a worker lost a morning's worth of unsaved work. But these days the network was so messed up that a jack going down was almost trivial. Let them get up here and debug it later.

He gave the line another pull and was able to haul in several feet of the wire. He did this again, holding the flashlight up until he was able to see the end of the cable, drawing a dark shape along with it. An odd fish being hauled in from the depths of a murky pond.

The fish made it up and over the top of three ceiling struts, drawing closer and closer until it got within fifteen feet and refused to budge. The wire had slipped into a groove and become wedged. Damn. He considered the thirty-foot drop into the atrium in the middle of the building. He might or might not be over that part of the building, but there was no other way. In order to retrieve the box, he was going to have to do a tightrope act.

He stretched a foot out to the nearest inch-wide strut and tested it with his weight. The strut was solid, and he could see where it ran over and was bolted to an I-beam. He checked both strut and the beams overhead with the amp probe, wrapped the red and black wires around the meter, and left it on the catwalk. Then he stepped out and began working his way sideways, reaching up and bracing himself for balance.

By the time he got near the box, Barry's left calf muscle had begun to quiver. He could feel the muscle jumping around against his pants leg. The box dangled below his right foot, and he eased down and took hold of the wire with one hand. The device was not heavy as he reeled it in, and he saw that the wire connected to it with a standard RJ-45 plug. This line would tie back to the network somewhere, while a second, smaller wire would be the phone connection. The device had a case made of black plastic with no logo or company name on the outside. It was a modem of some kind, Barry was sure. The quivering in his leg intensified.

He unhooked a long power cable that snaked off toward the edge of the building. These other two, network and phone, were the connections he would want to trace. Holding the box in one hand, he began to make his way back toward the catwalk.

It was a pipe that caused him to lose balance, sidestepping with only one hand for a grip overhead. He ducked to get underneath and the wires snagged. He gave them a yank, and he lost his balance. His whole body started to swing backward, pivoting on the axis of his right hand and its tenuous grip on the brace overhead.

He bobbled the modem gracelessly and tried to flick it toward the catwalk. Then he snatched at a pipe with his now free left hand and hauled himself back upright. Looping one arm up over the pipe, as though his arm were a giant hook, he stood there panting. He glanced in the direction of the modem, but could see only where the wire looped away out of sight. Other than that, it was all metal bracing, conduit, and shadows.

'It's Boeing,' Martoli said. 'The corporate tech support line logged the call at two o'clock Sunday afternoon.'

Tony carried his machine over and W. S. Dunn scanned the report. The customer was complaining about the latest driver update. They had run benchmarks and found none of the promised performance increase.

'Let's give them a call,' Dunn said. 'The contact's name and number are right here.' He hauled the phone over onto his bed and punched buttons.

The man who answered at Boeing was not the one whose name was in the logs. This guy was named Ted. But Ted seemed knowledgeable, so Dunn started firing questions.

When did you get the update file from Simtec? When was it loaded? And finally, Dunn asked if Ted would upload a copy to the Security Associates FTP site in Atlanta. And would he do it right now?

After a few questions of his own, Ted said, Sure. He was happy to.

Ten minutes later, Dunn logged into the Security Associates network himself. The home office had one high-powered Simtec server they used for testing. Dunn copied the Boeing file over to this server named Pigpen. Then he called on the phone.

'Linda? I need you to go in and reboot Pigpen. I need you to sit right there and tell me what happens. I wouldn't be surprised if we light it up.'

Linda did exactly as directed. 'Nothing unusual,' she said. 'What should I be looking for?'

'You'll know when you see it. Let's try some things. Change the date on the machine and set it for a month from now.'

Dunn could hear the tapping of keys as this was performed.

'Still don't see anything. Let me put you on hold and go to a workstation. I'll try some things and get back to you.'

Dunn still had the laptop connected to Pigpen, so he, too, began checking to make sure everything was in order. He began executing commands on the server and, after entering a disk utility program, he was staring right at his screen when the connection to Atlanta was severed. The keyboard on his laptop appeared to have died, also, but the laptop itself had come alive. Dunn leaned closer, holding the machine gently with both hands, listening, trying – as best he could – to discern what it was going through. Dunn's expression throughout was one of calm.

'Martoli?' he said at last. 'I believe we're onto something.'

Six minutes later, a breathless Linda was back on the phone. 'There's a problem,' she said. 'We do indeed have a problem.'

Dunn listened to what she had to say about the doomed server Pigpen, then he pointed at Martoli. 'You're going to Simtec,' he said. 'We need to hunt down Jim Seidler and Barry Shepard. I'll call ahead. We need to get their people in a room, isolate a machine, and demo this. We need to do it *now*.'

Barry regained the catwalk, sat down, and mopped his forehead. The modem was nowhere in sight. He stayed low and began looking, reaching tentatively into areas where it might have fallen. On a sweep off to the right he found it, resting against a vertical length of conduit. He scolded himself for being a damn fool, using his sweaty hands to paw around. Before sitting to examine the box, he used the meter to test the metal grate underfoot.

A standard net modem allowed someone to dial into the network from any remote location. Barry remembered the memo from Chris Jacobs, saying that he had cut off all incoming modem lines. This line was surely outside the Simtec modem pool and would have gone undetected. Now, though, he could have somebody track what the number was and where it came from.

Or he could see it through himself. Barry detached the phone wire from the modem and stared at it: he could do the trace right now. He made up his mind and wedged the modem into his pocket. Snapping the wire with his wrist, he followed where it ran off across the ceiling area. He stepped back out onto the supports and headed in that direction.

By stopping to check the path of the wire every few feet, he stayed on course and made slow progress. Simtec 4 was a large building, and by the time Barry saw the line dip toward the ceiling tiles, the catwalk was a long way away. He lowered himself to a crouch and trained the flashlight after the wire. Partially concealed by a length of return-air ductwork, he could see the splice. The wire he'd been following ran over and joined with one coming up from a wall. He had found it. After all, this wasn't magic, this coursing of transmissions that ran through a building. The signals weren't carried through the walls by phantoms. There were paths and rules to follow, just like the plumbing that carried water. More rules, really, and if you were willing to get dirty, to climb through pipes and dust and insulation, you could always find what had been done.

Right beside the splice, Barry lay on his stomach and

extended an arm toward the ceiling tiles. Each tile was settled down into its own metal frame and he couldn't get at the edge of one to pry it up. He considered breaking the tile in two with his fist; it wouldn't be difficult. But there was a better idea. He unhooked a medium-point Bic pen from his shirt pocket, and he used it now, skewering into the soft back of the ceiling tile and lifting it away. He craned his neck out over the hole and looked down.

Below, through the open square, Barry was looking down twelve feet onto a patch of burgundy carpet. He knew that carpet, and his heart began to pound in his chest. He stabbed another tile, lifted it aside, and found himself staring into the top of Jim Seidler's office. The light was on, but the door was closed and no one was there. Barry removed two more tiles and, with his palm, punched out the metal dividing braces. Then he grabbed the ceiling strut with both hands, swung down into the hole, and dropped. He hit the ground, rolled clumsily, and one shoulder came up hard against the base of Jim's desk.

Barry scrambled to his feet. It was irrational – comical, perhaps – but he turned and kicked the desk, swearing. His entry had left debris on the carpet, which made him think of something else, something he remembered seeing in Jim's office that, at the time, had seemed like nothing: little bits of ceiling tile. The tiny bits and pieces fell away like crumbs every time you moved a tile, and Barry had noticed them on the floor of the office before. He'd thought absolutely nothing of it. Simply that Jim must have had the place recabled.

But, now, it meant something else entirely. If the modem line had been spliced in above Jim's office, and it had been accessed *from* Jim's office, Jim could have plugged and unplugged the connection at will. The Ethernet address they'd been so desperate to find hadn't been used in two days – had probably been unplugged – until this morning, when Barry received the ransom message.

He glanced back toward the gap in the ceiling where he'd found the splice. You could control access to the network by simply moving a ceiling tile and detaching a connector. There was no other explanation. But Barry had known all that, intuitively, the moment he lifted the tile and saw the color burgundy.

He let out a long breath and surveyed the office. Over on a side table stood the Big Byte the technicians were supposed to be examining. Barry walked over and flipped it on, watching as the computer completed its Power On Self Test. Then it bombed out and would go no further in the boot process. It acted as if there were no hard drive at all, but the drive was there. He could see it.

Barry picked up the phone and dialed the manager of technical services.

'Hi, Jim,' the man said, picking up immediately.

'It's not Jim. It's Barry. I'm in his office.'

'Oh. What can I do for you?'

'Do you know about the machine Jim had you pick up from my office? We wanted someone to really go over the hard drive with a magnifying glass and tweezers?'

'Sure. We delivered that machine to Jim's office. He wanted it somewhere locked away. I sent two guys over to look at it, but they tell me it's a goose egg. Sounds like a low-level format.'

'Nothing on it whatsoever? Not one retrievable file?' Barry bit into the side of his lip.

'Apparently not. You want me to have someone else take a look?'

'No,' Barry said. 'Thanks.'

He set the phone down in a cold fury. Jim had brought the machine back to his office and had completely erased it. He had removed any hope of retrieval. Barry was staring at the useless box when someone rapped lightly on the door. 'Hey,' a voice said. 'Is somebody in there?'

Barry stomped over and ripped the door open. Jim's assistant jumped back out of the way. 'How'd you get in there?' the assistant said, looking surprised. He tried to get a look inside, past Barry's shoulder.

'I'm sorry, Mr. Shepard. If Jim's not here, he said no one was allowed into his office under any circumstances. I'm sure you understand, with everything that's been going on.'

Barry didn't answer. He headed straight out of the suite.

30

The heavy boardroom door opened and Barry Shepard stepped inside. Everyone was in there – Rowster, Cummings, and Chairman Jenkins, as well as Spakovsky and Karen Williams. Even a few staffers from the engineering and public relations departments. Some were pulled up at the table; others ranged about in scattered chairs. Jim was standing at the opposite side of the room, with his back to them, writing notes with a blue marker. Barry advanced to the boardroom table. He stood, reading the notes, and said nothing.

1. Announce interim CEO – Jenkins, 5 min.
   Statement
2. Trojan horse – Seidler, 10 min.
   Statement – scope of damage
   Brief disc – who, when, where
3. Tech talk – Mitchell, Simon, 10 min.
   How to get fixes, options
4. Q & A – panel, 5-10 min.

Jim was still finishing the last note as he asked, 'So, are we going to take questions about Diane during the Q & A? We could lay down some ground rules and restrict discussion.' Jim turned around and saw Barry. 'Welcome,' he said. 'We're drawing up the most important press conference in Simtec history.'

'Then you might want to add a number five,' Barry said. 'Call it, Explanations. Or maybe you should make that number one and bump the others.'

'Have a seat, Barry. This is no time to fool around. We're moving on this in ten minutes.'

Everyone else was staring at him, but Barry paid no

attention. His hair was flecked with bits of ceiling tile, his shirt streaked with dirt. He leaned forward and placed the modem on the boardroom table.

Jim's glance settled toward the box, then rose quickly. From behind the sunken features, the dark smudges under the eyes, came a jolt of anger. And now Barry sensed – perhaps it was in the eyes, or in that momentary wildness of expression – that Jim was on the verge of breaking.

Jim Seidler drew himself up and in an odd, squawking voice attempted to wield his authority: 'This is a hell of a time for an interruption, Barry. You need to sit down and bring yourself up to speed.'

Barry ignored him. 'I believe you recognize this little box. Don't you, Jim? I wouldn't be surprised if you built it yourself. The way it gets on and off the network, it must have some kind of automatic cutoff. Or do you just move a ceiling tile and unplug it?'

Jim set down the blue marker. He tried to give the others in the room a quick look of reassurance. 'I don't know what you've got up your sleeve, but it's ten minutes before show time, and this is not the place for it. I'm telling you to sit down. *Now.*'

'I don't think so,' Barry said. Several of the employees stared at him, aghast. 'Not until you remind us how heartbroken you were when Ben Cooper was electrocuted. Tell us how choked up you are about our customers. About watching Diane get thrown out. I'd like to hear that. While you're at it, you might tell us where we sent ten million dollars this morning.'

'Barry, either shut up or leave the room.' Jim's voice was scalding, but increasingly frantic. 'You've gone off the deep end. You must be drunk.'

'I could drink everything in your office and still not have come up with this. Not in my wildest dreams.' Barry's gaze swept the room, but the faces didn't register. If they had, he would have seen a portrait of shock and bewilderment. He pointed to the box on the table and addressed everyone. 'That modem has been allowing access into our network. The TechDirect shipments were changed via that device, and so were our master files. You plug it in and you're going to discover the one network address we could never locate. That's because the whole time it was tucked away in the ceiling above Jim's office. The modem was tapped into an old fax line that he hasn't used in years.' To Barry's right, the board members were frowning at one another, confused, even as Barry's voice gained in volume and hostility. 'We never would have found it, because Jim Seidler put it there. He's been the one responsible all along.'

What happened next in the room was a scene of utter confusion. Though he had been Jim's enemy since the beginning, Mike Spakovsky uttered a loud cry of protest. The accusation seemed so outrageous that the cry slipped out unbidden. Greg Mitchell jumped up and his chair went crashing over into a side table. Others in the room appeared frozen, only their eyes darting back and forth between the two men. Karen Williams rose to her feet, even as Jim Seidler headed toward Barry.

'That's a lie!' Jim said. 'I'm going to have security throw you out. I ought to break your jaw for that.' And as soon as he said it, he must have decided it was a good idea, because he shouldered Karen Williams aside and kept coming. He charged right up to Barry and delivered a raking blow.

Barry jerked his head back, deflecting the bulk of the impact. Then he pushed Jim backward with both arms.

'Look at you.' Barry said. 'You're a disgrace.'

At that, Jim lunged again, pinning Barry against the table and getting a hand up at his throat.

The two men began to struggle, engaged in a furious wrestling match. Barry slammed his forearm into Jim's chest, forcing him off, but Jim lashed out again. His lips were pulled back, snarling, and his fingers clawed and dug into the soft flesh of Barry's neck.

At the sight of live battle, Richard Rowster, who had been glued to his chair by the spectacle, leapt into action. 'That's enough!' he bellowed, to little effect.

Barry seized one of Jim's hands and bent the wrist, contorting it backwards until Jim gasped. Barry kept going, twisting the tendons until Jim's grip at his throat eased, and released.

Jim's face was red, and flecks of spittle flew from his lips. 'He's lying. Richard, you heard what he said. He's a goddamn liar. He deserves to have his tongue ripped out.'

Rowster didn't answer, peering stonily between the two. 'Let's get them separated. Someone get security in here,' he ordered.

Greg Mitchell had been coming toward them, but he instead headed out the door. Barry straightened his shoulders. His neck was marked with bloody gouges and he still held Jim's wrist in a lock.

Retaining his tight, unreadable expression, Rowster leaned in closer. 'That's enough cleverness for today,' he said. 'We're going to leave here and go into two separate rooms. Barry, you better be able to explain yourself.'

'I can.'

At this, Jim started to surge forward until Rowster cut him off. 'Jim. Keep yourself under control. Whatever's going on, you're only making it worse. We'll get it all out, understood?'

Rowster stepped squarely between them and removed Barry's grip from Jim's wrist. He quickly marshaled several feet between the two of them. He turned to Jenkins and said, 'Let's delay on that first announcement until we get this mess sorted out. The rest of it – the customer notification, the fixes and downloads – we need you to go out there and do it.'

Jenkins was wearing a look of pure shock, but he gave a slow nod.

Jim started to speak, but Rowster raised a warning finger in front of his nose. 'Not one word,' he said, and, to all present, it was clear that he meant it.

31

Just after twelve noon on July 24, the Simtec Computer Corporation issued a public appeal to all purchasers of its computer systems since June 1. The announcement was read by Chairman of the Board Peter Jenkins, and copies were faxed to major media outlets, as well as every reseller and dealer in the distribution channel. The wording of the announcement was straightforward and succinct: Several hundred thousand machines had been tampered with and were set to erase themselves on the following day.

Around the country, a number of news directors read the Simtec fax and considered it a hoax. Several hundred thousand machines? Come on.

But if it was a hoax, what was all this other information? One sheet documented the availability of a patch designed to remedy the problem. Simtec owners should be urged to acquire and run the file immediately. It could be downloaded from dozens of on-line locations, as well as overseas distribution points in Europe and Asia. A tech support phone bank had already been set up to handle questions and walk users through the procedure.

Then came a listing of Web sites, BBS numbers, reseller locations, and contacts. As a last resort, the file would be delivered on disk next-day air from Simtec itself. Recently purchased Simtec PCs absolutely could not be started prior to receiving the disk.

The news directors began to wonder. They tried to get through to Simtec's Office of Media Information. They phoned one another and began to realize that the Simtec story must be legitimate. At Simtec, a press conference was in progress. There was confusion over who was running the company, and the word on the street was that Diane Hughes was out.

The blood was in the water, and that great shark, the American news media, began to thrash its tail.

'The computer is blank,' Barry said. He sat on a swivel chair in the temp office where he'd been sequestered. Right now, he was telling Richard Rowster about the Big Byte. 'Everything that was there is now gone, erased, and there were plenty of files – you can check that with Bill Dunn.'

Which Rowster did. He also checked with the two support technicians who had come over to examine the machine at Jim's request. During the ten minutes Rowster was out of the office, Barry stared at the wall, continuing to piece it together. He went back over the Friday-night search for what they'd thought was the network address of a Simtec computer. He, Jim, and W. S. Dunn had stood in the hallway, while Dunn explained it to them: the computer had been turned off, which was why it disappeared off the network. He recommended a thorough and immediate search, and they had all agreed. Dozens of employees had been mobilized. They'd wasted hours, searched thousands of Simtec offices. All the while Jim would have known. . . .

Barry got up and began pacing the small room. All the damage that had been done. *The treachery of it.*

Rowster opened the door and slipped inside, along with a babble of voices from the outer room. He remained standing and tugged angrily at his shirt collar. 'I may not know what is going on here,' he said. 'But it happened on my watch, and I'm going to get to the root of it.'

'You talked to the technicians?' Barry said. 'That computer has been sitting in Jim's office the whole time. He gave his assistant orders not to let anyone in there. The situation ought to be pretty clear.'

'Jim says, if the files are gone, then you must have erased them. Or somebody else did. You had the machine in your possession, too, you know.'

Barry had to work to contain himself. 'Let me tell you something. I didn't have to erase any files. If I didn't want anyone to find that machine – the whole apartment where we *found* the machine – then all I do is keep my mouth shut about the phone. No phone call, no apartment, no computer. If you can't see that, you're blind. I should stop talking until I have an attorney present.'

Richard Rowster didn't say anything. He ran two fingers up and pinched the bridge of his nose. 'That's not necessary,' he said. And in a weary, somewhat saddened voice, he added, 'Let's keep going.'

And after another ten minutes of details, Rowster grew visibly upset. He left Barry and Jim in their respective rooms and went to confer with Cummings and Fitzhugh. The three of them went to Jim Seidler's office and stared up at the gap in the ceiling tiles. At this point, a joint decision was made and Richard Rowster called the Houston Police Department.

HPD agreed to send out a man, but when they heard about computer crime, they suggested he call the Harris County District Attorney's office. The DA's office put him on hold. Then they said it could be a federal interest case and they wanted to get the U.S. Attorney's office involved. Overlapping jurisdictions, they said. They'd have a conversation and get back to him. At this point Rowster let loose. He was suddenly squeezing the phone and yelling instructions into the receiver: Get somebody out here *now*, he said, and you can very well sort the rest out later. He punctuated this with an epithet designed to bring about some action. And it did.

Thirty minutes later, Barry would repeat what he had found for the second time, now flanked by a police detective and an investigator hustled up from the district attorney's office.

They set out a tape recorder and told Barry to begin at the beginning. Karen Williams was in the room serving as Simtec counsel, though Barry doubted this meant she was serving as *his* counsel. He went ahead anyway, and it took the better part of side A to get it all out. The investigator paid careful attention to the amount and types of damage done. He hadn't yet heard about Simtec's public announcement, and, when he heard the reason, he shook his head in disbelief. Meanwhile the police detective seemed especially interested in Barry's finding and taking a computer from someone's apartment, and his fight with a man who'd been hiding in the back room. He asked Barry to run back through that part a second time.

The district attorney's investigator was a quiet man named Thomas Pike. He jotted down page after page of notes and, when they got to the ten-million-dollar wire transfer, he left the room and started making phone calls.

When Pike came back in, he said, 'Some of your guys have apparently decided to set up a post outside the door. One named Greg Mitchell wanted to get word in here that they tested the modem.' The investigator was carrying a stack of pages, which he held up. 'Printouts of Ethernet packets,' he said. By the way he said it, it was obvious he didn't have the slightest idea what to do with them.

Barry held out his hand, but Pike withdrew the papers. 'Not so fast,' he said.

'It's the same address, isn't it? Every time we caught them on-line, they were using that modem.'

Pike peered tentatively at the top page. He flipped to the second, then the third, as if those might prove less mystifying. He looked back at Barry and said, 'Apparently so.'

Barry nodded and stood. One hand involuntarily went up to his neck, which had been tended to in a brief visit from a paramedic crew.

The investigator tapped his pen, watching. Several top executives of the Simtec Computer Corporation, as well as a Who's Who menagerie of other big shots on the Simtec board, affirmed that somebody – possibly even top dog Jim Seidler – had attempted to sabotage and defraud the company. That was all good and fine, but the fact was, they were now able to hold Seidler only on a misdemeanor assault charge, courtesy of his attack on Barry Shepard. To get a high bond and to put together a solid case against *anybody*, they'd have to come up with something better than what was currently on the table.

'Mr. Shepard?' Pike said cautiously. 'I'll be very direct with you about the evidence you're suggesting. We're not going to get any prints off that modem. It's been passed around like a football. The issue of access to the ceiling is somewhat useful. Especially if other people noticed pieces of tile on the ground. That puts us in Seidler's office with *something* going on. Maybe the only people who can unlock Seidler's office are cleaning people who wouldn't know a modem if it fell on their heads. But between you and me, what's going to come out is that anybody could have put that modem there. The same goes for the phone line – anyone could locate and tap into an unused line. They could do it like you did, by coming over from the catwalk.'

Barry Shepard turned slowly. 'I can't tell you how to build your case. All I can tell you is what I know, and what I believe you will find. You better start that tape again, because here's another part of it you're going to want to look into.' He went on to explain the connection between Simtec and the man who had been killed at a Galleria parking garage.

After getting this new piece, and hearing how Bill Dunn had found the professor at Rice University, Thomas Pike looked as though he were standing on a hot plate. Both he and the detective ran out of the room and made more phone calls. Karen Williams was staring in open amazement.

When Pike came back in, he said, 'The U.S. Attorney's office has been in touch, and they'll begin tracking the money down as we speak. We're also going to go over that Cutlass from the apartment. We'll take prints, and we'll follow those, too.'

He rubbed his hands together and looked appreciatively at Barry. He actually went out to the hall and brought Barry a glass of water.

By 3:00 P.M., the atmosphere around Simtec, on the Internet, and in computer dealers across the country had become a frenzy. A follow-up news conference held thirty minutes later was broadcast live on CNN.

The lead item was put forth to quash a rumor that Diane Hughes, Simtec CEO, had been ousted by the board. Unequivocally false, according to Chairman Peter Jenkins. Any assessment of company leadership on the part of the board would have to wait until after the current crisis. A panel of Simtec technicians followed at the podium with additional announcements and instructions. They stuck closely to the facts, and then fielded innumerable queries from the press. The panel was followed by a short, unscheduled appearance by CEO Diane Hughes. She read a terse statement and, according to eyewitnesses at the conference, seemed ill at ease. She did not accept questions.

After Barry had answered every question they could possibly think of, the investigators let him return to his building. He shunned the press spectacle going on next door, and instead went to stand in the middle of the three hundred temporary phone stations that now overran the TechDirect offices. Between noon and 7:00 P.M., an unrelenting crew of telephone sales reps, technical specialists, secretaries, analysts, and administrators were in the process of logging forty-seven thousand phone calls.

The word was getting out.

Efforts to track who had been contacted were, of course, flawed, and an additional fifty employees were culled from human resources and accounting to make verification calls to registered owners. Messages were left on machines, with wives and husbands, co-workers. Sometimes customers declared they were being contacted for the second time. No one seemed to mind.

Of course, there was no way everyone could be reached, and Barry met with Greg Mitchell to work on a fix that Simtec could mail to customers who missed the media barrage and tried to use their machines.

Garbage was being written to critical areas of the drive, and a team of engineers now dove into the task of resurrecting the data that had been scrambled. It could be done, and when it was, it could be replicated into a program.

That disk would be ready the following day, and it would eventually be used by 18,300 people. These people were irate. Some threatened legal action, but Simtec continued making every effort to see that they were reached and taken care of. The final tally would show that over four hundred thousand people had, through some means, learned of the problem before booting their machines on July 25.

A subdued, considerably more private ceremony was being conducted in another building. Bill Dunn had alerted Simtec of the counterfeit disk driver, and twenty Security Associates employees were dialing network administrators at hundreds of major corporations. They were discovering that every one of the contact names on Simtec's major corporate account list had received a disk mailer. The mailers were identical, and each included the Trojan horse disk driver created by Martin Milstead.

Security Associates personnel fought their way past voice mail and secretaries and people who were out sick or on vacation. Either the person listed on the account came to the phone, or someone who could verify the location of the Simtec disk mailer and whether or not it had been used.

Security Associates personnel didn't mince words. The disk driver was extremely malicious. For those who had loaded it, they must locate and unload it from all locations. Do it now, they said, and for every corporation, Simtec issued call tags for the mailer to be picked up by courier.

Bill and his team worked through each and every contact for Simtec's corporate accounts. Forty-two companies were found to have loaded the new driver. Forty-two companies were now on high alert.

At two hours before midnight, an exhausted Barry Shepard would look out at the desks, the phones, the chaos that had enveloped Simtec, and he would realize that there was nothing more he could do. He sat down in a swivel chair and twisted the cap on a liter of bottled water.

Barry was still in the chair, listening to the steady buzz of telephones and voices, when Thomas Pike sauntered back into the TechDirect offices. He caught Barry's eye and motioned toward a meeting room.

Pike was a tall, lean man who always appeared carrying a bulging, soft-sided briefcase. He closed the door behind them and sighed heavily. They had already had two such sessions, and, every time Pike left, Barry said, 'You know where to find me.' Every few hours, so far, Pike had done just that. He pulled out a chair and spun it around so that he sat down facing Barry.

'Your investigator Richard Green called,' Pike said. 'He gave me some information he'd put together on Seidler's finances.'

'Good. I asked him to hand over anything that might prove useful. I told him I didn't think I'd be needing his services anymore.' Barry let this trail off into a question. No response.

Then Pike said, 'I spoke to both Will Dunn and his son at the hospital. They appear to back you up, or so it seems to the extent I follow all this. I have one of our technical people going over to talk to Dunn tomorrow morning. He'll come talk to you, too.' Pike wiggled his fingers in the air. 'You guys speak the same language. You can sit down and go into all the details.'

'I do it enough times,' Barry said, 'I'll probably get good at it.'

Pike gave him a sharp look. 'He's got the tape of our earlier discussions, but I'm sure there will be follow-up.'

'That came out the wrong way,' Barry said. 'I'm tired.'

Barry knew the investigator was doing the best he could, but he was learning firsthand why Dunn had said it would be pointless to go to the authorities. So far, Barry had been handed around between several different people, and no one had appeared well equipped to handle the case. Pike included. The man was competent – he projected that air of confidence in the law and its ability to triumph – but he clearly didn't understand half of what Barry was talking about.

'I had a few follow-up questions of my own,' Pike said. He unsnapped the briefcase and extracted a pad of paper. 'I was speaking with your assistant.'

'Gwen.'

'That's it. We were going back over the calendar, and she recalled how, on Saturday morning – early, ten o'clock, she seemed to think – you suddenly went tearing out of the office in a mad rush.' He consulted his notes. 'According to her recollection, you came back an hour or two later.'

What was this about? Who cared what he was doing on Saturday morning? It was sounding more and more like *he* was the one under investigation. And perhaps he was. Barry searched the angular features of Mr. Thomas Pike. 'May I ask why it's important what I was doing at ten o'clock on Saturday morning?'

'Why don't you answer the question? Then we can get into the whys and wherefores.'

Even as Pike was speaking, Barry had begun thinking back. He knew exactly what he'd been doing on Saturday morning. It was the morning of Dunn's accident. He'd gone to Karen Williams' town house; then he'd met with Richard Green. He arrived at Simtec late and went straight to Jim's office. Shortly after that, he'd gotten the call from Claudia.

'All right,' Barry said. 'I got a call from my wife, Claudia, that my daughter wasn't in the house. I ran out of the office and drove home. We had received threats, so this was not as hysterical as it might sound. We were terrified.'

'False alarm, I take it?'

'Yes, it was. Caroline, my daughter, was down at a neighbor's house, hiding in a tree fort.' Barry started to say more, swallowed, and stopped.

Pike leaned forward, resting his elbows on his knees. 'The neighbor's name?'

'Frank Kline. He's four houses down from us. Caroline has played down there before. We just didn't think of it at the time. We kind of panicked.'

'Mr. Kline was home during all this? He would have seen you come home? Talked to you on the phone?'

'We were calling all the neighbors to ask about Caroline. It turned out he had seen her go into his backyard. My wife and I both went down to his house.' Barry's eyes narrowed. 'You can check all this with him, if you like.'

Pike finished jotting a note. He made a straight line under it and snapped in the pen point. Everything methodical and in its place. When he looked up, his face was impassive. 'The reason I ask, we've checked the beneficiary account for the wire transfer. It turns out that the account was opened at Southern Bank on Saturday morning at ten-thirty. Then I hear you went running out of here on Saturday morning. It's a curious coincidence.'

'Maybe I went running over to Southern Bank?' Barry said. 'Give me a break. What's the name on the account?'

Pike shook his head. 'Nobody's that stupid. It's a company account in the name of Micro Supply Inc. The signature's a dead end.'

An erasable white marker board filled one wall of the meeting room. Someone had scribbled a series of configurations and Simtec part numbers in scratchy green penmanship. Barry stared blankly in that direction. 'Let me get this straight. Someone went into the bank and opened the account on Saturday?'

'Correct. According to our reasoning, this would not be the account originally intended to get the money. Why wait until the eleventh hour, on a Saturday morning, and open it in person? There's no reason to take that risk. We figure maybe this ties in with the man in the parking garage. To open an account at the last minute, some part of the planning must have fallen through.'

Barry was thinking of something else. 'We use Southern Bank,' he said. 'Not for all our accounts, but that's where we transferred the payment from. Jim would have known that.'

Thomas Pike rubbed a thumb against the corner of his mouth, but he gave no sign of agreement. This was becoming, to Barry, upsettingly familiar. The investigator was unwilling to either mention or acknowledge direct suspicion of Jim Seidler. 'No doubt they chose Southern for just that reason,' Pike said. 'Ten million from Simtec to Micro Supply Inc. wouldn't raise any eyebrows. Also it's an intrabank transfer, so the money would go right through.' He adjusted his trouser leg. 'Of course, the Micro Supply account now has a balance of fourteen hundred dollars and thirty-two cents.'

He'd left the liter of water in the other room, and Barry swallowed a mouthful of thick, dry nothing. 'Fourteen hundred?'

'We have not yet determined where the rest of the money *is*, and if it's out of the country, Simtec can probably forget about it.'

'You say somebody came in to open the account?' Barry sat forward. 'An employee in the bank might recognize them. If it was Jim—'

'We'll do a photo spread. We'll check the bank forms for prints. All that stuff,' Pike said, though his tone was dismissive. He bent over, fumbling through his bag. When he straightened up, he was holding an ordinary-looking VHS videotape in his hand. 'The bank also has a surveillance camera. This is a copy one member of my team brought in a few hours ago.' He gestured across the room to one of the television/VCR combo units that equipped each Simtec meeting room. 'Shall we?'

They settled into chairs in front of the monitor and popped in the tape. Barry saw a black-and-white image of a branch bank office. The picture was slightly grainy, but adequate. In the foreground were the tellers, and the camera angle was such that you were looking over the shoulder of the one in the middle. A line of customers had queued up waiting for a spot at the counter. Beyond them to the left was a station for filling out slips. To the right was a desk where an account rep sat with a customer.

'That's the one,' Pike said.

Barry stretched out a finger, almost tapping the screen. 'Him?' he said with a grunt of disapproval.

'I might also mention that, at ten-twenty-one on Saturday morning, Jim Seidler was in his office on the phone to a supplier in California. You've got a heck of a nice phone system. It spit out a detailed call log for everything on Jim's extension. We cross-checked it by long-distance access code. That particular call lasted twenty-seven minutes. It's followed immediately by a call to Dallas that takes you up to eleven-sixteen. That's a pretty good alibi for Jim Seidler not being at the bank, anyway.'

Barry put his face up six inches from the screen. The bank employee was typing at a terminal. The customer appeared relaxed and unhurried. His dark hair was neat but longish, coming down over the collar. He sat sideways to the camera with his legs crossed, wearing what appeared to be khakis, a light-colored shirt, and tie.

Pike looked away from the screen toward Barry. 'You ever see the guy?'

Barry didn't respond, but his answer hung in the air anyway. He'd never seen the man before in his life. The tape was still running and, at one point, the man turned toward the camera. A woman had come into the bank, and he turned to look at her, giving a brief full view of his face. He wasn't young, not twenty-something, the way he might have been with the hair. He reminded Barry of Paul McCartney. He had the hair, but you knew he was no kid.

'How old would you guess?' Barry said. 'Thirty-five?'

Thomas Pike shrugged, and Barry folded his arms in disgust. 'I wish I could tell you I've seen him, but the truth is, I'm drawing a total blank.'

Pike nodded and punched the fast forward. 'This is all pretty much the same. When he gets up to leave, all you get is his back.' The tape went to snow for a few seconds and Pike took his finger off the button. 'Now we splice to what was on the outside camera in the parking lot. The camera pivots, so it's hit-and-miss.'

This image had a wider angle, and it was moving slowly to the right. There were lines of cars waiting in the parking lot to go through the drive-through. The camera got to the end of its arc and started back left.

'There he is,' Pike said. 'Would you believe he didn't even park in the lot? He walked over from somewhere else, the cagey bastard.' Barry picked the man up as soon as he came into view, already halfway across the parking lot. It was hard to tell, but he appeared to be of average height. The bank was situated at an intersection, and the man walked toward the corner with a swinging gait. He left the bank's parking lot and crossed a small strip of grass, then stepped into the street beyond. He was headed toward the shops, further down.

The camera was moving away now and he was about to go out of view. Barry glanced away from the man, across the street in the other direction. More shops. Lots of cars, all parked in a row. A woman with a dog on a leash. Something made Barry look back again.

It was one of the cars over in the other lot. More of a truck, actually, and it had a torn-up front fender. The man who had come out of the bank was headed in the opposite direction, but Barry knew that vehicle. It was a black Ford Explorer. His heart was pounding as he reached out and punched the rewind button. Pike was watching all this, measuring Barry's reaction, but he didn't say anything.

Barry watched the segment again, then rewound all the way to the piece where the woman came through the door and the man turned to face the camera. Barry hit play and watched. It was some performance.

Once you saw it – once you knew what you were seeing – it was like having the image come together in a 3-D illusion. The way the man swiveled at the waist, his shoulders erect. How many times had Barry seen Jim Seidler do that in a meeting?

As the man came about, facing the camera, Barry hit pause. The work was spectacular, just a touch here and there in the right places and you had a new individual. Younger. Different. But the Seidler part of the face was there, too. Barry had sat through a hundred of Jim's speeches, and even here in a bank, with a face meticulously altered, he could not disguise that demeanor that said, I'm going to open my mouth and you will listen.

Thomas Pike still didn't speak. The faintest wisp of a smile had formed on his lips, as though someone had whispered a mildly funny joke in his ear.

'I don't know how he did the phone calls,' Barry said at last. 'Maybe he set the computer to dial a number automatically. He could have an automatic fax go out, fifty pages to a supplier in California. That might use up twenty minutes. We'll figure that part out.'

Barry turned back to the screen and unpaused the image. He tapped the screen with his knuckle and watched quietly as an obsessed freak – a multimillionaire engineer, a mannequin Barry didn't even know – applied for his account.

32

It got easier in the following days. Call volume on the Simtec help lines began to decline. State and federal authorities, assisted by Security Associates and Simtec personnel, pursued their investigation, and on Friday, July 28, Jim Seidler was formally charged. Bail was set at twenty million dollars.

That evening, Barry Shepard went out to his car and began a slow and leisurely drive home. On his way out of the Simtec parking lot, the guard in the security booth straightened and gave an informal salute. Barry smiled and, for the next few blocks, tapped out a beat on the steering wheel. He'd been getting a lot of special treatment and, truth be told, it felt pretty good.

How long would it last? He didn't know. Six months from now, a competitor would start a price war, hoard some crucial part, or do God knows what to turn Simtec on its ear. Then they'd all be rushing to put out some other fire. That's the way the industry had always been.

When Barry entered his own neighborhood, he saw Caroline out by the garage with her red gym ball, shooting layups at an eight-foot portable hoop. He pulled halfway up the driveway and parked.

'Here, Dad,' she said, and tossed him the ball as soon as he was out of the car.

Barry tried to show off with a series of through-the-legs dribbles, but the ball was small and gave odd, rubbery bounces. He quickly thought better of it, sized up the basket and launched an attempt that caromed off the backboard.

Caroline shook her head and said, 'Dad, you shot a *brick*.' She darted off after the ball.

Claudia came through the gate from the backyard holding a trowel and a tray of something for the garden. She must have gotten home early, and she'd already changed into shorts and a sleeveless shirt.

Standing there in the driveway, her hair damp at the temples, pulled back and held under a blue baseball cap, she was the best thing Barry had seen all day.

'Hi there,' he said. He ducked under the brim of the cap for a kiss.

Claudia held up the tray of small flowers, each in its own plastic container. 'You caught me,' she said. 'I was going to plant these up front and see if you noticed.'

He gave them a speculative look and said, 'I'd notice they look half dead.'

'They're zinnias. They're supposed to be able to handle the heat, but I had them in the trunk for fifteen minutes, poor things.'

'Hey, Dad, let's play a game of H-O-R-S-E,' Caroline called. Barry and Claudia heard the ball hit the backboard with a *poing* and they both instinctively ducked.

Barry undid a second button at the top of his shirt and turned toward his daughter. 'Make it P-I-G,' he said. 'You shoot first.'

They were two letters into the game and Claudia was digging in the front bed when another car slowed and turned in at the end of the Shepard driveway.

'Who's that?' Caroline said. She and her dad both stopped to watch as the engine turned off and the door swung open.

'Oh, hey, it's someone I know from work. We'll finish the game in a little bit.' He gave his daughter a bounce pass and went down the driveway to meet his visitor.

Chris Jacobs was wearing jeans and a blue sport shirt, the sleeves tight around his muscular biceps.

'Hi, Barry,' he said, after they shook hands. 'I knew you lived over this way, and I thought I'd drop by. I hope that's okay.'

'Absolutely. I'm glad you did.' Barry flapped his open shirt collar with two fingers. 'Warm out here, isn't it? Let's go around to the back patio.'

Claudia had turned, watching, and Barry called over. 'This

is Chris Jacobs from the office. We're going to go sit around back.'

On the way, he introduced Caroline, who nodded somberly and stood holding the ball until her father and the large man behind him had passed.

They took a seat at a white patio table, but Barry popped back out of his chair. 'It's Friday evening. How about a beer?'

Chris started to protest, but Barry slipped through a door into the kitchen. He soon returned with two cold green bottles, handed one across the table and said, 'I guess you heard about Jim's bail.'

'I got a call right after.'

'Bail is often set at twice the amount stolen. Apparently that's standard procedure, or so Karen Williams told me.'

'The formula may be standard, but not the amount.'

Barry shrugged. He had decided to stop thinking about the money part of it. Ten million dollars that they'd probably never see again. What did it really matter? He remembered that moment when Diane Hughes held up her piece of paper that said 'Don't Pay'. He'd gotten a charge from that piece of paper. They all had. They were going to lock arms and fight. That was what mattered, the locking arms.

'I've been using some hindsight,' Barry said. 'Do you ever think back to those very first meetings with Diane? Remember when she waltzed in and knew nothing about computers?' Now it seemed hard to believe, but nine months ago, as the new CEO mapped out her plans, the other executives had flashed glances across the table: *How are we going to get through this?*

'I don't know what was worse for Jim,' Barry continued. 'When Diane came in and didn't appear competent for the job, or a month later when she started to make things happen. He wanted that spot more than any of us ever realized.'

'So, he went out and hired this James Dupree in order to make Diane look bad? Is that what you think?'

'I believe he agreed to supply information. He paid money out of his own pocket – two hundred thousand dollars. They've got a payment from Jim's bank records.'

Apparently this was new information, and Chris cocked an

eyebrow. 'That's not a bad piece of work, leveraging two hundred thousand into ten million.'

Barry was shaking his head. 'That's not the point. Jim didn't care about the money.'

'How do you figure?'

'It was enough to embarrass Diane. If Jim spent his own personal money and Simtec got out of it with a few scrapes, he'd figure no harm done.'

'But if Simtec didn't pay . . .' Chris paused.

'I'm saying he didn't intend for us to pay. In the beginning, it wasn't about money. As one of the investigators told me, going to the bank was careless. Why wait until the last minute? I don't think he decided to take the money until right at the end.'

Chris still didn't appear satisfied and Barry added, 'You should have seen the look on his face when we totaled up the corrupt machines. Jim was devastated. It went far beyond what he ever intended.'

Chris thought about this and then shrugged. 'Either way,' he said, 'that man did a lot of harm to a lot of people.'

This was a statement with which Barry could agree, and the two men sat quietly.

At last, Chris said, 'You've got a nice place. Nice family, too. My daughter's a little bit younger than Caroline. Shame we never once got together while I worked for the company.'

Chris hadn't returned to Simtec, and Barry hadn't known which way it would go. 'So that's it, then?' he said.

'Oh, yeah.' Chris waved a hand in the air. 'I'm done with all that. You get to a point where you can't go back. Even if you do, it isn't the same.'

Barry didn't answer. He traced a groove in the table with his finger.

'I'm okay with it,' Chris said. 'The company's giving me a nice enough deal. I've got to believe you had a hand in that, and I want to thank you for it.'

Barry shrugged.

'Really,' Chris persisted. 'You've always dealt with me straight-up. Now you're Simtec's man of the hour, and you deserve to be.'

'Man of the minute, I'd say. Right up until we hit the next crisis.'

Chris looked down and scratched at his beer label, taking off a neat row of paper with his thumbnail. He eyed Barry for a moment before he said, 'I'm going to tell you something. What I've been thinking about all week.'

Chris shifted in his chair and leaned in closer to the table. 'As soon as I heard about Jim – I think it was six Monday evening when I got the call – I sat out in the backyard and thought about it for two hours. I spent two straight hours staring at the swimming pool, then most of Monday night staring up at the ceiling. Thinking about passwords.'

'What about passwords?'

'You see, Jim must have had all the passwords. Every single one.'

'That's not too hard. He could ask for whatever access he wanted. Over time, he could accumulate passwords on every system without drawing attention.'

'That's what I found odd. Jim never went around asking about passwords. He's not a password kind of guy. He was lucky to know his own, and he didn't keep track of anyone else's. He expected me, or other people, to take care of that. The funny thing is, a couple of months ago, Diane asked me to compile a list of passwords and do a security audit. I thought it was a good idea. So did Jim.'

'Caspar. We heard about it. I was interviewed about my area, but I hadn't realized the scope. I guess a lot of us kicked in bits and pieces.'

Chris nodded. 'I was doing revisions, tabulating everything into a kind of white paper. I gave Diane a preliminary copy, and she immediately passed it on to Jim. She said she wanted him to review it first. Here she's commissioned this study and we've done a great deal of work. We're coming close to a finalized version and, to my knowledge, she ignored it. Not even a glance.'

'That's peculiar,' Barry said. 'If only because Diane is so thorough. But she's not very technical. It doesn't surprise me she wanted Jim's advice.'

'You know the expression about giving someone enough rope to hang themselves?'

'Yes.' Barry thought he could see where this was headed, and his pulse quickened.

'Well, suppose you're Diane. Suppose you learn, or suspect, one of your people is setting up trouble because he wants to make you look bad. He's your main rival, and it's too late to do anything about it. You don't know a damn thing about computers, and he's got most of the company in his pocket to begin with. You don't know what you could ever prove, if anything, and if you start screaming and pointing fingers, you're going to look like a hysterical witch. So, instead, you make a terrible gamble.'

Chris had a far-off look in his eyes. Perhaps the same look he'd had during those hours staring out at the swimming pool. 'One of my neighbors a few years back, a woman, was in the grocery store parking lot and a man came up to her with a knife. He told her to get back in the car. You know what she told him? She said, "No way. You can stab me right here, but I'm not getting in that car." And guess what he did?'

'Nothing.'

'Right. He ran off. She was going to make what he did so public that to go ahead would draw all kinds of attention. He'd almost assuredly be seen. That's the gambit. You can see what's coming, so you throw open the doors. In our case, you make it easy for your rival by providing a security study. You basically line up the targets. You get reckless, and perhaps you leave town so nothing can be done to stop the damage. You make him leave town, too. You're desperate, but you're trying to make a ball start rolling. A crisis that, once it gets going, it's so huge, it's coming so fast, even the guy who pushed it can't get out of the way. He's going to get caught. That's the way you'd hope it would work, anyway.'

Barry listened to the story about the grocery store parking lot and it sounded like a story Chris had already told him. Only he didn't remember it as being Chris. He envisioned Diane telling the story. Why would that be, Diane and Chris both telling a similar story? The cold bottle felt slick and wet in Barry's hand. He set it down unsteadily. 'Is that what you're telling me happened? Diane learned what was coming? She maneuvered so that Jim would be caught?'

Chris Jacobs leaned onto one elbow and stared out at the backyard. His eyes came slowly back toward Barry. He gave a dismissive toss of the head. 'Nah . . . that's just a what-if,' he said.

Barry could feel his heart thumping away inside his rib cage. His mouth had gone dry.

Chris was watching, and now he said flippantly, 'Don't worry about it. With Will Dunn coming in, they would have caught him regardless.'

'And without Dunn?'

'Look what did happen. You caught him. Who knows? There were probably footprints all over the place.'

Barry exhaled, long and slow. He glanced toward the side fence. He couldn't see Caroline, but he could hear the twang of the rubber ball. Every so often, it shot up in the air toward the backboard.

'That's a hell of a theory, Chris,' he said. Barry picked up his beer and fingered the label. He raised his bottle up in the air, in Chris's direction. 'Cheers,' he said. 'Here's to your new life.'

'And yours,' Chris said. 'And to yours.'